A Fire in the West

A FIRE IN

THE WEST

HARRY JAMES FOX

LUCIA MUDGWAY

FOXWARE PUBLISHING LLC

LAS CRUCES, NEW MEXICO

A Fire in the West

Published by Foxware Publishing LLC, 1156 Cave Springs Trail, Las Cruces, NM 88011.

Editing by Codi Ribitzki
Cover Painting by Evelina Valieva
Cover by Jay John Bennington
Map by Silvia Dobreva

Cataloging Information:

Dewey Decimal Classification 813.6
ISBN-13 978-0-692-14704-7
Library of Congress Control Number: 2014911739
Printed in the United States of America.
10 9 8 7 6 5 4 3 2 1

To

Our Families

Sic semper tyrannis
(Thus always to tyrants.)

Marcus Junius Brutus

MAP OF STONEGATE

CONTENTS

Map   ix
Preface   xiii
Chapter 1 An Incident on the Cash River   1
Chapter 2 The Academy   9
Chapter 3 Home Fires   15
Chapter 4 Green River Surgery   22
Chapter 5 The Beginning of Troubles   28
Chapter 6 Tension in Stonegate   36
Chapter 7 Secrets, Secrets, Secrets   44
Chapter 8 A Hasty Decision   52
Chapter 9 Whispers in the House of Healing   59
Chapter 10 A New Marshall   65
Chapter 11 Captive   74
Chapter 12 A New Love Unfolds   82
Chapter 13 A Plan is Hatched   90
Chapter 14 A Missing Person   100
Chapter 15 History Repeats   107
Chapter 16 A Prisoner in the Palace   112
Chapter 17 A Great Disappointment   119
Chapter 18 A Journey South   128
Chapter 19 The Weapon Smiths   135
Chapter 20 A Revelation for Robby   145
Chapter 21 Horse Troops   153
Chapter 22 A New Kind of Prison   163
Chapter 23 A New General   167
Chapter 24 Casualties of War   176
Chapter 25 Of Arrows and Guns   184
Chapter 26 A Cry for Help   195
Chapter 27 The Dream   201
Chapter 28 War on the Border   213
Chapter 29 A Day of Executions   218
Chapter 30 The Redemption of Robby   223
Chapter 31 The Invasion   229
Chapter 32 The Great Escape   238
Chapter 33 Of Gunpowder and Poison   250
Chapter 34 The Law of Reciprocity   264
Chapter 35 The Witch Is Dead   276
Chapter 36 A Fire in the West   286
Chapter 37 Triumph   297

The Ballad of Carla   313
Afterword   315
Family Tree   317
Maps

Contents

PREFACE

This book is the third in the Stonegate series. The first, *The Stonegate Sword*, was published in 2015 and received multiple awards, including a bronze medal in the 2016 Global eBook Awards. It tells the story of Donald of Fisher and how he came to change course from being a lore-man, or scholar, to a soldier and his adventures along the way. The second book, *The False Prophet*, continued where the first left off but contained enough background information to make it stand on its own. It received a silver medal from Literary Titan and other awards as well. This third book takes place a generation later and can also be read as an independent novel.

Lucia Mudgway from Australia and Harry James Fox from the United States are coauthors. For those interested in the setting of the novels, to include a mention of place names, these details are briefly mentioned in the afterword. Included in the final pages are also a family tree and additional maps of the Stonegate area.

We want to give credit to people who helped us bring this third work to completion:

Our principal editor, Codi Ribitzki, deserves much credit for refining and correcting the final product. She certainly made our job much easier. Other skillful editors were Leila König and Alice Lunsford.

Thanks are also due to Carroll Fox, who used her expertise as an English teacher to find and fix many errors in the early drafts.

Finally, we want to thank the many readers of early proof copies for their insights and suggestions. Mike Rundle was one. For the rest, you know who you are.

CHAPTER 1

†

An Incident on the Cash River

Look, it will be like a lion coming from the thickets of the Jordan to the
watered grazing land.
Jeremiah *49:19 HCSB*

The great cat lay on a granite ledge surrounded by clumps of ryegrass as
tawny as his fur. His belly was full, and he had hidden the remains of
a tender doe that would be good for several more meals. But that did not
mean he was uninterested in the prey that stood several long bounds below.
He was very interested. A human observer would have been amazed at his
patience as he crouched with only his whiskers twitching.

He knew nothing of the concept of patience. When he observed prey,
time passed with the speed of a hummingbird's wing. His brain was hard-
wired to recognize prey. It had something to do with their nervousness, the
fluttering ears, and the large eyes searching for threats. These particular
prey were big, bigger than most, but still prey, and they held his complete
attention.

But there were others there as well. They had a strangeness, a wrongness
about them. They were tall, as if standing on their hind legs, and they had
none of the mannerisms of prey. Their movements were deliberate, and they
seemed to act like hunters, rather than the hunted. They made him uneasy.
He caught their strange odor, and it had a wrongness as well. He could smell
a hint of something else—another kind of wrongness, but of a familiar sort.

The cat had smelled it before, from charred vegetation, turned black. He had even seen the strange red flowers that flickered and glowed and seemed to eat growing things. The smell was distinctive, and these others, the not-prey, had a whiff of that strange odor about them.

For all his size and strength, he was a cautious creature. The prey were tempting, but he had no intention of moving closer. He kept his eyes fixed upon them, watching, waiting, waiting, watching. Even when some of the wrong-things moved away toward the water hole, he continued to lay still. Time meant nothing to him.

†

The breeze blew down-canyon as it often did in the morning. It softly caressed her tanned cheeks. She was glad that she had not used the stinky scent-blocker that Robby used, since it did not matter now. Her green eyes focused on a nearby serviceberry bush. She could just see the tips of the antlers of a mule deer buck. They had been stalking him for two hours, and they were very close.

Ari Westerly had been hunting several times with her cousin, Robby Fisher, but it had been frustrating. For one thing, they had to go a day's ride from Stonegate before they had seen many tracks. Deer were scarce, closer in, and there had even been talk about setting up a hunting season like the ancients had used. Even here, hunting was not easy. The big bucks, particularly, were wary and understood very well that humans were a deadly danger.

The antlers moved and the tips of the gray ears came into view. She could see the shape of the large antlers now. They were a dark gray at the base, corrugated, but shaded to beige, then bone-white toward the tips, which looked as sharp as daggers. Then she saw the black nose and the muzzle, and the large, dark eyes. She froze, motionless.

She and Robby wore dull brown tunics, and she wore dark green tights on her legs and matching sleeves. They had both daubed their faces with green and brown hunter's paste and branches dangled from slits in their clothing. She usually kept her blonde hair in a tight braid that hung down the middle of her back. Her body was thin and wiry, and she knew she was strong for her size. The bow she used had a heavier draw weight than most girls her age could manage. She knew that deer had keen vision, but for some reason, they did not seem to see motionless things as a danger. The buck stared at them for a long minute, then turned away and took a bite of browse.

He took another step with his dainty legs, then threw his head up and looked at them again. She held her breath, trying to avoid blinking her eyes. Then he took another step and another. He was almost completely exposed. The buck lowered his head and turned slightly away. She started to draw her bow, but Robby motioned "no" with his right hand. She froze again.

He took another couple of steps and was completely exposed, perhaps thirty yards away. He turned his head to look up-canyon as if he smelled a scent from that direction. Robby smoothly raised his bow and drew it. She followed his lead, bringing the thumb of her right hand to her cheekbone. They both loosed their arrows at the same instant. It was noisier than she expected, since the silence was so profound. There was a sharp *snap-twang*, and she saw her arrow arch up, perfectly in line with her target just behind the buck's shoulder, and disappear.

The buck jumped, and with a springy, bouncing lunge disappeared behind some small pines. Then everything was quiet, except for a branch that she heard crack farther to the left. She lowered her bow and allowed the tension to start draining from her arms and legs.

"I think we missed," whispered Ari. "I can't believe it. He was well within range."

Robby turned and smiled. His face looked comical, streaked with the brown and dull green smears, and his nose was sunburned and peeling. "We didn't miss," he said. "That was a good shot, Ari. I think we got two pass-throughs."

"Let's go and see," said Ari, starting forward. But Robby put a hand on her arm.

"Not yet. Let's sit down and wait awhile." He proceeded to do just that, lowering himself to the pine needles and resting his back against a tree. She also sat beside him, shaking a cramp out of her left arm.

"Why can't we go look?" she whispered.

"We don't want to scare him. He has been hurt, but if we don't chase him, he will feel weak and will lie down. But he will keep watching behind him. In time, when he has lost enough blood, he will go to sleep. Then we can follow his tracks."

"How long do we have to wait?" asked Ari.

"Oh, about as long as it takes to eat breakfast," said Robby. "But since you always gobble your food down, we will have to wait even longer than that."

She punched his arm. "That wasn't nice. I don't gobble my food," she said. "But it takes you longer since you eat enough for two normal people."

"Ouch," said Robby. "Don't keep doing that. But don't worry. I expect if we find our arrows, they will be bloody."

They sat in silence, listening to the breeze in the treetops. They heard the scolding cry of a Steller's jay. A short time later, they saw the busy black shape of a pine squirrel, frisking on a branch. Robby pulled out a water bottle and offered her a drink. She accepted with thanks and enjoyed the taste of the spring water even though it was warm.

Robby was nearly twenty years old and was almost exactly a year older than Ari. They were first cousins but had been raised almost as brother and sister. They had been involved in many adventures and were nearly inseparable. But Robby had been attending the military academy at Stonegate for two years now, so she did not often get to see him. It was August, the academy was taking a holiday, and she and Robby had decided to go deer hunting. She had been practicing archery every day for weeks, getting ready for the trip.

Carla, Ari's mother, was an artist with a bow and arrow. She had a gift and made it look easy to put an arrow in the middle of the target. It was not easy for Ari. She had to work at it. She knew that she was a decent archer. She also knew that she could never match her mother, even though her mother was on the edge of old age, over forty.

Robby was probably a bit better than she at hitting targets, and his bow had a much heavier draw weight. He was about six feet tall, and his shoulders and arms were muscular, developed by years of hard work on the farm. His hair was almost black, with reddish highlights, and curly. This was strange, since his mother's hair was still a pale blonde and his father's ash-brown with blonde highlights, though he had gray at the temples. Ari loved her Aunt Rachel and Uncle Don almost as much as her own parents.

Robby touched her arm and motioned ahead. They stood, placed arrows on their bowstrings and began cautiously walking to where the buck had been standing. They searched for a few minutes. Robby was annoyed that he could not find his arrow, but they found hers right away. It was sticking in a small hummock, and, as Robby had predicted, it was glazed with dried blood. Nearly dried, that is—a few drops were still tacky to the touch.

"My arrow probably slid under the pine needles," he said. "We might never find it. Let's follow his tracks."

The trail was not hard to follow. The buck had been running hard, and his hooves had left dark scars on the forest floor. They also found a small drop of blood here and there. But there was not much. Ari became concerned. Surely, if the buck had been mortally wounded there would be more blood to find.

"I think we only scratched him," said Ari. "There are only a few drops once in a while."

"Yes, but look here," said Robby, and he pointed to a small oak brush. "See the frothy blood here? He blew that out of his nose. He has been hit in the lungs."

A few minutes later they found a patch of matted leaves, soaked with blood. But the buck was gone, and the tracks were indistinct. It was as if he left walking rather than running. Robby now looked worried, and they puzzled for a while, trying to find his trail. Ari found more drops of blood farther up the hill, and they continued on.

"I had hoped to find him where he had laid down," said Robby. "I don't like seeing him get up and go on farther."

But then Ari looked ahead and saw a tan shape under some low-growing juniper. It was the buck. They approached him cautiously, but it was clear that his life had slipped away. Ari lifted his head by tugging on his antlers. It was surprisingly heavy. His eyes no longer glistened. They seemed to be covered with a thin film, much like a frosty window on a winter day.

"He's beautiful," whispered Ari. "Robby, why did we do this? It seems so wrong, now. Why didn't we just let him live?"

"I know," said Robby, giving her a hug. "There is a wrongness about death. I feel it too."

†

Ari ran back down the trail to find Charlie, who had stayed with the horses. Charlie was at least ten years older than Robby and worked for her parents on Westerly-stead. He was big and strong—and slow. It wasn't just his large body that was slow moving. His mind seemed to work slowly, too. Some people thought him backward, yet she knew he was really quite intelligent. But it was as if time ran more slowly for him than normal people. He was clever in working out problems, such as figuring out the proper saw-cuts to build rafters. Her father, Howard, often said he did not mind that Charlie was slow since he always came up with the right answer in the end.

Charlie was patiently waiting in the shade, holding the lead ropes attached to the horses' halters. He saw her coming and stood. "Hello, Miss Ari," he said. "You seem to be in a hurry. Did you get one?"

"That we did, Charlie," she answered. She was a bit out of breath and did not say much. She took her horse's rope and slid her bow into its case. "Robby is field dressing him. He is a nice buck. I think Mum will be a bit surprised."

Charlie tightened the cinch on his horse, a tall, rangy black. He wrinkled his brow. "What will surprise her?"

"You know what," she answered. "We've gone out several times and always returned empty-handed. But not today."

"Maybe you should catch your breath," Charlie suggested. "There is no hurry."

"I know. You are never in a hurry. But we need to get him back home and hanging in a cool shed. We don't want the meat to spoil."

On the way back, Charlie pointed out the paw-prints of a mountain lion. "He looks to be a big one."

"I didn't see him," said Ari, scanning the hillsides above them. "But the track does look fresh."

"You almost never see them. But he is up there somewhere. Probably watching us right now."

†

Butchering animals and caring for the meat was second nature to Robby. He had the buck dressed and almost skinned when Ari and Charlie rode up. Charlie removed the panniers, which were large canvas bags, from Peg's pack saddle.

Peg was a tall bay mare. She did not like the smell of blood and refused to go close to the fallen buck. She snorted and stamped a forefoot. Ari groaned. She did not want to deal with a temperamental mare.

"Easy, there, Peg," said Charlie. He spoke in a soothing voice and patted her neck as she danced in place. Ari took the meat sacks from the panniers and passed them to Robby.

"I hope she doesn't cause trouble," said Robby as he finished the skinning and wiped the blade of his knife. He took a hatchet and divided the carcass into quarters. The small blade made chopping noises like a man splitting wood for a fire.

It did not take long to get the panniers filled. Ari took Peg's lead rope so Charlie could lift the first pannier. He approached Peg from the off, or right, side. Peg tossed her head and snorted again while sidestepping to the left. Her eyes showed white at the margins. Robby stepped forward and took hold of her halter so that both he and Ari could hold her in place.

Ari patted Peg's nose and kept speaking to her. "Easy girl. It's all right."

Charlie hooked the leather loops of the first pannier over the wooden X-shaped crossbucks of the pack saddle and let Peg take the burden a bit at a time. She seemed unsteady.

"Robby," said Charlie, in his slow, measured voice. "Come here and lift part of the weight. I'll get the other one and we will balance the load."

Robby did as he was told. When Charlie approached with the other pannier, Ari gently twisted Peg's ear to distract her.

She remembered an old horse trainer telling her: *A horse can only keep one idea in his head at a time. Twist his ear and he won't think of anything else.*

Peg did settle down as soon as both panniers were in place, and Robby helped Charlie transfer the hide and head to the center of the pack saddle. Then they covered everything with a tarp. When the load was secured with a pack cinch and rope and the hitch was tied, Charlie checked their work. Finally, after his deliberate inspection was complete, they mounted and took the trail toward home. It would take five hours, but it was downhill—an easy ride.

Ari went first, riding on Rusty, her little roan gelding. He was not a sprinter, but was agile and had endurance. She also liked his easy gaits; he was smooth and collected.

The trail led easterly, and they crossed from the first valley to another by angling upward to cross over a rocky ridge. Patchy brush covered the slope.

Robby spoke from behind. His voice was low, but his tone was urgent. "Quick," he said, "we've got to get out of sight. Turn left and get behind those bushes."

Ari looked back. Robby had been bringing up the rear, but he was spurring forward in a trot. She saw him pointing and reined in that direction. She urged Rusty into a gallop as they dashed toward cover.

Once hidden, they turned their horses to face each other. "I saw riders on the far ridge," said Robby. "I don't want them to see us."

"Why not?" asked Ari.

"Because they look like Raiders."

CHAPTER 2
†

The Academy

Since they have led My people astray saying, 'Peace,' when there is
no peace...
Ezekiel 13:10 HCSB

Donald of Fisher scratched his head, then closed his eyes as he squeezed the bridge of his nose. He looked up at his niece, Arielle. "Are you sure, Ari?" he asked. He kept his tone neutral, but she heard a note of doubt, and she felt her cheeks grow warm.

"Uncle Don," she said, "of course I'm sure. Who else could they have been? They had their shaggy dun ponies; they were armed for war..."

"But what color were their shields?"

"Some red, some black, some red and black. That is the colors the Raiders use, isn't it?"

"Yes," answered Don. "Yes, it is."

Ari stood and faced him. "You are going to say that the Raiders are a thing of the past, aren't you? But I know what we saw."

"Very well, Ari, I believe you. Please sit down."

She complied and Don continued. "But we have had reports like this before."

"Maybe those other reports were true."

"I don't think so. There have been attacks on travelers—on caravans. But the attackers always turned out to be common thieves."

Ari said nothing. Don looked at her and sighed. She set her jaw. *The problem is not convincing him. He knows me. Convincing someone else will be the problem.*

"Where is Robby? Why did you come alone to tell me?"

"Mum asked Robby to help her drive some cattle out of the orchard. Then he was going to see if you were at the academy. I told him I would come here to see if you were in the lore-house."

"That makes sense." Don stood and took his floppy felt hat from a peg. "Let's go to the academy. I want to hear this from him, too."

✝

Twenty years before, the Raider attacks had ceased. The decisive defeat of the False Prophet's army had ended not only open warfare but also the raids from the West. Don had hoped that the scourge of the Raiders would never return.

The Raiders were mercenaries, paid by the False Prophet to spy, harass, and sow confusion among the towns and cities east of the mountains, called the Western Wall. In the lands farther west, they served as the Prophet's tax collectors and enforcers of his will.

But even though the Prophet's army had been defeated, his rule had not ended. Many had hoped that the collapse of the Prophet's grandiose plans and his humiliating defeat would cause his long-suffering people to rise against him. In fact, there had been word of insurrections, even an attempted palace coup, but the Prophet had crushed them all.

✝

"Uncle Don," began Ari as she gathered her things. "What do you think this means?"

Don looked at her as if his thoughts were far away. He stared at her for a long moment. He had a faint smile on his face.

"Why are you looking at me so?" asked Ari, rubbing her cheek. "Do I have dirt on my face?"

"For once, no," said Don, giving a chuckle to show he was making an attempt at a joke. "No. I was just thinking that if you had red hair, you would look just like your mother the first time I ever saw her."

Ari had heard that story many times. She knew he had first met her mother, Carla, when he and several friends had rescued her, Ari's Aunt

Rachel, and four other girls from a Raider camp where they were being held as prisoners. Rachel was now Don's wife and Carla his sister-in-law since Carla had married Ari's father, Howard, Rachel's brother.

She sighed, smelling old books, a musty hint of mold and old leather. Don was filling a saddlebag with a notebook and some items from a drawer. The room had many bookshelves crammed with books, and one wall was nearly covered with swords and armor—old battle trophies. "I suppose," she answered, finally. "But why would the Raiders come back? How did they get past our patrols?"

Don threw the saddlebags over his shoulder and led his way toward the stable. He walked with a limp, his hair was shot with gray, and there were deep smile lines on his ruddy cheeks, but she thought he looked young for his fifty-odd years. "I am afraid that our patrols are not likely to have seen these Raiders, if Raiders they are. We send them out too infrequently, and most of the watchtowers are no longer manned."

At the stable, Don saddled his horse, Skipper, and led him out into the square between the lore-house and the Quill and Sword Inn. Ari led her mount out behind him. They tightened the girths and then mounted. He and Ari rode down the wide street leading to the Gate of Weeping, the north-facing gate leading out of Stonegate. Ari admired Don's mount. The blood bay color was striking. His shiny red coat contrasted with his midnight-black mane, tail, and stockings. The only white was a tiny star in the center of his forehead. She liked her horse, Rusty, but he was a full hand-and-a-half shorter, and his coat had none of the glossy sheen of Skipper.

They spoke little except for a few pleasantries, but Ari was comfortable with silence. She knew her uncle often seemed distant, lost in his own thoughts. But at other times he was warm and friendly and seemed to dote on her.

Leaving the gate, they took a narrow road to the northwest that passed by a prominent grassy mound. It did not look significant, unless one knew it was the mass grave of thousands of men who gave their life trying to conquer Stonegate, long ago. The victims were nameless, but a black granite tablet stood nearby, inscribed with words wishing they would sleep in peace.

Halfway between the burial mound and the horse troop barracks stood their destination. The academy was a two-story building with two wings.

It was quite modern, built of white stucco with a pitched red tile roof. The wings half surrounded a grassy lawn that nestled invitingly before it. Another principal feature was a large parade ground where cadets drilled and did weapons practice. A low wall surrounded the campus, perhaps ten feet high. The wrought-iron gates were open and a lone guard in a small guardhouse waved them through, giving Don a snappy salute.

†

They left their horses in a stable which stood beside other outbuildings behind Academy Main, the principal structure on the campus. Robby's horse was tied there, switching flies with his tail.

They entered through the back door and went directly to Don's office, at the end of a short hallway. Voices murmured, but they could not make out the words. They entered the room, Ari a couple of steps behind Don.

The office was large enough for a desk and a small conference table. A window with real glass panes gave light enough, so the lamps were unlit. An elderly man with a weather-beaten face was sitting in a side chair. Ari recognized him as Gray John, an old battle companion of her uncle and chief military instructor at the academy. Robby was leaning against the desk, arms folded, his face set and somber. Two other men sat at the table.

"There you are, Robby," said Don. "We've been looking for you."

"I thought you would be here, Father," said Robby, looking at the floor. He seemed withdrawn, almost sullen. He did not smile.

Don directed Ari to a chair and sat down himself. "Ari told me what you saw. Why don't you tell me your side of the story?"

Robby looked up. "I don't have a side. We identified a patrol of Raiders in full armor heading west, away from Stonegate."

Don turned to the man next to him. It was Thomas of Longmont, Stonegate council member and another old friend that he had fought beside. "What do you think, Thomas?"

"We have been discussing this with Robby, here. It is hard to believe, but… I take it you witnessed the same thing, Ari?"

"Yes, I did," answered Ari. "We know what we saw. And Charlie saw them too."

"Well, I for one don't doubt you in the least, lass," said the third man, whom Ari knew was Colin McCoy, another family friend. "That is not the issue with me, and I hope you understand that."

"I think I hear a problem coming," said Don. "So, what is the issue?"

"The main issue is what we should do about this news. The problem will be convincing Stonegate to do something about it." He turned toward Ari and fixed his blue eyes on her. She noticed that his hair was as red as her mother's and only had a few flecks of gray. But he was burly, while her mother was slight. *I wonder if Colin and my mother are related.* After a pause, he continued, "No offense, now, but people will say you young people let your imaginations carry you off. And Charlie, you know he's slow. My mother would say he's slower than creeping ivy."

"But Mister McCoy, it seems to me what matters is what's true," said Ari. She wanted to say more but held her tongue with an effort. "And Charlie may be slow, but he's not stupid."

"Not a bit of it, lass. I wish Charlie was helping us here at the academy. As for truth, that was well said. In the end that's all that matters. But people will believe what they want to believe, and they won't want to think that the Raiders are back, with all that might mean."

✝

Don and the others questioned the two young people for perhaps a half-hour. Then they took a break to find some lunch. Most of the staff were away on holiday, but they found bread, sausage, and cheese, and brewed tea to go with it. They ate at the conference room table and tried to decide on the best course of action.

Don noticed that Robby seemed tense and tried to set him at ease. "Tell me, Robby," he said. "Why were you and Ari riding up there in the first place? I don't remember you saying anything about it."

"I'm sorry, Father," said Robby. "Ari and I have been planning a hunting trip for weeks. I'm sure Mother knew all about it. I assumed you did, too."

Don glanced at Gray John, then looked back at Robby. "I see," he said. "I will discuss this with you later."

"I know. Never assume," replied Robby. "It won't happen again."

Thomas of Longmont cleared his throat. "That's all well and good," he said. "But we have a problem here. Two problems, actually."

"Let me see," said Gray John. "The first problem is the False Prophet. Sending out his Raiders again means he has something in mind, and he is willing to risk alerting us. Why would he risk that unless he feels very confident?"

Don nodded. "I see what you mean. We need more information about what is happening in his dominion."

"What you are all talking around," said Colin, "and forgive me for being so blunt…" He paused for a long moment. "You know it will be very difficult to convince Stonegate to take this report seriously."

"We have not been talking around it," said Don. "We have bludgeoned it to death."

"We have two votes on the council," said Thomas. "Mine and Rachel's. You won't have a problem convincing us."

"Yes, and thanks," replied Don. "But every faction on the council will have reason to put off a decision, and two votes won't be enough. They will all say Rachel is siding with me and her son. They know we are close friends, so your vote will also be seen as biased. The mayor's father regarded me as his bitter enemy until the day he died. Everything I suggest, he opposes, just as his father did before him."

"There is one bright spot," said Gray John. "The commander of Stonegate's horse troops does not need the council's permission to send a patrol west. Hamway is a good man. I trained him myself. I will speak with him."

Don looked at Gray John and smiled. "Well, old friend, if anyone can convince him to investigate, it's you. I'm just sorry that you aren't still leading the horse troops, yourself."

CHAPTER 3
†

Home Fires

A time to love and a time to hate;
a time for war and a time for peace.
Ecclesiastes 3:8 HCSB

The stable was quite small; it only had four stalls. But there was a breeze-way down the center wide enough to hold a wagon and a four-wheeled carriage. So it served as a carriage house as well. Don unsaddled Skipper and placed the saddle and blankets on a stand in the tack room. Then he led him out the back door and down a lane to the horse pasture. When he removed the bridle, Skipper nodded his head as if in appreciation, then walked a few paces, lowered himself to the ground and rolled. He obviously was enjoying himself.

Don watched him and was suddenly reminded of Old Robert, who had taught him most of what he knew of horses. Robert had been commander of Ariel's horse troops during the war against the False Prophet, long ago. The old man had taught him much, and he remembered the day he had died in battle, a crossbow bolt in his side. Don still blamed himself for his death. Robby, his son, had been named for his old mentor, and Don told stories about him to his children.

He did not want Robert to be forgotten, not that there was much chance of that. He lay buried in the nave of the largest church in Ariel, and he was still considered a folk hero by the people of the area. Don rarely thought about it, but he knew that he, himself, was famous in song and story as the

Lore-man on the Red Horse. He had traveled there several times with Rachel and had been warmly received. The elders of Ariel had asked if Don might be buried beside the old warrior. They even showed them a vault that had been prepared for that purpose.

No one likes to think about their own mortality and still less those they love. Rachel had been strangely upset, and the elders had quickly assured her that she would tender them a great honor if she gave permission to be buried there, too, at Don's side. They had both thanked them and promised to give the matter serious consideration. They had discussed the matter several times and had yet to come to a decision. Rachel considered the subject morbid even though she understood that it was considered a great honor. Don was tempted to give permission and even write it into his will since he was not held in great esteem by many Stonegate leaders. But Rachel had a family plot at Westerly-stead and that complicated matters.

Skipper rolled completely over on one side then back over to finish on the other side. Robert had said that this was a good sign. *If he rolls to one side, then completely over to the other, he's a good horse.* Don did not know if that was true, but Skipper was a good horse. But he was no warhorse like Snap who had carried him safely through many battles. The sad thing about owning and loving horses was that they died too soon. Snap had been put out to pasture when too old to ride. Don had himself found him dead, lying in knee-high grass. His great heart had failed him, at last.

Don hung up the bridle and walked to the house. It was a modest two-story dwelling, built of brick. The black grillwork over the windows contrasted with the white shutters and front door. He did not climb the two granite steps in front but continued to a side door that gave access to the kitchen. He entered and saw Sara, his daughter, kneading a bulging mound of dough. She turned and smiled. "I can't hug you, Daddy; my hands are covered over in flour."

Don gave her a hug and kissed her cheek. "That's fine. I can hug you," he said. "Where is your mother?" Sara was a happy twelve-year-old with rosy cheeks, full lips, and beautiful golden chestnut hair. She was just starting to show some graceful curves, though she still had the figure of a wood sprite. She was a girly-girl, with little interest in outdoor things, though she did enjoy horseback riding with her big brother. She also enjoyed teasing him unmercifully.

Sara told him that Rachel was in the study, so he walked that direction, lobbing his floppy hat at a hat rack in the hall. He met her at the study door while in mid-stride. They almost collided, and Don took advantage of the moment to steal a kiss. "How are you, Blue-eyes?" he asked.

She patted his cheek. "I am glad to see you. Robby stopped by. He was upset about something. He said he didn't want to worry me, but of course, that made me worry." She paused for a moment as she led the way to two easy chairs between their two desks. "Oh, he said they got a nice buck. I will look forward to some venison."

Don followed her and they both sat. "As will I," Don said, after a moment. "But you had reason to worry. I don't know why he did not tell you—or why he did not tell me about the hunting trip, for that matter."

Rachel put her hand to her mouth and her blue eyes widened. She had her blonde hair pulled back in a bun, and there were a few snow-white threads at her temples. Otherwise, she could have passed for a young woman in her late twenties. Time had been kind to her, despite the grief she had endured. "Oh, Don," she said in a whisper. "I'm sorry. I knew about it and forgot to mention it. Going hunting, I mean. But what else happened?"

Don told her the whole story. He had no problem convincing her that Robby and Ari had seen a Raider patrol, but she saw instantly that they could not easily translate that information into decisive action. She relaxed a bit when Don explained that Gray John was sure he could convince Commander Hamway to send out a patrol.

Don and Rachel discussed the bad feelings that Mayor Billings bore, approaching hatred toward Don. "I don't think he hates me," said Rachel. "He and I often disagree, and he chafes at a woman being on the council. He often says my Christian beliefs always encourage sentimentality and weakness. He says I avoid the hard decisions. But his father has poisoned his view of you."

"I know, dear," said Don, rubbing his brow. He looked out the window and could smell the newly mown hay. The memories came rushing back. He remembered the plan of the present mayor's father, also called Mayor Billings, and Lord Allen, the marshall of Stonegate, to mutilate the prisoners of war before sending them home. They believed this stern action would cause them to fear, and that would prevent any future invasions. Don and Rachel had opposed this strongly, and the rift that this created had never healed. It was all the more galling to the leaders that Don and Rachel's views had won the day.

Rachel put her face in her hands. "I can hear them now," she said. "If you had only not been so weak and sentimental, we could have prevented another invasion, forever."

"Now, Rachel," said Don, as he patted her shoulder. "We don't know they plan to invade. This could just be a probe. They may just be trying to gather information. We need to be doing the same."

"No, darling," said Rachel. A tear formed at the corner of her eye. "It is beginning all over again. This time the False Prophet will have learned from his mistakes. I fear for us all."

†

That night at supper, Don chatted with Robby and Ari, briefly reviewing once more what they had seen. Ari often shared a meal with them, so it was no surprise that she did so this night. Sara insisted on sitting at Ari's side. Don blessed the food and invited God's presence. As usual, there was lively chatter, except that Robby seemed a bit subdued. They spent little time talking about the Raiders, nor even what should be done about them.

The room was a comfortable one, with a high ceiling supported by rough-cut beams. The table glowed with beeswax, and the cutlery was sterling silver. An antique crystal vase held several fresh-cut roses, and the remains of a pot roast, carrots and potatoes held center place. The window was open, and a gentle breeze blew through the room. Ari then asked about the academy and Robby's first year there.

"You see Robby all the time, Ari," said Rachel. "Don't tell me he never talked about his first year."

"He never has, Aunt Rachel," said Ari. "But we have him trapped now. So tell us, Robby, how was it?"

Robby looked at Don for a long minute. "I will be glad to, Ari, but first let Father explain why he started the academy in the first place."

Don hesitated for a long moment. It seemed that he might make an excuse and not answer the question at all. Finally, he spoke, "Not too many people have ever asked 'why,' Robby. Now that I think about it, that does seem a bit strange."

They all had heard the story of the war with the False Prophet many times, so Don talked about the first years after peace had been restored, and the army had been demobilized. The allies of Stonegate had returned to their homes, and Don and Rachel began married life together. Don had, for awhile, kept himself busy around Westerly-stead, the combination farm-ranch owned by Rachel's family. The estate had been evenly divided between Rachel and Howard and their two younger twin brothers, Levi and Lucas. But Howard gradually took over most of the daily management of the property. Then Don and Rachel had built their own home about a half mile from Westerly-stead. Don began spending more time at the lorehouse and bought a half-interest in that institution. But he found that the world of study and learning did not interest him as much as it had before circumstances forced him to take up arms.

It was Gray John that suggested he establish an academy to train young men in military science. Don was skeptical, thinking there would be little interest in this kind of training. But he finally agreed to start a trial class on strategy and tactics, trying to capture the lessons learned in their recent struggle. They had no buildings, and the leaders of Stonegate offered no assistance, but they set up a six-week camp and invited twenty youngsters from good families to attend. It combined weapons training, horsemanship, and classes on how to lead men in combat. They even taught the rudiments of gunnery and allowed the trainees to load and fire the field artillery.

Tuition barely covered the cost of feeding the appetites of the young trainees, but the first session was a great success. Many prominent citizens encouraged Don to set up a longer program. And the academy was born. The faculty was chosen from men with combat experience, men like Don, who were looking for a challenging profession now that fewer warriors were needed for defense.

Don looked at Rachel as he finished explaining. "Your mother, Robby, encouraged me to do this," he said. "I think she was tired of me being underfoot."

"Not at all, dear," said Rachel with a smile. "But as soon as this house was finished, I could see you needed something to do. I could tell that the lore-house was not going to be enough."

"It was a risk," said Don, with a bit of a smile. He mopped up a bit of gravy with a crust of bread and chewed it. "We took most of our savings to buy the land from the city and build the campus. Even now, the academy does not make much profit. We could probably have made more money if we had simply left it with the money-lenders."

"That was interesting, Uncle Don," said Ari. "But no more excuses, Robby. Tell."

"It is not that it is a secret or anything," said Robby. "But unless you have been through it… It's just hard to explain. But the first year was hard; it was very hard."

"Was it the hazing?" asked Rachel. "We warned you about that, son."

"The hazing was part of it. But there are strict limits on that, so it was not too bad. The upperclassmen are not allowed to make slaves of the grunts, so we did have time to do our studies. Part of it was the lack of sleep. We had to stand guard on a twenty-four-hour rotation. But part was the competition. I thought I would have no problem doing well, but everyone in my class was as good as me, or better, in almost everything. It was discouraging. I wanted to make you proud, Father, and I was far from the top of the class."

"Not that far, Robby," said Don. "And you did make me proud. You did not give up even though I knew it was harder than you expected.

Robby brightened a bit at that. "Thank you for saying so."

Robby told a few stories about his experience and even made jokes about his problems, which caused a ripple of laughter around the table. He also mentioned that twelve of the first-year students had dropped out. But that was about average, and that was why the academy allowed sixty to enter the first year. After that, they kept the class size at around fifty, which meant that a little over 400 cadets were enrolled.

"Uncle Don," began Ari, "I don't understand why the cadets are all boys…"

"There are many reasons for that," interrupted Don. "A practical reason is that parents would never allow their daughters to attend. I am sure you know the other reasons. Young men hope to make practical use of their training. Women have no hope of a military career, so they would not invest so much time for no good reason."

"Yes, I know very well what you mean. But my mother proved that she was the equal of any man when it came to archery."

"She certainly did, Ari, but she is one in a thousand."

"Why couldn't you put on a short course for girl archers and let my mother teach it? If the class was all girls, parents may not object if their daughters dearly want to go." *I hope Uncle Don can see that I am right, and we can never have too many trained archers.*

Sara spoke up, "What a good idea, Ari."

Don and Rachel looked at each other for a long moment. Rachel winked at him.

"I think she has a point, dear," said Rachel. "You have a good head on your shoulders, Ari. We could hold school when the young men are away on maneuvers."

Don smiled at her and Sara. Ari felt satisfied. She would love to attend such a school, herself.

CHAPTER 4

†

Green River Surgery

You are going to hear of wars and rumors of wars. See that you are not
alarmed, because these things must take place, but the end is not yet.
Matthew 24:6 HCSB

Abel stood and massaged a knotted cramp in his lower back. His examination room was really a tent and the afternoon sun made it uncomfortably warm, even though he had rolled up the back wall had to provide some ventilation.

He stepped out to view the line of waiting patients. They were all sitting on low benches under several cottonwood trees. A young nurse, Anna, sat under a canopy behind a wooden camp table. She was recording patient information in a ledger as he approached.

"Anna," said Abel. "I need to take a break. Hold my patients for a half hour."

"Of course," she said with a smile. "We only have twelve waiting, and you certainly have seen more than your share." She reached for an hourglass and turned it over.

Abel nodded and walked behind the stone building that held their supplies and the tiny operating theater. He came to his own tent and poured a glass of water. He wiped his brow and sank into his folding chair. His gray tunic was stained, he noticed. *I probably should change into a clean one.* He rubbed his thumb over the embroidered crimson cross over his right breast. *At least here the Prophet's poor folk can see the cross on display.*

The Green River Surgery had been set up eight years ago. Abel had convinced the chief surgeon of the House of Healing that the Prophet's lands were closed to them and that was not likely to change. The Gray Pilgrims, sent out as roving healers to many isolated villages, had been expelled. The Prophet was sure they were spies as much as healers, and there was much truth to that. They did collect information and sent regular reports on conditions they encountered.

Desperate people, seeking medical care, had continued to take the long road to the House of Healing. But the way was difficult, and those who most needed care often found the journey impossible.

Abel was the one who conceived the plan of setting up a semipermanent surgery far to the west on the very border of the Prophet's lands. It had taken several years to put it into full operation, but it had been a success.

The sick, injured, and diseased could reach the Green River in a few days' travel from Prophet City. Abel had feared, at first, that the Prophet would drive them away by military force. But he had chosen to allow them to stay, unmolested.

Like the wandering Gray Pilgrims, the surgery had medicines based on formulas and compounds dating from the elder days. The healers were trained in a rigorous course of study and understood much of the ancient medical lore. Even though the surgery looked rude and primitive, the medical care they provided was far better than anything found in the Prophet's lands.

But there were limits. Their antibiotics could cure many infections, but they could not save a leg black with gangrene. Treatment often required amputation, which they could perform on-site. The medical books of the ancients enabled Abel and the other healers to diagnose many diseases, but that did not mean they could always cure them. They knew much, but they also knew how much had been lost. It was often frustrating.

Abel walked back and told Anna to send him the next patient. A tall young man with a full beard entered. His left arm was wrapped in a bloody bandage. Abel carefully unwound the black, crusty cloth to expose a mangled hand. The arm was swollen, red, and angry-looking.

"We will be able to treat this," said Abel, "but it was good that you did not delay, Mr...."

"Logan," the young man responded, "Tom Logan."

"Mr. Logan," said Abel, "we will have to clean this up and put you on some strong medicine. Did you have any trouble getting here?" He took a swab and began to clean the wound.

"No trouble, but there were, well, a few bad moments."

"What bad moments?"

"The road was blocked for a long time by a thousand horsemen in full armor. But that was not all."

"What else?"

"There were a lot of little cannons on wheels pulled by horses. At least a dozen. It was hard to get around them, I can tell you."

†

After sundown, they stopped seeing new patients, and the healers made the rounds of those who were in bed. Then they had their common meal. With guards, nurses, healers, and attendants, the cooks usually had about forty mouths to feed, in addition to the patients. The surgery had become an open-air hospital.

Thad, Abel's oldest friend, kept the records. He was a better administrator, allowing Abel to focus on patient care. Thad was also an excellent surgeon, and he performed several procedures a day in the operating theater.

Thad and Abel retired to Abel's tent and discussed the problems of the day, as they usually did. The western sky was red and mauve as they lit an oil lamp and relaxed over cups of hot tea.

"Any items of interest from the West?" asked Thad. He flexed his long fingers and brushed back a lock of dark hair.

Thad has surgeon's fingers. I wish I had his skill with a scalpel.

"As a matter of fact, yes," answered Abel. "You know we have often heard rumors of a military buildup. Reports of cannon fire, and the like."

"No doubt about it. I have read your reports—the ones you send to the chief surgeon. I wonder if anyone else reads them."

"Yes. It is like dropping a rock down a deep well and listening for a splash that never comes."

"Something new today?"

"What would you say about a report of a dozen field artillery pieces on maneuvers with one thousand heavy cavalrymen in full armor?"

"You don't say. By all that's holy—Abel! That would have been enough to turn the tide of battle in the last war." Thad's face went pale, and he sat bolt upright in his chair. "You have to do more than file another report."

"I shall write a report tonight, but this time I will also send a message to Donald. Stonegate has to know about this."

†

Five wagons loaded with food and medical supplies had arrived that day and would be returning to the House of Healing in the morning. They would be carrying three seriously ill patients and the money that they had collected in fees over that last two weeks. They would also carry Abel's report, which was almost ready. Most of the document consisted of information about patients treated and a list of needed supplies. Information relating to the Prophet's dominion, and especially military matters, was usually included in a coded addition. Abel wrote the message about the heavy cavalry and field artillery on a scrap of parchment, encoded it, and then made a clean copy. He folded it in a parchment envelope and sealed it with red wax.

It was dangerous to send an uncoded message, but Abel had no choice when he wrote the next one. He had never set up such an arrangement with Donald. If the messenger was intercepted and the Prophet learned that he was reporting such sensitive information, reprisals would be swift.

Abel remembered the communications that existed twenty years before. In those days, there had been an elaborate system of heliograph stations and messenger pigeons. *If only the old system had been kept up, Donald would have the message in hours instead of days.*

Abel wrote the message in a long letter to his old friend, but he dared not be too specific. He and Donald had ridden far together and had shared the dangers and hardships of battle. He felt like a prophet of doom, but Stonegate must be warned. War was coming. He felt it in his bones.

†

The Gray Pilgrims traveled through many wild and hostile lands and were only very rarely robbed. They were armed with a sword and crossbow, but these were for defense against wild animals. Even the most hardened highwaymen knew the Pilgrims would treat them with no questions asked, so they allowed the roving healers to pass unmolested. But Abel was sure that this truce would not hold for the Green River Surgery. For one thing, the surgery charged a fee, and that meant gold and silver. The supplies of drugs and medical equipment had value, also, much more than that carried by the Pilgrims.

The chief surgeon was a pacifist, but even he realized that the surgery would need a security detail. Abel had recruited a dozen guards, each armed with crossbow, sword, spear, and musket. They helped keep order among the patients seeking treatment and provided a guard throughout the night. He also insisted that the surgery must be guarded by another dozen horsemen, armed and organized in the Stonegate fashion, to patrol the vicinity. This made sure that no hostile force could approach undetected.

Abel was mostly concerned about bandits, but he wanted to be warned well in advance, if the False Prophet should ever send a military force against them. Two dozen men would be a formidable force, enough to discourage criminals, but would be of little use against the Prophet's mighty army.

The commander of the security forces, Quentin, was a middle-aged warrior who had served many years in a Stonegate horse troop. Abel did not want to use him as a messenger, but he had a young assistant, Jason, who was a recent graduate of the Stonegate Academy and who knew Donald very well.

Early in the morning, before breakfast, Abel met with Quentin and told him about the latest information. Quentin, whose nickname was "Hawk," was troubled and agreed that a message had to be sent to Stonegate as soon as possible.

"It's a good three hundred miles, you know, Abel," said Quentin. "Jason is little more than a lad. Perhaps I should go."

"No, Hawk," said Abel. "I need you here. Perhaps you could send a couple of troopers with him and two pack horses. They could use the pack horses as remounts if it comes to that."

"Aye, well…Needs must. Best if he starts this morning."

"I agree. I have a letter for Donald, but I worded it so that the message is not too clear, in case someone intercepts him. He will have to know what it means so he can explain it. Have them get ready, and I will talk to Jason before he goes."

Quentin walked away. On the ground, he walked with a hobbled gait, the result of an old war wound. Mounted, though, he rode with the grace and élan of a centaur. Both he and Jason had the lanky long-legged look that so many horsemen seemed to have, though Quentin was burlier through the shoulders.

Less than an hour later, Jason came to Abel's tent. "Lord Abel," he called out. "Did you want to see me?"

Abel raised the tent flap and emerged, wiping shaving soap from his face with a towel. "That I did. Let me tell you."

CHAPTER 5
†

The Beginning of Troubles

At that time Michael the great prince who stands over your people will
rise up. There will be a time of distress such as never has occurred since
nations came into being until that time. But at that time all your people
who are found written in the book will escape.
Daniel 12:1 HCSB

A full moon was hanging suspended in a black night sky like a perfectly
formed circular lantern giving light to what remained of the old Empire.
A cascade of nearby stars twinkled and sparkled like cut diamonds, as a band
of a dozen men made their way on horseback through the ruins that lay
south-east of Goldstone. Silhouetted against the night sky, their shadowy
figures moved quietly and quickly from their secret camp. No one cared to
visit the ruins anymore, not since peace had now endured for twenty years
after the horror of war. The inn was alive with the sound of fiddles, women's
laughter, and men's voices, happy that the False Prophet was just a legend
from the West. It was as if they could not seriously imagine him entering
the town and conquering them. During the day, people went about their
affairs, avoiding thoughts of war. On nights such as these, with a few stout
ales, the men let loose, forgetting their troubles and fears.

In Goldstone, one part of the town held a community, students and
educated men of wisdom, who studied the old lore books from the Days
of the Elders. Tonight, it lay fast asleep, the lore-men complacent in their
comfortable lives. None could envision that tonight invaders would break
the long peace.

The riders had dun horses and carried red and black shields, but in the shadows of the night, they showed an arrogant confidence that no one would see them as they rode into Goldstone. The town gates were open. It was almost midnight when they neared the lore-houses which lay in the center of town, and it was there that they were heading. All was quiet as they entered the grounds of the old buildings where precious books of knowledge and history were kept.

They dismounted their horses and crept in silence across the lore-house grounds toward the back entrance. A dark cloud had hidden the moon, making it difficult to see their way, but finally they found the entrance they were looking for. It was padlocked as expected, but they had come prepared with an axe to break the lock.

Within minutes they had entered the lore-house, straining to see what they thought would be in there—a library full of precious books. Books that the Prophet had ordered them to steal and bring to him. Books that would finally provide him with the knowledge to destroy his enemies in the East. Books that were the pride of Goldstone.

But to their dismay, there were no books. Instead, there was a stone wall in front of them with a thick wooden door covered in a wrought iron grille which was securely chained and padlocked. There was no way of gaining entry to this library, not even with their axes. It had obviously been fortified. Their information was outdated. Frustrated and afraid of the Prophet's wrath, the disheartened band of men admitted defeat and mounted their horses for the long ride home to Prophet City.

†

Morning seemed to come too slowly for Martin Abaddon, the Prophet of Prophet City, who had endured a restless night full of anxiety, crippling thoughts, and worrisome dreams when he finally did manage to fall into a fitful sleep. The shock and humiliation of being defeated by Donald of Goldstone twenty years earlier had never left him, acerbated by the courier delivery of the head of his cousin, commander of his Raiders, Balek Brown.

On top of that, his youngest servant, Isabella, who was his personal maid and later his concubine, had escaped from the palace. Rumors had reached his ears that she had run to Donald of Goldstone for help and was now secretly living in the House of Healing where she had immunity. It was one place where he did not want to meddle, not yet.

"Damn you, Isabella!" the Prophet muttered under his breath as he remembered that not only had this Donald defeated him in war, but he had protected many others who had betrayed him by fleeing. "I promise you one thing Donald of Goldstone…the next time I attack will be with force and vengeance. I will cut short your worthless life, and I will rule my new empire!"

The impact of defeat and humiliation had affected more than the Prophet's ego. It had a disastrous impact on the people of his capital, Prophet City. No longer did the Prophet come out on his balcony and give gifts and coins to his people, for his shame over the loss of his men and his defeat was too great. Instead, the people had been reduced to near-slavery. Much of the money he extorted in taxes was used to restore his military and build weapons.

The community festered with subdued grumbling, but anyone who spoke openly against the Prophet risked public execution. The headsman silenced the majority, but a small group of Christian believers had formed a secret society which planned to overthrow the Prophet. The Liberty Soldiers consisted of men and women who had suffered persecution as people of faith. Most of the Prophet's subjects knew that the Prophet was an evil tyrant interested only in power and greed. But this small group was gradually making plans—not just plans for the Prophet's downfall, but for the government that would come later.

After Isabella disappeared, the Prophet had blamed his favorite concubine, Selena, accusing her of aiding and abetting Isabella's escape. As punishment, Selena had been imprisoned in the palace tower, but in mysterious and unexplainable circumstances, Selena too had somehow escaped, never to be seen again.

"Damn women!" Martin Abaddon screamed out of the palace window where outside the sun was making its upward way into a blue morning sky. At least Shakti, his chief dancer, had never betrayed him and had now replaced Isabella as his personal maid and political advisor. It was Shakti who entered his room with his breakfast tray.

Time had not been gentle to Martin, who at sixty-two had aged in ways that made him appear older. His black hair had now turned a silvery white with auburn streaks which once had been reddish highlights. His feet and ankles were swollen, and his face was somewhat bloated. Yet Shakti, like a good bottle of wine, had aged well and blossomed into a very attractive forty-year-old woman whose grace and seductive figure still held Martin spellbound. She could still perform a dance as well as she had twenty years ago. Her advice was often useful.

"Sit, Shakti, please sit," Martin gestured to a chair. His voice had softened from his earlier ramblings, something that often happened when Shakti appeared. She seemed to have some kind of spell over him which almost made him appear gentle. It was quite a contrast to his real character which was aggressive and ruthless. "Please…join me for breakfast."

"Thank you, my lord. I would be honored to," Shakti said, flashing a smile that revealed white teeth which contrasted with the vividly red color painted on her full lips. She lowered herself onto the ornate tapestry-covered chair beside Martin, flicking back her long, dark locks of hair as she met his troubled eyes. "Why do you look so worried, my lord?"

"Please, Shakti, we have known each other for a long time, and you have served me well in every way. Please call me Martin. If anyone has earned the privilege of addressing me by my first name, it is certainly you."

"Of course…Martin. So what is making you look so sad?"

Martin sighed as Shakti poured him a steamy cup of tea to which she added milk and honey as he preferred. "Well, just before you arrived, Shakti, I was cursing women. You know, it is one thing to be beaten in war by men, but it is a worse thing for a man to be thwarted by two silly women. They escaped and put me to shame. You know, Shakti, I have never forgotten what Isabella and Selena did to me, even though it was twenty long years ago. And yet, here you are with all your kindness and beauty…you have been the only woman in my life who has truly shown me loyalty. You, out of all of them, are the only one I can trust."

Shakti looked surprised but pleased and a little confused. In all her time with the Prophet, she had never heard him share his innermost thoughts with anyone. Maybe old age and being humbled in war had softened him somehow…at least regarding her. Somehow, it seemed strange that this bitter man had any feelings at all, other than those of hatred for the East or contempt for his own people, the commoners. Something was amiss. *Maybe he has some different agenda.* Shakti knew him too well, knowing in her heart he could never be trusted, despite the fact he had just claimed he trusted her. Nobody trusted the Prophet anymore…not even his own men. He had many of his generals and colonels executed after the war because they had failed him. She thought he had become the most feared and hated man in the world.

"Why, Martin, thank you," she said after a brief pause. "It is my willing duty to serve you. Here, I have brought you some freshly baked bread and cheese as well as some fruit. Do not let these past events upset you, but rather think of today and tomorrow and eat your breakfast. You must stay strong if we are to defeat our enemies in the East."

I must be cautious, was Shakti's gut feeling. *What is he warming me up for? What will he have me do to appease the beast in him?*

Martin took Shakti's hand in his, stroking her long slender fingers, which were adorned with gold rings set with precious gemstones, gifts from him over the years. "You know, Shakti, I am no longer a young man, but I can still raise a powerful army to defeat my enemies. I believe that now is my time. My only desire is to annihilate Donald of Goldstone and all of Stonegate and those foul Southerners, the Sonora Clan and the Diné people. Soon, my army will be ready. They are finishing their final training now. I have not been idle for these last twenty years."

Shakti squeezed his hand in affection. "I know, Martin. I know your dreams and plans and hopes for the future. I have seen you long at work these past years and I feel that the time is ripe to strike against the East."

"How clever you are, Shakti, to have observed such a thing. Not just a beauty but blessed with brains and courage."

"You are too kind, Martin. It is common knowledge in Prophet City that you are building a vast army of soldiers, spies, and assassins. One would be a fool not to realize that you are planning to attack and very soon."

"You are no fool, my dearest Shakti. You have surmised correctly. I am indeed planning an imminent attack. The East has become complacent, apathetic, and completely unaware of my intentions. Therefore, I shall take them all by surprise. In fact, I have established secret camps all throughout the East where my Black Caps and Raiders have been spying on our enemies. And last week I sent Raiders on a highly secret mission to confiscate certain books from the lore-houses of Goldstone. These books contain specific information about ancient weapons of war. I want those books."

"Brilliant, Martin," said Shakti, moving closer. "And when will these Raiders return?"

Martin took a sip of tea and turned to look through the long windows of his private chambers. A band of Raiders was galloping at full speed down a long avenue. "Look, I do believe that is them now riding towards the palace. They should be here very soon."

"In that case, I should leave you to dress for your meeting with them." Shakti rose to take leave, but not before Martin took her arm and patted the chair.

"Yes, of course, my dear, but before you go I need to ask you a huge favor."

Shakti froze, realizing now that all of Martin's kind words had most likely been just a pretext to something more sinister. Her gut feelings had been right all along. Her heart skipped a beat as she wondered what this huge favor entailed. She resumed her seat.

"I have said many times that your beauty is timeless and your seductive ways, no man can resist. I just realized last night that no one in the East knows you or what you look like except for Isabella who rumor has it is safely tucked up in the House of Healing. Therefore, I need your help to gather the information I need about Stonegate, and especially about Donald of Goldstone and his family."

"Oh, Martin," Shakti said unsure of what he was implying. "Are you asking me to go from being your maid and dancer to your spy?"

"Correct, again, dear Shakti. Yes, that is exactly what I am implying. No one would ever guess that I have a female spy. They killed my last spy in their inner circle, a man named Bobby. But that was long ago, and I doubt they would see you as a threat."

"Oh, dear…I don't know."

"Hear me out. One of my spymasters sent a plan for my approval. It requires a woman who is clever, beautiful, and most of all, absolutely loyal. I immediately thought of you. You can do this, and you would earn my gratitude. Are you willing to hear more?"

Shakti nodded, but she felt like a mouse in a trap.

"I need you to find a man called Charlie who works at Westerly-stead in Stonegate. He is around thirty years of age and single, and some say he is a bit slow. I think he would fall for your charms very quickly and would be a perfect source of information about the people he lives and works with."

Shakti shuddered at the thought of leaving the palace and venturing into unknown territory. The palace was the only life she had known. She had spent her life pleasing the Prophet because she knew no other way to survive. Being used as bait to trap some innocent soul disgusted her.

"But how will I survive in Stonegate? Where will I live?" Shakti wrung her hands in anxiety at the thought of being alone with strangers in a strange world, a strange town.

"I do get regular reports from Stonegate. Many traders provide information, for example. Now, this plan is very specific. There is an inn, the Quill and Sword, that is looking for a housemaid and waitress. Upon my orders, one of my spies sent a letter to the inn. The letter said that you were moving from a town called Loveland to Stonegate and needed work. I won't go into the details, but they offered you a job. So, it is really not difficult. The hardest part, I'm afraid, will be your journey there. You will need to leave immediately and travel as fast as possible. Go to Stonegate, take the job, and make friends with this Charlie. Maybe you could become more than friends. As clever as you are, you should be able to learn much from him. There is really little risk for you, my dear, or I would not agree to send you."

Shakti knew full well that the Prophet was giving a command. She did not dare refuse.

At that moment, the leader of the Raiders entered and bowed low, one knee on the floor. The Prophet turned to receive his report, so Shakti withdrew to a corner of the room. The embarrassed man was finally able to speak and revealed the bad news that they had not been able to steal the precious books from Goldstone.

"Stand up and quit mumbling. You are saying that you failed? You could not access the library?"

"No, sir," said the chief Raider. "This mission was impossible. They have fortified the library with new inner stone walls, grilles, and chains. Penetration of the library was impossible. It would take an explosive device to bring down those walls or even access the grilled door."

Rage burned hot as the Prophet realized that there was no way he could get hold of those books unless they attacked Goldstone with full force. "I'll deal with you later. Get out of my sight!" he snarled. The man fled.

The Prophet beckoned Shakti to come closer. "Bring some refreshments, then go prepare for your trip to the East. I intend to have a meeting with my generals. It is nearly time to go to war."

CHAPTER 6
†

Tension in Stonegate

When they say, "Peace and security," then sudden destruction comes on them, like labor pains come on a pregnant woman, and they will not escape.
1 Thessalonians 5:3 HCSB

The late August nights in Stonegate were beginning to get cooler even though the days were still pleasantly warm. It was late afternoon, when the sun had lost its heat, that Rachel ventured out into her vegetable garden to harvest beans and corn. Ari and Robby were close by, chattering and laughing as they collected chicken eggs and fed the ducks and geese which were wandering around honking loudly. The sun was sinking below the mountain peaks in the west, leaving behind a trail of orange streaks which painted the fading blue sky.

The peace was shattered by the sound of a running horse. Don arrived in a hurry. Skipper snorted as if in protest at being ridden so hard as Don dismounted near Rachel, a troubled look in his eyes.

"For goodness' sake, Don, you rode in here like you were being chased by the Raiders. What is wrong? Has there been another sighting?"

"Yes," said Don. "But it is not urgent. I was just giving Skipper some exercise."

Don gave his stallion an affectionate rub on the nose. Despite the dirt on Rachel's face and hands from digging a new garden bed, Don pulled her in close for a kiss on the cheek. Their affection for one another had never diminished over the years. "I just heard troubling news from Goldstone. Apparently, a recent attempt was made to rob their lore-houses. The front door had been broken into, but thank God there was no way anyone could break into the library, itself. There is no evidence of who was responsible, but I doubt that this was the work of bandits. Bandits want gold or jewelry, but the Prophet might see things differently."

A worried frown crossed Rachel's fair countenance as she remembered the recent sighting of the Raiders and now this break-in, which seemed to be too much of a coincidence. "I fear you are right, Don. It appears that it was the Raiders, and if that is the case, what will they do next? The Prophet must be planning something."

"Lord John has been collecting writings and manuals about ancient weapons of war."

"About guns and gunpowder?"

"More fearsome weapons than that. If it was the Prophet behind this, he failed."

"Goldstone…isn't that where you were born and raised, Father?" Robby spoke as he and Ari walked over with puzzled looks.

"Yes, it is, Robby. Your grandfather, Gerald, was the lore-master there, and he served Lord John for most of his life. He was a man of great wisdom but lacked faith in God and also opposed lore-men taking up arms. I grew up in his shadow, sorting through musty volumes in badly lit rooms. That's how I remember it, anyway. I worked long hours as his scribe and assistant. When I was your age, Robby, I knew absolutely nothing about weapons or warfare."

"Maybe your father wanted to protect you," suggested Ari.

"Perhaps. I remember now with regret how we disagreed and argued about different interpretations and meanings in the ancient writings. It was Lord John who put an end to our arguments by suggesting I study elsewhere, so they sent me to Stonegate."

"Yes, I remember you telling me that story, Father, when I was young," said Robby. "You met Mother shortly after, and then the wars started, and the False Prophet murdered my other grandparents."

Tears glistened in Rachel's eyes as she recalled that terrible time. "Yes, Robby, thank God we've now found peace, and for most of your life no one has seen or heard from the Raiders or the Prophet…"

"Until now," Don interrupted in a firm tone. "We have to convince Stonegate to be ready for trouble and prepare for the possibility of war. And the biggest worry is that the Prophet has had ample time to build up a powerful army and develop new weapons. But we are weaker now than we ever have been."

"We'll have to mobilize, won't we father?" asked Robby. "I hope they will allow the cadets to go to battle."

"Mobilize, yes, if we can convince the leaders to do so. We'll have to see about the cadets."

"Well, this is all the more reason to start training our young women to shoot a bow," said Ari, thinking of what an expert marksman her mother was. "Didn't you say that it is a good idea?"

"I, too, think that is an excellent idea, Father," said Robby. "I think we should also send cadets up to Goldstone for its own protection. I would be willing to go to scout around Goldstone to see if there are any of the Prophet's forces up there."

"I think they can protect themselves," said Don.

Rachel nodded. "Remember. They will be on guard, now."

"I barely remember the place," said Robby.

"The last time you were in Goldstone was when you were a baby. Your mother and I took you to visit your grandfather. We heard he had fallen ill and could be dying. I needed to reconcile with him before he passed away, so we made the trip and stayed for three weeks until he finally left us. Thank God, we were able to put aside our differences and arguments and he passed in peace. We spent endless nights praying over him at his bedside and reading him stories from the old Holy Book which he had never believed in. Then on the night before he died, he told us that an angel of the Lord had visited him in a dream telling him he had come to take him home. He cried out in one of the ancient languages, '*Nunc dimittis servum tuum, Domine.*'"

"What did that mean?" asked Sara, who had joined them, and had been listening to every word.

"It is a quotation meaning something like 'Now dismiss your servant, Lord.' Your grandfather died saying the words, 'I believe, I believe.'"

†

Mayor Billings was in his council chambers reflecting on the latest news. Seated with him at the large polished table were Commander Hamway, Gray John, Thomas of Longmont, Colin McCoy, and Don. Loud voices echoed as they discussed the sighting of the Raiders and the Goldstone incident. The marshall, military leader of Stonegate, was too ill to attend.

"You must understand, Mayor Billings," Commander Hamway was saying, "that these events need to be taken seriously. As Lord Don has already pointed out, if we were to be attacked by the Prophet, we are not prepared to defend ourselves. It is obvious to me even from this small amount of evidence that the Prophet is planning something, and we cannot ignore the dire consequences if he is. The East has had peace for twenty long years, and not one city here is prepared for war. We have become apathetic and complacent, which puts us in a dangerous position if we were to be attacked from the West. As commander of Stonegate's horse troops, I suggest we send a patrol west and eliminate the Prophet before he can act. That is our only hope of survival against his forces."

Gray John put forward his thoughts. "Commander Hamway is correct in what he says. We need to be one step ahead of the False Prophet and plan a strategic attack on his palace. I now have a confession to make which must never leave the walls of this room. Unbeknownst to Lord Donald or anyone else, mainly for security purposes, I have secretly trained twelve men of the Red Axe troop for special operations such as this. These men are commandos who are taught to work by stealth and strength. They possess the capabilities of penetrating the walls of the Prophet's palace and capturing him. This action would not only save the East, but it would also save his own people who are suffering under his harsh regime. Many people in Prophet City are living in prison camps, surviving on bread and water, and working long, brutal hours until they eventually die from hard labor. Everyone who opposed him has been executed, the Gray Pilgrims have been banned from Prophet City, and many orphaned children survive only by begging in the streets. I suggest that the commandos go out with Commander Hamway's troops and we eliminate this problem."

Mayor Billings grunted in frustration. "That would be a crazy overreaction. Impossible. Provocative."

With a stern tone in his voice, Commander Hamway spoke. "With all due respect, Mayor Billings, I do not need council's permission to send a patrol west."

A look of annoyance flashed across the mayor's face, his forehead wrinkled, and his cheeks flushed crimson. "A patrol to gather information is well within your authority. But any sort of hostile action without proper authority is not. If you do anything rash, I will demand that you be relieved of command! The best I can do is to bring up your concerns during the town meeting in the City Hall scheduled for this Saturday evening. Let the people of Stonegate decide if they want some immediate action! Now, I declare this meeting adjourned."

With downcast faces, the men left the council chambers. Commander Hamway was defiant in his resolve. "Saturday is three days away, gentlemen. If we receive any more news about Raiders or suspicious activities nearby before then, I may have to consider sending out my troops in secret."

Gray John nodded. "I'm with you, Commander. Your commandos are also ready. I was glad to train them for you."

†

Ari and Robby again spent time hunting in the forest, armed with bows and arrows as they crept over rocks and through tall grass. Something had alerted their prey. They heard the snapping and crashing and snapping of frightened animals bolting. It sounded like a herd of elk. Surrounding them were aspen, spruce, pine and fir trees as they made their way to a small lake where they knew that a few moose liked to graze. It had been a few days since they had heard the troubling news about Goldstone.

"What do you make of all this?" asked Ari, as they stopped to catch their breath in a small clearing near the lakeshore where they found a rocky ledge to sit on. A few gnats buzzed over a mossy cove.

Robby looked straight into Ari's clear blue eyes, noticing how beautiful she was with her long blonde hair and her pinkish cheeks, flushed from the long walk. A small voice in his head said, *she's your cousin*, reminding him that as much as he wanted to take her in his arms and kiss her, that could never happen. "I think Father is right, that there is trouble brewing for us.

But I am so annoyed that he wouldn't let me go out to scout for Raiders. Actually, Father has been annoying me a lot lately, Ari. We argue about most things, and he has even suggested that we stop seeing each other so regularly. He thinks we are becoming too close for cousins."

"Bit late now, Robby. We've been inseparable since we were three. If you weren't my cousin, I would think about marrying you. I can't imagine my life without you in it."

"Are you serious?" Robby asked, wide-eyed. "Maybe that is what Father is worrying about. We can never marry, Ari. I hate the fact we are cousins. Sometimes I get angry and argue with God about it. How could God let me feel these things about you that cousins are not supposed to feel? It is hopeless, Ari. And now I know you feel the same way as me."

"Oh, Robby, this is truly hopeless. But I have trust in God that something will happen, and it will all work out. I don't know, I just always get this gut feeling that we will end up together."

"Well, it's a cruel God who put us in this predicament and all that will happen is that we will forever live wanting to be together, but unable to. I fear we will both die of a broken heart."

"Oh, Robby," Ari said in a soft voice. "Don't lose your faith in God. He loves you."

"How can I believe in a God who is so unfair? And look at all those stories of the war with all its horror and killings. If there was a God, there would be no wars...or an evil False Prophet who creates them!"

They sat in silence as Ari pulled out some bread and cheese from her knapsack and a flask of water sweetened with a squeeze of apple juice. A hawk flew overhead, cruising in circular motions, circling the sky.

"Look, it has found prey," said Robby, as the majestic bird swooped to catch a small waterfowl in its talons. "How wonderful!"

"Yes, cruel, but wonderful." Ari turned away with a smile, taking Robby's hand in hers. "It's so peaceful here. I can't imagine anything destroying our world."

"Well, I can," snorted Robby remembering the incidents of the last week. "I think that peace in Stonegate is about to end."

†

Saturday night had come around too slowly for Don and Rachel. The only positive thing that had happened was that Carla had agreed to start a training class for women archers at the Academy and was pleasantly surprised by the quick response by the girls of Stonegate to join. It was possible for news to travel fast, thanks to a new printing press. Rachel had printed out flyers advertising the new archery class, and the cadets had somewhat reluctantly distributed them to most homes in the area. The council had also printed flyers letting the community know about the town meeting on Saturday night, and the community was abuzz with rumors.

Mayor Billing was dressed in his finest…a golden tunic with red lapels and pale green leggings. He cleared his throat before addressing the crowd. "Good people of Stonegate, we are assembled tonight to inform you of a few incidents that have occurred here in the East and to ask for your input into what, if any, action should be taken. Over a week ago, Raiders were sighted by a few members of our community, who were hunting about five hours west of Stonegate. Then, a few days ago, we heard that the lore-house in Goldstone was broken into, but thankfully, nothing was stolen or taken. There is no evidence whom the perpetrators of this act were, but there is, according to Commander Hamway and his associates, speculation that it could have been the Raiders. I have this week engaged in a meeting with Commander Hamway and his group who suggested that military action should be taken against the Prophet as they believe that these incidents are of a sinister nature and that the Prophet is planning some kind of military action against us. My decision has been to put this information before you and ask for a vote on this issue. My personal view is that these incidents do not warrant a call for arms and warfare. However, I will leave it to you, the good people of Stonegate, to decide. Please consider it thoughtfully and discuss your thoughts before you vote."

An elderly man sitting in the front row put up his hand. "Well, Mayor Billings, I think that as a Christian, I need far more evidence before we decide to go to war. We have blessed peace now and we have much to lose if we overreact. Our community has never been more prosperous. Trade has never been more vigorous or profitable. War will destroy everything we have built since the last war. I say no to any military action unless we are attacked."

"Hear! Hear!" the vast majority of the community echoed in agreement.

Only one small female voice spoke up from the back of the room. "Forgive me for disagreeing with you, my good sir," the woman said. "I am new to Stonegate, but in my short time here, I have observed the beautiful city you have and the freedom to live how you wish. I fear that Commander Hamway is correct in his suspicions about the West. If the Prophet does attack and he probably will, you will lose everything here and perhaps even your lives as well. I urge you all to consider what your military people are telling you."

Mayor Billings whispered, "Who is this woman?" Then he spoke aloud, "All right, stranger, we have heard what you have said. Now, pray tell us your name and the nature of your business in Stonegate!"

Clear as a chime her voice rang out for all to hear. "My name is Shakti, and I am the new maid and waitress at the 'Quill and Sword.'"

CHAPTER 7

†

Secrets, Secrets, Secrets

Stand, therefore, with truth like a belt around your waist, righteousness
like armor on your chest,...
Ephesians 6:14 HCSB

In the hidden bowels of a dark mine beneath the mountain on the eastern
edge of Prophet City, a group of five young men gathered to conduct the
business of a secret society. The Liberty Soldiers had pledged allegiance to
all that was good and to combat all that was evil. All five, in their early twenties, were orphans from the last war. The Prophet had ordered the summary
execution of the few Christians in Prophet City who openly practiced their
faith, and that had included their parents. He thought that he had eliminated
all the people of faith in his capital, but he had only driven most of them
underground. He would have been surprised to know that many people
remained secret Christians, even some in positions of influence.

The Prophet continued to hold impressive ceremonies in his elaborate
temple near the palace in the old city. Some fervently believed the rites there
brought good luck and gave offerings to secure it. Others came for spells
to bring themselves fortune or calamity on their enemies. Fortune-tellers
promised to lift the veil of time and allow devotees to know the future, for
a price. Most pretended devotion to the False Prophet's cult, and doubtless,
some actually believed in it.

It was a cool night with ominous signs in the sky. The moon had turned
a crimson red, spiking fear in the hearts of men who believed something

sinister was unfolding in the world around them. All had noticed this as they traveled by different routes to their place of meeting.

Caleb, Elijah, Jeremiah, Josiah, and Arrow James (the youngest of the five) had helped form the Liberty Soldiers a year ago. All realized that the malignancy of the Prophet had to be stopped. They had all been brought up in an orphanage set up with the Prophet's grudging permission, but in a twist of irony, of which the Prophet was certainly unaware, the orphanage had been run by Christians—remnant Christians who had escaped execution by keeping their faith silent and hiding the old Holy Books.

After the war, the Prophet had ordered the oldest part of the city to be secured by an imposing stone wall, which controlled who could enter or leave. But the remnant Christians had discovered an old storm drain that ran under the wall. With quiet determination, they had cleaned out decades of rubble to make a passage that ran nearly to the old mines where they could meet and secretly practice their faith. And now, it was through this tunnel that Liberty Soldiers, such as these five, were able to come and go without interference.

"Hold fast, brothers," Caleb said as he addressed the others who were all younger than he. He was tall and wiry with red hair and freckles on his face. His hands and feet were big, and he looked fit and strong. "Time is running short, and we have much work to do. The Prophet is getting ready to take over the East at any time now. We must do what we can to stop this, or all those lands will also fall under his evil rule."

Josiah, a chubby-cheeked lad with brown hair and brown eyes, suntanned, and an athletic build, spoke up. "We need to somehow convince the people of Prophet City to overthrow the Prophet and storm the palace. There is much discontent now amongst us all, and it would not take much to create a coup d'état. Although the Prophet has a strong military now, it is only the Prophet and his high up commanders who have all the wealth. The ordinary soldiers, like the rest of us, are going hungry and surviving without warm clothing or decent shelter. If we can overthrow the top end, the soldiers might very well turn against their own leaders."

"That's my hope," Arrow James joined in. With his dark hair and gray eyes, he set a handsome figure who, despite his slender physique, was as strong and wiry as a cable. "I've heard it rumored amongst the field hands that they have had enough and want to see the Prophet gone, and a better ruler put in place…someone who has the people's interests at heart."

"I've heard that some would prefer to join with the East and enjoy the freedom and prosperity they think the Eastern people have," Elijah added, shaking his long, curly ash-brown locks in frustration about the whole situation they were in.

Jeremiah nodded in agreement, his piercing blue eyes shining with the thought of the possibility of freeing Prophet City from its oppressive and much-hated ruler. "Yes, we all yearn for freedom…and peace. We want to practice our faith. And we will never have that as long as the Prophet sits on that throne in his sumptuous palace while the rest of us struggle to stay alive!"

Caleb looked around at his little band of "brothers" as they so often called each other, and added, "I have found out that the Prophet has sent Shakti, who we know is his closest female servant, to Stonegate to spy on them. He is obsessed with taking revenge on that city and a man called Donald of Goldstone. It is said that this Donald is the key of Stonegate and that God led him to victory in the battle as prophesied by Carl the Elder."

"Ah, yes, I remember that legend. We used to imagine that Donald would come and set us free," Elijah responded, "but he must be an old man now. I wonder if this is the same Shakti who helped that other woman escape. I remember Mother Tess at the orphanage discussing it one day, when I was young, saying how she had prayed for—I think her name was Selena— to escape and that she had asked someone named Shakti to help her."

"Yes, I remember that," Arrow James said. "But it was so long ago. I also remember something strange about Shakti. Mother Tess had said that she was a good actress and had played her role at the palace well, whatever that meant."

"Come to think of it," Josiah said, with a quizzical look on his freckled face, "I saw a woman that must have been Shakti with Mother Tess several times as I was growing up, and they seemed very close. I thought it was peculiar since she lived at the palace, and Mother Tess is a Christian, but maybe they were just good friends. They often took tea together."

Jeremiah rubbed his forehead as though he might be getting a headache, "I think I remember her too; once she said that her excuse was to visit the orphanage to see the children, but it was really to see Mother Tess. She came to see her for some reason, not us."

"Well, she sometimes popped into my class," said Arrow James, "to bring sweets from the palace."

"I'm sure they weren't from the Prophet, Arrow James," Caleb said. "Shakti must have taken them from her own store of gifts, most likely given to her from the Prophet and never meant for us."

"Yes, it is curious, isn't it? And just who is this Shakti, really? She saves Selena from the tower, yet does it in a way that the Prophet never finds out, and then she befriends Mother Tess, spends time here in some kind of secret meetings with her, and then hands out sweets to the younger orphans? Very strange, indeed!" Josiah was indeed puzzled as he recalled these events from his childhood.

Jeremiah surmised the situation. "Well, unfortunately, we may never know who she really is and what she is up to...Mother Tess passed away last year, as we all know, and all those secrets will have followed her to the grave."

Caleb addressed his small group as midnight approached and sleep beckoned them all. "Unfortunately, our meeting tonight must end. But tomorrow, we will speak quietly to our small groups. We need to finish our plan of action, and quickly, before the enemy does. Good night, my brothers, and may God be with you tonight and always."

Shakti was enjoying her first two days leave from work after a week of learning how to be a waitress at the Quill and Sword inn. Unlike her initial concerns about moving to the East to a strange city where she knew no one, she had been pleasantly surprised to find how easy it was to settle in to her new work and accommodation. It was hard not to feel safe and secure when the people at the inn had welcomed her with open arms and treated her with kindness and respect.

The contrast between life in Prophet City and Stonegate was obvious. Life in Stonegate provided freedom, and here the average, ordinary citizen of this remarkable city was prosperous and well dressed. The cobbled streets of the town were tree-lined, flanked by colorful gardens, unseen back in the West.

Shakti sighed with joy and contentment. Never had she seen people live like this. The only life she had known was within the palace where she had lived in total submission to the Prophet. It was little better than a prison. Outside the gated walls, she had seen poverty, starvation, people suffering, and orphaned children.

Today, Shakti was embarking on a carriage ride to explore all of Stonegate. She'd never seen such beautifully crafted horse-drawn carriages. But they were the usual form of transport around town for the people of Stonegate. Silk and satin lined the carriages, with plush red velvet cushions for seating, and curtains tied back with golden ribbons. In the West, only the Prophet ever rode in such a carriage. Ordinary people could never enjoy such an experience—the closest things were the passenger coaches that ran between major cities, and they were expensive.

"Please take me first to the lore-house, driver," Shakti requested. She was fascinated when she learned of the school and university connected to the lore-house, educating ordinary people and not just the nobility.

The driver, wearing a gold tunic with a red waist sash and white leggings as well as a red feathered hat, was happy to oblige. "So where do you hail from, Missy? I haven't seen the likes of you before."

Shakti knew she had to be careful about disclosing her past, so she repeated what the Prophet had instructed her to say. "Oh, I've been a bit of a gypsy most of my life since my poor husband died, and I have been spending time living in various cities trying to start a new life. My last home was in Loveland, but I was restless there, and a friend informed me that the owners of the Quill and Sword were looking for a maid, so I applied for the position, and I was delighted when they wrote to say I could have the job."

"Well, I hope you enjoy our lovely city. Since the last war, we have made a lot of progress. We now have a military academy as well as the school and university, and we have an active trade with distant cities far to the East on the other side of the Great Plains. We even get some exotic dishes from the East such as crab and goat's cheese. However, we have had to defend our trade routes from bandits as we also have some expensive goods in demand here such as silk scarves and linen material which our women love to use to make new tunics and dresses."

"How interesting," Shakti said, wondering how much of this information she should report to the Prophet. Being his spy had put her in a dangerous and unwilling position. She knew she would have to use all her wiles to stay alive as the Prophet would not hesitate to retaliate against her if he discovered anything amiss in her reporting.

"Where in the world do you get silk?" she asked. She had a vague idea it was made from caterpillars or some kind of insect.

"We import the raw silk from somewhere far to the south. There are shops that make the scarves and other things here, then they resell them locally or to traders."

Shakti was more surprised at that than anything else. No ordinary person in the Prophet's lands could have afforded such an extravagant luxury, yet here it was within the reach of many. If news of this ever reached the Prophet's people, it would subvert their loyalty without a doubt. *I think tangible things like silks and satins might mean more to them than fancy talk about freedom.*

There had been no sign of Charlie at the inn, but everyone there knew him. Shakti was worried that she would have nothing to report about Westerly-stead unless she and Charlie met. She certainly couldn't approach Donald or anyone else for information, as it would look too suspicious, she was sure.

"Here we are, Missy. We have arrived at the lore-house and school."

"Oh, do drive on, please, I'd like to see the academy and perhaps stop there for a while."

The driver did as he was bidden, and soon they arrived at the long building where the cadets were trained. The driver had mentioned that a woman named Carla had started classes for female archers. He obviously thought the idea was ridiculous, but he had also mentioned that Carla was some sort of heroine in the last war.

Training girls in the arts of war was a strange and somehow unsettling idea to Shakti, too, and she found herself agreeing with the driver. Still, she decided to learn more about this unusual activity. She asked the driver to wait while she investigated. She entered the academy grounds and walked along a gravel path next to what must be the parade ground. There seemed to be no male cadets in the area, but she did see a line of targets, and some slender figures that must be the girls the driver had mentioned.

"Can I help you?" a female voice asked as Shakti approached.

"Oh, yes, yes," Shakti answered as she turned to face a woman around her age with vivid red hair.

"I'm Carla," said the woman with a warm smile, "and I teach the women the skills of archery. Are you perhaps interested in joining our classes?"

Shakti caught her breath in surprise and neglected to introduce herself although they clasped hands. "Well, I've never considered archery, and I only have two days off work from the Quill and Sword. I'm afraid that won't be enough time for me to learn how to handle a bow and arrow."

"I see. We have classes every midmorning whenever the young men are away. You are more than welcome to join us when you have time. After all, every woman should know how to hunt, if for no other reason."

Shakti thought for a moment before deciding, thinking how this would be a good opportunity to meet other women in Stonegate and make friends. "I would be delighted to join. Can I start tomorrow?"

"Of course," said Carla. "I would be pleased to have a mature woman join us. Most of my students are teenagers. The cadets are away on maneuvers just now and will be for another week or so. Just take home these forms and bring them back tomorrow filled in and we can begin straight away."

"Thank you, Carla," Shakti said, feeling enthused by Carla's obvious passion for her sport. "Oh, and by the way, my name is Shakti. See you tomorrow."

On the way home, Shakti's mind drifted. She wondered whatever had happened to Selena after she had helped her escape from her prison in the palace tower. Had she come to Stonegate after all? It was the one place that she had said she would feel safe. Shakti would never forget the words Mother Tess had said in a pleading voice: *You must help her escape, Shakti. She is with child by the Prophet and once he realizes that, he will surely take the child at birth, and have Selena executed. You must help!*

It had been a hazardous task to release Selena from her prison…a task which entailed putting sleeping potion in the Prophet's nightcap, taking the keys to the tower from his chambers, and delivering a frightened and terrified Selena to the orphanage where Mother Tess had organized to send Selena to Stonegate.

"We have a secret tunnel that leads to the caves in the west of the city. And from there, Selena will be escorted on horses to her destination...Stonegate," Mother Tess revealed. Shakti never forgot that night, or the fact that Selena was pregnant with the Prophet's child.

CHAPTER 8
†

A Hasty Decision

Don't consider yourself to be wise; fear the Lord and turn away from evil
Proverbs 3:7 HCSB

*D*ear Father,
  I have decided to head up the Cash River to scout around for the Raiders. I know you won't approve of my actions, but I need to do this for myself and for Stonegate. All the politicking with the mayor and the civilians will not help protect us from the False Prophet. I hope to find out where the Raiders are camped and what they are doing. Do not worry about me. I will return as soon as I have some news.
  Your son,
  Robby

Don read the letter aloud to Rachel and Ari as soon as he had found it on the table in the hallway…a letter, folded once and simply addressed, "Father." It was suppertime and Robby had not arrived for the family meal. The letter explained his absence but brought alarm with it. A fragrant aroma of freshly roasted venison with herbs and new baby potatoes wafted through the house, but despite that, no one felt hungry.

The sun had already set, and the dining room was lit with candles and an oil lamp which gave off an eerie pale-yellow glow, adding to the unsettled atmosphere in the room. Rachel wrung her hands in despair at the thought of Robby riding out alone.

"Oh, Don, what should we do? Should you go after him?"

Don bowed his head, wondering what the best decision was. Ari interrupted, "I should go…I know where we went hunting, and I could find him sooner than anyone else. But I will leave first thing in the morning, early before the sun rises. I will take my bow and arrow and some light provisions and…"

"No, Ari," Don interjected, "You cannot go alone. It is too dangerous now, especially as we know that those Raiders are out there somewhere. We need to make a plan, a sensible plan. Charlie and I will go with you. You can lead us to where you were hunting and can show us where you spotted the Raiders."

Ari nodded her head in agreement. "Well, if we are to leave early tomorrow, you need to talk to Charlie now. I believe he went off to the Quill and Sword."

Rachel took Don's hand in hers. "Please, Don, we must eat first, even if we have little appetite at a time like this. We must remain strong, and once you've eaten, then by all means go and speak to Charlie. We must find Robby before the Raiders do. God forbid what would happen if they came across him alone and without protection."

Don remembered the horrors of the last war and the evilness of the Raiders, but he tried to put away those old memories and respond to Rachel. "You are right, Rachel, my love. We should eat. After all, you prepared a splendid meal which should not go to waste. Charlie will still be at the inn by the time we have finished our meal."

Ari gave Rachel a comforting hug, aware of the fear gripping her heart. "Don't worry, Aunt Rachel, and don't underestimate Robby. I know he can look after himself. He is brave and determined when he sets his heart on something."

"I hope you are right, Ari, my dear. I hope you are right," Rachel responded with tears turning to salt wetting her pale cheeks. "I just pray that Robby stays out of trouble."

✝

It was a moonless night and as dark as the inside of a cave when Robby arrived at the place on the Cash River where he and Ari had gone hunting. He shuddered with a mixture of cold and apprehension as he remembered sighting the mountain lion's paw tracks the last time he had been here. It was now around midnight, and Robby hoped he might see evidence of the Raiders in the area. Surely, they would have a campfire going, despite the late hour. Any fire would stand out like a beacon. But there was no evidence of anything amiss or unusual, just the forest closing in on him with dark shadows and a blackened sky. The stars burned with cold intensity.

He looked around for somewhere to camp and snatch a few hours' sleep before continuing to scout the area. It had been a long ride, but Silver, his favorite white mare, had handled the trek with ease. They had gone across rugged hills and dipping valleys with confidence and a good speed, almost as if she was keen for an adventure herself.

He was glad that he'd packed a thick rug for himself, as well as provisions of dried meat, fruit, and a flask of brandy to warm his body and help him sleep. Soothing sounds of a nearby stream and the occasional hooting of an owl lulled him into a gentle sleep, a much-needed reprieve from the tension of the past few weeks. The constant and increasing disagreements with his father, Don, was one reason he had to escape for awhile the life he knew. The sighting of the Raiders was another reason, but the most important reason was Ari. He needed time to think about their lifelong friendship and reconcile himself to the fact that the woman he had grown to care for as more than a cousin or friend, could never be more than that. The last thing on his mind as he slipped into an exhausted sleep was Ari.

He awoke to the sound of twigs breaking and the low neighing of Silver nearby. Startled, he sat up, wondering what was happening. Then he heard it again…the rustling of something in the nearby scrub, and the sound of something moving closer towards him. Silver neighed again as Robby stood up, grabbing his bow and arrow in readiness for any peril.

The sky had lightened now, so Robby guessed that the sun was already beginning to rise far away in the east. His heart was pounding fiercely in his chest as he strained his eyes to make out any shapes or figures that may be prowling around him. He turned in all directions trying to determine where the sounds were coming from.

He raised his bow and arrow in readiness to protect himself if necessary. Then he saw a form emerge gracefully from the darkness of the woods in front of him. It was a young deer peering inquisitively at him. He let out a sigh and a peal of laughter in response to fear leaving his body as quickly as it had come. For a second, he had thought it was the Raiders, but seeing the innocent creature in front of him flooded him with relief.

Putting down his bow and arrow, he packed up his primitive camp. "Come on Silver," he said, giving her a gentle rub on the nose. "Time to get out of here. Let's go looking for Raiders!"

†

The Quill and Sword was abuzz with lively chatter, and the sweet squealing sound of a lone violinist playing a jig for those who came to enjoy the music, as well as a light ale and a dance. The aroma of beef stew was streaming from the kitchen, tempting diners to order a mouthwatering dish of herbed meat and vegetables swimming in a rich gravy which was mopped up with a freshly baked cob of buttered bread.

Charlie finished his dinner with complete satisfaction, emptying the last of his glass of ale as he saw Shakti approach him with a smile on her face that lit up the room. "Would you like another glass of ale, sire?" she asked, knowing he always enjoyed a few more after dinner.

Charlie wiped his mouth with the white table napkin and returned her sweet smile. "I surely would, lass. But please call me Charlie. I've seen you here nearly every night for the past two weeks, so I think we can get to be on more friendly terms."

"Of course, Charlie," Shakti blushed. "And you must call me Shakti. It would be nice to have a friend in this town. I haven't been here long."

Charlie looked into her large dark oval-shaped eyes. "Yes, I have noticed that. If you finish early tonight, perhaps I could buy you a drink?"

Shakti blushed, noticing Charlie's strong body and quiet masculinity. "I would love that, Charlie. I finish at nine tonight."

He watched as she left to fetch his ale, noting by the clock on the mantle that it was already eight o'clock. Out of the corner of his eye, he spotted Ari and Don moving towards him. He saw a look of urgency in Don's face, as if there was trouble brewing at Westerly-stead. "What is it, Lord Don? You seem to have the worries of the world on your shoulder." He motioned to Ari to sit down next to him as Don pulled up an extra chair.

"Well, Charlie, you seem to have a kind of intuition about you, that's for sure," Don replied. "It's Robby. It seems that he is determined to find those Raiders you saw, and he has left a note saying just that. Of course, Rachel is worried sick, as am I. Ari has suggested that we go up the Cash River early in the morning and look for him. Maybe we can bring him home and to his senses. You know where you saw the Raiders, so we should head off that way just before sunrise."

Charlie looked concerned, his brows furrowed into a wrinkle. "You can count on me, Lord Don. We should leave as early as possible. But, maybe we should keep this a secret. I'm sure the Mayor and the civilians would say something about it...perhaps accuse Robby of looking for trouble and even stirring it up. You know, many of the townsfolk just want to stick their nose in the sand and avoid confronting the possibility of trouble."

Don nodded. "I couldn't agree with you more, Charlie. Meet us in the Westerly-stead stables before dawn in the morning. But before I go, I may have an ale with you. Ari, would you care for a light ale or a cold wine?"

Ari shook her head, "No, I would much prefer that new drink from down south...I think it's called Sangria."

Shakti arrived with Charlie's ale and took orders for drinks all round. The music began to echo around the room as people danced to new songs written by the students of the music school in Stonegate. Ari swayed in time to the rhythm, wishing Robby was here with her for a dance. *Please God, let him be okay*, she prayed under her breath.

It was nearly nine when Ari and Don left the inn. Shakti watched them leave, glad she could have Charlie all to herself. The only man she had ever known had been the Prophet, and she knew only too well his evil character. She had before never met a man like Charlie, and it surprised her that she felt a flood of warmth and caring in his presence.

"Well, I have finished for the night, Charlie," she said, joining him at the table. "So, do tell me everything. I am so interested in hearing about your life in Westerly-stead."

Charlie smiled as she sat down to join him. He had never seen a woman as beautiful and lovely as Shakti ever before. Her long dark hair perfectly framed her oval face, highlighting her flawless complexion.

A singer stood and struck a chord on his taro, a stringed musical instrument. He began to sing in a clear tenor voice:

When Carla was a lass, she rode the mountain pass.
She hunted far for game.
With Rachel by her side, she wild and free would ride.
Until the Raiders came.
The Raiders came and burned, to steal what others earned.
They stole six beauties fair.
But brave men rescued them, and they returned again,
And escaped that evil lair.

The song went on to tell how Carla had defeated a band of Raiders and became a heroine of renown. Shakti listened to the tune with rapt attention. "Tell me, Charlie, have you heard that song before?"

"Many times. I know Carla well. In fact, she is the mistress of Westerly-Stead, the farm where I work. The tune does not lie. She is more accurate with a bow than anyone I have ever met."

"She is famous?"

"Indeed, she is. Everyone has heard the song. Some may think it is a tall tale, I suppose. But it is quite true."

"Interesting," said Shakti. "This intrigues me because on my last two days off work I ventured around Stonegate in a carriage and in my determination to explore this lovely town I actually met Carla training girls in the bow and arrow. She invited me to attend some lessons, and I have agreed when I have time. I had no idea how famous she was. But, for now, I actually want to know all about you and what is happening in your life at Westerly-stead."

"Well, I'm afraid that all is not well there, Shakti," he confided, feeling as though he had known her for years instead of a few weeks. "Lord Don's son, Robby, has gone missing, so tomorrow we are setting out early to try to find him."

"Pray, do tell me....why would he go missing?" she asked, wondering if this was something she should mention in her next report.

"Well, as you know, there was a recent sighting of the Raiders. I believe I saw you at the community meeting, and I was most impressed with you for speaking up. Well, it was Robby, me, and Robby's cousin Ari who spotted the Raiders along the Cash River. And Robby has gone looking for them."

Shakti's heart sank in her chest. She knew the cruelty of the Raiders more than anyone and how dangerous it would be for Robby if they found him alone and snooping around. "Oh, God, Charlie, you must find him before the Raiders do."

Shakti realized that she had fallen in love with her life in Stonegate and all it represented...kind, gentle people, freedom, and peace. She had to do something to stop the Prophet from destroying the beauty of life in the East, no matter what it might cost her.

"Sure, Shakti, we will do everything in our power to find Robby tomorrow. I don't think it will be too hard. In the meantime, would you care to dance?"

The music was intoxicating. Shakti was very unsure of herself as they began to dance. The music was vastly different from the rhythm of palace music which inspired harem dancing and she had no idea how to move to the unfamiliar beat. Charlie tried explaining the dance steps as he held her tenderly and close. "It's called a waltz. I've only just learned it myself. I'm glad I'm not the only one new to this."

Shakti allowed herself to relax in his arms, feeling his strength through his tunic. In the palace, she had danced alone or with the other young women for the Prophet's pleasure using exotic steps. Here she could just be herself...a single woman in the arms of a gentleman who appeared to care about how she felt. The only thing preventing her from relaxing completely was the knowledge that soon the Prophet would demand her report on what was happening in Stonegate.

CHAPTER 9
†

Whispers in the House of Healing

My God, my mountain where I seek refuge. My shield, the horn of
my salvation, my stronghold, my refuge, and my Savior, You save me
from violence.

2 Samuel 22:3 HCSB

D on took his sword down from a peg in his study and drew it from its
sheath. The metal gleamed with an oily sheen. There had been nicks
in the blade, and it had seen hard use, but careful file-craft had mostly
smoothed the imperfections to a wavy edge. He tested the blade with his
thumb, and it was still sharp. "My blade is ready, at least," he said aloud. "I
don't know if I am." The ache in his hip, caused, he thought, by miles in the
saddle, often caused him to limp, and it was worse in the evening.

He retrieved his saddlebags from the tack room in the stable and filled
them with things he would need for two or three days in the field. He
wrapped two wool blankets in an oilskin slicker. Then he went to the kitchen
to see if there was any trail food.

"What do you have for a hungry man traveling fast?" asked Don.

"If you don't want the trouble of cooking, I have dried biscuits, dried
meat, and dried apples. Quite a dry diet."

"That sounds good. Better add extra for Ari. She may not think about
food. I know Charlie will not forget."

"Do be careful with Ari, Don," said Rachel, putting her hand on his arm.
"She thinks she is all grown up. But she has not learned caution, and…truth
be told, is more than a little stubborn."

"Remind you of anyone?"

"Yes. You. And Robby."

"I was thinking about you."

"No, dear, I am firm, Robby is stubborn, and you are pigheaded."

Don laughed. "Now that you have set me straight, I must confess that my conscience is bothering me. We should have—well, let Robby in on some family secrets. We—I have kept putting it off, I fear."

"Oh, Don, I know," said Rachel. She leaned against the table as if she was dizzy and put her hand over her mouth. "I know we must, but I dread it so. I know we did the right thing. Yet, it was all so cruel and deceptive."

"We did deceive people, but if ever a lie can be a good thing, then…"

"If we had only shown more faith. A lie is always a sin. But he would have been shamed everywhere he went if we told the truth. But to tell him, even now. I can hardly bear the thought of it."

✝

Don had his sword and equipment stacked in the hall by the side door, ready for an early start. Sara was already in bed, and Juliet was tidying up the kitchen. Don and Rachel were sharing some cherry tarts just before an early bedtime. They were sitting close to the dying coals of the hearth-fire, and Don gazed at the ruddy glow on Rachel's sad face. He patted her hand.

"We have had more than one frightened refugee show up at our door," said Don. "Do you remember Isabella?"

"Of course I do," said Rachel. Her head bobbed up, and she looked him in the eyes. "How could I forget? What a night. We were still living in the farmhouse at Westerly-Stead. She arrived just before a terrible thunderstorm. Who was that young man who brought her to us?"

"You remember. Calvin, the courier. He was the one who carried Balek Brown's head to the False Prophet. I had not wanted that, you know. Colin and some others were behind it, I think."

"Yes, it was ghoulish, but it served him right. They both told us that the evil man screamed like a woman. He was expecting it to be your head, dear."

"It nearly was. And it would have been except for Philip. Brave lad. And Howard was also brave. Sad times, but God was in it, to be sure."

"Isabella was such a sad, frightened little thing when Calvin brought her to our door. He said he did not know where else to take her. She was one of the False Prophet's maids and was daring enough to make her escape. She was quite a good cook, I remember that."

"That was not the only young girl that he brought to us. A clever man and fearless, Calvin was. He had many sources in Prophet City and was trusted to carry messages by both the East and the West. But it finally became too dangerous. I believe he commands one of our small garrisons, now. Far to the east. I am sure he appreciates a quieter life, with nothing more to worry about except a few bandits."

"It was kind of you to personally take her to the House of Healing."

"I could not think of a better or safer place for her. It seems strange that going closer to the False Prophet's lands actually increased her safety."

"Yes, I am sure that evil man searched far and wide. But in the confusion of the war he failed—its aftermath, I mean. I am glad it all worked out so well. I hope her life there has been happy."

"Much happier than she would have had in that foul cesspool of a palace."

"Yes. Time for you to get to bed, big boy. You need to make an early start. I pray you can find our son."

†

The fragrance of lavender, rosemary, and mint was wafting through the air from the outdoor herb garden at the back of the hospital in the House of Healing. Isabella was inhaling the aromatic scents as she planted garlic and parsley which were frequently used in preparing herbal medicines. Many other useful plants grew and thrived in a sheltered spot in the garden which captured the sunlight for most of the day.

Exactly twenty years today since I found my freedom, thought Isabella as she remembered that exhilarating trip through mountains, canyons and gorges between Stonegate and this place where she had lived since escaping the clutches of the Prophet. It seems like it was only yesterday.

There had been a thick fog surrounding them most of the way as Don had escorted her on horseback to her new home. She'd ridden one of Don's gentler mares, a golden colored horse named Heidi, who kept a good even pace behind Don and Hardtack, Don's sturdy sorrel. At one point they rode through the bottom of a deep, dark canyon where the sunlight was blocked by sheer cliffs that rose from all sides. Isabella had felt the cold eeriness of her surroundings which made her shudder from the gloominess and starkness of the stony landscape around her.

They had continued on around sharp bends and winding rivers until the canyon widened revealing a lush green valley to the left and a widening road ahead which forked in opposite directions. Don took the road to the right which led directly to a stone-walled settlement with a huge portal displaying a red cross on the wall.

"Well, we're here," he'd said, as Isabella breathed in the fresh, cool air and admired the rows of red flowers and tall poplar trees planted along both sides of the track leading to the main building. "This is the House of Healing, Isabella, where healing is given to all, even those in Prophet City. However, there are two separate clinics which attend to patients, those from the East and those from the West. You will have political immunity here anyway, but it would be best for everyone that the False Prophet never knows that you are here."

Isabella had gaped in awe at her surroundings as they entered the hospital where they hoped to meet with Chief Surgeon Kerik. Light flowed into the building through wide, airy windows, bouncing off white stone walls and ceilings. The floors were tiled in bright red slabs and a dark wood cross hung on the door of Kerik's office. Inside, the room was simply furnished with a large wooden table and several wooden chairs and another low table by the window with a bowl of freshly picked red flowers. Kerik greeted Don warmly. It was the first time they had met since the end of hostilities.

"Come in, come in, my good friend Donald. What a pleasant surprise! And who is your lovely companion?" inquired Kerik.

"Forgive me for not introducing this lovely lady immediately, Kerik. This is Isabella, who has escaped from Prophet City and is in need of protection and a safe refuge. Isabella has many skills in cooking, cleaning, and organizing a large household as she was the False Prophet's personal attendant. I was hoping you could find work for her here as well as a place to live."

Kerik stroked his red beard thoughtfully as he made his decision. "I am certain we can find ample work for Isabella. The Gray Pilgrims keep busy compounding the medicines and attending the sick, and there are accommodations for them and our nurses. We do have a few spare rooms that would be suitable for a lady to stay in, and we may consider training Isabella to help in the hospital, in the clinic for Eastern people, of course. If that would be agreeable, Isabella."

Isabella had sighed in relief and could not control the tears, "Oh, thank you, Kerik, thank you so much. I promise you I won't let you down. Oh, and thank you too, Lord Don, for bringing me here to start a new life. I will never forget you…or Rachel…or Calvin."

Now, the memories of those days flooded in. Isabella recalled her delight at discovering the hot springs in the courtyard and the kindness of the Gray Pilgrims who had taught her all about herbal medicine and the strange medications from the Elder days. Much had changed in twenty years. Isabella became a senior nurse in the clinic for patients from the East, but she had over time, lost her fear of meeting with those from the Prophet's dominions. She was easy to talk to, and she was able to gather much information about what was happening in the West. Still, she had to be careful never to let them know her name since they also suspected that some were spies.

Kerik was now in his early sixties with graying hair and beard and ever-deepening wrinkles in his face. However, he was still as fit as any young man and continued his heavy workload as a surgeon as well as he had done twenty years ago. He approached Isabella as she was at her hobby, finishing planting garlic and parsley, wiping down her dirty hands in an apron already smeared with earth and bits of grass from weeding the garden beds.

"I must speak with you, Isabella. I appreciate the summaries you drafted for me. You have an analytic mind, and you always seem to be able to find the nuggets among the volumes of what is little more than gossip."

"Thank you, sir. There have been many whispers in the House of Healing lately from new patients from the West. We also get reports from the Pilgrims in the field as well as the field surgeries. Malcolm was having a difficult time keeping up with it all, so I volunteered to help him."

"Yes. It was much easier in the old days. We used to actually have Gray Pilgrims serving in the Prophet's palace. But no more. They have been banned from his lands entirely. But some of his relatives, even members of his household, come as patients here. They try to conceal their identity, of course. But we nearly always know who they are."

"It is wise to open the clinics to people from the West. It makes the Prophet think twice about ever attacking us here," said Isabella. She wondered what Kerik was getting at. He usually had little time for small talk.

"It has worked out that way, yes," said Kerik. "But we decided from the earliest days that these doors would be open to all. Not because it would benefit us, but because it would please God."

Isabella realized that she had been gently chided, so she said nothing. She nodded with a smile.

"I have invested some of our funds in maintaining the roads. Otherwise, the wretched people from the West would have a difficult time journeying here. Now, even an ordinary farmer's wagon can make the trip. Many of them are too ill to travel by horse. But I fear my thoughts are wandering. I wanted to thank you for your efforts and to let you know that we intend to take action."

"Thank you, sir. It is nice to be appreciated."

"Malcolm, as my military advisor, suggested that we pass this information to our friends in the East. I have decided to send him and Harold, the master of our walls, to Stonegate. They will take your summaries along. I will ask them to see Donald of Goldstone, your old friend."

"Oh, I wish I could go along. But I will ask them to give Donald my best wishes."

"Of course. I am also sending the same information to other friends to the south. They are also at risk if the Prophet is intending to go to war again."

CHAPTER 10
†

A New Marshall

Provide justice for the needy and the fatherless; uphold the rights of
the oppressed and the destitute. Rescue the poor and needy; save them
from the power of the wicked.
Psalm 82: 3-4 HCSB

Everyone in Stonegate attended the funeral of Marshall Allen. For forty-five years he had overseen the military defense and also enforced the law and dispensed justice. He had been loved and respected by the community who recognized that he was a man of fairness, compassion, and loyalty towards the people of the township. Since the war, he had quietly encouraged Stonegate to help the poor and afflicted, and the desperate and weary who needed a fresh start after that last dreadful war. Orphanages were established for motherless children, and work was provided for the destitute.

The sound of women sobbing could be heard above the voice of Pastor Landon as he took his turn, among others, to honor the memory of this courageous and beloved man. "People of Stonegate, we are gathered here today to put this exemplary man, Marshall Allen, to rest…a man who will never be forgotten by any of us for the work he did in keeping Stonegate a peaceful and progressive place for the last twenty years. But let us not weep in sorrow any longer, but rather rejoice that he has finally earned his resting place in Heaven where there are no more tears, no more sorrow, no more pain, and no more suffering. I am sure that Marshall Allen would agree with me that this is not a time for sadness, but rather a time to celebrate the wonderful achievements he has made in his life, and how he did everything for his people here with love and great consideration and regard for each and every one of us."

The sun was beginning to lose its heat as it silently sank toward the misty horizon. Women pulled their shawls closer around them as the crowd trickled away after the funeral service. Don and Rachel held each other close with a long embrace before making their way to their carriage which would take them back to their cozy house that stood near the farm of Westerly-stead. Apart from the sadness of losing Marshall Allen, Don and Rachel were gripped in their own dilemma about the disappearance of Robby.

"So, no sign of him? None at all?" asked Rachel again, as Don helped her into the stylish carriage complete with red velvet curtains and cushioned seats.

"No, my love. As I said to you earlier, Ari, Charlie, and I searched for nearly three days and only returned when it seemed fruitless to continue any further. All we found was the site of a recently used campfire, but if Robby had been there earlier, he was now long gone."

Rachel could not stop a sudden shudder. "Oh, I know, Don. You've done all you could. Who knows where he is now? He could be anywhere, and we have no idea where to look. All we can do is pray and trust that Robby comes to no harm."

Don nodded in agreement as Charlie took the front seat of the carriage to guide the horses home. "You are right, Rachel. After all, he is a young man of nineteen now, not a child. I pray that his training at the academy will have provided him with enough skills to help him defend himself if need be."

Rachel squeezed his hand as they sat in silence for a while, both lost in their own private thoughts and hopes. "Well, on a different note, Rachel, my dearest, Stonegate now has a new marshall, and he has brought with him his son as his assistant."

"Yes," responded Rachel, realizing that new things lay ahead for the township. "I believe his name is Levi Jackson and his son is called Isaiah."

"You are on the council. What did they tell you about them?"

Rachel gave a quick shake of her head as if she was shrugging off the nagging worry about her son. "Yes, let me see…these two have a good reputation. They served in Ariel, then in Steamboat and Longmont. Neither has actual battle experience, except for some skirmishes with bandits. But they are not fools when it comes to the False Prophet's menace or how he used the Raiders in the past. Perhaps they will be useful to us in meeting the current threat."

"I sincerely hope so, love. If they will start sending out patrols, they well might find Robby while they are out there and talk some sense into him… or at least if he intends to continue scouting, he can join one of our patrols. There is far more safety in numbers."

"You are right, Don. Perhaps tomorrow you should make a visit to the new marshall's office and discuss this matter with him. He has the authority to take action."

"A good idea," said Don. "I really think we could have brought Marshall Allen around to see reason if he had not been so ill. He and I were often at odds, but he changed as he got older. Less hostile and more caring. If he had been spared, I think we could have been reconciled."

As the carriage finally pulled into their drive, two horsemen were dismounting in the shade of a cottonwood near their stable.

"Well, it appears we have unexpected visitors," Rachel said, wondering who could be arriving without notice.

As they pulled up closer, Don recognized the men immediately. "Why, it's Harold and Malcolm from the House of Healing. Something must be urgent for them to come all this way to see us."

Don and Rachel greeted the two visitors warmly. They were old friends, and Don had great respect for their judgment.

Despite the warm welcome, a somber mood hung over the four of them as they entered the homestead where an open-hearth fire warmed the front room. Charlie stopped by briefly after unhitching the team and tending to the visitor's horses. Then he said goodbye and left for the short walk to Westerly-stead. Judith, Rachel's helper, emerged from the kitchen and helped hang up jackets.

†

Ari and Sara had not attended the funeral earlier, preferring instead to take a horseback ride together. Since Robby's disappearance, Ari had reached out to Sara and they had shared their forlorn feelings with each other.

"I miss him every moment," Ari was saying as they collected logs from the woodpile to prepare the fire in the dining room. "I feel as though part of me is missing, and I pray every day he is safe. I also fear that he has become doubtful about his faith. He was angry for weeks before he wrote that note to your father, and I'm upset that he never even said goodbye to me before he left."

"Maybe he didn't want to say goodbye to you, Ari. Maybe he couldn't," Sara gave Ari an encouraging hug. "Don't worry. I'm sure he'll come home soon. As soon as he gets cold at night and hungry for mother's cooking. Here, let's put these logs in the woodbox and you can help me light the fire."

✝

A warm, crackling blaze was soon alight in the large dining room, throwing out rays of heat, just as Don and Rachel entered, showing Harold and Malcolm a tour of the house.

"Mother, Father, oh, it's so lovely to see you home. Look, we've made a fire for you, and Ari and I can collect some fresh vegetables from the garden for dinner if you like," said Sara.

Rachel gave Sara a loving hug, "That would be lovely, Sara…and make sure you pick plenty. Judith is fixing a late lunch. Our guests will be hungry and will probably stay over."

As the girls left for the vegetable gardens, Rachel wished the visitors would cut short the polite conversation and explain what was so important for them to come such a long way. She knew it was not a social call. Her feelings of impending doom returned, feelings that had hung around her like a gray fog ever since the news of the Raiders, but growing worse after Robby disappeared. *Is there more bad news for us?*

"I insist you both have lunch and stay for dinner too, and since you have come a long distance from the House of Healing, you must enjoy a stay here overnight. Goodness knows, we have rooms here for guests to stay and you are always most welcome," Rachel said.

Malcolm and Harold nodded. "Why thank you, Lady Rachel," said Malcolm, "but we don't want to impose. We can stay at an inn in the city."

"We would not hear of it," said Don. "It is not often that we see old friends from the Haven area. We will want to hear the latest news. Rachel does get a note occasionally from Isabella, though."

"Oh, yes," said Harold. "She sends greetings. As a matter of fact, she has been very useful in gathering military information from patients from the West. She knows exactly what questions to ask, and since she is a nurse supervisor now, she can travel freely through the wards and converse with many. She helped pull this summary together, as a matter of fact."

Malcolm laughed. "She is much better with a pen than we are. My old fingers are much too clumsy. But we do have some unsettling news and wanted to talk to you to decide the best way to share that with your military leaders here."

"We thought perhaps we should speak to Mayor Billings," said Harold.

"Why don't we all relax first," Don suggested, "and we can discuss it all over lunch. We have news in Stonegate about some troubling matters."

The men were more than happy to sit around with a few warm drinks of hot spiced cider while Rachel and Judith heated up a hearty meal of roast beef ribs with golden potatoes crisply baked in duck fat and served alongside a steaming platter of freshly picked vegetables.

During the meal, Malcolm summarized the information they had brought. "As you are both aware, the House of Healing has always been a good listening post for news from both the East and the West. And recently, in the last few days, we have heard firsthand accounts from our patients from the West, which has convinced us beyond doubt that the Prophet is planning an attack on the East. So Kerik thought we should come here to Stonegate to see what action could or should be taken. He has also sent messengers to our friends, the Diné."

Don and Rachel looked at each other. "We have had a sighting of a Raider patrol just to the west of here. Also, someone tried to break into the library at Goldstone," said Don. "I think they were trying to steal the collection of military books held there."

"That fits the pattern," said Harold. "Isabella compiled her information, and it clearly points to a military buildup in the West. Young men have disappeared from the towns and farms. All recruited by the Prophet. The patients report seeing large units marching on the roads. They all have heard much cannon fire. Most disturbing of all was a report from Abel that we just received. There were reports of huge units of heavy cavalry maneuvering with batteries of field artillery. It appears that this is all quite menacing."

"I couldn't agree with you more, Malcolm," said Don, "And I am so pleased that you and Harold have shown such concern to alert us. However, I must let you know that Mayor Billings does not believe that the recent Raider sightings or the incident in Goldstone are enough to warrant any military action against the False Prophet. It was Robby, Ari, and Charlie who saw the Raiders. Now, since Mayor Billing will do nothing about it, our son, Robby has disappeared, leaving a note that he has gone scouting for the Raiders."

"Oh, heavens," Rachel interjected with a terror-struck look on her face, "If all this is true, then Robby is indeed in grave danger. We must make Mayor Billings and the new marshall see some common sense and take action."

Don shook his head in disagreement. "Rachel, Mayor Billings is a stubborn man who does not like to be proved wrong. I suggest that tomorrow, you all accompany me to the office of our new marshall, Levi Jackson, to discuss this. Any military man will have a great mistrust of the False Prophet. Rachel knows I was going to speak with him tomorrow anyway…so it would be best if we all went together. We must convince someone to do something before it's too late. And we need to protect Robby as much as we can."

†

Marshall Levi Jackson shook his head in annoyance and scowled. "So, you say there have been a few incidents around here lately that sound to me like trouble brewing, and yet Mayor Billings is reluctant to investigate or act?"

Isaiah Jackson, the new marshall's son and assistant, had been speaking to Don and his group outside in the foyer before agreeing to speak to his father, who was settling in to his new office by Stonegate Civic Square. "Yes, that's right, sir. And I have a group here to see you, one of whom is a hero of this town, Donald of Goldstone."

"Of course," said Levi as he remembered the songs of the *Lore-man on the Red Horse*. "It would be an honor for me to meet him. Who else is in this group, Isaiah?"

"There are two men from the House of Healing. One is Harold who is the master of the House of Healing walls, and the other is Malcolm, who is their chief military advisor. There is also Lady Rachel of Westerly, a councilor of Stonegate, who is Don's wife."

"Please bring them in," instructed Levi. "I am keen to meet them."

Isaiah ushered them in, and Levi motioned for them all to take a seat. The room was silent except for the voice of Don, who spoke for all of them, recounting the troubles of the past few weeks. Levi Jackson stood up when Don had finished speaking, a look of anger sweeping his face. "So, let me get this straight. There is evidence the Prophet is planning an attack on the East, and local incidences have also pointed to that, but the Mayor will not send out a patrol to investigate?"

"With all due respect to the Mayor," Don said, "he is not aware of the whispers from the House of Healing about the False Prophet's plans. But we thought it would be best to inform you of everything since the mayor has not been interested in responding. In view of the additional news, we are hoping that your office will take necessary action."

Rachel added, "Yes, it is vital now. Our son, Robby, is out there scouting for Raiders who by all accounts have set up secret camps all over the East. It is obvious to me that the False Prophet is planning to attack, and it could be any day. Our son's life and the lives of the rest of us in the East are in danger. We cannot continue to be complacent."

"I agree with all of you wholeheartedly. This calls for an urgent meeting of all those involved in protecting Stonegate. I can't imagine what the military leaders here were thinking. It is obvious that Stonegate does not have a large or strong military, and if we went to war, it is most likely we would lose. No, we have to find another way to fight the Prophet. I believe he has become thoroughly despised even by his own people. It would not take much for a coup d'état to overthrow him. Lady Westerly, I am not familiar with the politics here. Perhaps you could advise me on that. Clearly, this is a time to think coolly and act fast."

As they left the marshall's office, Don felt some relief. Levi Jackson had been the right man to talk to. He remembered how Commander Hamway had pleaded in vain with the Mayor to send a patrol west. Perhaps that would now be possible.

"Things are looking a little more positive for us now, my friends," Don said as the group entered the Quill and Sword for lunch. "In the face of all this, the mayor will have to back down…before it's too late."

The inn was packed with hungry townsfolk ordering ales and lunch as if the peaceful lives they lived would never end. Rachel noticed the gaiety and carefreeness that embraced the inn…and wondered how long they could keep this peace before the Prophet decided to act against them all.

"Well," said Malcolm as he ordered an ale for each of them, "it looks as though we'll be staying with you folks for a few more days until we sort this out."

"You are more than welcome," Rachel answered. "In times like these we must stick together. And we need to act quickly before the False Prophet does."

Suddenly, she wondered where Robby was, and how he was traveling… and her heart broke in fear.

†

In a dark mine west of Prophet City, the young men of the Liberty Soldiers were planning their next move. "I say that one of us needs to go to Stonegate to find this man, this Donald of Stonegate, and tell him what we have planned. There is no way the East can win against the Prophet this time… they do not have the strong military necessary to defeat him," Caleb was saying.

"I agree. But we need help to overthrow the Prophet. And they just might be the ones to do it," Josiah added.

The moon had fallen behind a dark cloud as the whispers grew louder inside the blackness of the cave, a blackness illuminated only by a few tall candles struggling to give any light at all. Arrow thought for a while before answering. "I'll go. I'll go to Stonegate and find this man, this Donald. No one would notice if I went missing for a few days. We must act fast. Time is running out for all of us."

Jeremiah agreed. "You are right, Arrow. It is time, time to act and you are swifter on horseback than any of us. Godspeed and good luck. We will have a fast horse ready for you by the break of day."

As they ended the meeting, they bowed their heads in prayer, wishing Arrow a safe journey…and success for their plans to rid the world of the evil Prophet.

CHAPTER 11

†

Captive

Then they may come to their senses and escape the Devil's trap, having
been captured by him to do his will.
2 Timothy 2:26 HCSB

It was late in the day, just before dusk, as two weary travelers made their
way north from Glenwood to Stonegate where they planned to spend two
weeks as a honeymoon. Newlyweds, Willy Oliver and his petite young wife,
Daisy, had planned this trip for months, getting their horses conditioned for
the long trek, packing saddle bags with necessary provisions, and planning
their journey with a map of the area.

"The best way is through these mountains and along the Cash River,"
Willy had said a few days earlier as Daisy watched him trace out a line along
the map. "There are a few farms along the way here where we can buy extra
provisions if need be, and there is some very pretty country along this route."

Daisy was excited at the prospect of a romantic, adventurous experience
with her beloved Willy, the man she had loved since she first met him at
school. And as the sun was setting on the fourth day of their trek through
wide valleys and a rocky mountain pass, they were only a couple of days
away from Stonegate. "I can hardly wait to get there," Daisy said. "Everyone
says the honeymoon suite at the Quill and Sword is splendid…the perfect
romantic getaway."

"Shush, stop, Daisy," Willy said, interrupting her daydreams, "There's a
band of men approaching…could be bandits. Quick, hide behind this rocky
outcrop before they see us."

Daisy did exactly as Willy asked, sensing an urgency in his voice. They slid in behind a thick cluster of towering gray boulders which shielded them from the main road, just as a group of a dozen men passed below them, heading south.

"Strange," said Willy as the group disappeared into the distance. "They did not look like bandits, since they were wearing some kind of uniform and had swords and shields. Some also carried bows and arrows. I remember my Uncle Harley, God rest his soul, telling me about soldiers that were assassins for the False Prophet. When I was a young boy, he told me many tales about when he fought in the last war. I remember very clearly. He mentioned that the emblem of the Prophet is three lightning bolts. I swear those men had three lightning bolts on the back of their tunics. God forbid, surely they were Raiders!"

Daisy froze in a kind of fear of disbelief. She too had heard stories about the last war, which ended just before she and Willy were born. There had been stories of horror about the cruelty of these men and the many battles that the East had fought against them in order to claim victory. "But why would they be traveling around here now?" Daisy asked, curious about what they had just witnessed.

"I don't know, Daisy. But it cannot mean anything good. We must report this as soon as we arrive in Stonegate. There is a man who lives there. Uncle Harley never stopped speaking of him. They fought together against the Prophet. He made me promise him that if ever I went to Stonegate, I must look him up and give him his regards. He is a living legend now, and his name is Donald of Goldstone."

"Of course, I remember that name. Everyone in Glenwood talked about him when I was growing up. I would love to meet him. We must visit him while we are in Stonegate."

The sun had set, and a billion stars were twinkling in the night sky above them. Usually, they had found a suitable campsite before it was dark, but a full moon gave visibility. Silvery rays of moonlight showed the outline of trees. Ahead, Willy noticed a wisp of smoke and the glow of a small campfire. "Stay here a minute, Daisy. I'll steal up and see who is camping out here. We don't want any trouble with bandits or Raiders."

Daisy watched as Willy moved quietly ahead. She shuddered as the cold night air wrapped its shivery fingers around her. She longed to be around a blazing campfire, herself. Voices in the near distance confirmed that Willy was talking to someone, but to her relief, the conversation sounded amicable. Within minutes, Willy reappeared and beckoned her to follow him. "It's safe. It's just a traveler from Stonegate resting for the night. He says we're welcome to join him. He hasn't talked with anyone for days and would like some company."

As they approached the camp, Daisy noticed he was a man about their age, and he was busy cooking something. It proved to be a brace of wild ducks he had bagged earlier in the day. The smell of freshly cooked meat was irresistible. Neither she nor Willy had eaten since midday.

"You must join me for dinner," the man said, then proceeded to introduce himself. "I have been traveling alone, but I am from Stonegate. My name is Robby, son of Donald of Goldstone. Unfortunately, my mission here is serious. I am not sure this route is safe for you. I believe that there are Raiders in the area because I myself recently sighted a group of them. I am trying to find where they are camping."

Willy and Daisy were concerned, but glad to hear Robby confirm what they had seen. "You too?" asked Willy. "We just saw a group of men who might be Raiders. We have heard of your father, Donald, and had planned to mention it to him, if we could find him. Our plan is to stay at the Quill and Sword Inn. It's our honeymoon."

Willy's story fascinated Robby. He asked the two to describe the men, how they were dressed, and the arms they bore. "I knew they were around this area somewhere," Robby finally said. "It was well that you kept your heads and quickly hid. But I wonder why you took the risk to travel this way without an escort. Did you not know it is dangerous?"

"There have been no attacks on travelers recently, as far as we know," answered Willy.

"Perhaps not, although the other route is surely much safer. But I agree that this is important. You must deliver a message to my father when you see him. Please tell him I am well and that I will be home in a few days. Mention what you saw."

"We will be glad to. But would he see us? He is a great lord and we are nobody special."

"Of course he will see you; don't be concerned. I am afraid that I have caused him some worry. He will be glad to get your message."

The moon was gliding higher in the sky as they finished their meal of duck and a few potatoes baked in the campfire. Daisy boiled up a billy of tea to take off the chill as they talked well into the night. Sleep came easily as the trio of travelers finally settled into their wool blankets around the fire.

"Time to wake up, Daisy," Willy whispered as he felt a pinprick of sunlight pressing on his eyes. "We have a long ride ahead of us before we arrive in Stonegate."

Daisy rolled up the beds and tied them behind the cantles of their saddles while Willy and Robby prepared a quick breakfast of tea and cornbread. A fine, cloudless day rolled out before them as they said their goodbyes and prepared to travel in opposite directions.

"Stay safe, my friend," Willy said as he and Robby shook hands in farewell. "I look forward to seeing you back in your hometown in a few days."

"Enjoy your stay in Stonegate," Robby responded. "The Quill and Sword Inn is the best in town, and I am sure you will have a pleasant stay there. They provide hearty meals and fine entertainment most nights of the week. I promise to have an ale with you when I return."

The sun was well up when the travelers set their paths in different directions. "I think we've made a good friend," Willy said as they headed down in the direction of Stonegate.

"I believe we have, Willy," Daisy said, praying under her breath that Robby would come to no harm and that in a few days they would all be enjoying a good time together.

†

Robby reined his sturdy mare, Silver, toward the area where Willy and Daisy had been the day before. He believed he knew of that large outcrop of gray boulders where Willy and Daisy had hidden from the Raiders. At least, that would be a starting point for trying to pinpoint where the Raiders were setting up camp.

A few blue jays flew above, traversing a perfect azure blue sky. Meeting Willy and Daisy had been a stroke of luck, confirming his suspicions. There was a shortcut through some rugged terrain up ahead which few travelers used. It was fairly isolated from the main route and quite a challenging trek for an unseasoned traveler. Robby decided to take a chance and head off that way.

Robby felt sure that he would soon come across some evidence of the Raider's whereabouts. In the past, his intuition had always been a strong point that often led him in the right direction in life, but now an ominous feeling fell over him. *Maybe I should have stuck to the main route.* He entered a dense stand of lodgepole pine, which made it difficult to travel anywhere except one narrow trail.

The trees gradually became denser, and in several places the branches were so high that they created a canopy that almost blocked out the sun. An eerie sense of danger surrounded him as he wondered if the Raiders could be possibly hiding out here. It would be a perfect place, quite hidden from the rest of the world. Robby's regret about taking this shortcut was confirmed when he heard horses' hooves behind him.

He looked back and saw nothing. Not wanting to be seen, Robby spurred Silver faster ahead, hoping to avoid whoever it was. Silver snorted as if in annoyance at being pushed ahead through a thicket of dense bushes, but Robby kept her going at a steady pace, still concerned that he was being followed.

Up ahead, he could see the trees thinning out and the landscape opening up into rolling green hills and a valley with far less bushland. He feared that this was not necessarily a good thing as it would give his pursuers clear visibility ahead. He urged Silver to go faster as they headed out into the open terrain, hoping that if he wound his way around the next hill, he might find a place to hide.

"Come on, Silver, go!" he muttered as he dug his heels into her flanks, calling for full speed. Behind him, he could still hear crashing sounds and hoofbeats.

†

Willy and Daisy arrived in Stonegate early in the afternoon after a pictur-esque journey through a rugged and beautiful valley. Stonegate also lived up to its promise as the most elegant city in the East as they made their way along its cobbled streets bordered by colorful floral gardens. They followed the instructions on their map of Stonegate to direct them to the Quill and Sword Inn which was a beautifully constructed building with a thatched roof and raised rose gardens around the welcoming entrance.

After settling in to their accommodations, they decided to honor their promise to Robby and deliver his message. They got directions to Westerly-stead, which was to the north, not far from the outskirts of town. It proved to be a straightforward route along the main road.

Before too long, after passing a few smaller farms and pastures, they came to winding driveway and a gate with a small sign that read "Westerly-stead." "Well, we're here, Daisy," Willy said as they rode up the dirt track to the entrance of the farmhouse. "Let's hope that somebody is home."

As they tethered their horses to a railing, a young girl stepped out onto the porch. "Hello, can I help you? Are you looking for someone?"

Daisy noticed that she was about their age. She had long golden hair braided into a pigtail and intensely green eyes in a small, delicate face. She smiled at them as Willy answered. "Yes, we are looking for Donald of Gold-stone. We have a message for him from his son Robby."

At the mention of Robby's name, the girl's face turned ashen, and she stiffened as if she had been struck by a lightning bolt. "Robby? Did you say, Robby?" She asked in a hoarse voice almost choked with raw emotion. "I am Ari, his cousin. He lives next door, but I spend a lot of time there. Forgive me for my reaction, but Robby has been missing for days, and we have been very concerned for his safety. Thank God you have seen him. Is he all right, then?"

Daisy was surprised at the intensity of her reaction. "Yes, he is fine, Ari," Daisy replied. "We came across him two nights ago. We were on the way from Glenwood to here and spent the night camping with him. He asked us to deliver a message to his father to say he is well and would return home soon in a few days."

"Thank God," Ari said wringing her hands in her apron as tears of relief sprung to her eyes. "We have all been so worried, hoping he was safe. I know the Raiders are out there somewhere. We saw them recently."

"Yes, we saw them too, Ari. In fact, Robby wanted to know exactly where we saw them, and he set off in that direction looking for them," Willy said, causing Ari to gasp.

"Oh, dear God, no!" Ari exclaimed as if fearing the worst. "If the Raiders feel they are being scouted, God knows what they will do. You must tell Uncle Don all about this, but he's not home. He and my Aunt Rachel are at the council chambers and will not be back until late tonight. Perhaps I can tell them where you are staying, and he can come and talk to you later on."

"That is fine with us," said Willy, hoping that this news had not been too distressing for Ari, who seemed so visibly shaken. "I am called Willy, and this is my bride, Daisy. We are staying at the Quill and Sword and will have a meal there tonight. We look forward to the meeting with your Uncle Don."

Ari seemed to recover her composure and took them both by the hand, thanking them several times. Then they took their leave.

As Willy and Daisy left, Ari ran straight out to the stables to saddle her horse. She decided she had to ride into town and tell Don and Rachel straightaway what the travelers had told her. She could not sit around and wait for them to return. As she rode towards the council chambers, all she could see was Robby's face.

†

It was perhaps the fastest Robby had ever ridden in his life. Adrenalin flowed through his body as his heart thumped in his chest. It was now certain, beyond a doubt, that he was being pursued by a group of men. For what seemed an hour he had led them through a maze of rolling hills, hoping to get them off his trail but the country was too open to find a place to hide.

He scanned the landscape around him, hoping to find a canyon or thicket that would provide refuge, but the land was now flattening out into open plains with scattered clumps of trees. Nearby, a small stream was flowing and alongside it willows were dipping their branches into the water's edge. His only hope was to ride down close to the stream and find cover behind the line of willow and cottonwood trees.

Silver was noticeably tiring as they sped down to the stream. The sound of hooves was closing in on him as he reached the water and tried to hide behind a row of trees growing thickly together. Sweat was pouring down his face; it was trickling into his mouth in salty drops and pouring into his eyes, blurring his vision.

All of a sudden, men were shouting behind him, and an arrow *whizzed* by, barely missing his back. Fear engulfed him as he reached for his sword. He was convinced that whoever was chasing him wanted his death.

"Stop!" a loud voice yelled as another arrow struck him, lodging itself painfully into his right leg. "Stop or risk your life!"

Robby ignored the command, continuing to urge his mount along the bank in a frantic effort to escape. Another arrow barely missed his neck when he was overtaken and surrounded by a dozen pursuers. They were Raiders.

"Surrender or be killed!" said a large burly man who appeared to be the leader. "We have been watching you for days. What are you up to, young man?"

Robby sat on Silver and raised his hands, trying to stay conscious, as the searing pain from the arrow nearly overcame his senses. "I am a hunter," he managed to say in a weak voice. "I mean you no harm. I had no idea anyone was out here. I just came to hunt for wild game."

"So you say, so you say," said the burly leader. "Well, mister hunter, you are now our captive and we will take you to our camp to ask you a few more questions. Seize him!"

A trio of Raiders came forward and pulled Robby off Silver, who had become nervous and agitated at the scene developing around her. They cut the arrow out of his leg, which only made it bleed so profusely that one of the Raiders had to wrap it tightly in a piece of dirty cloth. They tied his hands, and he was forced to ride double behind one of the Raiders, making escape impossible. Silver followed behind the group as they began to retrace their tracks.

The pain from his wound was throbbing and his head swam. All Robby could think of was Ari.

CHAPTER 12

†

A New Love Unfolds

Oh, that he would kiss me with the kisses of his mouth! For your love is
more delightful than wine.
Song of Solomon 1:2 HCSB

Shakti was dressing deliberately and carefully. She had chosen a creamy
colored lace dress that was tucked tightly around her slender waist
and flared out into a full skirt with sewn in pearls around the hem. Long
sleeves flowed down into a bell shape, accentuating her slender arms and
long delicate fingers with pearly fingernails. She tied her hair up in a soft
bun with caramel-colored ribbons that flowed around her shoulders, giving
her a sultry, soft romantic look. She lightly powdered her face with a warm
bronze shade of makeup, giving her cheeks a soft glow. On her lips, she
applied a light pink gloss that sparkled when it caught the light.

The night was a special occasion. It was the first time that Charlie had
invited her to have dinner with him. She finished work early, just after lunch,
giving her time to take a long, perfumed bath and enjoy a few hours beauty
sleep before getting ready to meet him. It had become a regular thing for
them to have a drink and a conversation after work, but tonight was different. There was a feeling of romantic anticipation in the air as Shakti made
her way downstairs from her small but tidy bedroom to the dining room.

Already, a nice crowd of people had arrived for dinner, mostly local
folk, but also a few visitors to town and a young newly married couple from
Glenwood who were staying in the honeymoon suite for a few weeks. Shakti

remembered them because she had served them drinks earlier, and now she could see them locked in a sweet embrace as they sat at a table for two in a secluded corner. She smiled as she passed by, remembering how she felt when Charlie held her. She was longing to see him and feel his strong muscular arms around her again. They had enjoyed learning the waltz together on previous nights, laughing as they tripped over each other's feet while they twirled around the dance floor.

Shakti had slowly come to realize that Charlie was special. He had a warmth, tenderness, and sincerity about him that the Prophet lacked. His large brown eyes were like warm wells of affection when he looked into her eyes, unlike the cold steel blackness of Martin Abaddon's gaze. Her heart skipped a beat as she saw him waiting patiently at the bar, sipping on a dark ale.

"Why, Shakti," he said as she arrived. His voice was slow and measured. "How lovely you look tonight. I guess I haven't seen you all dressed up before. You certainly take a man's breath away."

Shakti blushed, pleased that her hours of getting ready had the desired effect. She longed to spend the next few hours talking and dancing and experiencing her new life in Stonegate. She had guarded her true feelings every day in the palace at Prophet City. Extreme caution was necessary to survive under the Prophet's unpredictable temper and moods. *Perhaps tonight I can relax and just be myself. Though even here I must be cautious.*

Charlie was dressed in a fine gray tunic with dark charcoal-colored leggings and shiny leather boots. He gave her a soft embrace before leading her to the table he had reserved by the fireplace where a robust fire was blazing away with an occasional hiss and crackle of timber logs burning. A vase of long-stemmed flowers made an attractive and fragrant centerpiece for their table which was covered in fine white cotton and set with shiny silver cutlery and sparkling wine goblets.

"I've taken the liberty of ordering a fine bottle of wine that comes from down south where the Sonoran people live. They are famous for producing some of the best wines in the East, so I hope you enjoy this one. It is a new blend called a rosé which is slightly red in color, but not as dark as a regular red wine," Charlie said as he pulled out a chair for Shakti and poured her a glass.

"Why, thank you, Charlie," Shakti said, feeling a little spoilt and unused to being treated with such consideration. At the palace, it was her duty to pour the wine for Martin Abaddon, something he never did in return. "I am sure I will enjoy it."

"So, it is fortunate you have this evening off work. I have been longing to enjoy dining with you since I met you, and now here we are..." his voice trailed off as he locked eyes with hers, as if drinking in the flawless beauty of her sweet face.

"Why, Charlie, you are certainly gallant. I'm not accustomed to hearing such endearing words from a man before."

"Well, I find that very hard to believe, Shakti. A woman of your astounding beauty must have had a lifetime of compliments. Didn't you say you were a widow? Surely your husband would have spent his days admiring you?"

Shakti remembered with a jolt the story she had fabricated. She was spying for the Prophet, and tomorrow she was embarking on a journey to Loveland to meet with a few of his Raiders to deliver her report.

"Oh, yes, of course. Initially, my husband was very affectionate, and complimentary, but he became ill, and he was not a man of many words towards the end of his life." She hated having to lie to Charlie. It felt so wrong, stirring up her conscience in a way that bothered her. Every part of her longed to tell Charlie the truth, and she promised herself that someday she would confess to him the real reason she was in Stonegate and assure him that she had no love for the Prophet, or a desire to return to Prophet City.

Charlie picked up the menu, sharing it with her as they perused a wide array of choices for dinner.

"I was thinking we should make this a special night and indulge in three courses. After all, this is our first real date together, isn't it?"

"So it is, Charlie," Shakti smiled as she responded. "You know, it is such a treat to enjoy a night dining and dancing. I haven't enjoyed myself like this for a very long time. But what about you, Charlie? Surely, you've been dating some of the lovely women in Stonegate? I've seen how they look at you. After all, you are still young and handsome...and single. Why have you never married?"

Charlie took a sip of his ale as he took her slender hand in his. "Well, Shakti, it's like this. When I was a young man, around twenty, I did have a sweetheart. In fact, she looked a lot like you, but in all honesty, not quite as beautiful. She lived near Westerly-stead and we spent a lot of time together. I thought I had her heart, but it was not to be. She gave her heart to another. In fact, it was my best friend that she longed for. She was hanging around with me just to get closer to him, I think. Eventually, he took notice, and they ran away together one night. They eloped and went to live in Steamboat. I was pretty much heartbroken after that, so I threw myself into working around Westerly-stead, and no other woman has really interested me since then…until you came along, I must confess."

"Oh, Charlie, I'm so sorry to hear that. I hope your broken heart has truly recovered by now. And if not, maybe I can help it to heal." She squeezed Charlie's hand with tender affection, glad to hear that there was no one else in Stonegate he was interested in.

"So, what do you say? Do you like the sound of any of these exotic entrees?" Charlie asked.

Shakti nodded as she replied, "As a matter of fact, I have been longing to try the quail's eggs with homemade creamy mayonnaise and a bed of salad leaves. And for the main course, I must sample the baked rainbow trout in an almond sauce with roasted potatoes and wilted beans."

"Sounds good to me," Charlie added, "but I feel that I would like to try the pumpkin and cheese tart for an entrée followed by some roasted venison with baked parsnips and spiced cabbage. I was eyeing those strawberries and cream for dessert. What do you think?"

"Oh, Charlie, I have been wanting to sample the cheese and fig platter for ages for dessert. I have heard the cheese comes from the House of Healing where they have done more than preparing medicines. Cheese making is their latest venture."

"Well, we certainly must share a platter of their fine cheeses, but I am also going to add those strawberries with clotted cream."

Charlie went off to order the meals as Shakti sat in a dreamy haze, experiencing feelings she had never felt before. Charlie was so different from the cold Martin Abaddon. With his many wives and harem dancers he had little time or need to express real love and affection for just one woman. *I wish this night would never end*, she said to herself as the tingling effect of the rosé wine began to relax her a little

Charlie returned with another dark ale and a large beaming smile. "Here's to us…and a good night ahead. May there be many more like this to come, my sweet."

They made a toast to the night ahead as the inn began to hum with the sound of flowing conversation and laughter. An atmosphere of heady gaiety filled the dining room as the musicians arrived to offer fine dancing music as the guests finished their dinner.

"So, I believe that you have two days off work tomorrow," Charlie said as the entrees arrived on well-presented plates. "I was hoping we could go riding together and enjoy a picnic by the river that runs close to town."

"Well, Charlie, perhaps we could do that the next time I have a few days off. Unfortunately, I have some personal business to attend to in Loveland tomorrow, so I am arising early to catch the coach for my journey. I am afraid I will not be returning until late the next day…but it will be lovely to see you when I return."

Charlie looked disappointed. "Of course, my dear. I understand. It will just make it all the more special to see you when you return. I hope you have a safe and enjoyable journey there and back."

Shakti hoped so too. It was a journey she was reluctant to make, and one in which her news about Stonegate would most likely disappoint the Prophet. Her report simply stated that life in Stonegate was predictable and normal. People worked hard, frequented the inn, the town was peaceful and nothing of importance was happening. She would not disclose that Don and other leaders were suspicious of the Prophet's motives and that there had been sightings of Raiders.

As the main course arrived, Shakti noticed the young couple from Glenwood on the dance floor, holding each other close in the bliss of newlywed love. She envied them, thinking how wonderful her life could have been if she had met Charlie when she was younger or that perhaps someday she would enjoy a romantic holiday somewhere herself, with her new love.

"A penny for your thoughts, Shakti. You look as though you are far away, my dear."

"Oh…just thinking how lovely that young couple look on the dance floor. They are newlyweds from Glenwood, just staying here for their honeymoon. How lovely they look…and so in love."

"Well, I guess that love is in the air tonight, my dear," Charlie said softly, as he reached for Shakti's hand. "But since you mention the word 'love,' I have a confession to make. I know it may be a little early for this gesture of affection, but Shakti, I was hoping you would accept a gift to celebrate our newfound friendship."

Reaching into his pocket, Charlie produced a small engraved silver box. "Open it," he urged, as Shakti could not stop herself from expressing a small gasp of delight. Her eyes glistened with misty tears of joy, as with trembling fingers she lifted the lid of the box to reveal a shiny gold ring with a beautifully polished pearl set in gemstones.

"Oh, goodness, Charlie. Of course, I shall accept it and I shall treasure it always."

Charlie placed the ring on her finger as he added, "It is a friendship ring to begin with. I am hoping we can begin our future as good friends with a splash of romance here and there. On that note, would you care for the next dance?"

The band was having a break and did not recommence the music until well after they had devoured the cheese platter and strawberries.

"What a delicious meal," Shakti said, finishing off the rosé wine with her last mouthful. "We must do this again, Charlie, when I return. And let's have that dance now. The band has just started again."

Charlie led Shakti onto the dance floor where others were now twirling around to the strains of a beautiful melody. Her dress billowed beautifully as she moved in time to the rhythm of the taros. Charlie held her close to his heart. It was almost eleven on the inn clock when the band stopped playing and they resumed their seats at the table. Charlie ordered coffee for two as Shakti yawned in a contented state of tiredness.

"Oh, look," said Shakti. "Look who's just arrived looking a little worried... why, it's Don and Rachel."

Don moved towards them with Rachel by his side. Dark shadows were obvious under her eyes making her look as though she had not slept well for a few nights. She managed a smile as she saw Charlie and watched Don pull up two more chairs.

"I hope we're not interrupting, but do you mind if we join you for a quick ale? We are actually looking for a young couple from Glenwood who

I believe are staying here and who have asked us to see them. They have brought news with them from Robby."

"Really?" Charlie asked as if surprised by the news. "Well, Shakti just pointed them out earlier…they are sitting right over there in the corner by the bay window."

Don and Rachel glanced over to see Willy and Daisy Oliver stealing a quick kiss together. "Oh, if you'll just excuse us for a moment, Charlie, we need to talk to them. We'll be right back to join you once we get the news about Robby."

"Of course. We shall be here with a fresh ale for you. I am glad to hear that someone has seen Robby at last. What a relief!"

Rachel nodded. "Yes, I have been worried for days. But this appears to be a good omen."

Charlie and Shakti watched as Don and Rachel introduced themselves to Willy and Daisy. They could see a smile of relief cross Rachel's face as the four of them conversed.

"Oh, I do hope that Don's son is safe," Shakti said, knowing full well the ruthlessness of the Raiders. "And that he returns soon."

"Aye," said Charlie in agreement. "We all miss him around here. Especially his cousin, Ari, as they grew up together and are as close as a brother and sister. Ari has been moping for days without him."

"Oh, dear," Shakti continued. "Let's hope we see him return here soon. I can see how upset his poor mother Rachel is."

The coffee arrived with a few fine chocolates on tiny plates. It was the perfect ending to a wonderful night in which Shakti could not stop looking at her new pearl ring from time to time. People were trickling out of the inn as they made their way to their homes to enjoy a good night's sleep so they could face another day. A day in which Shakti dreaded having to leave Stonegate.

Don and Rachel arrived back, beaming at the good news from the Olivers. "Robby sent word that he intends to be home in a few days. That should put a smile back on Rachel's face," Don said, putting his arm around Rachel, who did appear a little happier.

It was almost closing time at the inn, and Don and Rachel had just said their goodbyes to Charlie and Shakti when a young stranger burst through the door looking disheveled. "I'm looking for Donald of Goldstone," he said to the young girl at the bar.

She pointed toward Don and Rachel. "See, that is Donald of Goldstone over there, sitting at the table by the hearth. He is the older gentleman with the fairish graying hair."

"Oh. Thank you, miss. And could I have an ale, please? I have come a long way, and if there are any meals available still, I would be grateful, as I have not eaten all day."

"Well, you are in luck, sir, as we always have a pot of hearty beef stew on the stove for latecomers. I will certainly bring you a fine serving with a freshly baked cob of herbed bread and our homemade butter. Please make yourself at home."

The stranger took his ale as he walked towards where Don was seated. "Hello," he said extending a hand to shake. "You must be Donald of Goldstone. I hate to disturb you, sir, but I have come a long way to find you. I must talk to you regarding an urgent matter. Oh, allow me to introduce myself. I am Arrow James from Prophet City."

CHAPTER 13
†

A Plan is Hatched

When you go out to war against your enemies and see horses, chariots and
an army larger than yours, do not be afraid of them, for the Lord your God,
who brought you up out of the land of Egypt, is with you.
Deuteronomy 20:1 HCSB

A somber mood hung over the conference room of the academy. A group
huddled around a large oval table talking in low voices. The meeting
was chaired by Marshall Levi Jackson, naturally, since the topic was military
strategy. He called them all to order and began with introductions. Seated
there were Mayor Billings and Rachel, representing the civilian leadership.
Military leaders were the marshall's son Isaiah, Commander Hamway, Don,
Gray John, Thomas of Longmont, and Colin McCoy. Invited guests were
Malcolm and Harold of the House of Healing and Arrow James of Prophet
City.

"I want to first hear from a young man who has traveled far to be here,"
said Marshall Jackson, opening the discussion. "Following his message, I
will invite a former cadet of the Stonegate Academy to share another report.
Is that agreeable?"

No one objected, so Gray John cleared his throat. "This is Arrow James
from Prophet City," he said. A murmur came from many lips, and Rachel's
eyes widened. "Arrow has come to tell us of the plans he has made with his
group. He wishes to enlist our help in executing his plan. I should add that
he represents a small group that calls itself the 'Liberty Soldiers.' Donald and I
have had a long chat with him and think he offers us an interesting proposal."

Arrow was dressed in a simple blue tunic of rather coarse weave. His dark hair was untidy, but his gray eyes were clear and direct. He was slim and youthful, hardly looking old enough to even be a first-year cadet. He glanced around the room, but he seemed to be composed and calm. His voice was clear and carried well. "Gentlemen, lady, I am honored to be invited here to meet you all. I feared that no one would bother with me or my strange request. To be asked to speak—well, it is more than I could have dreamed of.

"I am here to tell you that the time is ripe to overthrow the Prophet. This is not simply based on some grumbling of ordinary people in the West. Discontent runs deep. There is cause for discontent, of course. Taxes are ever-increasing, which creates unbearable hardships for most families. Everywhere there are spies and secret police, the Black Caps, which create terrible fear and mistrust. No one's life, liberty, and property are safe. Families hide their daughters when the Prophet's enforcers or tax collectors show up. I think you can guess why. Excuse me, Lady Rachel, if my words were indelicate."

Rachel said nothing. He paused for a moment and calmly took a sip of water. "I am sure that none of this is a great surprise. You probably know that our evil tyrant is loathed by nearly all. But I can tell you that even those holding high positions have had enough. Even though any act of defiance is quickly stamped out, things are nearing a breaking point. More executions seem to only add to the simmering hatred."

Marshall Jackson stopped him. "I am not at all surprised at what you say. But I am amazed, frankly, at how well you express yourself. Tell us, what does your small band intend to do? Do you have arms? Are you organizing an insurgency?"

"The Liberty Soldiers are a group of young men and women, Christians, all. But I really represent a small planning team, just a few men. I am the youngest. We have been speaking to people about overthrowing the Prophet. Of course, we have to be very careful. But there is an underground network of secret Christians that trust each other with their lives. That helps because that means we actually have a network of hundreds. We have been spreading the message that the Prophet and his henchmen live in palaces, in luxury, gorging themselves on wine and lavish banquets while ordinary people are almost starving. It is like throwing grease on a hot fire. The people have had enough! Our words strike a chord."

Gray John interrupted. "That is all very well, but the False Prophet has a well-trained army. Any mob attempting to storm the palace would simply be swatted down like flies. Are you ready for bloodshed? Probably futile bloodshed?"

Arrow James nodded. "You are correct, Gray John. The army has grown quickly and has probably doubled in the last year alone. The Prophet promises all young men who join a good wage, warm barracks and plenty of food. Many men have the choice of the army or one of the prison camps. But we have no intention of simply stirring up a mob."

"Exactly what do you propose?" asked Marshall Jackson. There was an edge to his voice.

"Hear him out," said Gray John. "Tell us about your maps and the storm drain." Everyone sat up straighter and looked at each other.

"I will do that," said Arrow. "Everyone says that I talk too much, but I thought some background might be helpful." He produced a rather small scroll and laid it on the table. It was rather dirty, and the draftsmanship was crude. "This is a map of the palace and surrounding grounds. We have entrances marked with the number of guards and when the shifts change. There is a wall around the old city and another surrounding the palace grounds. But we have discovered an old storm drain that leads from outside the city to quite near the palace and beyond. Some Christians have for some time been using it to slip out of the city. There are some abandoned mines to the east that allow groups to meet in secret. We did some digging and were able to connect the major drain to a storm sewer in the palace courtyard. See, it is marked here."

"So, your plan is to use these storm drains to get into the palace?" asked Hamway.

"Well, yes. But that is the problem. We could easily raise a few dozen young men besides ourselves. But none of us have weapons besides knives, and we have no real training, either. We can gather information. We can make plans. But we need your help to carry them out."

"I see," said Marshall Jackson. He sat in thought, looking at the map. "Are there any questions?" He waited for a moment, then continued. "I think that is enough for now. I am sure that we will want to discuss this in more detail." He held up the map. "Can we keep this?"

"Of course," said Arrow. "That is why I brought it."

"I can take it to the lore-house, if you wish," said Don. "We have a cartographer there, and we could have him make a copy."

"Blast!" said Marshall Jackson. "I should have invited Lore-master Duncan. He has a wise head, I understand. But we can fill him in later. Yes, by all means, have a copy made, perhaps at a larger scale." He turned to face Arrow. "Thank you, Arrow James. Kindly go and relax and take some refreshments. Someone can direct you to the small dining room." Arrow nodded, expressed thanks, and left the room.

Shortly after, another, slightly older man was escorted through the door. He wore a padded tunic with the typical network of rust spots from wearing mail. His leggings were mud-splattered, and his hair was matted from wearing a helmet. It looked as if he had just ridden in, with no chance to do anything but shed his heavy armor.

As before, Gray John did the introduction. "Kindly welcome Jason, a former student of mine. He arrived early this morning with an urgent message from the frontier. We have had only enough time to get a hot breakfast into him and his men before I had to join this meeting. He has significant news. He shared the essence of it to me, but I will let him tell you in his own words."

There was a buzz of conversation as he took the seat vacated by Arrow. Don was surprised. He remembered Jason very well since he had graduated from the academy the previous Spring. Jason looked him in the eye, and they both nodded.

"Jason was sent by Abel," continued Gray John. "Many of you know Abel well. He is a Gray Pilgrim and a skilled healer. He is in charge of Green River Surgery on the very borders of the False Prophet's dominions." Gray John looked directly at Jason. "Go ahead and tell this group what you told me."

Jason rose to his feet and cleared his throat. He seemed to not know what to do with his hands, so he finally clasped them behind the small of his back. "Yes," he began, tentatively. "Abel wanted you to know that one of our patients saw a large cavalry force, perhaps one thousand, in the field with many field artillery pieces. They were apparently conducting maneuvers."

"One thousand?" blurted Mayor Billings. "Surely a wild exaggeration."

"I agree we can't rely on a civilian's estimate of numbers," said Marshall Jackson. He looked around the room. "But any large force of heavy cavalry exercising with field artillery is very worrisome."

"Decidedly so," said Don. "It was our field artillery that helped us defeat the False Prophet's cavalry in the last war. It was also vital in choking off his supply lines. It seems likely that our advantage has been lost."

Malcolm raised his hand. All eyes turned towards him as he spoke. "We received the same report from Abel, and other indications confirming it. But you, Jason, must have been delayed. We got the message days ago."

"Aye. That we were. I have three horse troopers with me, but we met a much larger band of Raiders on the way. It was a close call, but we finally lost them. It cost us three days. I'm sorry, but we got here as fast as we could. I have a written message for Lord Donald, but it says what I just told you. Although, I understand the message is put in guarded terms."

Jason passed a folded note to Don. He quickly scanned it. "Yes," said Don. "Jason is correct. Thank you for explaining the exact meaning. Thank God, Abel recognized the significance of this sighting."

"Hmm," said Marshall Jackson. "Very well. Thank you, Jason. Well done. I was not comfortable with Arrow James hearing our discussions, but you are welcome to stay if you wish."

"The Arrow lad seems trustworthy to me," said Commander Hamway.

"Even so, he could be a creature of the False Prophet," said Jackson. "He is a clever man and would be capable of trying to bait a trap. But at this point, we should take a short recess. I need to stretch my legs."

†

When the meeting reconvened, Marshall Jackson gestured toward the foot of the table. "Now we will hear from our friends from the House of Healing," he said.

"Thank you," said Malcolm. "Not all of you know us. I am the chief military advisor, and Harold is master of the walls. He commands the House of Healing levy in case we are under siege. Recently, my main task has been to gather information to give us warning of threats to our medical center, our healers in the field, and those traveling to seek our aid. You know our healers as Gray Pilgrims, of course.

"I have here a summary of the intelligence we have collected from many sources. Abel's report you have already heard. It is already included in the summary. We conclude that the Prophet has accelerated his rearmament and now has a greater force at his disposal than ever before. We know that the Raiders are gathering information, too, and are the advance guard of an invasion which could be only weeks away. I will leave this document with you."

"Thank you for such a complete analysis," said Marshall Jackson as he accepted a thick bundle of documents. "We have reached much the same conclusions, but your work certainly confirms what we already suspected."

"We have also sent messengers to our friends in the south. The military threat is a danger to us all. We also sent pigeons, so we will soon have a report of their meetings."

"And you brought more of your pigeons to us. We will send you back with more of ours. Rapid communications may be vital in the days ahead. Too bad we lost the heliograph network. Some thought it was too expensive to keep up, apparently." Marshall Jackson paused and gazed pointedly at Mayor Billings, then he turned back to Malcolm. "Thank you for your help, and please pass on our grateful thanks to Chief Surgeon Kerik."

The floor was then given to Commander Hamway. "We all agree, then, that a worrying indication has been the Raider activity," Hamway said, by way of beginning. "It has been established now by various eyewitnesses that there are Raiders in this area, especially in a location along the Cash River, and most probably somewhere close to Goldstone, as well. Just yesterday, a young couple from Glenwood reported seeing a band of them. We can safely assume that the Raiders have set up camps close to many major towns in the East. In view of this, I propose that our first line of action is to eliminate the enemy by destroying the camps and the Raiders in them."

"And how do you propose to do that?" asked Mayor Billings. His face was flushed. Don suspected that he was searching for something to justify his inaction. No politician would want to be accused of placing them all in peril.

"We are bringing our horse troops back from the garrisons along the trade routes and are activating those that have been on standby," explained Hamway. "They will require some refitting and additional training. But I have worked with Gray John all summer. We used the academy facilities for training some of the finest members of the Red Axe troop to enable them to carry out special operations. These men are capable of working by stealth and surprise to find and perhaps even eliminate small Raider bands. Looking ahead, these men would be ideal for working with Arrow James."

"How many do you have?" asked Marshall Jackson. "Of the special operations troops, I mean?"

"We have two groups of twelve each," answered Gray John. "Not a large number, but we have given them extensive training in camouflage, scouting, hand-to-hand combat, musketry, and explosives. One man in each group has one of the ancient weapons and knows how to use it."

Hamway raised his hand to stop him. "We know that only you can allow the use of our precious store of ammunition for the old rifles, Marshall Jackson. For that reason, they have not had live-fire training. Now that I mention it, we suggest that these two men be issued at least twenty rounds each."

"Good Lord," said Mayor Billings. "Do you have any idea how valuable that old ammunition is? I would have to strenuously object."

"That ammunition has no value locked in storage cans," said Rachel. "This is a military decision, and you will be in for a fight if you try to interfere."

"I agree," said Thomas of Longmont. "My vote would be against you. Do not test the will of the Stonegate Council on this."

Mayor Billings' face turned red, but he only said, "That was uncalled for."

"I will make the decision," said Marshall Jackson. "The law is clear on that. But I will have to learn more about the supply of this old ammunition."

When the murmurs in the room quieted, Gray John pulled out a large map of the East and laid it out on the table. "As you can see, on this map I have pinpointed the most likely areas that the Raiders would have set up camps in the East. These areas are close to most of our towns, but have the benefit of being heavily wooded or isolated. They are off the main roads where most travelers would not venture but are perfect spots to hide out."

Commander Hamway agreed. "These do seem to be likely areas to investigate. I recommend we send out the special groups immediately. They can start the search and our regular horse troops can go out and join in when they are ready.

"Thanks to your staff who did most of the planning," said Gray John. "We all need to remember that it will be a secret and dangerous operation. The planning team calls it Operation Ochre. If we hear that name, the meaning should be clear, and details will not need to be discussed elsewhere. If you all agree, and upon the order from the marshall to proceed, your groups can be sent out with little delay."

There was little more to say, and all signaled agreement with the plan, even Mayor Billings. Marshall Jackson asked if there were other items before they adjourned. There was silence for a moment, then Thomas of Longmont raised his hand.

"I do have a suggestion," Thomas began. "I have a foot in both camps, being a Stonegate councilor and also still on the military rolls. My concern is that the average person in Stonegate does not have the information we have discussed. It would not be wise to share any details, but we must alert them to the danger. If my dear friend, Gray John, can have Operation Ochre, I propose a plan to be named Operation Information. It would be quite simple since the new printing press is available. We should prepare a warning to travelers that Raiders have been seen. We should suggest that people take up arms, travel in groups, and report any suspicious sightings. These will be printed as handbills and we will distribute them to every city and town."

Rachel agreed. "Of course, Thomas, I could organize the printing and bundling of those handbills. I am sure I can enlist the help of Carla and the women's archery club."

Mayor Billings spoke up. "Now, no one can say that this is not my area of responsibility. We should not use the local printer. Too expensive. The council has a small printing press. We should use that."

"That sounds sensible," said Marshall Jackson.

"At last," someone said.

"I heard that," said Mayor Billings. "And I see no reason we should print enough for the larger cities. Hightower has several printers and better paper makers than we do."

"But the small towns don't," said Rachel. "Lives are at stake. Let's think about that more than pinching pennies."

"We don't have time to discuss all these details," said Marshall Jackson. "Mayor, Lady Rachel has offered to help, but if you will take responsibility for informing citizens of the danger, I will only ask to review the wording so that military secrets are protected. Are there any other suggestions?"

"We should place travel bans against anyone traveling alone, at least on the more dangerous routes. We already have checkpoints set up, and we can order our men to turn back solitary travelers," Don suggested.

"That is a good precaution, Lord Don," Commander Hamway said. "We must be cautious in the face of danger and also be one step ahead of the Prophet. But we don't control some of these roads, such as the Great Highway going west from Hightower. Nor the road over the Western Wall that leads from Estes Park."

Malcolm spoke up. "We could suggest that our sister cities take the same action. But I was thinking about the huge amount of traveling and work it will take to distribute the handbills. Perhaps our Gray Pilgrims could assist in this distribution, since they travel extensively, anyway."

"That is an excellent idea, Malcolm. Would your Pilgrims take them to our friends in the South: the Diné People and the Sonora Clan?"

"Of course, But this will take some time."

At that, the meeting was adjourned. Many planned to have lunch back at the Quill and Sword. Don and Rachel took charge of the visitors.

✝

It was early afternoon, but the air was crisp, and a light breeze was blowing as Don, Rachel, Malcolm, Harold, and Arrow returned to the home near Westerly-stead.

"Well, we haven't had so many visitors in a long time," said Rachel, as they arrived to the warmth of a roaring fire in the living room hearth. "You must all be hungry. I think Judith has fixed a lunch. We will have a more substantial meal at suppertime before retiring to bed. It has been a very long morning."

Malcolm yawned. "Yes, and tomorrow Harold and I will make haste back to the House of Healing. I hope we can have an approved handbill to take with us. We will see that copies are sent to our friends in the South, the Diné people and the Sonora Clan."

"Yes," said Don, trying to stifle a yawn himself. "And a nap after lunch will not go amiss. Please send our regards to our treasured friends down there. We fought a good war last time, with them at our side. Let us see if we can do it again, but this time in a different way. We do not have the manpower to defeat the False Prophet in open battle. We will need to use all our stealth, skill, and cunning."

Arrow nodded as Judith brought in steaming hot cups of spiced cider. "I truly believe that a few men can capture the Prophet. Once he is in our hands, his armies will not protect his interests. They will be glad to be rid of him."

Rachel nodded. "So, Arrow, are you really leaving us early in the morning? Surely you need to rest a few days. It is a long ride back to Prophet City."

"Yes, I must return as soon as possible before I am missed. We have much to do. Gray John thinks he can arrange for the special Red Axe troopers to meet with us in secret. There are still many details that we need to arrange. We need to think beyond the Prophet's capture to what will come afterward."

The afternoon passed pleasantly. All the men followed Don's example and took a nap. Afterwards, they all enjoyed a chicken dinner. Their time together ended with handshakes, hugs, and goodbyes as young Arrow was planning to leave long before Rachel or Don awoke. A full moon was hanging high in the sky as if promising change to all their lives. Don and Rachel crawled into bed and drifted off to sleep, but not before hugging each other for comfort and warmth. The last thing that Rachel thought about was Robby.

CHAPTER 14

†

A Missing Person

Sustain me with raisins; refresh me with apricots, for I am lovesick
Song of Solomon 2:5 HCSB

The coach from Loveland was already late as Charlie waited patiently for Shakti to arrive back in Stonegate. He held a dozen red roses in his hands with a small card attached that read, *I have missed you, Love, Charlie*. It was late in the evening and the streets of Stonegate were quiet, but he could hear music and merriment coming from the Quill and Sword on the corner. He looked at the big clock again, feeling a sense of impatience as the coach finally arrived in town.

He waited for Shakti to alight, his heart beating a little faster at the thought of seeing her again. Yet, as the last person left the carriage, there was no sign of her. "Excuse me, sir," he said to the coachman. "I was expecting my lady friend to arrive on this coach this evening. I am sure her return journey was booked and paid for. Her name is Shakti, and she has long, dark hair and a slender build."

The coachman looked Charlie up and down. His eyes lingered on the red roses in his hand and he said, "Oh, sorry, sir. Yes, we did have a lady by that name booked to return on this coach. But she never arrived at the stop in Loveland. We waited quite some time for her, which is why we are late. But, we could not wait forever."

Charlie could not conceal his disappointment at the news. "Well, perhaps you could tell me when the next coach arrives here from Loveland. Perhaps she had some reason to stay in Loveland longer."

"Perhaps," agreed the coachman as he moved to the boot to unload luggage. "But the next coach does not arrive until this Saturday evening. Three days away."

"Oh," was all Charlie could say. "How strange. You see, she has to start work again at the Quill and Sword tomorrow. Odd that she would miss the coach unless something has happened to her. I must tell them at the inn that she has not arrived."

"Of course," the coachman replied. "Well, good luck. I hope your lady friend is fine."

Charlie hurried to the inn, wondering what could have befallen Shakti. The owners of the Quill and Sword were old family friends who had known him since he was a young boy. Alice Cartwright and her husband, Joseph had run the inn since the end of the last war and were kind both to their staff and their patrons. He spotted Alice serving the newlyweds from Glenwood, and she smiled as he made his way over to her.

"Well, hello, Charlie. Are those glorious roses for me…or for that new love of yours, Shakti?" she joked.

"Well, as a matter of fact, they are for Shakti, Alice…but I'm afraid that she somehow missed her coach. And the next one from Loveland arrives here in three days' time."

"Oh, dear," said Alice. "I do hope that there is nothing seriously wrong. She promised that she would return this evening. She did say that she had some urgent things to attend to."

"Yes," said Charlie, continuing to puzzle about what could have happened. "That is exactly what she told me. By the way, did she leave you an address in Loveland? I may be going down that way next week, and so if she doesn't return on Saturday, I could inquire at her address."

"Of course, Charlie. That she did. She said she lived there before she started working here. I think it is 123 Clemmons Lane, Loveland or something like that. Let me pour you an ale while I check the records. You certainly look as though you could do with one. And here, let me take those pretty roses and put them in water. Perhaps they will last until she returns."

Charlie sipped a much-needed ale as he waited. She bustled back with a beaming smile on her face. "Well, I'm sure glad I checked the address. It is 125 Clover Lane, Loveland. So, if she doesn't return, you could inquire there."

Charlie took the small snippet of paper and put it in his pocket. He decided that if Shakti did not return on Saturday, he would go to Loveland.

†

Rachel and Carla were busy organizing the printing of the handbills at the council office. Ari and Sara were helping by putting the flyers into boxes ready for delivery. It was late Saturday afternoon when they finally finished after three days of hard work.

"Whew," said Rachel, wiping her sweaty brow. "I do believe we can stop now. And thank goodness we won't have to work tomorrow, as it is Sunday, and we all need a good rest."

"Yes, thank goodness," echoed Carla, "I'm tired of being stuck in the printing room for three long days, instead of managing things at Westerly-stead or training the archery students. At last, we can go home and relax."

"Yes," Rachel said, "I'm also relieved that this task is completed. And it's a good thing we put on that beef stew early this morning…or none of us would be eating tonight."

"Well, we could have gone to the Quill and Sword for dinner if you hadn't prepared the stew," said Ari. "You know, I might just go over there after dinner to say goodbye to the Olivers. Willy and Daisy are leaving on Monday and I don't want them to leave without me saying goodbye. You know they have invited me to stay in Glenwood sometime and visit them."

"I'm afraid you might have to postpone your travels for a little while, Ari," Carla said. "You know no one is allowed to travel alone. It is no longer safe."

"Yes, but I wouldn't go alone," said Ari. "I would take the coach. It has other people on board and only travels on the main route. And Willy and Daisy are riding back home. Charlie and Colin have some sort of errand to do in Ariel, so they will all travel together. See, I do understand the danger."

"Yes, well, speaking of that, I think it would be safe enough to go to the inn tonight. You might be able to go with Charlie. He is hoping that Shakti will arrive on the coach tonight. For some strange reason she missed her coach last time," Carla said, as they locked the doors to the printing room and made their way to the council stables where their horses were tethered.

"I don't know what he will do if she doesn't return tonight. He hasn't been himself the last three days, making himself sick with worry."

"Well, I know how he feels," Ari said, thinking of Robby and wondering why he hadn't returned by now as promised. "We are all missing Robby. And you, Aunt Rachel, especially. I don't think that any of us have had a good night's sleep since he disappeared."

Rachel put an arm around Ari. "Yes, I'm afraid you're right, Ari. I am beginning to think that something is amiss. He did tell the Olivers he would be home soon, in a few days, and it has been almost two weeks. I can see that Don is terribly worried as well."

"Well, all we can do is pray for his safe return," Carla said. "I say we head home now and hope for the best. For all we know, he could be back there right now enjoying an ale with Don."

"Oh, I hope so...I do hope so," Ari said as she mounted her little roan gelding, Rusty. She blinked back the tears as they sped home to Westerly-stead.

†

Charlie was trying not to think the worst as he waited patiently for the next coach from Loveland to arrive. The nights were becoming cooler now, a bit like the chill in his heart at the thought of never seeing Shakti again. He had picked a fresh bunch of daisies from the garden at Westerly-stead, uncertain if the roses had survived. It was just after ten o'clock when the coach pulled up at the rest stop and a half a dozen people alighted from the carriage. Charlie's heart stopped in his throat. There was no sign of Shakti.

With a heavy heart, he made his way to the inn where Alice was watching. His glum face and stooped shoulders showed that there was no good news. "So, no sign of Shakti?" she asked Charlie as he ordered a dark ale.

"No, no sign. This is very peculiar. I don't know what to make of it at all. I have no idea what has happened to her."

"I'm so sorry, Charlie. I am worried about Shakti too. She obviously had every intention of returning here. Her clothes and belongings are still upstairs in her room. I can't imagine why she has not returned. Such a fine woman and a very good worker too."

"Well," said Charlie. "She certainly was all that and much more. On another note, however, I will be traveling with the Olivers to their home in Glenwood on Monday. On the way there I can make some inquiries at the address you gave me."

"Of course, that will probably work. God be with you when you travel, Charlie. The Olivers are such a lovely couple. You know that Willy is Harley's nephew? He fought valiantly against the Raiders in the last war and was a treasured friend of Lord Don's."

"Yes, I remember him…a big hulk of a stocky man…strong as a bear and solid as granite. He was one of the best fighters in the East, or so he said. I met him once when I was about ten years old and never forgot him."

"Yes, Harley was unforgettable, all right. And everyone he met loved him and respected his strength and courage for battle. Do be careful now, dear."

The inn was now bustling with activity as the band began to play the waltz that Charlie had taught Shakti. He ordered another ale as Ari arrived to see her newfound friends, Willy and Daisy. She waved and smiled at Charlie as he sat reminiscing about every wonderful moment he had spent with Shakti at the Quill and Sword. All he could see were her beautiful eyes staring into his the last time they had danced.

†

Shakti arrived at the address on Clover Lane in Loveland to find two men waiting for her. She was surprised, since she had been told to drop off her written report and return immediately to Stonegate. The taller of the two men demanded the report and read it while she stood there, knees shaking. She realized that the spymaster was a dreaded Black Cap.

He seemed angry. "You say this source of yours—the one in the very household of Donald of Goldstone—is nothing more than a field hand and knows nothing of significance. Correct?"

Shakti nodded. She had tried, when writing, to protect Charlie by minimizing his importance.

"The Prophet gave me orders to pull you out if this proved to be the case. So, it's back to Prophet City for you, little lady."

Shakti was stunned. She was trapped and did not know what to do. She could hardly say that she had lied. Now her own report was going to tear her and Charlie apart, perhaps forever. Her mind seemed frozen as the men led her to some ruffians who had a spare horse. They were Raiders.

For the second time in her life, she felt like a prisoner. She watched with silent anguish over several days as the landscape of the East changed to a rugged range of mountains bisected by a high pass overlooking Prophet City. What would Charlie think? Would she ever see him again? She fingered the pearl ring he had given her, wishing that this was merely a bad dream. But as the horses passed through the palace gates, she knew with a sinking feeling that she was indeed back and that she might never see Stonegate again. For the first time, she prayed to the Christian God and begged to be set free from the Prophet.

†

Martin Abaddon was waiting in his chambers, pleased at the prospect of seeing Shakti again. She still was his favorite harem dancer, and he realized with dismay that while she had been in Stonegate he had missed her. Sending her as a spy had at first seemed to be a good idea. But he had regretted it almost at once. He had been pleased, rather than angry, when the messenger pigeon had brought her report and word of the decision to recall her.

He wore his favorite purple and gold tunic with a tasseled sash around his waist and cream-colored leggings to impress her. His new maid, Alicia, served some of the most exotic wines in his collection and a banquet of cheese, various fruits, and thinly sliced toast.

Shakti arrived, looking tired and disheveled from her long ride. "I will have Alicia pour a perfumed bath for you, my dear, and allow you to freshen up. I have instructed her to place a new gown I ordered especially for you on your bedside table. I am sure you will love it as it is in the latest fashion."

"Why thank you, Martin, how kind and thoughtful you are to think of me," Shakti responded. She slipped back into a role, pretending affection to please the Prophet. "I am sure that a bath will relax my weary bones and refresh a tired body. Thank you for the gown…I am sure it is perfect as your taste in everything is so impeccable."

The Prophet smiled, revealing a new gold tooth made while Shakti was away. "How delightful you still are, my dearest Shakti, even when you are tired. You know I have missed you more than you can imagine." Then he turned away and allowed her to go to her room.

Shakti also smiled, relishing the thought of a hot bubbling bath where she could be alone to think of Charlie. There had to be a way to escape from this palace, somehow. As she undressed, she thought of Selena, and how Mother Tess had organized an escape route. But Mother Tess was long gone now and all her secrets with her. She sighed, allowing the fragrance of lavender to calm her senses as she soaked in the bath.

The gown Martin had ordered for her was exquisite; it was made from a fabric that she had never seen before. A soft, lightweight cloth it was, that moved with her body as she walked. Flaming red and gold colors sprang out in the shape of flowers against a pale green background. She could not imagine a more glorious creation—something fit for a queen. She shuddered, hoping that the Prophet was not meaning to take her as one of his many wives…surely not. But a nagging fear enveloped her.

CHAPTER 15

†

History Repeats

For the eyes of the Lord range throughout the earth to strengthen those
whose hearts are fully committed to Him. You have done a foolish thing,
and from now on you will be at war.

2 Chronicles 16:9 HCSB

*H*istory *always repeats itself, first as history, second as farce.* Don could
not remember the source of the quote, but it seemed apt. The report
from Abel, that told of one thousand heavy cavalry and ten field artillery
pieces on maneuvers to the east of Prophet City, had struck a nerve, finally.

Don's home, once so warm and welcoming, was now as cold and fragile
as an icicle. Rachel had dark circles under her eyes, and little Sara kept asking
when Robby would come home. Don had even saddled Skipper on one
occasion and started to ride west on a one-man rescue mission, just as he
had so many years before when Rachel had been kidnapped by the Raiders.

This time, though, he had only ridden for a few miles before reality came
crashing down like a felled tree. He had no idea where to start looking. He
was no longer young. And he had responsibilities that he could not abandon.
He had reined Skipper homeward, and a stiff afternoon breeze had not been
enough to dry the tears that ran down his cheeks.

†

Don had suggested that they invite Carla, Howard, and Ari to Friday night
supper. As an afterthought, they also invited Carla's mother, Betty, who lived

alone and would welcome an outing. But things nearly fell apart. Don had planned to take the afternoon off, but problems at the academy held him up until late afternoon. When he rode into his courtyard, he found Betty's carriage parked by the stable.

Don unsaddled Skipper and turned him out into the horse pasture and walked though the kitchen door. He was greeted by the warm smell of a beef roast in the oven of the cookstove and Betty and Rachel's maid, Judith, busily making preparations.

"Hello, Betty," said Don. "Where is Rachel?"

"Hello, Donald," replied Betty. "She was called away to a council meeting. Sounded urgent."

"You mean you had to get the supper ready?"

"I don't mind. Makes me feel useful. I came by early with some fruit and vegetables. Judith has been a big help."

"She is a treasure, to be sure. What can I do?"

"You can best help by staying out of the kitchen. But you can make sure we have enough chairs. Let's see, besides your three, we need four more. I guess seven will do it."

Don went to the dining room and found that seven places were already set. He realized that she just wanted him to be out of the way, so he retreated to his study for a half hour before he heard the sounds of someone arriving.

He stepped outside to greet Howard, Carla, and Ari. Carla had a large hamper which smelled like fresh-baked bread mixed with the scent of apple pie. Then he helped Howard tie the team in the shade, and they all went into the house.

Howard had filled out his lanky frame and was even a bit thicker around the middle than he had remembered, since he had not seen him for nearly a month. But Carla was as trim as ever and her red hair just as striking. Ari looked pale and drawn and had little to say, though she offered her cheek for Don's kiss of greeting.

"Any word of Robby at all?" asked Carla, taking him by the hands and gazing deep into his eyes.

"I'm afraid not. Rachel is worried sick."

"We know," said Howard. "Ari has been beside herself."

"We have our best people searching," said Don. "But let's try to just enjoy a meal together."

Don showed them into the living room, but Ari and Carla immediately left for the kitchen. Ari soon returned with two glasses of chilled tea, garnished with mint. Howard and Don accepted them with thanks, and they sank into two comfortable chairs.

"Rachel should be along soon," said Don. "She had to go to a meeting of the Stonegate council."

"Any idea why they called a special meeting? They don't usually meet on Friday, do they?"

"I imagine it is about the news of the False Prophet."

They sat in silence for a few minutes, sipping their tea. Don had grown close to Howard over the years though they had little in common. Howard's life was in the management of his family's farm and herds of cattle. He was proud of his breeding program and his orchards and fields. Don, on the other hand, was focused on the academy and training the next generation of military leaders.

"What are you going to do?" asked Howard.

"I have no idea," said Don.

They were washing their hands and face by a water barrel and washstand near the back door. Then they heard hoofbeats and the jingle of harness and turned to see Rachel drive in. She had a light buggy, and the mare pulling it had a dark sheen of sweat. She clearly had been in a hurry. Don helped her alight and Howard tied her mare in the shade next to his team and wagon.

"How did the meeting go?" asked Don as he followed Rachel into the house.

"They are frightened and confused," said Rachel. "They understand that the False Prophet is building up his forces, and that probably means he plans to invade."

"Yes, that is good, I suppose—good that they are waking up to the threat, I mean."

"It is, but they really don't want to face all that might mean."

"It will mean rearming and great sacrifice."

"Exactly. Nothing a politician wants to hear."

"It strikes me that it is for the best that your seat on the council is hereditary."

"Why is that?"

"If you had to run for office, you would be a politician." Don smiled.

She punched his arm. "Be serious. Anyway, they did the only thing they could think of."

"What was that?"

"They called for a study."

†

The meal was delicious. The roast beef, grass-fed from Waverly-stead, and topped with a creamy horseradish sauce, was as good as anything Don had ever tasted. Carla's bread with fresh butter and the side dishes were equally delicious. But the mood was somber, and they mostly ate in silence.

"Any word at all from Robby, dear?" asked Betty, putting her hand gently on Rachel's arm.

"They did find his tracks—that of his horse. We know he was heading west."

"If he planned to scout the False Prophet's lands, he had a long way to go," said Howard. "To do a proper job could easily take six weeks."

"It's possible that he has been delayed," agreed Carla. "We could be worrying for nothing."

"I suppose it's possible," said Don. "But my heart tells me that something has gone wrong. I pray to God every day for his safety. I wish we could do more."

Ari looked at Don, her large eyes brimming. "I am so afraid."

Don turned toward her and clasped her in a strong embrace. "We all are, Ari. We all are."

†

After the dishes had been washed and put away they left the final straightening up to Judith. Sara wanted to show Ari her new dress. Betty declared that she would like to see it, too, so they all went upstairs to Sara's bedroom.

Don and Rachel invited Carla and Howard to the back porch where they all enjoyed a chilled fruit punch.

"What kind of study did the council call for?" asked Don.

Rachel explained the council's reaction and if Carla and Howard were surprised, they gave no sign of it.

"They charged Hamway to consult with his best military advisors and come up with a plan to combat the threat at the least cost possible," explained Rachel.

"I see," said Don. "Not necessarily the best plan from a military standpoint. Just the cheapest."

Howard shook his head in wonder. "They still don't really understand. Our very existence is at risk, and they are counting pennies."

"Oh, I almost forgot," said Rachel. "Marshall Jackson told me to tell you that Operation Ochre has been launched."

Howard and Carla looked at her with a puzzled expression.

"Nothing serious," said Don. "A military matter. Some students we trained at the academy."

"I hope it finally means we are doing something," said Carla.

CHAPTER 16
†

A Prisoner in the Palace

I was naked and you clothed Me; I was sick and you took care of Me; I was
in prison and you took care of Me.
Matthew 25:36 HCSB

Robby suddenly awakened as he struggled to see through dimness. He
tried to focus on looming shapes and shadows, but all he could see was
moonlight just visible through a long, narrow window. He was shivering
on a coarse straw bed with only one thin blanket. The room was strange;
circular it was, with stone walls. Where was he? His head throbbed with a
dull ache as he tried to remember what had happened. There was a gash on
his forehead and a rough cloth bandage on his left leg which also throbbed
when he moved.

After rising from the rough straw, Robby limped over to the window,
wincing in pain when he put pressure on his left leg. Outside he could see
a huge stone building with turrets and many windows. It was some kind
of palace surrounded by a high stone wall. In one of the windows, a dim
light glowed, but all else was in darkness. He thought it must be well after
midnight, and the people of the palace were well and truly asleep…except
maybe the occupants of one room.

As he surveyed the view, Robby's memory began to recover. With horror,
he realized that the Raiders had taken him prisoner and brought him here.

With no doubt he knew he was now a prisoner in Prophet City. He remembered the mocking voices of the Raiders taunting and threatening him.

His thoughts turned to Ari and his eyes felt wet. He wondered how she was and wished that he had never disobeyed his father and taken off on the spur of the moment. He knew too well that his mother and father would be sick with worry by now. They would all be asleep in their comfortable, warm beds where the hearth was ablaze, food was plentiful, and love was abundant. His heart sank as he thought that maybe he would never see his loved ones again. His future was bleak here where the Prophet was known to execute most prisoners without a fair trial.

He felt a sharp pang of hunger, adding to his distress. Would he be fed or starved to death? Would he be tried for some kind of crime, or would he be sent to one of those notorious prison camps? How he missed the academy and all his friends. But most of all he missed Ari.

†

Ari and Sara were busy harvesting fall crops in the garden at Westerly-stead. Both were silent as they worked. Ari had become fond of gardening, as it gave her a chance to spend more time with Sara. Sara had noticed that her cousin missed her brother and kept saying that surely he would soon return. It had been over a week since Willy and Daisy Oliver had returned to Glenwood accompanied by Charlie and Colin McCoy. Despite her brave words, Sara had eaten little and had begun to cling to Ari's side like a baby sister.

"Do you think that something has happened to Robby, Ari?" Sara said breaking the long silence between them. "I mean, the Oliver's said he would be back in a few days."

"Sara," Ari said with tenderness, "we mustn't think of the worst. We have to believe that Robby will return any day now. One day, some day soon, Robby will return to us. I can't bear to think otherwise."

"Oh, Ari, you really do love him, don't you? Just as much as I do. It's just so awful not knowing where he is or when he will return to us."

"I know, Sara. Sometimes I think I love him too much. But no matter what happens, we must have faith. I have been praying for him every night. Anyway, it's getting dark soon, and we should finish up here and go help

Aunt Rachel in your kitchen. She has invited the new marshall, Levi Jackson, and his son, Isaiah, for dinner tonight. I believe that Gray John is coming as well so there will be plenty of cooking to do."

Sara took Ari's hand in hers as they skipped the half-mile to Sara's home. They tried to talk about other things but were mostly silent.

"Mother, we're here to help you," Sara exclaimed as they entered the warm kitchen where Rachel, Judith, and Carla were busy peeling potatoes and chopping pumpkin.

"Well, thank you, girls," Rachel responded, "but I believe you need a good wash and a change of clothes before you start working in here. You're both covered in dust and dirt, so go on and be quick. Our visitors are arriving soon."

Ari and Sara giggled as they ran off to the bathroom for a warm soapy bath and a fresh change of clothes. "We're just like sisters, aren't we, Ari? We can share a bath and even wear each other's clothes. I'm almost as big as you now so most of my new tunics will fit you as well"

"Thanks, Sara, you are tall for your age. That saves me rushing home to get some clothes, but I just thought, I do have some clean clothes here anyway. I washed them the other day and hung them in the spare room. Let's get ready. I can hardly wait to see Gray John. He's always been like a dear grandfather to me."

"Me too," Sara acknowledged. "And he has so many great stories to tell about the last war and how we won, and how father led the horsemen."

"Yes, Sara, your father will always be a legend and never forgotten for his bravery. Let's hope we don't have another war because I know that Gray John is worried about that."

"I know. I read those travel ban flyers. Oh, I do hope we don't have another war."

"Let's not dwell on it, my little love. Here, let me pour this bath and fill it with lavender oil and we can relax and pretend that tonight Robby will arrive home and that peace will continue forever."

It was dusk when Gray John, Marshall Levi Jackson, and Isaiah arrived. They were greeted by two excited girls, Ari and Sara, as well as the tantalizing aromas of roast duck and stewed venison wafting out of the warm kitchen.

Don had just arrived from the academy and helped welcome their guests while Rachel and Judith set a long table in the dining room.

"Welcome, friends," Don said as he seated them at the table, now laden with chilled tea, jugs of earthy colored ale, and a few elegant bottles of amber-colored wine. "Please make yourselves at home. Ari and Sara, please bring out some cob loaves of herb and garlic bread. We will be eating soon, but, in the meantime, you have a choice of what to drink."

Gray John smiled. "It is always a pleasure to visit and enjoy the very best of hospitality in Stonegate. Since it is your first time here for dinner, Levi and Isaiah, I can promise you won't be disappointed. Rachel and Carla are fine cooks and the wines are home brewed."

"You are right as always, Gray John. Carla has an old retainer who has mastered the art of making elderberry wine. It's an old recipe, and I hope you enjoy this particular drop," Don said. He began pouring each of his guests a generous glass.

"Well, we are pleased to be invited here, Don," Levi said. "Your reputation from the last war has made you something of a mythical legend. We are honored to be here as your guests."

Don smiled as they toasted their glasses. "Why, thank you, Marshall Levi, but I simply did what any one of you would do in that situation. Let's make a toast to the future, the now pressing fight for peace...and to the final destruction of Martin Abaddon, so-called Prophet. I propose peace and safety." All took a drink.

There was a chorus of "Hear, hear."

"And let's hope is Robby safe..." Rachel added, as Judith entered the room carrying hot, steaming platters of vegetables and a pot of stewed venison. Ari and Sara followed with a few more platters of roast duck and potatoes.

"Of course we share that hope," Marshall Jackson acknowledged. "It is a very strange dilemma that we have two people missing from Stonegate and no idea where they are or what happened. I believe we need to send a full horse troop to the area where Robby was last sighted. A special group did find his tracks, but then lost them."

"Well, that might be helpful," Gray John said, stroking his gray beard as he spoke. "I have already dispatched a skilled tracker to assist that special group. He can try to pick up Robby's trail while they try to find the Raider camp. If they do find Robby, they have been ordered to see that he gets safely back to Stonegate."

"Oh, thank you, Gray John," Rachel said touching his hand in real affection. "I have barely slept a wink since he left home. Knowing those men are out there looking for him brings me great comfort."

"Do not fear, Rachel. I promise you one thing. If Robby is anywhere near the spot he was last reported, my men will find him and bring him home. I can assure you of that."

"Thank you, Gray John, once again," Rachel said wiping a tear away from her cheeks. "I will leave this in your capable hands, but for now let us eat."

Just after Don offered a blessing for the meal, they heard knocking at the door. It was Howard, reporting that Robby's mare, Silver, had returned.

"Oh, thank God!" Ari screamed as she ran to the front door. "Robby is home at last!"

But they all spoke at once, making it hard to learn more details. Howard finally explained that it was only Silver, alone and scared—and without Robby on her back.

✝

Everyone in the palace had gone to sleep well before midnight…except for Martin Abaddon and Shakti. Martin was pacing around his rooms in an agitated state. Prisoners from the East were unusual enough, but this one especially preyed on his mind. The keeper of the tower had been so guarded and withdrawn that the Prophet sensed something was amiss.

"You see, Shakti, my dear, this bothers me. The Raiders said this young man was behaving in a suspicious manner quite near to our camp there. There is every possibility that someone had previously sighted my Raiders and raised an alarm. Are you sure you did not hear of any suspicions in Stonegate…that perhaps my men were in the area?"

Shakti felt her heart flutter, knowing full well that word of the Raiders was widely known in Stonegate. But she had mentioned nothing of this in her report. Fear forced her to lie to his face, even though she knew it made her situation even more dangerous. She carefully worded her answer, opening her eyes wide and looking directly at his face. "Perhaps some might know, but I heard nothing of such matters. Stonegate is living as if peace will last forever and they have no suspicions at all."

"Well, I always knew they were a bunch of fools and imbeciles!" Martin said with a sneer. "Are they so arrogant that they truly believe that one day I would not exact my final revenge? Doubly so on that lore-man, Donald, and all those that oppose me?"

"From what I saw, Martin, the people of Stonegate are so immersed in their own lives and business that war is the last thing on their minds. There is a new generation of young people now who never experienced the last war, and I never hear anyone talk about it. People have forgotten what happened and moved on to raise their families or just want to forget the past."

The Prophet took a large gulp of new juniper wine before exclaiming. "How wonderful for them! Well, it is high time I reminded them of who I am, and that one day I will rule what is left of the old Empire, including and especially that most hated city of Stonegate! Surely, you did not enjoy your stay there, Shakti?"

Shakti knew that when he was manic, he was as dangerous as a pit viper. Any wrong word could provoke the Prophet into an uncontrollable rage. "Well, Martin, I can honestly tell you it was an experience like no other. And yes, life in Stonegate was very strange and unfamiliar to me. It was difficult for me and hard to fit in, but I knew I was there just to observe the people and report to you. I wish I could tell you more, but there is not much to say."

"The whole plan was a bad one. I will have words with my spymasters. But I want to know more about this prisoner and why he was snooping around. The Raiders said he refused to identify himself, saying he was the son of a poor farmer in Stonegate. I think you might be able to find out exactly who he is and the truth of what he was doing there. Tomorrow morning you can take him some breakfast and an extra blanket to soften him up. Also, I believe he has a few injuries. You need to attend to those wounds and perhaps with a gentle, womanly touch he will reveal everything to you that I need to know."

"I see," said Shakti, shuddering with a silent fear. She'd heard the news from Charlie of Robby's disappearance and how Don and Charlie had gone looking for him to no avail. Surely this prisoner could not be the same person…Robby, the son of Donald of Goldstone?

✝

Robby could not settle back to sleep once he'd realized the gravity of his situation. He wondered what had happened to Silver, and if she had made it home. She had vanished in the night, soon after he had been taken. The only concern he had was the reaction from Ari and his parents if and when Silver did make it back to Westerly-stead…without him.

Despair clutched at his heart as the hopelessness of his situation hit home. He was gripped with a panic so intense that he couldn't breathe and for the first time since he told Ari that he no longer believed in God, he cried out to that very same God.

"Oh, Father God!" he called from the depths of his broken heart. "Forgive me for not believing in you. I confess my sins to you and ask that you come into my heart once again and lead me through this terrible ordeal. I am so fearful, Lord, of what will happen to me, but it is what will happen to Ari and my parents and my sister Sara that is more important, Lord. I know now that my actions have caused them pain and for this, I am truly sorry. Lord. I call on you from my heart to forgive me for all the suffering I have caused them."

Suddenly, it seemed that a white light appeared in the darkness, growing closer and totally enveloping him with a radiant warmth. A peace came upon Robby that was unexplainable and magnificent as he could almost feel the arms of God wrap tightly around him—and in the stillness of that glorious moment he heard a voice, "You are my child, and I will protect you."

CHAPTER 17
†

A Great Disappointment

Delayed hope makes the heart sick, but fulfilled desire is a tree of life.
Proverbs 13:12 HCSB

Willy and Daisy kept laughing and teasing each other as they rode south towards Loveland. They were in no hurry and did not push their horses. Even at a fast walk, it was at most a three-hour ride. Dark, angry thunderheads were building to the west, but that did nothing to dampen their mood.

Colin could not keep a smile off his face. Daisy kept chattering and pointing out things that the rest of them would have missed. *It would be sweet to be young again and in love.*

"I think we are going to get wet, Willy," said Daisy. She giggled, then glanced at Charlie and Colin, who were riding behind them. "Look at those clouds."

Willy was leading their pack horse, which was loaded with a cage of pigeons, a box of handbills, food, clothes, and camping supplies. He looked at the western sky with a frown. "I hope not, sweetheart," he said.

"Loveland is only fifteen miles away," said Colin. "We might be able to find shelter there before the storm hits."

"I don't mind rain," said Charlie, after a long pause. "But that might be sleet. It is getting colder."

"There is a fairly good inn," said Colin. "Perhaps you two could wait there for a bit. Charlie wants to stop and try to find his lady friend."

"Of course," said Daisy. "We all liked Shakti, and I know you are concerned about her. Take your time. We might even have an early lunch, and I would not mind being indoors if that storm comes this way."

"Aye. I am worried, and that is the truth of it," said Charlie. "It is a mystery to me. I gave her a friendship ring, and I know she was keen to return to Stonegate. She left most of her belongings at the inn."

"Maybe you should report this to the authorities," said Willy. "The town watch, perhaps."

Charlie nodded but said nothing.

"Charlie has an address," said Colin. "We will ride over there, while you wait at the inn. Perhaps there is a perfectly simple explanation."

Before long, Loveland was before them, laid out with a sprinkling of outer farm houses and horse-filled pastures before the township of closely connected houses and other dwellings appeared. They could see the yellowish-gray walls dimly through a cloud of blowing dust.

The gusts of wind were cold, and the four travelers had put on heavy coats to keep from being chilled. But only a few raindrops had dampened their faces when they arrived at the gates of Loveland. Colin remembered the way to the Loveland Inn and led the way. Charlie gave the impression that he had never been there before, and he looked around the narrow streets with interest.

"Strange," said Charlie. "Loveland looks very much like Stonegate, but different, somehow. The streets are narrower, for one thing."

"I don't know," said Daisy. "Some back streets in Stonegate are pretty narrow."

"I mean the main street."

"Have you ever been to any town other than Stonegate, Charlie?" asked Colin. He was surprised that Charlie had never ventured to the closest town. Charlie was obviously from a good family and had lived north of Stonegate his whole life. Perhaps he was, at heart, an outdoorsman.

Charlie wrinkled his brow. "Well, Mister Colin, I have ridden far afield, but never had reason to go to any of the nearby towns. Strange, now that I think on it."

"Oh, Charlie," said Daisy, "It is so sad that we are not planning to go through Hightower. Willy, couldn't we go a bit out of the way, so Charlie can see the old buildings? The ones so tall?"

"We can think about it, dear," said Willy.

Willy tossed a small coin to the stableboy so their horses could be sheltered from the storm. Then he gave him another so they could have oats with their hay. Willy and Daisy walked toward the front door. There was a brick chimney on the side of the building and dark smoke was being blown east. "Brrr," said Daisy. "It's freezing. Maybe we should just stop here for the day."

Colin followed them in and saw them settled in the common room. Then he spoke to the innkeeper. Their host did not know Shakti, but had heard of Clover Lane, which was outside the city walls, but nearby. Then Colin gave him some of the handbills and asked him to spread them around. "I will be happy to put this up for travelers to read," promised the innkeeper. "And I will send a boy to the market to hand them out. Thank you for the warning. I don't like the sound of this. Raiders again. Who would have believed it?"

Colin returned to their horses and took his reins from Charlie. He was talking to a slender fellow with a close-cropped white beard. The man was pointing to the west.

"Strange," said the man, looking intently at Charlie, "Everyone in this town knows everyone, pretty much. But I've never heard of a woman called Shakti. And Clover Lane is on the far outskirts of town. Just a few old farmhouses out there. But I think they are all sitting empty since the last war. They were wrecked and too far gone for repair. No one has lived out there for years. It is off the main route out of town. I can't imagine a lass living there, though a drifter might take shelter there once in a while."

†

Once again, a sinking feeling clutched at Charlie's heart. None of this was making sense, and he feared that he was going to face disappointment once again. He and Colin left the inn, going in a westerly direction out of town. He had memorized the directions and kept muttering them as they left the town by the west gate, right into the face of the wind. They had to make several turns, which they identified by landmarks. Some tumbleweeds came bouncing by and a flock of blackbirds was sped along by a tailwind.

A few abandoned farmhouses appeared before them just as an old sign read *Clover Lane*. It was rusty and hung at an angle but was clearly legible. Charlie spurred his horse to a trot, his heart racing in time with the hoof-beats. A few old cherry trees stood lonely and unloved in an abandoned fruit orchard and a small, muddy ditch creek flanked both sides of the road.

"Here it is," Colin yelled out from behind Charlie. "You almost went past it."

Charlie's jaw dropped, and he gasped as he rode into the unkempt, weed-covered property. It was marked with a faded number on a broken letter-box—*125*. "Surely this cannot be possible," he mumbled as he tied up the horses to a post. Colin had already ventured inside through a door that swung crookedly by one rusty hinge. The door posts were rotting and inside was a stale, musty smell. Charlie followed, to find a gloomy interior with some broken, charred pieces of old furniture. The kitchen had some dirty crockery left in a sink next to an old wood stove. The rusty firebox had charcoal in it and looked as though it may have been used recently. There was kindling in a coal bucket and a stack of split logs next to it.

"Well, someone has been here recently," said Charlie, noticing plates and cups on the table and a coat flung over a chair in the corner. Picking it up, Charlie noticed it was red and black with an emblem of three lightning bolts on the back.

Before he could say anything, Colin uttered, "Oh, dear God in Heaven! That is a Raider's coat!"

✝

Rachel and Don could not speak when they learned that Silver had returned without Robby. But Ari uttered a fearful cry as the realization sank in. Where was Robby? "Oh, God help us!" she screamed as tears of grief flowed down her cheeks. "Oh, Daddy! Oh, Aunt Rachel! Surely, this cannot be happening!"

Rachel ran out to comfort a very frightened Silver who was now whin-nying at the other horses in the pasture. She stroked her long white nose and embraced her neck, her tears falling into her fine, shiny mane. "Where,

Silver?" she asked as the whinnying began to calm down. "Where is Robby? I wish you could speak!"

Don walked over to calm both Rachel and Silver. Howard had put a halter on him and led her over from Westerly-stead. She still had Robby's saddle and bridle on, though the reins were broken. Don could find no blood on the saddle or any sign of injury to Silver, though she was muddy and looked drawn.

Gray John followed to offer his friendship and support. "This is alarming, Don," Gray John said in a firm voice, "but we must be strong in the face of adversity. At least we now have proof, if proof was needed, that Robby is in some kind of trouble. Perhaps the tracker I mentioned can retrace Silver's trail. I will see if his dogs can pick up her scent."

Carla had also arrived. Rachel tried to speak between muffled sobs as Ari clung tightly to her hand with Carla now embracing both of them. "This calls for action, I believe," Carla said. "Tomorrow, Howard and I will go up the Cash River and see what we can find. We cannot leave it any longer."

"No!" Don said. "I understand that waiting here is the hardest thing to do. But Gray John has already organized the search. We must leave it in the hands of Hamway's men, now. You keep training your archers, and I will focus on the cadets."

Rachel sniffed, sobbing silently as she sought refuge in the arms of Don who held her tight as he stroked her hair. Ari held Sarah, who also had tears flowing down her cheeks. Marshall Jackson and Isaiah remained silent until the ladies had settled down and the tears had run dry.

"Howard and Carla," said Marshall Jackson, "the good thing is that special operations troopers are already scouting the areas most likely to be Raider camps. I believe that with all our resources out there, we will recover the missing boy."

Rachel whispered her thanks and then returned to the house with Sara and Carla. "Come," she said. "We can pray for his safe return."

"I'll take Silver to her stall in the stable," said Ari, gently patting the mare as she nuzzled Ari's face. "I think she would love a good feed of hay and some fresh water, and a good rest."

"That would be a big help, Ari," said Don. He stood and watched her lead the bedraggled Silver to the stable, then escorted his guests out of the cold."

Don led a prayer after dinner just before the visitors departed. "Lord, we pray that wherever Robby is that you are with him and will protect him from harm. And that he is safely returned to us soon."

Rachel seemed glad to have Don all to herself and kept clinging to him. "Will you be going out with the trackers?" she asked.

"I would if I thought I could do any good. But for the next few days, I must help with training the cadets. Colin was sent with a message to Ariel, so we are now shorthanded. Gray John is organizing the senior cadets into a regular horse troop, and most of the third-year boys will be equipped as mounted scouts. Marshall Jackson is recalling every available artilleryman and will be starting gunnery training. So much to do."

"One more thing," he added. "One of Howard's field hands will be coming over every day to exercise Skipper. He is out of condition, and I don't have time to ride him as he needs."

As Don put on his nightclothes, he felt compelled to look out of the window toward the West where evil loomed like a dark shadow of dread. "Even though you are not going, I worry about you. Promise me you'll always be careful, Don," Rachel said as she lay cuddled in Don's loving arms in the safety of their own comfortable bed. "I couldn't bear to lose you too!"

†

Neither Charlie nor Colin said anything aloud, but Charlie had no doubt that they had solved part of the riddle. Why she had listed an abandoned house as her former address was a mystery that he could not unlock. He would have to puzzle over that later. But it seemed clear that she must have been captured by the Raiders. They searched the house for any sign of her but found nothing except a hairpin. It looked new but could have belonged to any woman.

Lightning flashed, and thunder rolled. But they continued their search behind the house. Just beyond the fence, they found numerous hoofprints and manure. Horses had been here, and the tracks were fresh—recent enough to have been made when Shakti disappeared. Colin spotted something trampled into a muddy spot and picked it up. When he shook the mud off, it proved to be a thin scarf, blue and pink, of a closely woven fabric.

Colin held it up. "Do you recognize this, Charlie?"

Charlie took it carefully in his big fingers. It did look familiar. "I am almost sure this is Shakti's. It must be hers. These must be tracks of Raiders. Dear Lord, they must have taken her captive." He turned to face Colin. "Come on. We have to follow these tracks."

"Wait, Charlie," Colin "Let's think this through. There are over ten sets of tracks. We could be riding into a hornet's nest."

"I am not afraid of them," said Charlie, as he untied his horse. "We both have swords. Gray John said the Raiders were not difficult to defeat."

"Not if you are a fully armored horse trooper on a warhorse," insisted Colin, "And even then, twelve to two are not odds I would like."

"You have armor," said Charlie. "Anyway, if you won't go, I will go alone. I have to try."

"I have a mail waistcoat. Not much. We have no helms, no shields, and these are not trained warhorses. Be sensible."

Charlie said nothing. He deliberately mounted and reined his horse to face west.

"Very well, Charlie," said Colin, finally. "We can follow the trail for a ways, to see where it leads. But the first sign of trouble, and we will have to clear out. Getting killed won't help Shakti."

The trail was easy to follow at first. After a mile, they began to enter the first foothills and saw two sets of tracks leave the main trail and go north. They stayed with the main set of tracks, leading higher toward the mountains.

The rain finally came, just sprinkles at first. They stopped long enough to pull oilcloth slickers over their coats and then continued on. Then the storm hit. Ran came down in a torrent, and within minutes the trail that they were following had become a stream. Then the rain came down even harder yet, and it was turning to sleet.

"Charlie," shouted Colin. "We have to get out of this. Find shelter."

Charlie shook his head stubbornly, but he knew Colin was right. Finally, shoulders slumped, he nodded. They found a grove of stunted oak brush next to a rock outcrop. They dismounted and crouched under the trees.

The rocks gave them some shelter from the wind, and they waited until the leading edge of the storm front had passed.

Charlie led his horse back to the trail, and his heart sank. The tracks were gone, completely obliterated. There was no way to find Shakti now. And he realized that even if he found her, they were hopelessly outnumbered. The gusts of wind were like millstones grinding his heart until he was filled only with dregs of despair. He had lost her and even worse, he had lost hope.

†

They arrived back at the Loveland Inn in the evening. The rain continued to sprinkle down, but the sleet had passed. They stabled their horses and entered the inn, hanging their dripping slickers on pegs by the door. Daisy and Willy had been concerned and listened in awe as they told their story. In fact, their voices had carried, and a small crowd had gathered to hear the tale.

This was obviously the most exciting news that had reached the common room crowd in many a month, and soon the entire room was buzzing with the news. "Imagine," someone said. "Raiders in our own back garden. And kidnapped a beautiful woman."

Colin carefully drew a sketch map of the house on Clover Lane and the trail they had followed. Then he wrote a detailed report to Don and sealed it in oilskin. The innkeeper promised to put it on the morning coach to Stonegate.

Charlie did not feel like talking, and he rode in silence for days. He said he did not want to go to Hightower, so they took a cutoff and hit the Great Highway west of that city. Willy and Daisy had heard of the ancient tunnel through the mountains. They had been told as children that giants had built it, and they could see how that story had gotten started. But it was only one of the amazing things that caused Daisy to exclaim with delight.

Their sturdy mounts seemed glad to see the stable at Glenwood where they could be rested and watered. The tree-lined streets welcomed them as they alighted in the center of town where the Glenwood Inn promised a fine meal and a good night's accommodation for Charlie and Colin.

"Thank you so much for escorting us safely home," Willy said, shaking hands with Charlie before heading off to their new marital home in a newer part of town. "We would gladly have accommodated you, but as newlyweds, we have only the one bed and no other sleeping quarters as yet. However, I am sure you will find the inn extremely comfortable. The roasted pig is their specialty as is their honey mead ale. Daisy and I will see that the handbills are distributed. May God protect you as you continue in your travels."

Colin and Charlie bade them farewell before entering the inn. It was already alive with the hustle and bustle of lively patrons feasting on succulent meals and enjoying the ale. They joined in gladly, and the food was as good as they had been told. The night was yet young, but they were tired from many days on the trail and planned to have a busy tomorrow.

Charlie's mind had been untangling his questions about Shakti and why she had given an abandoned house as an address. Then a most unwelcome thought struck him like a maul. *Suppose she was not captured by the Raiders. Suppose she was meeting them. What then, O God, what then?*

CHAPTER 18
†

A Journey South

Then they said to him, "Please inquire of God so we will know if we will
have a successful journey." The priest told them, "Go in peace. The Lord
is watching over the journey you are going on."
Judges 18: 5-6 HCSB

It had been twenty long years since Eli and Jesse had traveled south for any
reason. The last time they had visited Danny Yazzi of the Yazzi Clan in
Diné and Señor Reuben Ramos of the Sonora Clan was to deliver medical
supplies as well as to warn them about the threat of war from Prophet City.
As Gray Pilgrims, they had been able to travel south without being robbed
or ambushed and without suspicion that their visit south was anything other
than a routine care for the sick.

Now, it seemed as though history was repeating itself, and under Kerik's
instructions, they had been ordered to inform the communities in the South
that once again the Prophet was making his evil plans to attack the East,
mainly out of retribution for the last war in which he had been humiliated
and beaten.

The scenery had not changed since they'd last ridden through here with
a band of Pilgrims. Now, it was just the two of them, spurring their horses
hard through the rocky landscape. Eli had visited Danny Yazzi then, and
Jesse had taken a turn at the crossroads leading towards the Rio Grande to
see Señor Reuben Ramos. But this time they would see Danny Yazzi together
to suggest that strategic action was needed to protect the East from a military
force greater than anything they had ever known.

They made their way to a collection of four *hooghans* with doors that all faced towards the rising sun and surrounded by branch-covered arbors and corrals. "Well, this is it," said Eli as he and Jesse tethered their tired horses to a rail in the front yard which was filled with beds of succulent plants and flowering cacti. "I remember it so well, almost as if it were yesterday."

A young-looking woman came out of the front entrance, an arch with a dark timber frame, and observed the unexpected visitors with a mild curiosity. She had a ruddy skin with long, black wavy hair cascading over her shoulders, looking very much like a younger version of Danny's wife, Aiyana.

"You look familiar to me," she said to Eli, wrinkling her forehead.

"Oh, you must be Carmen, Aiyana's daughter. Of course. I remember you, though you were just a very young girl when I visited here before. But that was long ago now so I am surprised you recognized me at all."

"Oh, yes," Carmen said, a wide smile spreading across her delicate-featured face. "Of course, I remember you now. You came to see my father and bring him medicines, but you also came to tell us about the threat of war with the West. Please tell me you bring good news, not bad. Is there really trouble brewing in the West?"

"Sadly, yes. Carmen, I wish it were good news, but the False Prophet is planning another evil attack on all of us, and we have come to alert the South of the possibility of imminent war."

Carmen's face turned pale as she heard the news. "Good Lord in heaven! You must come in. Mother and Father are resting in the shade out the back. I am sure they would be delighted to see you and offer you their hospitality. Mother will certainly insist you stay with us for a few days to recover from such a long journey. Please come this way."

Eli and Jesse followed Carmen through the traditional *hooghan* into a backyard garden full of shade trees and flowering succulents. Bees buzzed peacefully amongst the desert flowers as Danny rose to his feet, a huge smile filling his round face. "Big surprise to see you, Eli. Long time now since I saw you last. Please, come, sit. Tell us your news. Aiyana and I want to hear your voice."

Aiyana rose gracefully to embrace Eli in a warm, welcoming hug, happy to see their old friend again after such a long time. They knew it was the traditional greeting of the Diné who followed the Jesus Way. "Please sit, both of you. Let me fetch some cool drinks and some refreshments from the kitchen. It is always warm in *Dinétah* this time of year. We get cooler weather later than you."

"Thank you, Aiyana. And Danny. So good to see you again also. I have brought my friend, Jesse, with me this time. He was the one who visited Señor Reuben Ramos last time we ventured south, and I am afraid I have to tell you that the reason for our visit this time is the same as last time. It has become evident that the evil Prophet is planning to attack us any time now. There are rumors he has built up a powerful army of one hundred thousand men, forty thousand more than last time. We have no chance against such a force if we were attacked."

Danny sat silent for a few minutes. It was as if he was struggling with the thought of another war. His guests did not interrupt him as he stared into the distance as though trying to see something far away.

Aiyana and Carmen arrived with tall glasses filled with a fruity punch and platters of tortillas and tacos. "Please eat, drink, our honored guests, for you have come such a long way to deliver this sad news. Danny gestured towards the refreshments. "Another war, you say?" Danny asked. It seemed as if the creases on his face deepened.

"Thank you," said Eli and Jesse, at the same time. They began to sample the food.

"I know this is bad news, my good friend," said Eli. "That is why we ask for any help you can give us. They will kill without mercy and enslave the survivors. When they finish with us they will come for you."

"That is truth, friend Eli," Danny replied. "Let us talk about this. It is long since I have been in battle. Not so with the young men. Every spring many go south to fight on the side of our friend Rueben's people. Some do not return, but this way they learn how to fight."

Eli and Jesse looked at each other. Their eyes widened, and their jaws dropped. "Why?" asked Eli. "Battle against whom?"

"Bandits come from the far South—come up the big river. Big problem for the Sonora people. Our young men are the best scouts. In return, Rueben's people send things we need. Cattle, chiles, beans, and other things."

"So, your warriors are well trained?"

"Yes, and also the lancers of Reuben's people. They have not grown soft. They have learned war as a man must—in battle against a cruel enemy."

"How many men could the Diné send against the False Prophet?"

"Maybe more than last time. One thousand, if most agree to go."

"And Reuben?"

"About the same. What he sent before. All heavy lancers. But there is one more thing."

"What is that?"

"We have young men. Yes, and women too. They are a different kind of warrior. They go to teach the Jesus Way to people in darkness. They bring light to dark places. For years now, they go into Dixie. That is the bad Prophet's southern country."

"I—we knew nothing of this," said Eli. "Wonderful. Has there been a response?"

"Yes, friend Eli," said Danny, smiling at last. "The darkness draws back, and many people there follow the true God."

"Wonderful, as I have said. But I am not sure how that would help very much—against the Prophet's invasion, I mean." Eli looked at Jesse, who took a drink from his glass and stared at the ground.

"Do you think that this people coming to the light means nothing?" said Aiyana. "Faith is more powerful than even the False Prophet's big guns. You Pilgrims, of all people, should know that."

Eli squirmed in his seat. "Of course. Of course, you are right. But still..."

"Take this word to your chief surgeon," said Danny. "Send it by bird's wings to the Stonegate people. We will help, and friend Reuben will help. I am sure about that."

"But what, exactly...?"

"Do not underestimate us. We will go into the Black Prophet's lands. If the people there will join with us, we can drive out his warriors."

"Yes, that might be a distraction—force him to split his army. But you are lightly armed, and he now has many field guns."

"But we have speed and...What is the word Aiyana?"

"Stealth, dear. Stealth," said Aiyana, with a hint of a smile.

"My friend, Reuben and I have talked long about this. We are almost ready. A few days and we will begin to move. Even now our scouts are south of Junction. I had planned to send warning to you. By sunrise, two days from now, we will move our main force. Reuben will not be far behind."

"We had hoped you might take action, but this is more than we could have dreamed," said Eli. "I will suggest to the Chief Kerik that we send our mobile surgery towards Junction. We have it ready for emergencies. Perhaps we can help treat any wounded."

"That would be very good. We have men that can bind wounds, yet your healers are the best. But here is one other thing, friend Eli," added Danny. "This time we will not be riding north to fight by your side. But if the Black Prophet cannot be stopped, tell our friends that they can send their women and children south to us. We have places of refuge in the desert. Tell them their precious ones would be welcome here."

"You would give safe haven to women and children?"

"Yes, gladly."

Eli, Jesse, and Danny shook hands before kneeling down to pray. They knew deep within their hearts that the only one hope really was in the victory that only Jesus could give them.

†

Rachel had been waiting patiently for Don's return. Despite what he had insisted, he had changed his mind and left with a six-man patrol that accompanied the tracker and a dog handler with a brace of hounds. It had been three days now of not knowing where her son and her husband were and wondering if they were safe or even alive. Every day she prayed for news, and so it was with a joyful heart that she saw Don riding up the lane.

Throwing herself into his arms as soon as he had dismounted Silver who Don had hoped would take them back to where Robby was last seen, Rachel could not contain her tears. "Oh, Don, is there any news of Robby?"

Don held Rachel tightly before answering in a somber voice. "I'm afraid there is some news, my dearest. But I will need to take you inside and settle you down in a comfortable chair before I can tell you."

Rachel's heart sank. This was not good news. In her heart, she feared the worst. "Oh heavens, Don, please don't tell me we've lost him forever?"

"Now, now, Rachel, let me take you inside where it's warm and we can have a quiet drink and a long talk. All is not what it seems, so we must stay positive…at least for Robby's sake."

Dan settled Rachel down into a large armchair by the fire, placing a warm knitted blanket over her knees. "Here, my love. Let's partake of a fine brandy together. For the news I have to tell you may be upsetting to you. I have discovered news about Robby and where he is…and that there is still hope for him."

"Oh, Don, do you truly know where he is, then?" Rachel asked, taking a sip of brandy that sent slivers of heat racing through her body. "Please tell me everything that happened while you were away and what you know about our son."

Don took Rachel's slender hand in his as he said, "Well, then, let me start from the beginning."

Rachel took another sip of the strong drink, knowing it would help dull the pain of finding out any bad news about Robby.

Don cleared his throat as he began, "Well, after we left you, we headed to the place where Robby was last seen. Two of the special operations troopers met us and had already scoured the immediate area. We found signs of a recent campfire on our first day, but it could have been made by anyone. But the dogs picked up a scent, which we followed farther into the woods and there we found evidence of a huge campsite."

"Was it a Raider camp?" asked Rachel.

"It proved to be. There was evidence of a battle and there were scattered weapons, blood and camping gear strewn around. While we tried to decide what it all meant, we saw riders approaching. It was the rest of the same special operations group. They were startled to see us there because they had just attacked and destroyed a group of Raiders in that very place. A couple had fled, but they had finally chased down the last of them."

"Did any of the Raiders survive?"

"No, they fought like demons, apparently, and only the leader was taken alive. He did answer a few questions before breathing his last. But this is the important thing. They found out that Robby had been taken prisoner and had been sent under escort to Prophet City."

"Oh, my God, Don, this can't be possible! Please tell me it isn't true! Surely it's some kind of mistake? Why would they do that?" Rachel said, fearing she would faint.

"Rachel, I don't know how they got the Raider leader to talk. I really don't want to know. But he said that the reason they took Robby back to Prophet City was because of his appearance. The dying man said he had never before seen a young man who was a mirror image of the False Prophet, not even among his many sons. He was afraid to kill a young man who could possibly be a relative of the Prophet, so he ordered him to be taken alive to Prophet City."

Rachel nodded, knowing full well what Don was thinking; it was about their family secret. "When the False Prophet sees Robby, there is no doubt he will know who he is." A tear trickled out of her eye as she remembered a night, twenty years earlier, when a young pregnant woman had been brought to Westerly-stead. She had been spirited out of the palace and taken, even though heavy with child, to the safety of Stonegate, to Westerly-stead. It was the same person who had taken Isabella there just months before—Calvin the courier.

"At least there is a good chance he will not be executed if the False Prophet believes that Robby is his son...and maybe he will realize then that it was Selena who gave birth to him."

"All we can do is pray, Don, and hope for a miracle that, like Isabella and Selena, he too will find a way to escape and return to us."

CHAPTER 19
†

The Weapon Smiths

Those who oppose the Lord will be shattered;
He will thunder in the heavens against them.
1 Samuel 2:10 HCSB

Charlie followed Colin McCoy as they traveled down the lane heading toward the gates of Ariel. The way was crushed gravel, but it turned to rounded granite cobblestones a quarter mile from the town. Steel wheels of freight wagons had cut noticeable grooves in the granite, indicating that the surface had been there for many years.

They had bypassed Hightower on the trip from Stonegate, so Ariel was the largest fortified town that Charlie had ever seen outside of Stonegate. The city of Stonegate was much larger, but Ariel's walls were higher, and each angle of the wall was crowned by a square-angled watchtower.

As they approached the gates, Charlie commented, "I have never seen better stonework."

"Right you are, me boy," said Colin. "Ariel's masons are the best. The chief elder's name is Stonehewer. That should tell you something."

The gate guards eyed them curiously but made no move to bar their entry. Colin knew the way and they ventured through the narrow streets. There were plenty of people out, and the sidewalks were occupied by vendors with crude stands selling food and handicrafts.

"Is this market day?" asked Charlie.

"Every day is market day except Sunday," answered Colin. "Ariel is famous for more than edged weapons, but for now we will go to a smith's shop I know."

"Don't we have to give the message to the city fathers?" asked Charlie.

"All in good time."

They halted in front of a shop with a signboard projecting over the sidewalk. The painted sign had a scarlet sword with flames licking along the blade. There were two short stone columns in front with black iron rings for tying horses. Charlie started to dismount, but Colin signaled him to stop. "Let's go to the alley around back. They have a nice stable."

Colin led the way through a short maze of narrow passages and they soon had their horses stalled in a shady barn. They loosened the cinches and Colin gave them two forks-full of hay. "Is this all right?" asked Charlie. He was nervous about feeding someone else's hay without permission.

"That it is," answered Colin. "The owner is an old friend."

They entered the weapons shop through a rear door and a short hallway. They parted a curtain made of wooden beads on strings and found themselves in a workshop. A small, gnarled man was there, bent over a large grindstone. His body was thickset and his arms and legs were shorter than normal. Charlie realized that he must be a dwarf. He had heard of a city of dwarves in the mountains but had thought it to be an old legend. *Is this it?*

Colin embraced the diminutive man. "Good to see you, Matthew," he said. "You are looking well."

"As are you, old friend," said Matthew. He turned to Charlie. "I do not believe we have met."

"This is Charlie. He works for Rachel's family and is a friend of mine," said Colin. "Charlie, this is Matthew. He owns the shop and is the best weapons master in the land."

Charlie bowed, since Matthew did not offer his hand. Matthew returned the gesture.

"You are much too kind," said Matthew. "We have many good smiths in Ariel, and some of your Stonegate smiths do good work, too."

He led them through a showroom with ranks of swords, shields, spears, and other edged weapons Charlie did not recognize. Some were heavily engraved and inlaid with precious metal. Others were plain blued steel. All looked keen-edged and deadly. Matthew stopped and picked up a breastplate. It was beautifully polished and had a thin rope of gold trim along the edge. "This is one of our latest pieces. I must admit that I am proud of it."

They admired the workmanship. Charlie was impressed with the clean lines and the beauty of it. "I have seen nothing like it."

"So much mail was captured in the last war that it almost put mail makers out of business," said Matthew. "I mostly make swords, helms, and breastplates now. But come with me. There is someone you should meet before you do anything else."

He lit a candle and led the way downstairs to a large basement, lit only by two small arched windows high on the wall ahead. The room extended into darkness on their right. He led them that way and the ceiling changed from wood beams to vaulted stone. "We are under the street now," said Matthew. "There is another set of passages still lower down, but they are storm drains. These chambers were once used for storage. During the war, they were often filled with people."

"Why was that?" asked Charlie, trying to see in the dim gloom.

"The False Prophet's big guns shelled the city," answered Matthew. "But these old storage rooms were a safe refuge." The way ahead contracted to a tunnel that ran as straight as a plumb line. There were several passages that met at perfect right angles, but they continued going straight ahead.

They came to a set of stone stairs, climbed single file through two flights, and came out into a sunny courtyard. "I think you know where we are now, Colin," said Matthew.

"That must be Timothy Stonehewer's house," said Colin. "I knew about the tunnels, but…"

"I know, not often used, but useful when we want privacy. Some eyes and ears are not friendly. Elder Timothy has been expecting you. Actually, there is another passage that leads directly to his apartments, but perhaps we should use the front door."

"He must be quite old. I remember him as an old man, and that was twenty years ago."

"About eighty, I think. A few years older than me. This way, if you please."

The courtyard had a small fountain in the center. The tinkling splash of the water was pleasant to the ear. Stone benches formed an open square and a vine-covered trellis offered shade. The vine was covered with blue, trumpet-shaped flowers.

Matthew skirted the fountain and entered a doorway into a flagstone-paved foyer. The door was open, but he knocked as he entered. "Anyone here?" he called.

A rather stout woman in a dark-green dress and white apron entered from a side room. "Yes, who is it?" she called as she entered. "Oh, it's you, Master Matthew. I see you have guests."

"We do. Indeed, we do. All the way from Stonegate," said Matthew. "Mistress Gordon, you will remember Colin McCoy, and I would like to present Charlie—I'm afraid I did not catch your last name."

"Hahn," said Charlie. "Don't use it much. Most call me Charlie of Westerly."

"Well met, Charlie of Westerly," she said, offering him a small hand to shake. Her grip was firm and her palm was hard. This was a woman who used her hands for more than light housework. She turned to Colin and greeted him the same way. "I must confess that I do not remember you," she said, "although the name is familiar."

"It should be," said Matthew. "He rode and fought with Old Robert and Donald of Fisher during the last war."

Her eyes grew big and her hand covered her mouth. "Of course, "she said. "It is an honor, sir. Do come in. All of you. Do come in."

She bustled about and insisted that they follow her into a small sitting room with comfortable chairs around a low table. "Please sit down. I will have refreshments sent. Then I will announce you to the elder." She hurried out, leaving an inner door open.

It was not long before their host made his entrance. He was bald with a long, white beard. He walked with a stoop, leaning on a cane in his right hand. In his left, he carried a staff topped with a silver hammer.

"Good day, Lord," said Colin, standing in respect. Charlie also got to his feet.

"Hello, Colin McCoy," said the dwarf, for dwarf he was. "Welcome back to Ariel. And this is your friend, Charlie…"

"Hahn, Lord," said Charlie.

"I understand you serve the family of Lord Donald," said the dwarf. His voice had the scratchy tone of old age but was still firm and deep.

"This is Lord Timothy Stonehewer," said Matthew. "He is the chief elder of Ariel. We are honored that you would take the time to see us."

Colin and Charlie agreed that it was a great honor.

"I do serve the family of Lord Donald and Lady Rachel," said Charlie. "But Lady Rachel's brother, Howard, is my actual master."

"I see. Excellent. Now please sit down. You are my guests and I am no king. I am still chief elder, but not all that active these days. I certainly don't give myself airs."

They all took their seats. Elder Timothy's eyes glittered with keen wit. "It is good that you looked in on me before you speak to the town weapon smiths."

"Of course, we know it is common courtesy," said Colin. "We have a message from Stonegate. It has some unsettling news, I believe." He handed the elder an oilskin packet.

Elder Timothy took the packet. Breaking the seal, he pulled out a folded parchment and read it with a thoughtful expression. He took his time, and the others sat in silence until he had finished. Finally, he spoke. "Unsettling news indeed. Although I must be candid and tell you that there is little here that we did not already know. The report from the healer at Green River and the large force training nearby merely confirms some other information that we have recently seen. I fear we are entering a dangerous time. I am glad you came to see me so promptly."

"I had the idea that you wanted to see us right away," said Matthew.

"The smiths have certain secrets that they have been ordered to reveal to no one. This note from me will allow them to speak freely." He handed Colin a folded parchment.

"What secrets?" asked Colin.

"We have developed a new kind of cannon called a culvern. Actually, we developed it mainly for defense of our towns in Haven. But the culvern will be of great interest to Stonegate."

✝

The weapon smiths were to be found in a fortress within a fortress—a blockhouse east of Timothy Stonehewer's quarters. Colin and Charlie remained a few paces behind as Matthew went ahead to speak to a brace of guards. Charlie whispered to Colin a question that he was longing to ask: "Is this the city of dwarves I have heard about?"

"There are a number of dwarves here. They took refuge here during the time of troubles and left many descendants. But there is no city of dwarves; most people here are of normal stature. Still, old tales die hard."

They broke off their conversation when Daniel waved them forward. Colin showed the note from the elder and they were quickly passed through an iron grille to the left of the ten-foot-high ceremonial gate.

They were met in a narrow room that looked more like a laboratory. Stone tables were covered with glass flasks, and the walls were covered with shelves of books.

An elderly man dressed in a leather tunic and green trousers greeted them. He wore a spotted apron over his clothes. He was above average height—certainly no dwarf.

"I am David," he said. He had hair and a close-cropped beard that may have once been brown, but gray hairs gave a salt-and-pepper look. "I have been told, Matthew, that you have two guests from Stonegate."

Matthew made the introductions and showed him the chief elder's message. David read the note, scratching his beard as he did so. "I am glad to meet you both," he said, finally. "I am not sure of your mission, but it is clear that you need to see what we have been developing."

"Elder Timothy mentioned something called a culvern," said Colin.

"Yes, we have such a thing," said David. "And none too soon. Stonegate may not know it, but its warriors desperately need this weapon."

✝

Charlie was deep in thought as David led them through a larger workshop toward a large double door. *What in the world is a culvern? A new musket, or some kind of bomb, perhaps? Or perhaps a huge siege gun like the Prophet developed?*

They entered a large chamber with high ceilings, crowded with machinery. In one corner he saw a pair of horses hitched to a shaft that was connected to gears and drive belts. It seemed to be powering some sort of metal drill. There was almost too much to take in, but David pointed straight ahead, and Charlie's attention was drawn to a long-barreled cannon mounted on a gun carriage with ironbound wheels. It had the usual tail section that provided a firm base of fire.

"This is a culvern," said David, patting it like he would a nervous horse. "It fires a three-inch shell four thousand yards and is amazingly accurate. A good gunner can hit a saddle blanket at that range."

"By all the holy angels!" said Colin. "That is over two miles. Much farther than our field artillery can reach."

"We think it has the longest range of any artillery available. The old town guns with the old propellant could shoot farther, but that propellant is all gone, of course."

"Does it outrange the Prophet's huge siege guns?" asked Charlie.

"That it does," answered David. "But the siege guns fire a much larger ball. We had first thought to mount these atop our walls, at least the walls of Bethuel and Ariel. The House of Healing does not want them." Daniel paused and shook his head.

"Well, the Chief Surgeon considers these too much of an offensive weapon. But that is neither here nor there. As I was saying, the idea was to neutralize the threat of the siege guns and force them to stay out of range or be destroyed."

"I see how that would work," said Colin. He began running his hands along the cast bronze barrel, admiring the craftsmanship. "Our foundry in Stonegate can cast the small field artillery pieces, but nothing this large. This is an unusually long barrel."

"That is the secret of its range and accuracy, of course," said Daniel. "Unfortunately, it is harder to load and has a slower rate of fire."

Charlie joined Colin in examining the cannon. It was decorated with raised depictions of serpents with gouts of fire spraying from their mouths. The barrel was polished to a reddish-golden sheen, and the carriage was of varnished wood with blackened metal fittings. It was beautiful, if a weapon of war could be described in those terms.

"We are confident that they will be very effective and have already mounted two of these on each of Ariel's square-sided towers for all-around defense. The guns for Bethuel have been manufactured and will be hoisted into position very soon."

"I wish Stonegate had something like this," said Charlie. "We have mounted some of our small cannons on our walls, but they are no match for these—culverns."

"Well, don't forget that Stonegate has its town guns which we in Ariel and Bethuel never had. Even though you are now forced to use black powder in them, they are capable weapons." Daniel paused. "But I don't think Stonegate should put guns like these on city walls."

"Why not?" asked Colin. He turned to face Daniel directly, as did Charlie.

"These guns should be taken to the field. We have learned that the Prophet now has many pieces of field artillery and plans to use them against your defenders very soon, I think. A culvern can destroy his field artillery before it gets within range of ours."

"That would require a direct hit," said Colin. He rubbed his chin and wrinkled his brow.

"We can hit and kill enemy artillery at extreme range. We have proved it and have gunners that can train yours to do the same."

"I must say, that is good news," said Colin with a grin. He suddenly stood taller, as if a weight had been taken off his shoulders.

"I have even better news," said David, with an answering smile. "The elders of Ariel have agreed to loan four culvern batteries to Stonegate. They can leave with you whenever you say."

†

Twelve long-barreled cannons, with their crews, limbers and ammunition wagons make for a long caravan. The line stretched for nearly one-half mile down the Great Highway. Ariel had also dispatched a horse troop, the Lances, and a detachment of grenadiers, besides. Actually, there were thirteen cannons and an extra gun carriage, since Ariel sent spares.

Charlie had been impressed by the Lances. They were smartly turned out, with well-groomed horses, obviously in top condition. Their armor was similar to the Stonegate style, with breast and backplates over mail, though their helms lacked cheek pieces. Mail coifs protected their necks, instead.

They carried long war spears, befitting their name. Their horses had mail chest protectors, and some had steel plates with a short spike attached to their bridles giving them the appearance of a steel-horned unicorn. Besides their swords and lances, each man carried a bow or a case of javelins. They were well drilled and smoothly executed their maneuvers as they got into formation, ready to march.

The Lances had fifty horse troopers broken down into five mounts of ten troopers each. But the primary mount, in addition to the ten regular troopers, also included the troop commander and his assistant, as well as buglers, scouts, a healer, a cook, several horse-holders, and two messengers. These extras added about twenty more men, so the troop actually totaled seventy and took with them ten spare horses, or remounts, as well as eight pack horses that carried food and supplies. The cook acted as the horse wrangler, with the help of the horse-holders, and he was responsible not only for feeding the troopers, but also took care of remounts and pack stock.

Riding with the horse troop was a detachment of grenadiers, which carried gunpowder bombs that they could throw a considerable distance with a sling. They also carried crossbows. The grenadiers were very effective against massed infantry, and the exploding bombs could break up an enemy cavalry charge. There was nothing like an exploding bomb underfoot to terrify a warhorse, even if the flying pieces of deadly metal did not always kill or wound.

Some of the guns had weathered to form a light-green patina, but many shone with a golden luster—fresh from the foundry. The carriages carrying the new guns glowed with fresh varnish and paint and looked fit for a parade. Some older guns showed the marks of field service, and the horses that drew them wore harness darkened with sweat. The horses that drew the new guns had harness that was russet and glowed with beeswax, as if fresh from the harness maker. But all the guns were drawn by a four-horse hitch and the horses looked fit and strong. They drew the heavy pieces easily.

Charlie had learned that three guns formed a battery, each led by an officer—a battery commander. Five gunners were assigned to each culvern which meant that the artillery had approximately as many men as did the horse troop. Each gunner was armed with a musket and a crossbow, as well as a pike. The pike was a long spear designed to stop a charging warhorse.

The gunners were not mounted, except for the commanders. Most rode in the ammunition wagons or supply wagons. Several pigeon cages rode atop the supply wagons. The fleet birds could rapidly carry messages back to Ariel.

Clearly, the horse troopers, guns, and gunners were a generous loan. Charlie learned that the Lances formed about one-fifth of Ariel's active and trained horse troops, though there were other troops that formed a reserve force.

Charlie rode with Colin toward the front of the column, just behind the lead battery. The old highway made for easy travel, as it swept in gradual curves following the Eagle River. Blue mountains stood like sentinels to the south and east, and the near slopes were covered with a mix of pine and aspen. The sky was nearly cloudless, and a gentle breeze ruffled the tawny grass by the roadside.

Charlie turned to Colin, speaking in a low voice. "Ariel is generous," he said. "I wonder—why they were willing to weaken their defenses for us?"

"They realize that the False Prophet will attack along the northern route, when he comes," answered Colin. "These guns will be of more use up there than in Ariel. They have shown much wisdom, I think."

"Yes. I wish our leaders had more of this wisdom."

CHAPTER 20

†

A Revelation for Robby

In my distress I called to the Lord and He answered me.
Psalm 120:1 HCSB

It was well after midnight and the Prophet was still interrogating Shakti, almost as if he was trying to trick her into revealing more about what she had experienced during her stay in Stonegate. "So, you see, my dear, they sent you back here so soon because you reported nothing of significance. This farmer you tried to seduce was worthless. So, there was no use in keeping you there. Are you sure there is nothing more you can tell me? Does anyone in Stonegate suspect that I am ready to make war with the East?"

"I have already told you, Martin," Shakti lied but kept her story simple. She knew she was dealing with a clever and dangerous man who had an uncanny ability to smell out deception. "No one suspects anything. People are just getting on with life, unaware of your intentions."

Shakti feared that if she told him the truth, he would attack at once. She somehow felt she should encourage delay, but knew she was playing a dangerous game. "I understand you want to know more, Martin," she continued, "but as I have already said, life in Stonegate is very different. They are at peace and want only to stay that way."

"Good," said Martin, with his usual smirk. "That will make it easy for me to catch them napping."

Shakti tried to fake a yawn though her insides were twisted in a knot. "Master, it is getting late now. If you wish me to visit that prisoner, morning is only a few hours away. It was a long and tiring trip back here, and I am afraid that sleep beckons me."

"Of course, of course, my dear. You are only a frail woman, and the trip was long. But, just remember, I want to know who this prisoner is. I know that something is amiss but can't put my finger on it. I will arrange to see you tomorrow evening. But for now, I bid you good night."

It was with a huge sense of relief that Shakti fell into bed that night, hoping that the Prophet believed her...and that the prisoner in the tower was not Robby, son of Donald of Goldstone.

✝

Morning arrived far too soon, with a bright sun throwing its rays through an opening in the bedroom curtains straight into Shakti's eyes. For a moment, she forgot where she was, half expecting to find herself back in the comfortable room at the inn in Stonegate. With a groan, she realized that she was back in her own quarters in the palace in Prophet City. She instinctively put her hand over the ring on her left finger, feeling the smoothness of the pearl as a silent tear escaped from her eyes.

"Oh, Charlie, I promise I will find a way to get back to you. Please, do not give up on me...on us."

Reluctantly, she slid her body from beneath the silk bedcovers and hastily washed her face at the ornate ceramic basin. She dressed herself in a simple tan-colored tunic with black stockings and a wide belt which accentuated her small figure.

The warm palace kitchen was the first stop. She intended to set a tray for the prisoner's breakfast but discovered that the kitchen staff had already laid out a breakfast of fruit, cheese, and rye bread with some churned butter for her to take to the prisoner in the tower.

She made her way up the seemingly never-ending spiral staircase, lit only by an occasional loophole, that led to the tower prison. It would be easier, she thought, if the prisoner was no one she knew. A sullen guard turned a giant key to open a door. "He seems tame enough," he muttered, "But cry out if he bothers you." She nodded and carried the tray inside and heard the door slam. A tall young man was looking out of a barred window.

As he turned to face her, she almost dropped the tray, before composing herself with great difficulty. The young man, too, let out a gasp as he exclaimed, "I know you! Aren't you the tavern waitress from the Quill and Sword? I am certain I have seen you there. What are you doing here?"

Shakti was also taken aback, not just because he remembered her, but because the young man she was looking at was the very likeness of a young Martin Abaddon. The jet-black hair with the red streaks, the face, the muscular build, and the height—all matched. She had been a young girl when Martin was twenty, but there was no denying the mirror resemblance. She did not recall meeting him in Stonegate, but some nights at the inn were so busy she could not possibly see everyone there.

Coming to her senses, Shakti put her fingers to her lips. "Shoosh!" she said in a hoarse whisper. "We must speak quietly! These palace walls hear everything and both of us are in grave danger. Here, take your breakfast… and I will explain everything."

He seemed glad for the food and accepted the tray with grave courtesy. Then he began to eat, but not rudely as she might have expected.

"Please tell me your name," suggested Shakti.

"I am no one, really. Just a simple farmer," he said, fumbling around the tray as if looking for something. She realized that he was looking for a napkin and was somewhat embarrassed to realize that she had not given him one.

"I realize that you have no reason to trust me…"

"That's certainly true," he said, coolly, "Obviously you were a spy. Did you think Charlie would be able to tell you something?"

She felt her face grow warm. "I was a very bad spy, I'm afraid. But now, I'm nearly as much a prisoner as you. I truly care for Charlie, you know."

"Of course, and I am the reincarnation of Carl the Elder."

"Don't mock me," she said. "You are in serious trouble and are about to make matters far worse. I think I know who you are. You are Robby, the son of Lord Donald." She paused. "But I am not sure that even that is the whole truth."

His eyes widened, and his chin jerked upwards. But he said nothing and began to spread butter on the slice of rye bread. He only had a spoon but managed the matter neatly.

"Don't answer, then, it is all the same to me," Shakti said. "For God's sake, don't admit it to anyone but me. If the Prophet learned you were precious to Donald of Goldstone, death would be the least of your worries."

"Quite true, I'm sure. I don't think you are a very good interrogator, either."

"I don't think the Prophet knows that Lord Don's son, Robby, went missing, or that there was a great search for him. But you and I know the truth. Maybe the best thing is to tell you what I know. If you don't want to tell me anything, fine. I will still help you if I can.

"You see, Martin Abaddon—that is the Prophet's real name. Anyway, he is planning a surprise attack on Stonegate, and it could happen soon, perhaps even in days. The Raiders are not simply scouts. They are the first wave of the invasion."

"That sounds true," said Robby. "But you can afford to tell me the truth. I am in no position to tell anyone else."

Shakti ignored the comment and continued. "You are right about me. I was sent as a spy, and I deliberately made friends with Charlie. The Prophet wanted to learn what the leaders of Stonegate were doing, and they thought that Charlie would be their inside source. I was given no choice in the matter."

"If that's true, why are you back here?" asked Robby as he polished off the last crumbs of his bread and cheese.

"Because Stonegate won me over, and Charlie won my heart," she answered. "So, I made sure my reports contained nothing of significance. Then they yanked me back as useless, much to my dismay. By then, all I wanted was to be with Charlie. And he has given me this pearl ring as a token of our friendship. I want to get back to Stonegate just as much as you do, so we must make a plan to escape from here…and soon, before war breaks out."

"Why, that ring belonged to Charlie's mother," Robby said. "She gave it to Charlie in her will. You must mean a lot to him for him to give it to you."

"Oh, I hope so," Shakti said, wiping away a tear from her eye. "For he means the world to me, and I cannot imagine what he must be thinking since I disappeared from Stonegate." Then she realized what he had said. "But you just admitted that you know Charlie very well, didn't you?

Robby looked shamefaced. "Yes, I guess I did. Maybe you are a good interrogator after all."

"Oh, stop it," said Shakti. "You think this is just a clever game. It is not. Don't you see, you don't have to admit who you are? I could easily convince the Prophet that you are Robby, Lord Don's son, whether or not you admit it. But that is the last thing I want to do."

"Well," said Robby, "I would, of course, like to escape from here. But I fear that if we are caught leaving here, the False Prophet could very well execute us both."

"I am sure of it, Robby. He would have us both killed without hesitation. And when you meet him, don't call him the 'False Prophet.' He could fly into an ungovernable rage. However, there is something I need to reveal to you which might mean our salvation. This is a very peculiar, but first I must ask you if there could be any possibility that you were adopted?"

Robby recoiled as if struck in the face by a rattlesnake. "I beg your pardon? Why would you ask such a thing? As far as I know, Rachel is my birth mother, and Don is my true father!"

"That was not a trick, and thank you for confiding in me. I knew you were Robby, anyway."

"If it was a trick, it was a good one," mumbled Robby, rubbing his face with a shaking hand.

"I don't mean to upset you, Robby. But when I first laid eyes on you, I was startled by your appearance. I have lived in this palace since my birth, and I knew the Prophet when he was your age. Robby, you could be his twin. And when you meet him, and you will soon, you will also be shocked at his appearance. He now looks like an older version of you, but there is no mistaking the resemblance. It is uncanny."

Robby was momentarily at a loss for words. "But how can this be? How can it be possible that I look so much like him?"

Shakti sighed as she remembered things from long years ago. "Well, it could very well be possible, Robby. You see, twenty years ago in this very same prison was a lady who was carrying the Prophet's child. She escaped before the Prophet ever knew and to this day only a few people know that she was pregnant. Her name was Selena, and she escaped to the East, but I don't know what happened to her after that. All I can think of that explains the resemblance is that she gave birth to you, most likely, and your parents adopted you. There is no other explanation for the way you look. You look exactly the same as the Prophet."

Robby again sat silent. Shakti could only imagine his feelings. That he might be the son of a man that he hated—that everyone he had ever known hated.

"I do remember now," he said at last. "The Raiders who captured me were saying some strange things. I overheard them talking when they thought I was asleep, and one of them said it could be bad luck to kill me as I looked too much like somebody. I didn't know what that meant and so I dismissed it. But now it makes sense. If I look so much like the False Prophet, they would have seen that resemblance too."

"Of course they did. It is so obvious. There is only one answer to this puzzle…Selena gave birth to you in the East, and somehow you ended up at Westerly-stead being raised by Don and Rachel."

Robby wondered why his parents had never told him about this if it was true—that Selena was his birth mother. Then another thought struck him… if he was truly adopted, then there was no reason he could not marry Ari.

"We have to get back to Stonegate, Shakti…somehow we have to find a way to escape, no matter how dangerous it may be. There is someone I am desperate to see in Westerly-stead."

"Well, before we can even begin thinking about that, I have to report to the Prophet about who you are and what you were doing when you were captured."

Robby scratched his head as he thought for a moment. "Tell him my name is Daniel and that I am the orphan son of a poor working farmer from the rural areas of Stonegate and that hunting game is what I do to provide extra food for the family. And that all I was doing at the time of my capture was hunting. There is no way he can disprove my story. And if I do look like him as you say, and he thinks I am an orphan he may very well believe that I am Selena's true son, and therefore his as well. Perhaps this story will save my life."

Martin was keen to hear Shakti's report on the new prisoner at the end of the day when he had finished his strategy meetings with his generals and commanders. "So, who is this young man in the tower, Shakti? And why was he snooping around the Raider's camps?"

"Much is not clear, but I see why they sent him here to you. Although he is a farmhand who says that he was orphaned at an early age, there is something else. I must tell you that you will be shocked when you see him. He has an uncanny resemblance to you at the same age. However, he insists that his name is Daniel and that he is the orphan son of a poor farmer from the outskirts of Stonegate."

"What?" asked the Prophet with a gasp. "How can that be? That must be why they were afraid to kill him. And they couldn't let him go once he had seen them…so here he is. I need to see him for myself. I will order the guards to bring him here at once."

Robby was deep in prayer when the guards arrived to take him to the Prophet. The vision he had seen on his first night of imprisonment had not left him…a vision of white light and a presence of God, and a promise of protection. It gave him the strength to endure what lay ahead and face his fear of the unknown.

He was chained and roughly led down the spiral stairs out of the tower and into the palace itself. The rooms were so ornate and decorated in gold and gemstones that it took his breath away. Never had he seen such an opulent display.

The Prophet's chambers were even more splendidly decorated, but he did not have time to take in the view. Waiting there quietly was Shakti. "You can leave us now, guards," she said, "and wait outside. He seems securely chained. The Prophet will arrive in a moment."

The guards protested but were afraid to cross Shakti, so they left them alone. The minutes seemed like hours as Robby stood shackled in chains, nervously wondering if he did indeed resemble the Prophet, and what this would mean. A sound from the side corridor made him turn his head just in time to behold a man dressed in a military-style tunic entering the chambers. There was no mistaking it. They both had the same jet-black hair, red streaks, and muscular build, except the Prophet had streaks of gray beginning to show. Both of them let out a simultaneous gasp.

"How can this be, Shakti?" the Prophet asked as if Robby were not present. "Is this a cruel twist of fate? How can a man look into the face of another who looks exactly like him?"

Robby, too, was startled. Hearing something was not the same as seeing. He stared at the too-familiar face. He recognized himself in that face, so the possibility of being his son was real.

"Well, Martin," Shakti answered, "There can only be one explanation… and that is that Selena was carrying your child. She gave birth in the East… and that this is truly your own son."

The Prophet strode to the door and ordered the guards back in. "Unshackle this man. He will not be returning to the tower prison. He can be housed in the family wing somewhere until I decide what else to do with him. No son of mine will live in a prison!"

The guards unlocked the chains at once and stood at attention by the door. Robby did not know what to say, so he stood mute, rubbing his sore wrists.

The Prophet beckoned him. "Sit, sit, lad. I have many questions to ask you, and the night is young. Shakti, pour my son a fine wine and bring him something to eat. We will have to see that he is bathed, and I am sure you know why. No offense, being dirty is not your fault."

Shakti was surprised at the Prophet's response. She had not imagined that he would be so quickly convinced. As she left for the kitchen, she began to think ahead. She saw that escape might be easier with Robby in the family wing. Security was tight there, though mainly aimed at preventing access rather than escape. There were acres of gardens to wander through, containing many areas not viewable from the palace. Perhaps this was a good outcome. There was one disadvantage. She did not have easy access to the family wing.

Shakti returned with sausage, cheese, and toasted buns, along with a crystal decanter and goblets. Robby took a swallow of wine without hesitation, yet he seemed wary and confused.

"Drink, drink. There is a brave fellow. You have been through a hard ordeal, but as part of my family, you will find that life here can be pleasant. But, unfortunately, I can never allow you to return to the East. Your new life is here with me; forget your old life. That is over."

CHAPTER 21

†

Horse Troops

A horse is prepared for the day of battle,
but victory comes from the Lord.
Proverbs 21:31 HCSB

Ari stood in formation with Carla's band of forty girl archers. She was proud of what they had been able to accomplish in little more than a week. She did not know if it had been her mother's idea to use them as recruiters. She thought so.

But the idea was good. And so local beauties armed for war had gone out in pairs to the city of Stonegate and nearby towns and villages. They issued a challenge to the young men to volunteer to serve in the defense of their homes.

Their message was simple, and it was powerful. "If we young women are willing to take up arms, why won't you? Are you afraid?"

Long lines of young men began forming at every city hall, patrol station, and barracks throughout the region. They had the passion and enthusiasm of youth and would not be denied.

This was something the timid and vacillating politicians of Stonegate, Longmont, and Loveland had never experienced. They at first tried to discourage them, insisting that the matter was well in hand, and the fears of an invasion were exaggerated.

Ari recalled her parents discussing the amazing response and the discomfiture of the politicians. *They misread the mood of the public, that's clear.*

Four or five hundred young men had arrived at the Stonegate Academy grounds. Many were armed as best they could from weapons and armor handed down from their fathers. But some only had spears or axes and came in their work-stained tunics. Ari had noticed a score of gray-haired men in worn and shiny mail trying to herd them into some semblance of order.

Ari and the other girl archers, however, faced away from the mass of volunteers toward a file of horse troopers forming up to ride west. They were ready to depart. Upright war lances looked like a steel-tipped forest.

Commander Hamway bent low over the withers of his mount to hear something that Marshall Jackson was saying. Uncle Don sat astride Skipper a few paces away from her. He looked at her and gave her a quick smile. She smiled back, wishing she could run and give him a quick hug, but that would not have been proper. She held her place, standing as tall as she could with her strung bow by her side.

Gray John shouted at the senior cadets, "Get your horses in a single file. You are not herding hogs to the market. You are horse troopers."

The girls on each side of Ari giggled. Carla turned to give them a glare, and the noise suddenly stopped. Ari's ears felt warm. *I hope she didn't think that was me.*

Mayor Billings' remarks were finished, finally, and the horse troops passed in review. Salutes were exchanged, to the deep brass notes of the town band. With a shout and a stirring bugle call, the horse troopers left the academy grounds in columns of four. Stonegate was formally sending out its men to battle, at last.

†

Don rode between Hamway and Gray John in the midst of the column as the three troops headed north to the ancient bridge that spanned the Cash River. The cadet troop was impressive for polish and gleam. The coats of their mounts glistened, their armor shone like silver, and the leather of their tack glowed.

But Don knew that although the cadets all had long months of training, the young men had no real experience in combat. Even the Red Horse troop, famous as it was, had seen little of real battle. For several years, the troop had been broken down into four mounts of twelve troopers each and had manned patrol stations scattered along the roads running through the eastern plain. Their only combat had been against bandits and highwaymen who preyed upon travelers along the trade route.

It had been better than no experience at all, but poorly armed, disorganized bandits were certainly no challenge compared to the Raiders, and even the Raiders were poorly armed compared to the Prophet's heavy cavalry. *I wonder how our lads will fare against the False Prophet's best?*

"Did you say something, Lord Don?" asked Gray John. He reined his horse close so they could talk. Hamway urged his horse ahead, leaving them some distance behind.

"Talking to myself," said Don, with a chuckle. "An old man's quirk."

"Probably because old men want intelligent conversation," replied Gray John.

"I was just thinking that we make a brave show," said Don. "I fear that these youngsters would be no match against the old Red Horse troopers."

"To be sure. God, how I wish we had those lads back again. Stonegate never had large numbers. The False Prophet had us beat there. But man-for-man the Stonegate troopers were the best."

"No argument, and your old Red Horse lads were the best of the best. Hamway was one of them."

"Yes. Good man, Hamway."

"But our troopers from Ariel also did well. I wonder if they have kept their edge."

"I hope so. They might be better than us, now. Red Horse is not bad, but did you see the Black Eagle turnout?"

"Yes. Their horses are fat and sluggish, the men sit their saddles like sacks of potatoes, and their armor is rusty."

"Don't remind me."

The three troops and their baggage train followed the Cash River along the main highway that meandered northwest toward the mountain range they called the Western Wall. They only had made thirty miles when the daylight faded to dusk. So they made camp on a small meadow where the river made a bend, and the canyon swelled into a wider valley.

The cadets had recently returned from their summer vacation, but Don had insisted as a first order of business that they go on maneuvers for a week. It was a wise decision. The cadets had used the time well. They were used to the saddle and their horses had some conditioning. The Red Horse troopers and their mounts were trail hardened so the day's ride was no challenge to them, either.

But the Black Eagle troopers showed the effects of soft living and a lack of training. Don walked through their camp and saw sweaty horses and saddle-sore troopers on every side. Their grousing stopped when he walked by and they tried to make a brave show when he asked them how they fared. But it was obvious that they were woefully unprepared.

They had sent out scouts—thirty young lads who well knew the country ahead of them. They returned to the camp just as the kitchen began serving meals.

The two scout leaders reported. Both were senior cadets and started to make their report to Gray John. But he gave a negative hand signal, a downward motion of his hand, palm down. "Tell your tale to Commander Hamway. He is in charge here."

"We found fresh horse tracks and an old camp," the taller of the two lads replied. "But the ashes were cold and appeared to be several days old. And we found this." He handed over an arrow.

Hamway looked at it and passed it to Don. It was for a short bow. The shaft was cracked as if someone had stepped on it. The steel point was elongated into an acute tip. It was a hybrid—not a bodkin pointed to pierce mail, but not a broadhead for hunting, either.

Don passed it to Gray John. "It is a war arrow, I would say. What do you make of it?"

John looked at it, spinning it between his fingers. "It must be a Raider arrow. I don't know who else's it could be. No hunter would use this kind of point, and it is too short for Stonegate bows."

Hamway dismissed the young scouts and then turned to Don. "I want to clarify one thing," he said. "I would be glad to consider this mission to be under your overall command. You are the closest thing to a general that Stonegate has."

"Not true, I'm afraid," said Don, gesturing toward Gray John. "John is my old mentor and if anyone should be called a general, it's he."

Gray John shook his head. "Don't say that, when we all know otherwise."

"All that aside," said Don, after a long moment, "you are in charge, Hamway. I have no commission from Stonegate—so technically I'm a civilian. Marshall Jackson declared the cadet troop a Stonegate horse troop with John as its leader, under your command."

"Nevertheless," insisted Hamway, "I will put myself under your orders."

"No," said Don, after another pause. "A mission can have only one commander, and that is you. But you can consider me your military advisor, and I will give the best advice I can."

†

Gray John briefed the scouts on the location of the camp where Robby had been taken captive. His special operations unit was operating independently, far to the west, and they planned to link up with it near a village named Fox Park.

They arrived at the place of Robby's capture by midmorning. But the old campsite offered no new information, so they pressed on to the pass at the head of the Cash River.

The old watchtower stood proudly near the summit of the pass. Don left the column with Gray John and they rode to meet with the small garrison. Don noticed some recent repairs to the stonework, the fresh mortar contrasting with the weathered granite blocks. The breeze on the top of the pass was a stiff one, ruffling Skipper's black mane.

The young captain of the guard was a graduate of Stonegate Academy, so they knew him well. His name was Tommy, a tall, lanky youth with a full head of untamed brown hair. His face was wide and honest, covered with freckles. He looked much too young to be in his post. *But they all look far too young.*

"Hello, Tommy," said Gray John. They embraced, their armor clashing. "Anything to report?"

"No, sir. Not much," replied Tommy as he turned to greet Don. "Welcome, Lord Don. Would you have time for some hot tea? I have some spice bread that my mother sent up with the last supply shipment."

They accepted his invitation and entered the watchtower. The first floor was a kitchen and eating area, as well as the armory. They sat on benches next to a squat cookstove. Since Tommy had a kettle on, their tea and spice bread took only a few minutes to serve.

"We are finally getting the watch tower back in shape," said Tommy. "It had been abandoned for several years, you know. It had a bat colony living here. What a mess."

"It looks quite livable, now," said Don. He was impressed at the tidiness and organization. "You have been here, what? Two weeks?"

"That's right. And I don't have much to report. We don't have facilities for horses, but we have been running foot patrols. We have found fresh horse tracks a mile to the north, but they have been crossing at night."

"Have you reported this?" demanded Gray John.

"Yes, sir. I sent a report by messenger pigeon only yesterday."

"Good," answered Gray John and Don at the same time. Gray John continued, "Probably arrived in Stonegate after we had already left. Well, keep up the good work. It was a mistake to have abandoned these watch posts, but better late manning them than never."

†

They caught no glimpse of Raiders that day even though the scouts kept finding more horse tracks which seemed to show that scattered bands of horsemen were converging. All trails pointed to the northwest.

They camped that night in a rolling grassland, with scattered patches of purple sage. Fires were forbidden, and no bugles sounded. They put out listening posts on guard about a half-mile in every direction. Don had no wish to be surprised in the middle of the night.

They were up again in the gray light of early dawn. After the men had a cold breakfast and the horses on the picket lines had their oats, they set out again—following a trail churned up by fresh hoof prints.

It was nearly noon and Hamway had commented that it was about time to halt and take a quick lunch when a scout came riding back at a gallop. His horse skidded to a stop next to the Red Axe banner, and he threw a hasty salute.

"Riders approaching, sir," he said. "A dozen heading this way, and a much larger force chasing them."

"Good Lord," said Hamway. "I wonder if that's the special ops troopers we were supposed to meet."

He flashed a grim smile at Don. "I think we are about to see some action. Any advice?"

"Sound the charge," said Don. "The time for stealth is over."

†

The bugler for Red Axe troop blew the ancient call to action, and the buglers from the other troops sounded an echo as they spurred their mounts to a gallop. They crested a knoll and saw ahead a line of riders heading their way with a plume of beige dust rising behind them.

Still farther back was a line of horsemen with red and black shields coming on like wolves for the kill. Units riding towards each other at the gallop have a closing speed of nearly a mile per minute, so the Raiders only had seconds to realize that instead of chasing a few fugitives, they were meeting a well-armed enemy.

The Raiders sawed on their reins, trying to stop and reverse course, but it was too late. The Stonegate troopers were on them too quickly. All fleeing riders, their exhausted mounts white with foam, passed through the ranks of horse troopers and the battle was joined.

Don wished he was riding Snap, his old warhorse. Skipper was large and strong but completely untrained for battle. Don realized that his place was not to trade blows with Raiders. He had to help Hamway direct the action.

"We need to send a troop around behind them," shouted Don to Hamway. "We have fresh horses, and we want none to get away."

Hamway nodded. "Take Gray John and the cadet troop around to the rear."

Don raced to the right and saw that Gray John already had his cadets flanking the Raiders. The leading edge of the cadet troop was already engaged in battle, and others were sending arrows into the melee.

"Stonegate!" came the cry from a score of young voices, and the clash of arms on shields and armor rippled through the air.

Don rode toward the academy banner and shouted the order to swing to the left and take the Raiders in the rear. Gray John instantly understood and gave the bugler the command to swing left. At that point, the hundreds of hours of mounted drill paid off. As if on parade, the young troopers obeyed. They smoothly disengaged and rode past the tangled mass of Raiders. They went by in a blur of steel and horseflesh and found themselves looking at Raider backs.

A score of Raiders had already turned to flee, and some slipped through the closing net. Gray John detached a twelve-man mount to ride them down.

The rest of the cadets closed on the main body of Raiders. Don kept his place in the second rank, directing the inexperienced lads to fight in teams. Then two bearded men rode their dun horses through the line and came directly at Don. He had no choice but to engage them.

Don lowered his spear and spurred Skipper forward to meet them. His spear was partly deflected by the first rider's shield. It glanced off and struck him in the shoulder. He spun out of the saddle and hit the ground rolling.

The other rider came up on Don's left and aimed a sword cut at his head. He raised his shield, which blocked the blow, but the tip bounced off and slammed into the cheek piece of his helmet. He felt a sting on his face as he dropped his spear and drew his sword.

The Raider was well trained, and they circled each other, trading blows which they both caught on their shields. Then a cadet came up behind the Raider and gave a well-delivered cut to the side of his head. His helmet took the blow, but he lowered his guard and Don's sword sliced into his sword arm above the elbow. The foe's sword fell from his fingers, and he froze for a moment, before dropping his shield and raising his arms in the air.

Then Don realized that the ringing clash of battle had died down. Hands were going up all across the mass of Raiders. The battle was over.

✝

As always, the battle was over in minutes, but the aftermath took hours. They disarmed the Raiders and forced them to dismount. The three horse troops each had an assigned healer, and they were soon busy.

The better arms and armor of the Stonegate forces again paid dividends. The Raiders also had little, if any, actual experience in battle, so the inexperience of the Stonegate troopers was not crucial. Friendly losses were light, and Don was relieved that none of the young cadets had been killed. But a dozen had been wounded and of these, four seriously. The other horse troops suffered comparable losses though a total of three had been killed and four warhorses were lost.

The Raiders had numbered nearly two hundred, though of these about twenty were lightly armed scouts. The Red Axe troop had shown no mercy and accounted for most of the enemy dead. Fifty-two Raiders had breathed their last and another forty seriously wounded by the time the enemy had surrendered. The field had the look of a military hospital.

✝

That night they camped near the battlefield, since many were wounded too seriously to be moved. A messenger was sent back to the watchtower so that a message could be sent on to Stonegate. Don added a note requesting that wagons be sent their way to help transport the wounded. The healers had treated the friendly wounded first, of course, but then gave aid to the enemy. Don was the new owner of several stitches—to close a shallow sword cut to his cheek.

The Raiders had been stripped of arms and armor, and their hands were bound. Gray John had ordered the cadets to search the Raider saddlebags for food. Then they distributed enough to the prisoners to give them a scanty meal.

The commander of the Raider force had been captured, and Hamway ordered him to be brought to his campfire. Two large horse troopers led him up. He was of average height but was as thick as a beer barrel. His hair was greasy and matted in a ring around his head where his helmet had been. He had a large bruise under his eye and a bandage on his leg. His breath was foul.

"You will live to regret this," he said with a snarl. "The Prophet will feed you to his dogs, and people will be cleaning you off their shoes."

Ardmore, the Red Horse troop leader, stood and cuffed him across the face. Droplets of blood and spittle flew in a mist. "Show some respect or I'll…" said Ardmore.

"That's enough of that!" exclaimed Hamway. "Sit down, Ard."

"Untie me and we'll see if you're brave enough to do that again," said the Raider in a choked voice. A thin stream of blood ran down from one nostril.

"Keep a civil tongue in your head," ordered Gray John, "or you will be on a water diet. It does not look as if missing a few meals would hurt you any."

The prisoner lapsed into a sullen silence. They questioned him at length, but he would say nothing about what his force was doing there.

"You attacked us without provocation," he finally said. "Be proud. You have given the Prophet all the excuse he needs to wipe you off the map."

"You have kidnapped our people and were trying to kill our patrol," answered Don. "I would call that extreme provocation.

The prisoner shook his head and would say no more.

†

Don suggested that a detail of cadets identify and make a record of the names of the dead Raiders. They noted the names on a parchment, and Don placed it in the horn pen case on his belt. Two shovels were provided by the camp cook and ten unwounded Raiders were directed to dig a grave and bury their fallen on a knoll near the battlefield. The Raiders asked permission to raise a stone cairn over the grave, and they were allowed to do so.

The hollow ripping murmur of a shovel-full of earth falling on a coffin lid is a terrible sound. The field burial had no coffins, but it still reminded Don of the day when they laid young Philip to rest in the family plot at Waverly-stead. It was more than twenty years ago, and Don had heard the same sound many times since, but that day remained fixed in his mind. Philip was the youth that gave his life so that others might live. Don had mourned him like he would have for his own son. Sometimes life seemed unfair. He knew God had a plan, and His plans were always good. But the good was not always obvious, not to him.

CHAPTER 22

†

A New Kind of Prison

But I trust in you, Lord; I say, "You are my God."
Psalm 31:14 HCSB

Although the accommodations in the family quarters were comfortable, Robby still felt as though he was in prison. He had been given a small room at the back of the kitchen near the servant's rooms which was away from the main rooms in the family wing. In a way, this gave Robby some privacy where he spent time praying and longing for Ari, his parents, and his old life back in Stonegate.

It was a day with cold rain outside when Shakti came to visit him with news about the great army and the coming advance to the East. "The Prophet has told me that many units are going through their final training exercises. He also said something about many cannons."

Robby's heart froze in fear of what could happen if those cannons arrived near his hometown. The methodical planning seemed almost diabolical. "I don't like the sounds of that. It is all coming together too fast. Worse, we have no real plan of escape, and unless we do, we can't send a warning."

Shakti nodded her head in agreement. "Sadly, Robby, that is true. All we can hope for is that the Prophet loses the war, and that we can somehow return to Stonegate to live in peace."

Robby responded with what was in his heart. "Only God can save us now, Shakti. So, we must trust in Him. There is little else we can do."

"Yes, I have been also praying to your God, Robby, and it has given me great comfort. Did the Prophet question you again?"

"Yes. Over and over. He seems mainly concerned about my earliest memories. I couldn't tell him much. But I think he remains convinced that he is my father."

"Be very careful. Do not underestimate him. He may seem kind and jolly, but that is just an act. In the meantime, you must try to fit in here. At least we are safe within these palace grounds."

"Well, I'm not sure about that," said Robby, thinking about the several altercations he had experienced lately with the Prophet's two elder sons around his own age. "I have had a few battles here myself…with Adam and Martin Junior. Recently I was walking in the gardens when I realized I was being followed. I turned to see those two bullies coming up fast behind me. As I stopped to find out what they were doing. Adam accused me of being nothing more than a stray orphan from the East. And Martin Junior added that I was not wanted in their family—that I would be better off dead. Then they both attacked me. If it wasn't for my academy training, I would have lost. But I blocked their blows with a high knee kick and then managed to drop them both. They were only bruised and a bit bloodied. They ran off, threatening that they weren't finished with me yet."

"Oh, Robby, be careful. They could encourage some of their brothers to join them next time."

"Don't worry, Shakti. Gray John was the best teacher there is. I can take care of myself. Perhaps they will leave me alone if they try again and fail."

"I hope so, Robby. But be watchful and alert. Especially when you are alone in the gardens."

"I promise. I am determined to stay alive. Ari is the main thing I am living for and praying for. I live in the hope of seeing her again."

†

In the old mine near the city, the Liberty Soldiers were in a meeting with twelve from the special operation force of the Red Axes. They were working out a plan to enter the palace and seize the Prophet.

Caleb showed an updated sketch map of the palace and surrounding gardens to the leader, Noah. "There are usually four guards at the gatehouse any night of the week. Once we get past there, we follow a long cobblestoned path to the side entrance to the palace. This is manned by another four to six guards. However, you should be more than a match for them. We hope you won't need to kill them but do what you must do. Once we take out the six guards at the entrance, we will storm the palace and seize the Prophet. We must move quickly, as our success will also depend on surprise."

Noah interjected. "I promised Gray John we will try to find Robby and rescue him. Besides, he is a friend of mine." Noah looked Caleb directly in the eye. His face was set and his blue eyes were like glacial ice.

Caleb swallowed. "Well, we have a reliable source from the palace who tells us that Robby has been moved from the tower prison to the family quarters. It appears that he resembles the Prophet, who is now convinced that Robby is his son. We must make sure this coup is successful, and Robby is placed on the throne as the Prophet's rightful heir."

"With your inside information, we certainly have a good chance," said Noah, tracing the map with his fingers, following ink line showing the long storm drain that ran under the city walls.

"And once we have Robby safely away from the family quarters…" Caleb began to say.

"We bring him and the Prophet right back here," Arrow James finished the sentence. "The next step will be to put Robby forward as the leader of a new, reformed government."

"Suppose we simply put Robby on the throne as the Prophet's heir?" suggested Caleb.

"That would be a clever move, indeed," said Noah. "I know I don't clearly understand the local situation. But even if Robby is one of the Prophet's sons, wouldn't he be illegitimate? How could he be the rightful heir? Wouldn't his other sons have a far better claim? And, on top of that, since they are older, wouldn't they be first in the line of succession?"

Arrow thought for a moment. "In the normal course of things, yes. But, capturing the Prophet is not the end of this. We hope to stir up the people. With him gone, we hope the people will rise up to throw off his hated rule and anyone associated with it. But there is no central leader that they can look to. I believe they would seize on Robby to be that leader. He would by far be more acceptable than any of the other sons. All of those are part of this cesspool of corruption."

"I agree with this. But, Noah, we do need to discuss one problem," said Caleb. "The palace officials are bound to keep the Prophet's disappearance quiet while they move heaven and earth to find him."

"True," answered Noah. "His capture alone is not enough. That is one problem. And we will also need a diversion. We need something to distract the attention of the guards, or this plan will not work. But we can help provide the diversion. Stonegate will send a force to the West."

CHAPTER 23
†

A New General

They said to him, "Come, be our commander, and let's fight against the
Ammonites."
Judges 11:6 HCSB

Rachel's tears tore at Don's heart as nothing else could. There were glisten-ing streaks on her cheeks as she mounted the steps to the back porch. Don had heard her arrive and had gone to meet her, but when he saw her face he felt a pain like a dagger twisting in his liver. But the blade quickly turned to a frozen icicle. *Has she heard about Robby? Something bad?*

"What is it, dear," Don asked as he stepped forward and pulled her into his arms. He patted her shoulder, awkwardly, as she shook with sobs. "Is it Robby?"

"No…no," she said, her voice choked. "Not that."

"What, then?"

"I…it is complicated," she said, after a pause. "Oh, God." The last came as a prayer—not a thoughtless expression.

Don led her inside, and they sat facing each other. "The council meet-ing…" she began, wiping her cheeks with her fingers.

"Just a minute," said Don. He went to the kitchen, grabbed a clean dish towel and brought it to her. She wiped her face. Her fingers were shaking.

"Oh, Don, this is tearing me apart. I don't know if I should be proud, angry, or ashamed. But I am so afraid. I don't want to lose you…"

"Just start at the beginning," suggested Don, holding her hands and looking into her dark blue eyes. They were brimming like deep pools and her face was flushed.

"It is Mayor Billings again," she began. "He flew into a rage and accused you of starting a war."

"What? For saving the lives of the special unit?"

"He ignored that. I think he is afraid and lashed out in anger. He kept talking about sending emissaries to the Prophet to try to appease him."

"Doesn't he realize that it is the Prophet that wants war? Only our surrender would appease him."

"That is what most of us kept insisting," said Rachel, composing herself. "Then Marshall Jackson argued for the raid on Prophet City. The mayor almost became unhinged when the marshall pointed out that the mayor did not control military matters."

"Then what happened?"

"I—I can hardly bring myself to tell you."

"Do go on, dear."

"Oh, darling, he blamed everything on you. He said that you are...you are a coward. He saw that the votes were against him, you see."

Don felt his cheeks go warm. "Perhaps I should call him out. He has no right to slander me in public." He felt blood throbbing at his temples.

"No, that would not do. Let me finish."

Don was puzzled. He knew that there was bad blood between them. Most of Stonegate probably knew that much, he supposed. But what did enmity between him and the mayor have to do with military plans? "I am sorry," Don said, "I don't see—"

"Oh, Don," said Rachel. "The mayor insists that you lead the raid. That is the only way he would agree. If you refuse, he insists that the raid be called off, or he will take this to the streets and try to stir up his supporters. If he did that, there could be violence."

"Why me?" asked Don. "Why would he want me to lead? He does not respect me. He..."

Rachel held up her hand. "Because he thinks you will refuse, and that means he will get his way." She paused and buried her face in her hands. Then she lifted her head and straightened her shoulders. "Part of me wishes you would refuse. You are no longer young, and you have certainly done your share. No one would blame you if you declined. And I am afraid that if you do go I might never see you again."

Don searched her face. "There is more, isn't there?"

"I am afraid so," said Rachel. "The council voted that the raid would go on, but only if you led it. And that is how I voted, too. Now I am sure I voted to send my very heart to his death."

Sobs again filled the room as Don held her close. He murmured comforting words as he rocked her and let her weep.

†

The council had called a follow-up meeting at sundown that very day. Don wanted Gray John to attend, so Ari carried a message to him at the academy. Rachel and Don set off together in her carriage. Don reflected that it had been years since they had gone together to a meeting of the full council. The last time had been when Don had requested a grant of unused city land for the academy. He had finally received the grant, but the debate had been so acrimonious that he had not been back. In the end, he had paid the city the full price.

Rachel's place on the council was hereditary, and she had faithfully attended out of a sense of duty. Don was proud of her and was sure that her quiet voice of reason had served the community well. Robby was the one who they always expected to succeed her, but of course, that was now in doubt.

Gray John met them at the door, and Don explained the issue at stake. They had expected that they would be early, but the council chambers were almost filled when they entered. Eight councilors sat at a polished head table, along with the mayor and marshall. The mayor customarily chaired the council meetings since he was responsible for civil affairs. The marshall led in all things military, and logic would have suggested that he chair this meeting, but he did not.

Don sat at a long table that butted against the head table to form a tee-shape. He looked around the room. Hamway was there, of course, because his horse troops were the main component of the raid. A rotund man with a white moustache and a too-tight tunic sat next to him. Don knew he commanded the city levy, but his name escaped him. *I must be getting old.*

Lore-master Duncan was there since he was an ex officio council member and often attended. Gray John sat by Don's elbow. The meeting was closed to the public, but it seemed that prominent business leaders outnumbered the military by two to one. The mayor had obviously been busy packing the attendance.

Mayor Billings made a motion with his hands and two guards swung the ornate doors closed and turned a key in the lock. He tapped on a water glass with a penknife and called the meeting to order.

"We are gathered here tonight against my better judgment," said Billings. He went into a long preamble about the unfortunate events that had led to this point. He took a sip of water, and then concluded, "While I continue to believe that any further action to provoke our old enemy is most unwise, I find myself outvoted. Let the record show, however, that I am resolute in my opposition."

There was a loud chorus of "Hear, hear" from many in the room, mostly the businessmen. Some openly glared at Don. Don caught Rachel's eye from her place at the head table and she gave him a brave little smile. She was the only woman in the room, but Don knew she was used to that.

Then the mayor turned the meeting over to Marshall Jackson. He appeared to be nervous, as he tugged at his tunic collar to loosen it, and shuffled papers before him for a long minute.

"Thank you for attending on short notice," the marshall began. "Everything you hear tonight is extremely sensitive and must not be discussed where unfriendly ears might hear."

One of the well-fed businessmen raised his hand. "Can't I even discuss it with my wife?" he asked.

"That depends on whether you consider her ears unfriendly," broke in Thomas of Longmont from the council table. That got a good laugh. Even Rachel joined in, and the tension in the room subsided, just a bit.

"I think you all know what I mean," continued Jackson. "First, I want to thank you for attending on short notice. I don't intend to discuss the planned military operation. Those who need to know the details will be briefed on an appropriate occasion." He looked down at the papers again, then let his gaze sweep the room. "Nor will I reveal the timing of the operation, though preparations are being made even as we speak."

"Then why were we invited?" The shout came from a man that Don recognized as a wealthy shopkeeper. "I hope you realize that you will be putting our lives and property at risk."

"I don't know why you are here," answered Jackson. "That is a good question. But I understand the risks very well, thank you. Now, please hold your questions until we have finished our business here."

Jackson looked pointedly around the room which fell silent. "The council has agreed that Lord Donald of Fisher, commandant of the Stonegate Academy, should be commissioned as a general and be given command of this operation. He would, of course, be expected to lead our forces in the field."

Jackson looked at the mayor, who was staring at the table in front of him. After a moment, he turned his gaze on Don. "Donald of Fisher, do you accept this charge?"

"Before I answer," said Don, "I would like to know if you offer this commission because you feel I am best qualified or if there is some other reason."

"I suggested your name," said Mayor Billings. "I don't doubt your qualifications, but I frankly doubt your willingness to risk your life on a fool's errand."

"I wager he won't," came a voice from the back of the room.

"Turn them down, Lore-man," someone else shouted. "You can stop this."

"Order, order," shouted Jackson. "Any more outbursts and I will clear this chamber. I don't care who invited you."

Once more, the room fell silent, except for a low, rustling murmur. Jackson glared, as if trying to see who was making the sounds, then fixed his gaze on Don once more. "I ask again, Lord Don. Will you accept?"

"With God's help, I will," answered Don. He heard a stifled sob and knew it came from Rachel.

†

Don and Rachel traveled by carriage directly to the academy, in company with Gray John, who kept pace with them on horseback. They assembled a score of cadets and sent them off with a message for all unit commanders to attend a meeting to be held the next day at midmorning. Then they returned home and tried to sleep. But sleep was long in coming.

The call apparently came as no surprise. The mount and troop leaders of all the horse troops, the chief armorer, the artillery battery commanders, senior scouts, and a number of veterans from past wars answered the call. The only civilians present were Carla, representing the women archers, and Lore-master Duncan. Thomas of Longmont was there, and he was one of the council members, but he was there because of his military experience and was still on the military rolls. Rachel did not attend, and Don, pointedly, did not invite the mayor.

The assembly met in the mess hall of Stonegate Academy. Classes were excused, and cadets were used for security. Don wanted privacy. As the meeting opened, Marshall Jackson introduced Don as General Donald and turned the meeting over to Hamway, horse troops commander, to brief Don and the others on the operations plan and the current status of preparations. Don already knew that the plan involved a raid into the heart of the Prophet's dominions, to be supported by a diversionary invasion from the south. But the details had been a closely held secret.

"Gentlemen, um…lady, Marshall Jackson, General Donald," said Hamway, in introduction. He glanced at a large-scale map of the lands to the west, and then paused, looking decidedly uncomfortable. "Let me first apologize, General, for not keeping you informed. As you know, I led the planning team."

"Lord Don—I mean, General," interrupted Marshall Jackson, "to placate certain civilian leaders, I was forced to instruct Commander Hamway to tell no one about our plans, except for a few senior leaders. That was probably a mistake…"

"Very well," said Don. "Continue, Hamway."

"Yes, Sir," said Hamway. "The essence of the plan is to take a small force into Prophet City before the enemy can react and try to remove the False Prophet by capturing or killing him. We plan to use all five of our horse troops, five artillery batteries and two grenadier units. The special operations team from the Red Horse Troop will actually penetrate the palace."

He paused and picked up a piece of thin paper. "There has been a change, and with your approval, we will increase the force. I have here a message from Ariel. They are sending four more artillery batteries, one horse troop and a grenadier company. They should be here in two days' time."

"Who delivered the message?" asked Don.

"As you know, we recently sent two messengers to Ariel, and they took a cage of messenger pigeons. One of our pigeons returned with this message."

"How large will our force be, in total?" asked Don.

"About one thousand, all told."

"Very well. Go on."

"The plan calls for our allies, the Diné and the Sonora Clan, to advance into the Prophet's territory. They have already agreed to this. If possible, they will drive the enemy garrison from the town of Junction and then move farther into the area known as 'Dixie.'

"We hope that the population in the southern part of the Prophet's dominions will rise up in rebellion to his rule, but the main point of the diversion is to draw the Prophet's army, and particularly his heavy cavalry, away from Prophet City."

"Tell me what enemy forces we can expect," Don said, making notes on a piece of paper.

"We know that the Prophet has three training camps with about ten thousand foot soldiers in each, all within thirty miles of Prophet City. There are more training camps further north—we think four."

"Good Lord," exclaimed Don. "Seventy thousand?" He felt a lump in his throat.

"I am afraid so," answered Hamway. The room fell totally silent. Then muttering began and rose like wave noise on a windy beach.

"Quiet down," said Hamway. His voice was sharp, and the noise stopped. "I haven't finished. We do not have a good count on the heavy cavalry but know that at least three thousand are training in the vicinity of our objective, and perhaps as many as twenty batteries of light field artillery are operating with them in the field. That would be nearly one battery per horse troop, since their troops are larger than ours. Oh, there are also scouts and Raiders operating in the area, and various outposts and lookouts."

"Do we know how many?"

"Scouts and Raiders? I am afraid not."

Hamway continued the briefing, discussing logistics in detail. He revealed that supplies had already been moved as far as Steamboat, and all five of the Steamboat artillery batteries were in position there as well. Don had heard nothing of this and was surprised and impressed that the movement had been kept so secret. Then Hamway called a recess.

The participants all stood to stretch their legs and take refreshment. Water, cider, and sweet pastries were available on a side table, and men with grim faces helped themselves. There was little joking.

"I am glad you already have put forces as far as Steamboat," said Don to Hamway. "I hope that this will not give our plans away."

"Steamboat does not have divided loyalties like it once did. The people there have not forgotten that the Prophet destroyed their town. They have rebuilt and are much more alert to possible spies than we are. We put out the story that Stonegate is reinforcing Steamboat and that we will be training together. I think it sounds plausible."

"Do you think we can make this operation work?" asked Don.

"It is a desperate gamble," answered Hamway. "God alone knows."

✝

The final part of the meeting went over every detail of the mission of each unit. Hamway had prepared written orders which Don approved and signed. Then Don stood to say a few words. "I know you realize that this raid depends on secrecy and speed. The forces against us seem overwhelming. But I am sure that the last thing they would expect is for us to attack them. Since our objective is the False Prophet himself, we can simply strike and withdraw. Remember that Prophet City itself is mostly unwalled, though there is a wall around the old city, and apparently it has only a small garrison to handle civil unrest. We can deal with them. It is their heavy cavalry and artillery that is the biggest threat. But I agree with Commander Hamway that we have a good chance of success."

Don paused and looked at the faces of his command. There was a sense of tension; of coiled energy. There were no smiles, but he could not sense fear, either. "Questions?" he asked. "I will also listen to your concerns."

A hand shot up. Don nodded, and Ardmore, Red Horse Troop Leader, stood. "How do we deal with the thirty thousand infantrymen?" he asked.

Don motioned to Hamway, who answered. "They are thirty miles away at last report. We will have succeeded or failed and pulled back long before they could march that distance."

"Are cannons emplaced to defend the city?" came another question. Hamway answered in the negative. He added that the walls surrounding the palace did have a few small cannons.

Gray John stood and was recognized. "The thing we should most fear are the Raiders and enemy scouts. It will be up to our scouts to find them first and prevent them from giving the alarm. If we are seen, and they warn the False Prophet, we will face a warm reception."

Don looked around the silent room. "If there are no further questions," he said, "it is time to go to work. God be with you all."

CHAPTER 24
†

Casualties of War

So beware, the days are coming, declares the Lord, when people will
no longer call it Topheth or the Valley of Ben Hinnom, but the Valley
of Slaughter, for they will bury the dead in Topheth until there is no
more room.
Jeremiah 7:32 HCSB

Underneath their bloodstained medical gowns and caps, Eli and Jesse
were perspiring as they worked on their last surgical patient for the day.
For the last twenty-three hours, they had treated the most horrific wounds
on injured men, friend and foe alike. Injured civilians kept streaming in,
besides. Nothing in all their years as Pilgrims had been as intense as this.
Clement, the other healer, was sleeping the deep sleep of exhaustion. The
surgery had five nurses, not nearly enough to manage constant, day and
night care. They had to accept several young women who volunteered to
help. They wondered why and then found that the volunteers were part of
an underground Christian community. When the healers learned that, they
understood that it was Christ's love shining through them.

When Eli and Jesse had arrived back at the House of Healing, the mobile
surgery had already departed. Chief Surgeon Kerik had received the message
they had sent by pigeon from the land of Diné and had responded immediately. The surgery shipped in six wagons, which contained their medicines,
instruments, bandages, and tents. The nurses had traveled in one wagon with
the bedding for staff and patients. They only took enough food for a week,
but other supply wagons would follow. A mount of twelve horse troopers

from Ariel went along to provide security. Clement, a Gray Pilgrim who was familiar with the Junction area, was in charge. He had traveled widely in the area before the Prophet had expelled him.

Eli and Jesse had taken only enough time to have a good meal and take a cleansing plunge in the hot springs before they also departed. With fresh horses, they galloped west, along the Great Highway built by the ancients. The two caught up with the surgery at the border of the Prophet's dominions. Then they waited two days before the horse troopers brought back the glad news that Danny Yazzi and his forces had arrived and were attacking the Prophet's garrison. They moved the surgery as close to the town as they dared and set up their tents.

When Danny Yazzi arrived, he brought word that Señor Reuben Ramos from the Sonora Clan had already advanced to Dixie, several days' ride farther to the west. Battles were being fought daily, resulting in many dead and wounded. The mobile surgery was too far away to help the casualties from Dixie, though a few that could survive the trip arrived in the back of farm wagons acting as ambulances.

"I think we've done as much as we can, Eli," Jesse said as Addi and her inexperienced assistant nurse, Magan, directed the stretcher-bearers to carry the last sleeping patient into a crowded tent. A nearby carriage house served as an overflow ward, but space to shelter the wounded was becoming a critical issue. "We need sleep before the next lot of patients arrives. There is no more we can do today in the state we are in. I can't keep my eyes open."

"Aye, I agree," Eli said, glad to remove his medical gown and looking forward to soon retiring to his quarters. "Addi and Magan will have to take over now, and God knows we have a shortage of nurses."

"Yes, but we are blessed that some Christian women from Junction have arrived to lend a hand. Without them, this surgery could not cope. And there would be many more deaths from lack of care."

"Truly, it's a great blessing, old friend. I suppose there are believers in Dixie now. Most were pagans until the Diné mission workers went there to teach the people the Holy Book."

"Yes, and now these Junction women are reading verses from the Holy Book to our patients regardless of who they are. It brings the men comfort as they recover, and I have heard that many men from the West who once served the False Prophet are converting."

"Yes," Eli said, rubbing his forehead wearily. "It is strange how men in the face of death can lie together in the same tent here and become friends instead of enemies."

Jesse tried to stifle a yawn as they cleaned up and sterilized the surgical equipment. "Yes, we are certainly seeing some kind of miracle here, despite witnessing some of the most gruesome injuries ever. I was surprised to see the number of men who have lost a limb. I imagined that the Diné were skilled horseman and archers, but I did not realize that they were so skilled with the axe."

"They certainly put fear into the enemy. Their resistance broke quickly. I think the Prophet's false tales that the Diné are bloodthirsty barbarians actually worked to our advantage. The local people were astonished when our friends treated them with decency. I suppose they thought the Diné warriors would eat their children." Eli wiped a sweaty brow as he talked.

"We are still in an exposed position here," said Jesse. "Nothing much would stop a band of Raiders from attacking us if they avoided our scouts."

"Some nurses want to learn how to use the crossbows. They know we have extra weapons in one of the wagons. I told them to put their trust in our security detail. Then they reminded me of the legend of Carla and the songs that tell of her courage. They want to be able to defend themselves and their patients just as Carla did."

"Ah, yes. But Carla is a real person, not a legend. She is an amazing archer and helped defeat a band of Raiders, more or less like the songs say."

"So, should we allow them to learn how to use a crossbow?"

"I see no harm in it."

✝

Martin Abaddon, the Prophet, felt rage constrict his throat, and pain like red-hot hammers throbbed in his skull. *Betrayed once again!* He remembered, long ago, when he had opened a parcel to see his commander's head, Balek Brown's dead eyes had stared up at his. This news gave him the same sick feeling. His southern provinces were under attack, and his forces were fleeing like cowards. There were reports that his own people were welcoming the attackers and even fighting on their side. He was in a closed meeting with his top two generals, General Logan and General Walters, both as angry as the Prophet about the news that the barbaric Diné people and the horse-men of the Sonora Clan had actually taken the town of Junction and had occupied parts of Dixie.

"But Dixie has always been a hotbed of rebellion," General Logan exclaimed in a loud, agitated voice. "I am not surprised that they gave in so easily. And Junction was lightly defended. We withdrew most of our forces from there to add to our northern army."

"Yes, my dear general," Martin snarled in contempt. "Obviously you miscalculated. Perhaps we should have attacked those southern savages first. But it's too late for that. What do you plan to do about it? This is total humiliation!"

General Walters added his bit while he rubbed a forehead as though he also had a headache. "Yes. Exactly. I often said we should have attacked them. Thrown them off balance. Your strategic sense is unmatched, Sire!"

"I'm still waiting for a sensible suggestion. No doubt, we will have to move forces south," The Prophet said, drumming the table with his fingers.

"Unfortunately, my lord, that is not feasible," said General Logan. "Moving significant numbers to the south would take our focus from the invasion. We are nearly ready now. The training cycle would be disrupted. Our supply stockpiles are in the wrong place for a move south. And we need overwhelming force to insure a victory over Stonegate. If we can take Stonegate, the rest of the East will be easy to overcome."

The Prophet ran his hand through his graying black hair in frustration. "So, what do you recommend we do about this invasion? Ignore it?"

"These Southern barbarians can't do much more than they have done already. We can send a blocking force south to slow them, and they will have problems with supply. They won't be able to do more than hold what they have. We need only delay them a few weeks. Then this war will be over. Once Stonegate falls, we can crush the southerners at our leisure."

"Are you so sure?" the Prophet asked. "Some towns could present a problem to us. What about Ariel and Bethuel?"

"No, I believe not," said General Walters. "I believe we have an easy victory ahead of us. We can starve out Ariel and Bethuel. But there is one possible threat, indirectly relating to the enemy incursion in our southern province."

"What is that?" demanded the Prophet.

"Not at all likely, but if the rebellion spread and more and more towns turned traitor—that could create a problem. Perhaps we should march the city levy south. They are well armed, and they can commandeer food from every town they pass through. It is a sizeable force, Sire."

"How large?"

"Twenty thousand. We can easily send half that number south. They would greatly outnumber those invaders."

"But, general," said General Logan. "The levy is made up of old men and boys. That would mean sending boys as young as thirteen into battle. And if we send ten thousand south, all we would have here are the halt and the lame. Half the levy are paper troops, in case you did not know. They simply won't be there because they are sick, have died, or were made-up names."

"You knew that and did nothing, general," said the Prophet. "I am not pleased, and that is dangerous for you."

"I have reported this, Sire. Nothing was done because the commander of the levy is a relative of yours. I suggest you speak to him. Perhaps he is pocketing the salary of those fictitious soldiers."

The Prophet muttered something inaudible, then let the matter drop. "Very well," he said, finally. "Send a levy of ten thousand south. I don't want a single man taken from my invasion force. If you have to recruit every last man in this town to do it, then do it! Every boy over the age of thirteen is included in this order. We have no time to waste; do you hear me?"

General Logan and General Walters bowed their way out of the conference room. "Yes, Sire, we shall see to it at once!" General Logan replied as he left.

†

When the news swept through Prophet City that all young boys were to be immediately sent to the border to fight the warriors from the South, hatred for the Prophet intensified among his own people. Fear crept into the heart of every mother who knew full well that a thirteen-year-old child had no chance at all against skilled warriors. For years, the Prophet had been spreading tales about the Southern barbarians, and every parent believed them. But they were right about one thing. This was a death sentence for these boys.

The Liberty Soldiers sat huddled together with their maps and plans as they discussed the matter at hand. "This is certainly one of the worst orders the Prophet has ever decreed!" Caleb said. "We must do something to help these young men escape."

"Yes, but we can only save so many," Arrow James responded. "And we would have to use the tunnel. Christian lads probably know about it, but to expose it to a non-Christian would put all our plans at risk. Even if we get them through the tunnel to the East, then what? How will they survive out there?"

"We can perhaps find a way to get them to the Green River Surgery," said Jeremiah. "They might be willing to help. I know they have Gray Pilgrims there, but one of us will have to go and talk to them. We must convince them that lives are at stake."

"Well," said Caleb wiping a bead of perspiration from his brow. "I will be the one. After all, I was a patient there myself, as you know, a few years ago when I broke my arm in a fall. Abel knows me. I know I can talk to him, and I am confident he would be willing to help us. That man has a tender heart."

"All right then. It's agreed. Caleb, you should go," said Elijah. "We will help you pack and prepare things. You should leave in the next few hours before sunrise."

†

Shakti was resting in the gardens at the back of the Prophet's family quarters, happy to have found free time to visit Robby, who was not dealing with his confinement well at all.

"You know, I'm still a prisoner, Shakti, whichever way you look at it," said Robby. "And I find no acceptance from the Prophet's wives or children. They treat me either as though I don't exist or if the sons see me they try to start a fight. I miss Ari, my family, and Stonegate terribly. I feel as though my heart has been torn in two."

Shakti took Robby's hand in hers and looked into his eyes. "Listen, Robby, at least you are not in the tower. You are not in the torture chamber smelling your own burning flesh. Be patient. You revealed your God to me and told me about your vision. Trust in Him. Aren't you grateful He showed Himself to you?"

"Oh, yes I am, Shakti. I had given up on God before I came here and even stopped believing in Him. But evidently, He never gave up on me. And for that I am grateful. And I feel His presence when I am alone at night or in this garden."

"Well, we must think positive thoughts, Robby. We must believe in our own hearts that you will see Ari again...and I will see Charlie. Otherwise, we are lost."

"Thank you for your kind words, Shakti. You have become a good friend and my protector. I could not cope without your support...and that of God's."

Shakti placed a motherly kiss on Robby's brow as she stood to leave. "I am afraid I can stay no longer today, Robby. The Prophet has asked that I see him this afternoon, and I am curious as to what he wants. Strangely, he often seeks my advice. I will see you again as soon as I can."

Shakti made her way to the heart of the palace, forcing her feet to carry her to the Prophet's private chambers. He had sent a note asking her to come, as he had some urgent questions to ask her. She shuddered, hoping that nothing was amiss that would provoke his anger.

As she arrived, Martin greeted her with a half-smile. "Oh, do sit, my dear Shakti, but first pour us a chalice each of my fine red wine which has just arrived from my private winemakers."

Shakti noticed the silver jug and two fine-stemmed chalices into which she poured the crimson liquid. "Here you are, Martin," she said, handing him his drink with a warm smile. "And may I ask the nature of this occasion? Your note has made me quite curious."

"Well, Shakti, I have just been speaking to Generals Logan and Walters. The Southern barbarians have attacked. They moved into the town of Junction and an area called Dixie. I have been thinking about the timing, and I am convinced that the enemy somehow knew I am massing forces here near the city. Probably they suspected that I will soon attack to the east along the same invasion route. The question is, how could they know? Perhaps someone from Stonegate asked for their help. But you said that Stonegate suspected nothing. Have you been lying to me, my dear?"

Shakti burst out with a squeal of laughter, then covered her mouth for a moment. "Of course not, Martin! How could you think that? If the leaders suspected something, they naturally did not tell the commoners."

"But, Shakti, this is serious. Much depends on taking these cities by surprise, and I am wondering if that surprise is now lost. We will win anyway, of course, but I want to minimize the cost."

"Martin, if that is the case," Shakti said, glad to have a sip of red wine, "then it must be that our South was attacked in order to upset your plans. Your generals should be considering what other plans Stonegate may be making." Shakti laughed again, noticing that Martin's face had softened and that his eyes told her he believed her.

"You are right, as always, Shakti. Forgive me for doubting you. But now that this has been cleared up, I have something far more important to tell you. In a few weeks' time when I have won this war, I plan to make you my next wife. I will put you in first place. Most of my other wives are like cows, only useful for producing my heirs. And we will rule the entire East and West together. Until then, I will allow you your freedom to do as you wish, but mark my words…as soon as I claim victory, you will live here with me, in the palace and not in the dancers' quarters. You will be my last and most beloved wife of all."

Shakti tried hard to hide her feelings of fear and contempt as she took a huge gulp of wine. "Forgive me for blushing, Martin. It must be the wine… and the shock of your proposal."

CHAPTER 25
†

Of Arrows and Guns

"For I know the plans I have for you"—this is the Lord's declaration—
"plans for your welfare, not for disaster, to give you a future and a hope."
Jeremiah 29:11 HCSB

G ray John, Hamway, Marshall Jackson, and Jackson's son, Levi, met in
Don's office after the others had dispersed to carry out their orders.
The marshall rose from his seat and paced around the small room like a
caged lion. Then he resumed his seat and crossed his legs, but the elevated
foot would not stay still.

"When will the Diné and the Sonora Clan launch their attack?" asked
Don. They sat in padded side chairs along the walls. No one wanted to sit
at his small conference table.

"They have probably begun their attack already," said Marshall Jackson.
He seemed deep in thought but sat bolt upright, fingers drumming on the
wooden chair arm.

"Isn't that too soon?" asked Levi. "It will take a week at least before we
can begin our move and another twelve days to get our forces into position
to attack."

"Not at all," said Gray John. "Remember, the main point of the southern
incursion is to cause the False Prophet to pull his forces south to clear the
way for us."

"Is the plan to move at night?" asked Don. "Night movements are difficult. And if we are to move fast with the artillery, it will have to be on roads."

"That is the dilemma," said Hamway. "We would be harder to observe at night, but travel by road means we will pass small settlements, farms, and outposts. Even at night, we can't go unseen."

"Perhaps we don't have to pass unseen," said Don. He rose and looked out the small window. "I am beginning to get an idea. Perhaps the more obvious we are, the better."

†

The Black Eagle troop had gone ahead to Steamboat with the artillery batteries. But the remaining four troops spent most of the week engaging in mock battles. Since the state of training in two of the troops was poor, they needed as much practice as they could get.

Colin McCoy and Charlie arrived with the force from Ariel two days after Don had assumed command. Charlie's head was high as he and Colin led the culverns into the academy grounds and they parked them in neat rows. They rode up to Don and saluted.

"I hear that it's congratulations I should be offering, sir," said Colin.

"Maybe your sympathies would be more in order," returned Don with a smile. "What are these toys you have brought us?"

"I think we should take them to the gunnery range and find out," answered Colin. Charlie said nothing but nodded with a wide grin.

"Did you get my message about Shakti?" asked Colin.

"Yes, I did," answered Don. He turned toward Charlie. "Charlie, I am sorry. We sent a patrol out, a full horse troop. They found your tracks and another trail left by two horses. But the thunderstorm wiped out the other trail you were following. They think they headed West, probably over the Western Wall. If she was captured, she may be in the Prophet's hands by now."

"Thank you for trying," said Charlie, after a long pause. His eyes kept blinking. "It means a lot that you tried." He rode off alone. Don and Colin watched him go and sadly shook their heads.

They immediately, that very afternoon, took a culvern battery out to see a demonstration of its range and accuracy. If it could really counter the Prophet's artillery, it could tip the balance in their favor, and they needed all the help they could get.

Carla and her woman archers rode out with Don and the other commanders. She had insisted that they be allowed to show off their skills, and Don had to agree to keep peace in the family. *Carla is going to be disappointed when I tell her that her archers will not be going on the raid.* Don had always seen the women, no matter how accurately they might shoot, as defenders of Stonegate itself. He had never understood why Carla had insisted that they be mounted or trained as horse archers. Nor had he interfered.

"Thank you, Don," said Carla. She was riding a spirited sorrel, nearly the same size as Skipper. She wore no helmet, carrying it strapped to her pommel, and her red hair was tied back in a bun.

"For what?" asked Don. His thoughts were on the culvern bouncing along the narrow road just ahead of them.

"For giving my girls a chance to show what we can do," answered Carla. "I persuaded Giles, the head of the Ancient and Honorable Archery Company, to bring his men out to set up some targets for us and grade our accuracy."

"Very well, but we will want to see what the culvern can do, first."

"Of course. I am curious, myself."

By midafternoon, the three culverns had been positioned on a small knoll overlooking a wide valley that the academy used for gunnery training. A few stray cattle had been driven out of the way, and the range declared clear. On the far slope, three mock artillery pieces had been set up. They had been quickly constructed out of scrap lumber but were the correct size and shape. The closest was at one thousand yards, with another at fifteen hundred, and one at two thousand, which was an extreme range, well over a mile away.

The farthest dummy gun looked like a black dot, but Don could see it clearly enough through his binoculars. Eager gunners showed Don the sights fixed on the gun which were a simple groove and post. Fine adjustments to windage and elevation could be made with two heavy brass screws. Coarse adjustments were made by the time-honored method of moving the entire gun carriage with crowbars.

Their horses were held by several cadets to the rear of the gun emplacement. Don, Carla, Hamway, and a dozen others stood behind the guns, wadding in their ears. One gun fired at the nearest target. A puff of dust showed that the shell had hit low. The concussion staggered them and flattened their cheeks.

"We are firing solid shot, today," said the battery commander. "The explosive ones are a bit too dangerous for your exalted persons. I don't want to risk a mishap."

"That was a near miss," said Don.

"Close enough for an exploding shell to cause casualties among the gun crew, but still a miss. The gunners will adjust their charges and holdoff. It was directly in line. I will fire the entire battery now."

They loaded the guns and fired on command. This time Don could see the shells in flight, tiny dots arching up and then down. The target vanished in a ball of reddish dust. When it cleared, all that could be seen were fragments of wood. A cheer went up from the gunners and spectators.

"Good Lord," said a voice near Don. "The best our guns can do is eight hundred yards, and that is with the new powder and maximum elevation."

"And you are?" asked Don.

"Battery commander, sir," came the answer. "Field artillery."

The next target took two volleys to destroy and the far target, three. But it was obvious that even at that distance the culverns were effective. Don was impressed. "This is going to be an unpleasant surprise to the enemy," he said."

"At two thousand yards, it sometimes takes several volleys," said the culvern battery commander. "But get the guns we will."

†

Don had almost forgotten about Carla, but she soon reminded him. There was a line of straw dummies near the culvern battery, and the spectators moved so that they were in view. Carla and her girls, fifty strong, rode by at a gallop and repeatedly loosed arrows as they passed. A dozen men went running out and counted the arrows stuck in the targets. There were over one hundred hits. It was an impressive display of accuracy. The spectators discussed this among themselves as the spent arrows were gathered and returned to the excited girls.

Don congratulated Carla and told her he had never seen better archery—especially considering they were riding galloping horses as they went. Carla smiled, then reformed her unit and led them back to Stonegate. Don saw Ari with the others, and she waved at him as they all departed.

Giles walked up to Don and stopped by Skipper's shoulder. He leaned on his longbow and waited to be recognized. His men were busy retrieving the straw dummies and transporting them to a waiting horse and wagon.

Don looked at Giles after a moment. "Well," he said, "What was your impression?"

"Impressive," said Giles. His face was somber, and he appeared ill at ease. "My men are trained to use longbows in mass volleys. Our bows can outrange theirs, and we practice at two hundred yards. These girls were less than one hundred from their targets. But for pinpoint accuracy, I don't think we can excel them. And our bows are no good on horseback. Too long and awkward, though much more powerful."

"Yes, yes," said Don. "But are they good archers? That is what I want to know."

"Yes, they are. Very good."

†

That evening, Don and Rachel discussed the events of the day. Don could tell that Rachel was proud of Carla and Ari. Don was still not sure what place could be found for Carla's sharpshooters, but he found that their skill gave him a sense of pride, as well.

Then Don discussed his idea that just might make his force invisible in plain sight. He asked Rachel to organize the women to put a design on hundreds of shield covers. Others would be needed to knit a strange pattern out of white, gray, and red wool. He told her that the younger cadets at Stonegate Academy were to fashion large numbers of small accessories out of horsehair and glue. These were strange tasks, but all involved were to understand that they must be kept secret. No strangers in town must hear a word.

†

Wesley Fletcher's house looked much the same as it did the first time Don had seen it, many years ago. He had gone to Steamboat with a simple request from the weapons masters of Ariel—samples of the exploding shells from Steamboat's town guns. At the same time, he had returned Wesley's and Barbara Fletcher's daughter, Amber, rescued from captivity. She had been kidnapped by the Raiders, and Don had helped free her while he was freeing Rachel.

Much had happened since that time. Steamboat had fallen to the Prophet's army, and the town was nearly destroyed by fire, looting, and vandalism. Wesley's house had suffered much damage, along with the rest, but it was difficult to see the damage now. The repairs had been cleverly done, and even the inside looked much the same, though the furniture was somewhat different.

The years had been kind to Barbara. She had gracefully passed beyond middle age, but she was still trim and erect, and her face had few lines, though her hair was as white as a winter drift. Wesley was somewhat stouter, and his back was bowed, but the twinkle in his eyes was that of a youth. They had greeted him warmly and had set out a feast that five hungry soldiers could not possibly get themselves around.

"Welcome," said Barbara as he stepped over the threshold. "Thrice welcome, dear friend." She offered her cheek for his kiss.

"Thank you, Lady Barbara," said Don. "Good to see you, Lord Wesley." He shook Wesley's hand. The old man's grip was still strong.

"It is good to see you, Don," said Wesley. "Or should I say, General Donald?"

"Guilty as charged," said Don, with a smile. "And how are Amber and Crispin and the grandchildren?"

"All well," said Barbara. "They will stop by later. But young Wesley and Lily are no longer children. They are quite grown up. In fact, young Wesley would like to attend your academy next year."

"I am sure that can be arranged," said Don. "Can it be two years since I have seen them? Time gets away."

"That it does," said Wesley. He ushered Don into the sitting room and offered him a glass of wine. Don accepted, and they sat and sipped the ruby liquid as they caught up on all the family news.

"So, Don, why is a Stonegate general bringing a large force our way?" asked Wesley. "I heard that you are providing us some reinforcements. There was also something about a training exercise."

"There is more to it than that," said Don. "We aim to test the False Prophet's defenses, and perhaps set him off guard. Maybe we can make him think twice about invasion." *All true, but not the whole truth. I know Wesley can keep a secret, but the real objective can't be shared with anyone.*

"Be careful," said Wesley. "There are traders and the Lord knows who else here in town. Some could be spies. Worst of all, someone claimed they saw Buddy Burger near the market a week ago."

"Buddy Burger?" said Don. He remembered him as the rodent-faced councilor that had turned out to be a spy for the False Prophet. "I thought he was dead."

"So some believed, but probably not," said Wesley. "He is truly an evil man. Did you hear the story about Maitland Clarke and the other council members that could not escape Steamboat when it fell?"

"I don't think so. I know the enemy occupied Steamboat for a time and slaughtered many people."

"Buddy Burger kept a blacklist and helped the False Prophet's commander find everyone that opposed his rule. Burger identified Maitland and cheered when he was executed. But he did not escape scot-free.

"When the enemy forces retreated, Buddy Burger was riding out of town with them. Someone threw a flaming torch at him when he passed through the gates. His clothing caught on fire, and he was badly burned. Some say he did not survive, but there have been many reports that he lived and has been lurking in the False Prophet's realm."

"Why would he return to Steamboat?"

"He is probably seeking some way to revenge himself. That is the kind of person he is."

†

Don rode Skipper toward the west gate of Steamboat as soon as the dawn gave enough light to see. He knew an escort would be waiting there to accompany him back to the camp. The streets were nearly deserted. The town had been rebuilt and the walls restored, although they still bore the marks of war. Scorched places on brick would forever remain. But the shops were repaired as best as could be. The ancient plate-glass windows, that had survived the times of troubles and had been many a merchant's pride for generations, were no more. In their place were small panes of wavy modern glass in a wooden lattice. Shop windows still, they were defying the evil forces that had shattered the originals.

It had been pleasant to see Amber and Crispin. Amber was no longer the willow-waisted young maiden she had been when he had first laid eyes on her. But she was still a beauty. If anything, she was more witty and vivacious than ever. Crispin had gray hairs at his temples and was thicker in the midsection, but he was his charming self—still a shameless tease. It had been a delightful reunion, and the time had passed too quickly. Because they had stayed up so late, Don had accepted the offer of a guest room. It would be the last comfortable bed in a long time, he knew.

Six former cadets, his honor guard, met him at the gate and accompanied him back to his command. Busy hands were folding tents into the backs of wagons, and the cooks were pouring dishwater onto campfires. The scent of damp ashes and a barnyard smell hung in the air, still damp from a light dew.

Colin, who was acting as his assistant and aide-de-camp, met him at the center of a knot of officers. "Ah, it's grand to see you, sir," he said. "Did you have a pleasant evening?"

"I certainly did," answered Don. "Everything ready?"

"Indeed," said Colin. "The scouts left before first light, and I started the artillery down the road, escorted by Black Eagle troop. They need a bit of a head start. Oh, here is someone who wishes to talk to you."

Don looked up to see Crispin standing there, armed in mail, with a helm crafted after the Stonegate fashion, except that his had a tuft of red horsehair affixed to the tip. "What is it, Crispin?" he asked, as he dismounted. "Do you wish to come with us?"

"I neglected to mention that I command Steamboat's first horse troop. We have three, but mine was first formed and is the best, of course."

Don was taken by surprise. He hardly knew what to say for a moment. "I need to put you in charge of security, Crispin. You certainly kept that quiet."

"I am yours to command, General," Crispin said. "But I was given to understand that my troop and I would accompany you halfway. Until we reach the Green River, then provide security for the supplies that you plan to leave there. We are sending a culvern battery and two batteries of field artillery. A company of pikemen is riding with the guns as well. It is a small force but one that would cause the enemy some problems."

"Steamboat has a culvern battery?"

"Yes. A gift from Ariel. But the gunners are also from Ariel. We have not had time to train our own."

"Well, it sounds as if you have your orders, and I can confirm them," said Don. He stepped to Crispin's side and gave him an embrace. "It is good to have you with us. I know I can count on you to keep our food and powder safe."

"I can only modestly say that it will be in good hands," said Crispin. He gave a wide grin, and his dimples showed themselves for an instant. "That is, if you put me in overall command of the security force."

"Has that not been decided?"

"I am afraid not. It was left to you to assign a commander."

"Hmm," said Don. "I will call a meeting later and we will decide then. Fair enough?"

"Eminently," said Crispin. "Till later, then." He mounted his horse and rode to join his troop.

Don briefly met with his unit commanders and established the marching orders for the day. Then they started the supply wagons along the road, and the horse troops took the lead. Don rode with Gray John and the cadet troop. Carla and her archers rode in columns of two just behind them.

Wesley's words kept coming back to him—the sighting of Buddy Burger. *What was he doing in Steamboat, if that was him? We will have to watch for anyone that looks like a messenger heading west. They could be carrying word of our movements.*

†

Don had great difficulty deciding what to do with Carla and her fifty girls. He had tried to explain that life in the field was rough. They would not have much privacy, and their presence could cause problems with the men. Then he mentioned the possibility that they might be captured by the enemy. If that happened, they would be sure to be cruelly treated, no doubt violated and degraded. He did not mention it, but his worst fear was seeing these precious young women fall in battle. He simply did not think he was ready to face that.

Carla had listened to all these objections patiently. "I completely understand, Don," she said. "But I don't ask that you send us into the forefront of battle. Let us stay back with the guns. My girls can send a blizzard of arrows against enemy cavalry if they try to charge."

"Yes, that would be helpful," agreed Don. "We won't have infantry, since they move too slowly. Without pikemen to defend the guns, we are vulnerable."

"So you need me? Is that what you are saying? So why are you hesitating?"

"I think you know the answer. I don't want to be responsible for their deaths. How could I tell Rachel that you and Ari had been killed?"

"Don," said Carla. She had an edge in her voice. "Rachel and I have discussed this. If we go, Ari goes too. It would be cruel to leave her behind. She is as good an archer as any I have."

Finally, Don proposed a solution. He would put the matter to his commanders. If they agreed that Carla's girls could come along, he would raise no objections. He felt satisfied with this, and Carla readily agreed. Too readily, he saw in hindsight.

Much to his surprise, the commanders were not unified in opposition like he had expected. Even Gray John, traditionalist as he was, did not object. True, some were horrified at the idea, but as the discussion continued, more and more began to see advantages in taking them along. Don suspected that Carla had been quietly laying the groundwork for some time.

The final decision had been Don's, and he had reluctantly agreed. Carla and her girls would be allowed to travel as far as Green River which marked the boundary of the lands the Prophet claimed. If there were no problems, and if they proved themselves in the field, then they might continue on to provide security for the artillery batteries. But they could not go with the horse troops in their final assault on Prophet City. Carla had said she was satisfied with this.

†

Don's scouts had ridden up the low ridges that paralleled the route of the march to make sure that no enemy force had occupied the high ground. But they were looking for large units. They did not detect a party of three that was hiding on a ridgetop behind a screen of Gambel oak, perfectly positioned to view the valley below. Two wore the beards and armor of Raiders. Their dun ponies and another dozen of their party were well hidden a mile to the north in a grove of dense spruce. With them was a man who wore no beard, probably because the slick scar tissue on his right cheek and chin was completely hairless. His low forehead, thick brow line, and receding chin, together with a prominent nose, gave him a rodent-like appearance. But there was nothing wrong with his dark eyes as he scanned the valley below with an ancient telescope.

"There he is," the man said. "I see him as clearly as if he was right next to us. It is that cursed lore-man."

"I am not interested in who," said one of the other men. "I am more interested in how many and why."

"The lore-man would not be along if this was a simple training exercise," said the first man. "Word has it that Stonegate is sending some forces to help reinforce Steamboat and to train with them. But I don't believe it."

"I know you have old scores to settle, Burger," said the other man. "But we are here to gather information. That's all. Have you a count?"

"Yes," said Buddy Burger. He passed a scrap of parchment with neat columns of numbers to the other man. "Quite a sizeable force. You are a Black Cap. Could you slip into their camp at night and eliminate that man?"

"I probably could. But I have no such orders, and I might not get out again. That would not be to my liking."

"It is frustrating to be so close to my old enemy and simply watch him ride away. He is the Prophet's enemy, too, you know."

"Perhaps," said the Black Cap. "But our orders are to wait, watch, and report." He turned to the other man. "Go get a pigeon from the cage. I will draft a message. There are those in Prophet City who will be very interested."

CHAPTER 26
†

A Cry for Help

Do you really speak righteously, you mighty ones? Do you judge people
fairly? No, you practice injustice in your hearts; with your hands you
weigh out violence in the land.
Psalms 58:1-2 HCSB

It was three days' journey to Green River Surgery from the cave where
the Liberty Soldiers met. As soon as Caleb reached the border he felt
tension drain away. He did not want to go along the main road because an
outpost marked the edge of the lands the Prophet claimed. He did not want
to answer questions from suspicious soldiers. So he took a well-used trail
that avoided that outpost altogether.

The surgery was about forty miles beyond the last outpost, a prudent
distance away. There ahead of him he could see the familiar sight of the old
cottonwood trees that shaded the tents comprising the makeshift hospital.
A dozen men on horseback were heading towards him, obviously one of the
patrols who guarded the area.

A burly man headed the group and as soon as they reached Caleb, he
looked him up and down with suspicion. "Please identify yourself, young
man, and tell us the nature of your business here."

"My name is Caleb, and I have come from the West with news for the
commander of your security forces, Quentin, or Hawk as some call him. I
was a patient here a few years ago and know the Gray Pilgrims Abel and
Thad who treated my broken arm. I have come in peace with information

that you may find interesting. I ask you for nothing more than an escort to the Green River Surgery."

"Come on, young man," the leader said. "My name is Horace, and I can see you are no threat. Follow me and I will take you straight to Quentin. Mind you, much has happened since the last time you were here. We have been getting a few wounded from fighting, far to the south, besides those from closer by. Some have paid for their treatment by work. Some have helped bring in logs to build a new surgical theater as well as some smaller log cabins for incoming patients. We also have a small store."

The rest of the patrol continued down the trail as Horace took Caleb with him. The landscape in the area was high desert, but along the Green River was a narrow strip of lush green winding its way through the valley like a snake. There were no nearby forests, but scattered trees grew along the river, and the healers did find some plants there, as well, that were useful for herbal medicines at the surgery.

Caleb was surprised at the way the surgery had changed and was growing into what looked like a sprawling community. Just before they arrived there they passed through a new cemetery with freshly dug graves. A few women were there who seemed to be arranging flowers and putting up wooden markers naming the dead.

"Those women came up the river all the way from Dixie and stayed to lend a hand," Horace said in his gruff voice. "We have been blessed with volunteers lately. If there should be a great influx of casualties, we would need the volunteers to cope."

It was hard to imagine that farther down the river, battles were already being fought and blood was being shed. The sky had never been such an azure blue, Caleb thought, as they rode along past the cottonwood trees and clotheslines heavy with laundry. Some sheets had bloodstains that washing could not remove.

They rode up to a newly erected timber cottage, apparently used as a guardhouse and Quentin's office. Caleb remembered that he had been in a tent before. Horace confirmed this. "All the tents are being used now to house patients, although the very sick are being cared for in the new log cabins where it is much warmer."

"Hello, Hawk," Caleb said with a smile as Quentin appeared at the door.

"Is that you, Caleb?" Hawk asked, scratching his forehead. "I remember you, now. You came here a few years ago after falling off that wild horse you were trying to break in. What was his name, Wildcap, I believe?"

"Well, that's why they call you Hawk," Caleb said. "Never forget a thing. I had almost forgotten that horses name myself. Yes, Wildcap. And here he is now. But I changed his name. Now I call him 'Spirit' for he has a fine one."

Caleb dismounted his horse, giving him a fond rub along the nose, as Horace filled a water trough with a bucket from a nearby well. Spirit lost no time in dipping his nose in the liquid and start drinking with obvious relish.

"Come in, come in, Caleb," Quentin beckoned and opened the door. It led into a cramped room complete with a table and a few comfortable sitting chairs.

"I will return to my men, Hawk," Horace said. "Just as soon as my horse has finished drinking. We saw nothing of interest other than this young scoundrel." He winked at Caleb with a smile. "You never know what you might run into out there!"

Caleb smiled in return and they shook hands. "Thanks for your escort, Horace. Perhaps I shall see you again."

"Perhaps," said Horace as they bade him farewell.

"Very well, Caleb, find a seat. These chairs are rough, but they beat sitting on the ground. What news do you bring from the big city? I can see you are not injured so you must have come here on another matter." Quentin looked him up and down as if trying to answer his own question.

"So I have, Hawk," Caleb began, wondering where to start. "Much is happening in the Prophet's lands which you need to know about. For many years the Prophet has angered the people with high taxes and almost starvation as he builds his cannons and increases his military. At first, he decreed that all boys over sixteen must join the army or the Raiders, and for years they have been forced to train as soldiers for the next war. This angered many families, but all had to stay silent for fear of execution. But in secret, most curse the Prophet for the suffering he has caused. Now, he has made a decree far worse. Since he found out that the men from the South have occupied Junction and parts of Dixie, he has ordered that all young boys aged thirteen and older be sent to the border to fight. They are only children, Hawk. They stand no chance of surviving in battle against those skilled warriors."

A look of horror crossed Quentin's face. "That is inhumane!" he gasped.

"Exactly," said Caleb, glad that Hawk responded as he hoped he would. "That is why I came to see you and ask for your help. My brothers and I know of a secret tunnel that leads out of the city. We want to help some boys escape, perhaps as many as one hundred. But they need a place to go once they escape from the city. I hope you will give them help to come here. These boys are used to hard work and no doubt they could be of use to you around here in return for a safe haven."

Quentin kneaded his forehead as he listened. "I see. I see. In all good conscience I cannot say no. But food would be the problem. There is never enough, though we bring in some wild game, and the House of Healing sends supply wagons. The patients and their families rarely bring enough for more than themselves, if they bring that much."

"We will try to see they have enough food to survive the trip here," said Caleb. "But we can't do more than that. Does that mean you can't help?"

"Perhaps we can, Caleb. These boys have no chance of survival if they are sent to fight on the border. I need to speak to Abel and Thad, of course. But how to feed them?"

"Perhaps Abel could think of something?"

"It would be possible for our patrol to pick these boys up and show them the way here. We can get them by the outposts. You have my promise we will help you. I am confident that Abel and Thad will be glad of more hands to help with the workload. But why don't you start with ten, and we will go from there. When will we get the first intake?"

"Well, if I leave now, I can be back in the West in three days to talk to my brothers who will help me organize the boys to escape through the tunnel at night. So, you will see the first lot of boys arrive here in a week or so."

"Don't worry, leave it to me. These boys will be provided for. But, you are not going anywhere until you get a hot, hearty meal and a few hours' sleep. Then you can depart refreshed."

"Thank you, Hawk. I am famished and tired. And I am sure that Spirit will appreciate a rest."

"Good," Hawk said, shaking Caleb's hand. "It's a deal."

†

Danny Yazzi was feeling fit, even stronger than when he had parted from his beautiful Aiyana. He had lost the catlike reflexes of youth, but he had mastered the warrior way. In battle, the movements of an opponent's eye, a subtle shift of his weight, and Danny knew the next move he would make. His axe was swift as the flash of sunlight on water. But more valuable than that was his strategic wisdom.

A messenger from Señor Ramos reached Danny, just as he was opening the gates of the last prison camp near Junction. These were political prisoners, and he knew they would have no love for the Prophet. But they would also be in no condition to take up arms against him.

The message was encouraging. Not only had the local people in Dixie welcomed the Sonoran heavy cavalry, but some of the Prophet's garrison had declared themselves to be in rebellion against his cruel rule. The garrison had also revealed news that was profoundly disturbing. Orders by messenger pigeon had revealed that the Prophet was determined to send boys as young as thirteen to the south to put down the disturbances and expel the invasion.

Night was fast falling before Danny directed his warriors to find a new camping area for a rest and a hearty meal, a good ending to a day crowned with success. Many a man gave devout thanks that another bloody day was over. A few desperate people came by with wounded and sick on litters, and Danny ordered some young men to escort them to the field surgery that the House of Healing had sent.

Danny Yazzi's voice was clear as he addressed the weary men at the campsite. "Our enemy is sending young boys to fight us. We will try to spare them if it is possible. But we will not wait here for them to come to us. We captured many weapons and are arming any of the men of Junction that wish to fight. Then we will march north. May the God we serve continue to bring us success."

As the men finished the last of their meals and partook of the last drop of coffee, a dark cloud suddenly covered the stars and the moon and darkness enveloped them. "Not a good omen," said Danny Yazzi as he closed his eyes, glad at last to be in his rough camp bed where sleep came easily from exhaustion.

†

Robby was having a strange dream. In it, he saw his father riding toward the West with Ari and her mother Carla. He woke with a gasp. *If only it were true!* Sleep eluded him after that, so he made his way into the palace gardens near his room. Everyone else was asleep, and there were no candles or oil lamps lit anywhere so Robby guessed it was well after midnight. He looked up towards the heavens, but a dark cloud had obscured the light from the moon and the stars, enveloping him in a thick darkness.

He understood what had sparked that dream of hope, the hope of seeing his loved ones again. Shakti had visited him yesterday afternoon in such a distraught state that he feared she would collapse.

"Oh, Robby," she said, her lips trembling as she spoke. "The Prophet is convinced that the war will be over in two weeks, and that he will be victorious. Then he told me he intends to make me his last and final wife to rule with him."

"You have served him for many years, Shakti," said Robby. "But surely he has…I don't know how to talk to you about your personal life. I don't want to pry."

"The Prophet can have whatever he wants in the palace, Robby," said Shakti in a small voice. "But for some reason, he has never forced himself on me. And now, God forbid that this marriage should happen, as I shall never be with Charlie again!"

Her tears flowed, wetting her cheeks and lips as she sobbed like a small child. Robby took her in his arms to comfort her, not knowing what else to do. "We have to pray, Shakti. Pray that God intervenes and that this never happens."

"I will pray, Robby, I will," Shakti said between sobs. "But now I must get back, as Martin has invited me for a few drinks of his newest wines this evening, and I have no power to say no. I fear for my future, and for yours."

Robby looked upwards, remembering her words. But all he could do now was pray.

CHAPTER 27
†

The Dream

I will pour out My Spirit on all humanity;
then your sons and your daughters will prophesy,
your old men will have dreams,
and your young men will see visions.
Joel 2:28 HCSB

D on was standing at the foot of a vertical cliff made of rugged black basalt. He leaned back and looked up, but gray, swirling mist obscured the top of the sheer wall. This was strange since he was bathed in sunlight where he stood. He felt an overwhelming compulsion to climb up. He did not know why but knew that he must.

He was clad in his familiar armor and weapons but knew he could never climb while so encumbered. He stripped down to his under-tunic and even pulled off his boots. He began to climb, and at first it was easy. His toes and fingers found crevices and ledges that held him securely, and he progressed upward, getting higher and higher. As he climbed, the sunlight became dimmer and the mists closer. His fingers and toes were raw and sore, and the climbing became harder and harder. The rock was smoother, and it was difficult to find something to grasp.

Finally, he reached a dead end. The cliff above him was as smooth as glass. His toes began to slip, and he frantically clawed the unyielding face for something, anything, that would give him a secure hold. Worst of all, when he tried to descend, it proved to be impossible. Nothing could be seen below, and his toes found only empty air. He hung on as long as he could, then slipped and suddenly was weightless, with a wind blowing by his ears. He knew he was falling, and he fell for what seemed to be a long time. Then he felt strong arms grasp him under his armpits, and he was gently lowered to the ground as light as a feather.

He looked around but could see no one—only the dazzle of bright light. Standing there, panting, he tried to regain his strength. He heard nothing, but the compulsion to climb was even stronger, if anything. He moved along the cliff face frantically, looking up, trying to chart a route upward. Then he thought he saw a way and began to climb again. But everything happened just as before. He reached a point where he could not go on, found it impossible to descend, and fell into those strong arms again.

He tried a third time, with the same results. Then in frustration, he turned toward the light. "I can't do it," he cried, in frustration. "I know I have failed you, but I can't climb it."

Then he heard a voice. It was pure and deep, like the rushing of mighty waters but soft as the sound of a breeze in the treetops. "All you had to do was try," the voice said. "Sometimes success only comes by failure. Only when you are weak are you strong."

✝

Then Don awoke, the voice still so real that he was surprised to find those near him still sound asleep. The stars above were cold and bright, and he could hear the soft camp noises. A horse stamped a foot and he could hear someone snoring. He could smell the musk of a well-used saddle blanket.

What a strange dream. Is it an omen, a message? It may be, but if so, what is it? How could failure result in success? He fretted for a long time, trying to make sense of it all. Finally, he drifted off and awoke only when someone shook his shoulder. "I brewed coffee, sir," said Colin. "It is nearly dawn."

The cooks had prepared a breakfast of oatmeal and apples. They ate standing up and began the familiar routine of breaking camp. Teamsters were hitching horses to wagons, and the gunners did the same to cannons. The scouts departed to make a protective screen and the long column formed up along the ancient road heading due west.

Their journey could be thought of as three smaller journeys, all different, but all about one hundred sixty miles long. The first one was from Stonegate to Steamboat. There was little danger, and the passage over two mountain passes proved to be a good shakedown for the raid. They found and solved problems, and the inexperienced troopers became used to life on the trail. It turned out to be a practical training exercise more than a military campaign. At Steamboat, they made minor repairs and loaded supplies. Some of the draft horses pulling the culverns had gone lame, and they were able to trade for fresh work stock.

The second leg of the journey, from Steamboat to the Green River, was almost complete. They had first traveled through towns that were friendly and then over a long stretch of high desert that was mostly uninhabited, except for a few ranches. They had to be on guard, but they had seen no enemy forces. The way ran close to a river and there were springs that provided enough water for man and beast. But they knew that once they entered the Prophet's lands, the situation would be different.

The final part of the march would be through hostile territory. There would be plenty of water, but the inhabitants could not be trusted. Contact with enemy forces would be likely. They would leave half of their supply wagons just east of the Green River, under guard by a force from Steamboat. From there, the route led west, then northwest over a mountain pass, then down through a valley leading to the heart of Prophet City. The pace of march would have to speed up, since the success of the raid depended on surprise. The plan called for a rapid advance and an even more rapid retreat.

"I was a bit surprised about Crispin," Don said to Colin as they rode along.

"And why would that be so?" asked Colin.

"He seemed a bit young to assume command of all the Steamboat forces."

"Ah, but your age might be showing a wee bit. Most of his troopers probably consider him an old man. Plus, he's a charmer and fair-spoken. He will do well."

"I am sure you're right. I did not feel comfortable giving him command without a meeting. But there has to be one person in charge."

"Truer words were never spoken."

"The field artillery teams seem to be a problem," said Don, changing the subject. "I had assumed that the horses would be well conditioned from farm work. But pulling heavy loads around farm fields does not season them to long miles on the road."

"Hindsight is always a great teacher," said Colin "I wonder what else we did not think of. We will pick the best of the lot when we go on from Green River. We can leave the fat, lazy, and lame horses behind."

†

The scouts had spotted three riders on fast horses who tried to flee to the West. They intercepted and detained them all. The three had protested, claiming to be innocent ranch hands, but the scouts could not take the risk that they would carry a warning ahead of them. All would be held captive at the supply camp until the raid was completed.

Thomas of Longmont briefed the advance party that would cross the Green River and enter the large settlement nearby, a town called Vernal. The main body would cross to the south and never enter the town, but they could not pass unobserved.

"You probably wonder why you have been asked to grow out your beards," began Thomas. "The reason is that the enemy troopers favor the full-bearded look.

"We have carried with us a couple of score of enemy shields with the False Prophet's cursed three lightning bolts. You will carry them, together with an enemy banner. We captured many of these as trophies in the last war. Time to put them to use."

"Are we to pretend to be enemy troopers?" asked a lad.

"You catch on quick," said Thomas. "We are outfitting a mount of twelve in the full armor of the False Prophet's heavy cavalry, complete with the heavy, unwieldy, horse armor. You will go into Vernal and spread the word that we are a body of the Prophet's forces returning from a raid."

"What about the border guards?" asked another.

"You will ride right by them as bold as you please. We will take them into custody later on and replace them with our Steamboat friends."

"The cadets of the academy made up hundreds of false beards," continued Thomas. "We also have knitted wool armor that will make our horses appear to be carrying the False Prophet's heavy horse armor. The main body will have shield covers with the lightning bolts. We will bear banners with the same. We hope to appear as if we belong to the Prophet's army."

"Won't that cause confusion if we actually get into combat?" asked another.

"It certainly would. When and if we fight, the shield covers and beards will come off. When we depart the area, you will get your own shields back, and I see a razor in your future."

†

The ruse seemed to go off without a hitch. The small party spread the word in Vernal and returned just as another horse troop finished subduing the border guards. Steamboat infantrymen took their places, and the field artillery crossed over the ancient bridge. They did not plan to pass through town since they would be taking a shortcut a few miles to the south.

"You mentioned a surgery on the Green River, didn't you, Lord Don?" asked Crispin.

"Yes," answered Don, "but it is several day's ride up-river. Too far away to be of immediate help." He turned and looked ahead, observing the movement of the forces in front of them.

"It's all going according to plan, so far," commented Don.

"Let's hope it continues," said Crispin, scratching at his horsehair beard.

"There doesn't seem to be any large number of enemy forces in the area," said Don." I am sure that Vernal has some foot soldiers, but with your artillery, they should pose no threat to you. Just keep the bridge open."

"The townspeople might find it suspicious that the border guards are behaving differently."

"Bluff it out," said Don. "Time to use your gift of gab."

"You can count on me."

The Prophet's banners flew proudly over Don's force as he crossed the river and began driving into the Prophet's territory. Instead of the deserted plains behind them, the road ahead bisected plenty of small settlements. But the people simply gazed sullenly at them as they passed. They did not seem to be alarmed, but they certainly did not welcome them. Don found that to be a good sign. The deception seemed to be working.

They pressed on with a goal of traveling at least forty miles per day. The evening of the third day found them high in the mountains, near the top of a wide pass. The smaller road they had been following had joined with an even broader road which reminded Don of the Great Highway between Ariel and Hightower. They had fully expected to confront enemy forces, but so far, they had met none. Don was not sure if that was a good sign or not, but he was grateful for it.

They held a strategy conference before descending the pass into the broad plain that held Prophet City. The daylight was fading fast, and the assault forces were told to get some rest before they continued on. Don was torn about whether to take the artillery with them. They had always planned to leave the supply wagons and two batteries of artillery at the top of the pass. Carla and her girl archers would stay there as well. That was settled. But the road down the pass was steep, and the heavy artillery would be excruciatingly slow in ascending back up the pass. Don put the question to his commanders.

"I think we should leave the artillery behind," said Hamway. "The horse troops can race down, assault the palace, capture the Prophet and be gone before the enemy knows what is happening. The artillery would just slow us down, and I don't think we need them. The grenadiers have breaching charges which can blow the palace gates down as well as artillery."

Thomas of Longmont, who had command of all artillery, had other ideas. "But, General Donald," he said, "The culverns are our answer to enemy field artillery. Without them, you might find yourself in the same situation that the False Prophet's forces faced. If there are enemy horse troops with artillery, they can mass to charge you. If you mass to defend, their artillery will tear you apart."

Gray John spoke up. "If we take culverns down this steep hill, we risk their loss. If the enemy captures them, our secret weapon will be lost. We don't have to mass our horse troops since we can disperse and retreat. We don't have to defeat the enemy heavy cavalry if any should appear. We only have to avoid them."

"The problem with the culverns is that they must travel back up steep hills to return over the pass," said Hamway. "I am afraid they will be so slow that the enemy will have time to react. We will have to fight a battle that we could avoid."

"Very well," said Don. "We will leave the culverns behind. But I think we should take one battery of light field artillery with us. We can use four-horse hitches, and they will be able to return fast enough." Don quickly wrote out orders so that there would be no mistake.

"Thomas," said Don. "You will be in command here. I will take all the horse troops and the grenadiers. Your gunners are armed with muskets and pikes, and you have Carla's horse archers. That leaves you somewhat exposed, so find a good defensive position and await our return. We will leave for Prophet City well before dawn and try to arrive back here before sundown."

"Of course," replied Thomas. "You can count on us."

"This is all going to happen swiftly if it is to happen at all," said Don. "The scouts estimate less than thirty miles to go. I would think we will be back well before sundown. We might as well drop our disguises. I want to fly our own colors when we go down tomorrow."

"Perhaps we should stay disguised until we enter the city," said Hamway.

"No," said Don. "The False Prophet does not allow military units to enter the city, so even if we carried his flags, the alarm would be given just as quickly. He would fear it was a coup."

Everyone nodded and began to peel off the uncomfortable false beards.

There had been traffic on the road all day, but the lead troopers had simply ordered the wagons and coaches to pull to the side of the road and stop until Don's forces had passed. Don had not been concerned that they would be seen as long as they were traveling faster than anyone they met. As for riders coming up behind them, they had simply been ordered to stay to the rear. When they stopped for the evening, they blocked the road and allowed no one to keep traveling west, though they allowed east-bound travelers through. But it seemed that people avoided traveling at night. A few drovers grumbled but turned back to camp at a settlement a few miles away.

Carla's girls had drawn some curious looks, but they had also pasted on wispy beards, and their armor concealed their figures well enough that they could pass for teenaged boys. Don stopped by and had a quick word with Carla and Ari.

"You can send a note to Stonegate by pigeon, if you wish," said Don, speaking to both as the campfires were being lit. There was a smell of burnt hair as the men cast their false beards and shield covers onto the flames. "We have plenty of birds, and I am sure that Howard would like to hear from you."

"That is a kind thought, Don," said Carla. "But we don't need special privileges."

"What is the use of being in command if you can't tell someone to do what you wish?" asked Don. He spoke in a joking way, with a smile. "If you do as I say, then it is an order and not a privilege."

"Thank you, Uncle Don," said Ari. She laid her hand on his arm. Even close up, her downy beard looked quite realistic. Carla had enlisted the aid of a theatrical company, and their expertise showed. The beards of the horse troopers also looked fine at a distance. A few dozen had grown real ones, and they were the ones that contacted the people on the road. But they planned to shave tonight to prevent confusion in the coming battle.

"You can take your beard off, Ari," said Don. "Time to show your pretty face again."

She made a face as she stripped off the sticky hairs. "Ugh," she said. "I wonder if my face will ever be clean again. What I would give for a bath." They all smiled at her.

"Are you going to write to Rachel?" asked Carla.

"Yes. I want her to know she is in my thoughts," said Don. "I also must send my daily report and tell the marshall our final plans for tomorrow. So I had better get busy. Why don't you come with me to the pigeon keeper, and we can write out our messages?"

"Of course. Thank you again."

†

The birds disappeared into the night. Don knew they could fly at fifty miles per hour, so the messages would be delivered in the morning. Afterwards, they went to a prayer meeting where God's blessing and protection would be earnestly sought.

Ari and Carla bade him a good night after the meeting was over. Carla gave him a hug. "Stay safe, Don," she said. "Bring the False Prophet back in chains."

"I will do my best," said Don. "Keep us in your prayers."

†

At the end of the day, when everyone else in the camp was asleep, and Ari was worn and weary from long hours in the saddle, all she could think of was Robby. The moon was full as she looked up into the heavens thinking that under these same starry skies Robby was lying somewhere. Perhaps he was looking upwards and thinking of her. She had to believe that, or she would give in to despair.

"Are you asleep, Ari?" Carla said softly from the bedroll next to hers.

"Oh, Mother, you startled me. No, I am still awake. I was just thinking of Robby and praying he's safe."

"Have faith and trust that God will watch over him, Ari. We must continue to fight against the Raiders and win this war...it is the only way we will ever see Robby again."

"I know," said Ari remembering the day that Don and Rachel had told her the truth about Robby being kidnapped by the Raiders...and that he had been adopted as a baby.

"I am still thinking about what Rachel and Don told me about that woman Selena who came to them after escaping from the West. And how she was pregnant with the Prophet's child and made Don and Rachel promise they would bring Robby up in the Christian way if anything happened to her."

"Yes, I remember," said Carla. "It was Rachel and me who delivered Robby into this world. Selena sensed she was dying, and we stayed with her, praying until she breathed her last. The only people who knew our secret apart from me, Don, and Rachel are Howard and Charlie. Why, Charlie was only around twelve years old, and he had been hiding in the hallway outside and heard everything. When we found him shivering outside the door, we made him promise not to ever tell anyone in Stonegate the truth about Robby. Rachel got away with saying she was Robby's mother, and it was a good thing that when she was pregnant with Sara she hardly showed any sign of it, so people accepted what they were told. From the time of Robby's birth, Charlie took on the role of his big brother. He loved that baby and hardly left his sight. He has always been protective of Robby, fearing that the False Prophet could somehow one day take him away. Why do you think that Charlie always insists on going hunting with you two?"

Ari thought for a moment, and suddenly it clicked. *Yes, every time we went hunting, Charlie offered to come and help. And he was always hanging around Robby, keeping a watchful eye over him.* "Yes, Mother, you are right. It all makes sense now."

"And you know how some people think Charlie is a little slow? Well, actually, he is not slow. It is just that the shock of what he witnessed that night has made him cautious and slow to answer some questions or respond, as he fears he may say the wrong thing. He has been very guarded since that night…and very careful to keep our secret. He was only a child and everything he went through has affected him."

"Charlie is a real gem, Mother. There is no person I know who is so loyal to us and our family."

"Well, his parents died when he was just fifteen so that made him draw even closer to us…and to Robby. He was an only child as his parents were both elderly and had him late in life. In fact, it was a bit of a miracle, because they had been trying to have a family for many years and had all but given up when Charlie came along."

"He must have been very special to them and very loved," Ari said, thinking about the joy his mother must have felt to have finally conceived a much-longed-for child.

"Oh yes, he was. And that is why Charlie has such a heart of gold. He knows how to love. And right now, he is in love with Shakti."

"It's sad for both me and Charlie then, Mother. Both of us are separated from those we love. But at least I know where Robby is, and that he is not my cousin, so there is a chance for us to be happy if we survive this war."

"Yes, Charlie is devastated by Shakti's sudden disappearance. And then following her to her old address in Loveland and finding out that the Raiders had been there…one doesn't know what to think! But Charlie says he trusts Shakti and that someday the truth will be revealed. He is a man of great faith."

The stars were twinkling brighter than ever as the night stretched on and the thought of another day and a battle reminded Ari that it was time for some sleep. They did not speak for a short time and Ari thought of Robby. *Strange. I love him. But we have never kissed, not really. A peck on the cheek does not count. I have never held him in my arms. Oh, how I long to.*

"Well, we must persevere, Mother, Ari said at last." And tomorrow is another day. Let's hope we can fight a good battle and keep our enemies away from Stonegate. I so much hope that Uncle Don can find Robby."

"Yes, my darling Ari. Good night and good rest. We must be strong and ready when the morning breaks. This war is not in our hands alone…not by any means."

†

Buddy Burger gave his horse a lash along the flanks with his quirt. "That will teach you to stumble," he muttered. "They gave me the worst nag of the lot." He was still fuming from his humiliating, scornful treatment by the cursed Black Cap. The dolt had even gone so far as to laugh in his face at his sensible suggestions. The man had even admitted that he could have slipped into the camp and eliminated the lore-man.

"We could have had him," he said over and over in a kind of litany. *It would be sweet to eliminate that pompous Wesley Fletcher. But the Prophet's hatred is directed mainly at Donald of Goldstone. With good reason. Why couldn't the Black Cap see that?*

Burger had visited the Prophet recently, in response to an urgent summons. He had not seen him in several years. He was still handsome, but Burger's sharp eye had noticed a hint of a yellow color in his face, and he seemed to wince occasionally as if his side pained him. His legs looked a bit swollen, and his torso seemed a bit bloated. It could just be middle-aged fat, but Burger suspected he might have problems with his liver. Perhaps his dissolute life of excess was catching up with him.

"Burger," said the Prophet, after forcing him to partake of a small cordial, "I want you to go back and nose around for me. You know Steamboat well and could be a help to my men. I am sending a small team to keep watch over the area."

"Of course, Lord Martin," answered Burger. He addressed him in a familiar way, at the Prophet's insistence. "But my face is well known in Steamboat. I would not be very effective as a spy."

"You will be an advisor, more than a spy," said the Prophet, Martin Abaddon. "But I will give you a purse of coin—a heavy purse. Perhaps you can buy information. And there are others in the East that would be only too glad to help you. A bit of gold may make them gladder still."

Burger had gladly accepted. Anything was better than more years of futile exile, nursing his bitterness. He had expected to be rewarded for his service, even though it had ended in disaster. But a meager living and cramped quarters was all the reward he had ever gained. It was months after the war had been lost before the Prophet had received him, and although he was thanked, he was then ignored. But the Prophet had remembered him after all.

He remembered the Prophet's words about others that also hated the smug East and all it stood for. There was one who could, perhaps, be enlisted to help gain a measure of revenge. If so, he knew the Prophet would consider the money well spent.

He traveled light, since he could buy whatever he wanted on the way, and there were small communities along the way, protected by stockades, that often had rooms where a traveler could stay. He had not been this way before, and so his face was not known. But everyone knew where the old witch lived, and he would have no problem finding her. And he was sure she nursed a hatred as virulent as his own.

CHAPTER 28
†

War on the Border

I lie down and sleep; I wake again because the Lord sustains me. I
am not afraid of the thousands of people who have taken their stand
against me on every side.
Psalms 3:5-6 HCSB

The wind had been blowing hard from the west all day. Bits of sand had burned their eyes and blistered their cheeks. Even the toughest warriors had donned their warm jackets over their battle armor. Their horses kept wanting to turn their hindquarters toward the gusts, and their tails streamed between their legs. Tumbleweeds bounced by like thorny beige balls. Danny Yazzi and Señor Reuben Ramos were sitting around a robust campfire dealing with the four young prisoners they had captured. They had found eight young boys under fifteen who were fleeing, and now four more wide-eyed lads sat shaking before them, fearing whatever fate may befall them.

"Do not be afraid," Danny said to the group who were cold, hungry, and tired after a day of battles in the field. "We will not hurt you. Our men are followers of the Holy Book and our God does not allow the murder of children, only our enemies. Please tell us your names and about your life."

The eldest boy spoke up with a tremble in his young voice. "My name is Mika, and these are my friends from our village in the mountains north of here. This is Kya, Nord and Atlas. We are farm boys. We don't know how to fight. But the Prophet is making all boys our age to fight you. We don't want to go in battle, but it is death to disobey the Prophet. So, we ran away and left our mothers sobbing."

The aroma of wild rabbit stew was wafting over the campsite, reminding the boys that the hunger pains they were suffering were real and a result of not having eaten all day. As if reading their minds, Reuben stood up to bring back some hot tea and plates of simmering meat. "I am sure we will all feel better after a hearty meal. And a good night's sleep. But first, Danny, what are we to do with these boys?"

Danny addressed the young group as they tucked into a much-needed meal and a hot, sustaining brew of southern tea. "Boys, we heard about the Black Prophet's order. My men will not kill any of you youngsters if we can spare you. We plan to send you to safety."

Mika finished the last of his stew, sopping up the thick dark gravy with a slab of crusty bread baked in a ceramic camp oven. "We are all good hunters, sir. Perhaps we could spend a day hunting tomorrow. The rivers are full of trout at this time of year. We would be happy to help in exchange for your kindness. And if it please you, we could stay on here instead of going to the surgery."

Danny scratched his head. They could use food, but they were on the battle front. "Thank you, young Mika. Game is good, but our people do not eat fish. Another thing. It will be dangerous here. We chase the Prophet's men. Maybe you can help for some days, then you will go to a safe place."

Mika nodded and seemed to relax. "Thank you, sir. We have not had kindness from strangers before. All of us hate the Prophet. All those in our village, I mean."

"Yes, we have heard this. Other boys have said many villages are near starving. The Black Prophet takes all food to feed his army."

"Yes, sir, that is true. But, we have many caves by the lake, and it is there that our fathers have stored much food away from the eyes of the Prophet. So, in our village, we have food. But other villages are not doing so well, and many people are going hungry to feed the fat bellies of the Raiders and the Prophet's family in the palace."

Reuben brought back more hot tea for the boys and a plate full of sweet breads and cheese which the boys devoured in no time. There was also a platter of dried fruits and oatmeal biscuits, a treat that the boys enjoyed as the night wore on and a chill crept in through the night air.

Mika shivered as Atlas put more dried twigs onto the campfire, hoping to keep warm. The wind gusted and sighed as if sharing their emotions.

"Time to sleep," Danny said, noticing Kya yawning. "There are blankets in the wagon. Two of you can go there where it is warm. The other two can sleep in the tent. We have an early rise in the morning and another day of fighting while you go hunting. Pray to our God for protection against the enemy tomorrow and a good night's sleep tonight."

Morning broke with a crisp breeze still flowing through the campsite. Mika awoke wondering where he was, almost forgetting that he was no longer home in his village with his family and friends, which was what he had been dreaming about. Rubbing his eyes, he sat up and opened the tent flap to take a deep breath of fresh air.

Danny and his warriors prepared their horses for the day ahead. Danny intended to keep pressure on the retreating soldiers and drive them in the direction of Prophet City. He turned to Mika. "You boys stay well behind us. There may be fighting. You can work your way through the trees on that hillside and perhaps find some deer."

"Be careful, sir," said Mika. "The Prophet's army may have big cannons."

"We will. If they defend with cannons, we will just attack at night."

Danny turned to several leaders. Their bronzed faces and black hair caught the light of dawn. "I do not expect them to make a stand. The Black Prophet is losing his appeal, even to his own men."

"Yes," said Mika. "It is as I said. People are turning against him everywhere."

†

Robby had heard about the war on the border. It was as if the Prophet had made Shakti his private confidante now that he was planning to marry her when the war ended. But everything he told her, she told Robby, and together they had formed an unbreakable friendship.

"I believe it is the Southerners who have come to fight along the border," Shakti said as they sipped tea in the palace rose gardens. "Martin says he will annihilate those barbarians if it is the last thing he does. And already in the past week, he has been sending the young boys to the border to fight against them. God help those young boys!"

Robby shuddered thinking how difficult it would be for those youngsters with no experience or training in warfare. "I spent two years in the Academy, Shakti, and I know it will be impossible for those boys to survive without any military training. This is nothing more than a suicide mission for those children."

"Yes, I am afraid so. But, Robby, there is something far worse I have to tell you, and I fear that things may not end well. Martin has put out an order to kill Donald, your father, and he wants his head on a platter in return for what happened to Balek Brown. I suppose you heard about that. He has never gotten over that, and he never will!"

Robby's face went pale. "If I get a chance, I will kill the Prophet myself, with my own bare hands, before I would allow that to happen!"

"Yes, but you are banished to your quarters here and have no access to the palace. There is hope, though. I have some information that there are plans to eliminate the Prophet. Trust me, Robby, my source is very reliable. And I believe this will happen any day. Just pray that it happens soon so we can put an end to this war. If the Prophet is captured or executed along with his family, you will be the only heir and successor to his throne."

"What!" exclaimed Robby, wondering where Shakti got her information from. "Sometimes I wonder if you are not still a spy, Shakti. Where did you hear this?"

Shakti put a gentle hand on Robby's arm. "I will tell you, but you must promise me that this will be our secret, Robby."

"Of course, of course. I promise!" Robby said, anxious to know the secrets that filled Shakti's heart. "But, I would have to reveal it if keeping your secret meant harm to my family."

"Agreed. How should I begin? During the last war, I had a friend called Mother Tess who ran an orphanage for abandoned children. She was a good woman, God rest her soul, and it was because of her that I helped your biological mother, Selena, escape from the tower. She planned it all, and years after the war ended, she handpicked five young boys to form a secret society which they would run when they reached eighteen years of age. This group of boys is known as the Liberty Soldiers, and they are planning a coup against the Prophet. No one knows this except me, and what I have to tell you is strictly confidential."

Robby could not believe what he heard as Shakti continued. "I have to tell you this so that you are ready when the day comes. I will never be Martin's wife if this plan goes ahead. And, if it does, I believe you will be the next ruler of Prophet City…and the entire West!"

CHAPTER 29
†

A Day of Executions

When he entered his house, he picked up a knife, took hold of his concubine, cut her into 12 pieces, limb by limb, and then sent her throughout the territory of Israel. Every-one who saw it said, "Nothing like this
has ever happened or has been seen since the day the Israelites came out
of the land of Egypt to this day. Think it over, discuss it, and speak up!"
Judges 19:29-30 HCSB

Civil unrest was spreading throughout the West as discontent and
grumblings continued about the evil actions of the Prophet. News
had reached Martin Abaddon's ears that people were no longer afraid of
voicing their anger. Protests erupted in every town and village. The people
were goaded by the forced conscription of thirteen-year-old boys to fight
against the East.

"I will not allow it!" the Prophet screeched, his face turning purple with
anger and the blood vessels in his neck dilating as if they were about to
explode.

General Logan agreed. They sat in the main chamber of the palace
discussing recent events in the West. Logan responded with a firm plan to
prevent the continuing rise of protesters and to issue a warning to others
of the consequences of turning against the Prophet. "Have they forgotten
the last executions already?" the general asked, reminding Martin that the
people of the West knew the wrath of the Prophet when he felt betrayed. "We
need to impose a series of mass executions, a day they will never forget…a
day which will remind them not to continue their grumblings against us.

Here is a list of the names of those who are voicing their anger and stirring up the population. We could very well have a civil war on our hands if this business is not stopped!"

"I agree," Martin said, glad to receive a copy of the list from his general. "Right, these people need to be arrested straight away and brought to the palace tower. Next week we will begin a public display of mass executions of all those on this list. Anyone else not on this list who causes trouble in the rural and remote areas is to be hung from the trees in their villages as a sign that we will not tolerate those who are mischief-makers!"

"I will see to it, sir, that this is done. My men and I will round them up post haste and deal with these rebels. This will surely silence the mobs of protesters once and for all!"

†

Never had the streets of Prophet City been so awash with the blood of those who had spoken against the Prophet. Forty-five men were executed on a day that would always be remembered in the West as the day of executions. It was a day in which even the sun was afraid to shine, and a dark, gloomy cloud filled the heavens enveloping the hearts of men with an undeniable sense of despair.

In the rural areas, it was common now to see men hanging from trees and left swaying in the wind until grieving families cut them down to bury them as sorrow filled their hearts. Now men whispered in quiet tones about their hatred for the Prophet, and everyone wished the same thing—the death of the Prophet himself.

Inside a cave where the Liberty Soldiers regularly met, the final plans were being laid to eliminate the Prophet, yet even the rest of the Christians were oblivious to the secret business being conducted there.

"We must move quickly," Caleb was saying, as they laid out their maps of the palace grounds and buildings. "At the back of the palace are the family quarters where we will take the Prophet once we kidnap him from his private chambers where he lives and sleeps. But we must take Robby, the adopted son of Donald of Goldstone and the biological son of the Prophet, to safety. All must go to plan. We will also have the help of the Stonegate special operation forces in this coup, so together we can ensure that Robby is unharmed and returned to the palace as the new leader of the West."

Arrow James was keen to complete the plans and prepare for the planned mission. "I am reminded of my visit to Stonegate. Meeting Gray John there and his men since then has been a great honor. We must try to think of every possible pitfall. It would be a disaster if something goes wrong, since we will have only one chance. The special operation team should be here in a few days' time. We must work with them to coordinate our plans and movements."

Jeremiah cleared his throat as he spoke. "It is hard to believe that Robby is the biological son of the Prophet. The information I received shows that he is keeping to himself in the family quarters and living in solitude, spending his days and nights in prayer. Such a contrast of good and evil between him and the Prophet is becoming obvious. Donald of Goldstone must surely have brought him up well in the faith of the Holy Book."

"Yes," Elijah responded. "There is a great difference in their characters. The Prophet is the most evil man on this earth. Yet, Robby, his own flesh and blood by birth, is the complete opposite in character."

"However," Josiah interjected. "It was not always so. Our dear friend Shakti has said that for a long time Robby lost his faith, even turning his back on God until he had a vision in the palace tower of the revelation of God himself who appeared as a light. Shakti said that Robby told her that this changed his life and that since then he has become increasingly close to his God."

"It is a good thing then," said Josiah, "that the man we put on the throne will be a man of faith, like us. So, let us now pray, for the time is near for us to act. This time next week, the West will surely have a new ruler, and a great evil shall be eradicated from the face of this earth, once and for all!"

†

Shakti was frantic. The day of executions had left her torn with shame and grief. She could hardly bear to be in the company of Martin Abaddon. But she knew she must keep her feelings of disgust and contempt to herself. He had not hesitated to imprison Selena, his favorite concubine, in the palace tower when he realized she had helped Isabella escape. There was no doubt in her mind that she was now treading dangerous waters with Martin. If he ever found out she had betrayed him by providing information to the Liberty Soldiers and had also concealed what she knew about the plans that Stonegate had been making against him, she would certainly be imprisoned herself, or more likely, executed.

A shudder ripped through her as she made her usual nightly visit to keep Martin company and partake in a meal and some new wines with him. After all, he was still planning to marry her when the war was over.

"You look as beautiful as ever, my dear Shakti," Martin said, oblivious to her feelings of deepening hatred towards him, as she entered the room wearing a glamorous dress made of fine silk and a string of shining gem-stones around her delicate neck. "I see you are wearing my latest gift of fine stones. How pretty they look against your creamy olive complexion. And how lovely your new gown looks on your womanly figure."

Shakti couldn't stop herself from blushing. "Why thank you, Martin, how kind of you. I do love this new gown and my necklace. But, please, you must stop spoiling me. I'm overwhelmed with these continuous presents, but of course I am sincerely grateful and cannot thank you enough."

"Please, Shakti, do not be overwhelmed. I don't think I ever told you how much you remind me very much of my dear, dear mother. Perhaps that is why we have never been…close."

"I see…" said Shakti. She had thought that nothing he could do or say would surprise her, but she was surprised. "I wondered…"

"I know it has been torture for you—to be so close to me without the fulfillment you deserve. But, at last, I see you for what you are—a desirable woman. When you are my wife, you will receive so much more. But do tell me, how is my son Daniel faring over there in the family quarters? I believe you visit him from time to time?"

"Yes, I will give you the news about Daniel," said Shakti, remembering that this was the name Robby gave the Raiders when he was captured. "Well, his mood is fine, but he likes to keep to himself. He needs some time to adjust to his new life here, but I am sure that soon he will feel just like one of the family. Everything is still new to him."

"Quite new," said Martin. "After all, he was born in the East and brought up as an orphan. I am sure his life there was very different to his life here. So, do tell me, how does he occupy his time?"

"He spends a lot of time outdoors in the gardens...and he likes to read. There are many books in the family library that he enjoys."

"Ah, yes...books my men took from the East. And it is a pity they failed miserably to break into the lore library in Goldstone and bring me those military books for my collection. Never mind; they were severely punished for their failure and will never fail me again. When I win this war, those books will be mine."

"Of course, Martin," Shakti said as she poured him a fine glass of red wine from the new palace wine cellars. "What a lovely drop of red this is. Perhaps the best of all."

"Yes, my wine makers have certainly excelled themselves this time. But they claim it was a very good batch of grapes that are the secret of its success. Take another glass, my dear."

"Why thank you, I do believe I will."

Martin continued nibbling on cheese and grapes as they spoke about the great army which was finishing its training. "I just issued an order for the head of Donald of Goldstone."

Shakti shuddered. "Yes, you already told me that," she said, wondering if the Prophet was becoming forgetful. He had recently been repeating himself, not aware that he had already told her the same thing. Was he losing his memory, or was it the result of indulging in too much wine every evening? His legs were looking a bit swollen, and his face had a yellowish tint.

"I know you should rest more. These problems are wearing you down. I must say you look exhausted this evening," Shakti said noticing the dark circles under Martin's eyes.

"You are right, Shakti. Since the peasants have been revolting I have hardly slept. Still, the day of executions has certainly put a stop to that and any further riots. But perhaps I should retire to my bed early this evening."

Shakti was glad that she could escape. She simply wanted time alone with no more pretending, at least for a while.

CHAPTER 30
†

The Redemption of Robby

We have redemption in Him through His blood, the forgiveness of our
trespasses, according to the riches of His grace that He lavished on us
with all wisdom and understanding.
Ephesians 1:7-8 HCSB

For days, Robby had closed himself off from the rest of the Prophet's
family. He thought of his father and mother constantly. He prayed for
Ari, hoping that she would be safe in her rambling home in the shadow of
the blue mountains. The only person he spoke to was Shakti, except for one
more brief meeting with the Prophet. He sensed evil in him like a foul odor,
though the Prophet had been pleasant, trying to project an air of fatherly
kindness.

It was another cold, dreary day in the palace gardens where Robby spent
most of his time praying. He looked forward to the times when Shakti stole
a few minutes to tell him tidbits of news and offer encouragement.

"I cannot believe my birth father is Martin Abaddon," Robby lamented
as Shakti poured hot cups of tea into earthenware mugs. The steamy liquid
was comforting on these cooler days, and she often brought a treat of warm
buttered scones with homemade orange jam. They ate in the shade of the
elegant pagoda in the center of the rose garden where a screen of shrub-
bery concealed them from prying eyes. "I never met such a man. Is there
anything but evil in his heart?"

"Do not fear him, Robby, for he won't harm you, and do not fear that you are anything like him. You were raised by parents who love you as their own. I can only believe they must have promised Selena that they would raise you in their faith."

"Tell me about my mother, Shakti. Tell me everything you know."

Shakti poured another hot cup of tea from a silver pot as she began her story. "Well, Selena was a few years younger than me, but we knew each other very well, as we were Martin's favorite dancers. But, before she disappeared, Martin preferred her company far more than mine. Selena was enthralled with Martin and even once told me she loved him. When the last war was being fought, it was Selena who asked Martin to have his generals bring her the head of Donald of Goldstone."

Robby went pale and almost dropped his teacup. "So, it was my birth mother who wanted my father dead!"

"Yes, but Robby, you must understand. At that time she was only trying to please and impress Martin. Her life depended on it. But the night that the head of Balek Brown arrived, another servant, Isabella, disappeared. She was terrified that Martin planned to make her one of his concubines. I remember that night; how well I remember! After the head of Balek Brown arrived, Selena went to her room to get away. I saw her there. She kept trembling and was wide-eyed. She knew that Martin was likely to go crazy and perhaps lash out at anyone or everyone. Because Selena left the audience chamber at the same time as Isabella, she fell under suspicion. That night, Isabella was nowhere to be found. Martin blamed Selena for helping her escape. He thought Selena was jealous and was trying to eliminate her rival."

"Oh, dear," said Robby, as he nibbled the last of the scones. "Is that why Martin imprisoned her in the palace tower?"

"Yes, it was. It was a punishment for what Martin thought was her role in Isabella's escape. But during her time in the tower, something happened to her. She told me she had been visited by a person in a white robe who was surrounded by such a blinding light but who spoke gentle and comforting words to her, saying, 'You are my child and I will protect you.'"

"Can it be true, Shakti? That is the same exact thing that happened to me. In the same place. It is what turned me back to God. I knew, with total certainty, that I was in His glorious presence, just as Selena, my birth mother, was. And now all I want is to follow the way, the truth, and the light."

"Robby, there is something about you. I don't know...holy is the best way I can say it. God has a plan for you. You will rule here from this palace. I feel deep in my heart that Martin is losing his mind. He has little time left."

"I have no wish to rule anything," said Robby. "Only to go home. I have no interest in palaces or thrones."

"I know," said Shakti. "But you may not be able to escape your destiny. Perhaps that was the reason that your mother was allowed to escape."

"So, how did my mother, Selena, escape?" Robby asked.

"All I know is that after that vision in the tower, Selena begged me to help her escape and send her to Mother Tess. It was Mother Tess who later confided that Selena was carrying Martin's child. One night, when Martin was in a drunken stupor, I took the keys to her cell. There was a short time during the changing of the guard when the way was unguarded. I opened the door to her cell, lowered her down from the wall with a rope, and let her go. Mother Tess was waiting for her with a horse and they both rode off into the night. Mother Tess told me later that she had sent Selena to the East by a courier who knew the way."

"So, she must have arrived in Stonegate in a very distressed state," said Robby. "And then when she gave birth to me she must have either died or fled."

"Selena loved children, Robby. She would never have given you up. The only thing that makes sense is that she died during childbirth and your parents brought you up as their own."

"What a truly amazing story! So, Selena was transformed by her experience in the tower. I would like to think that at least my birth mother had a good heart."

"Oh, yes, Robby. Underneath the facade she put on for Martin, she was a kind and loving person. In fact, Mother Tess said that Selena asked if she could have a Holy Book to take with her to Stonegate so she could learn more about God. None of us believe a particle about the Prophet's cult."

"That gives me much consolation, Shakti, knowing that my mother died believing in the faith."

"Yes, and I was curious about your God, but it wasn't until I met Charlie that I really came to believe. And now I pray every night for peace and an end to the war. Too much innocent blood has been and is still being shed even as we speak. And outside these walls, the people are starving and rising up against the Prophet, who is fast losing his power and appeal in the West."

Robby finished the last of his tea as the day came to an end and an early full moon rose. "What a strange silver moonlight tonight. It is almost as if it is trying to send us a message of some sort, of change coming."

"Yes," said Shakti. "I noticed it too. That is not the only strange sign in the sky and the heavens. Perhaps the war will end soon, and we will have peace. The moonlight is comforting and perhaps ominous, but I feel there are good things to come."

"Yes," Robby said. "I hope you are right. I am not sure I can be patient much longer. I may have to try to get out of here even though I don't see a way. My beautiful Ari consumes my every thought."

"I miss Charlie in the same way and pray that somehow this will all end, and we will be reunited with those we love."

†

Martin was pacing in his private quarters as Shakti entered the room. "What is it, Martin? You seem to be upset?"

"Yes. I was very troubled over reports that Donald of Goldstone has crossed the border with a small army and coming this way. I have a plan to deal with him, but the audacity…"

There seemed to be a commotion of some sort in the outer court. Shakti turned her head toward the large eastern window, and there were the sounds of marching feet. "What is it?" she said. "It sounds like a body of troops in the palace courtyard."

"Don't be frightened, little Shakti," said the Prophet. "I merely ordered the palace defenses strengthened. I can't believe that this small force would be so daring as to come here. But I hope they do."

"Why?" asked Shakti. She tried to go to the window to look out, but the Prophet grabbed her arm and held her back.

"Because we are ready for them."

Cannon fire shook the palace. Shakti shook off the Prophet's hand and ran to the window. Ranks of armored men filled the courtyard. She had barely time to comprehend what she was seeing when the eastern gate was blown into pieces, which went flying towards her. She ducked, even though none actually hit the window.

The Prophet snarled. "We are being invaded as we speak, and I will bet you anything that Donald of Goldstone is in command!"

"But that is impossible, Martin. Don't you have thirty thousand foot soldiers out there protecting Prophet City?" A chill went down Shakti's spine as she prayed that Robby did not hear the news.

"Yes. More than that, actually. This is going to turn out very well. Although I still can't believe they were so bold. It seems almost as if they must have some other plan than a mad raid."

The firing grew louder and shook the floor under their feet. General Logan came striding in. His face was pale, but he appeared confident. "A raid, just as you foresaw, Sire," he said. "We have beaten them back and will trap them at the pass."

"Very good, general. Keep me informed." The Prophet waved him away, then seemed to be aware for the first time that many of the palace servants were clustered in the audience chamber as if to seek a place of safety. "All the rest of you, go back to your duties. This little problem is solved."

Martin led Shakti towards his large windows where the sky was streaked with columns of smoke. Empty now, the only troops visible in the courtyard were a dozen guarding the portal where the gate had stood. "I truly hope this Donald will be taken alive. But alive or dead, he will soon trouble me no more!"

†

Robby could hear gunfire outside the palace walls as he made his way back to his small room near the servant's quarters. He had trained for battle and wished he could join the fight, since it must be some kind of raid by forces from Stonegate. *Or could it be a revolution? Shakti would know, but I have no way to contact her.* He tried to go out the entrance to the courtyard, but four men in full armor blocked his exit and shooed him away.

Then he tried to shake off his frustration in the only way he knew. He returned to his room, turned to his Holy Book, and prayed. "Oh Father in heaven, keep my father, Don, safe from harm during this war. And if it is him and his men out there, give them victory over the evil enemy. Failing that, let them ride free from capture."

He turned to a page in the Holy Book which inspired him to keep praying deep into the long night. And the last thing he read before he fell asleep was, "The Philistine commanders continued to go out to battle, and as often as they did, David met with more success than the rest of Saul's officers, and his name became well known." 1 Samuel 18:30.

The thought ever in Robby's mind was the hope that his father, Don, would meet with success in battle and that his name once again would be known all over the land.

CHAPTER 31
†

The Invasion

Their horses are swifter than leopards and more fierce than wolves of
the night. Their horsemen charge ahead; their horsemen come from
distant lands. They fly like an eagle, swooping to devour.
Habakkuk 1:8 HCSB

The scouts left sometime after midnight. They were ordered to lead their
horses up narrow trails along the ridge tops that ran parallel to the main
body's move down the highway in the valley bottom. Another secondary
road also ran in about the same direction a few miles to the north, and
Hamway proposed sending the Black Eagle troop along that way. Don was
uneasy about splitting his forces, so Hamway showed him a rough sketch
map by the light of a candle.

"Look here," said Hamway, pointing with a twig. "The roads will join
before we spill out onto the plain. And this way we can be sure that both
routes are swept clean."

"Why can't the scouts check to the north as we go?" asked Don.

"There are many groves of aspen and spruce-fir, and the scouts won't
have time to clear them. A sizeable force could be concealed there. But a
horse troop can check as they go. I think this plan will improve security,
not weaken us."

Don thought it over. It was a last-minute change, but it seemed logical.
"Very well," he said. "Make it so."

There is a good reason that commanders dislike movements at night.
The moonless sky gave little light, and a few candles offered poor light to

saddle horses and hitch teams. The leaders of each mount carried a small lantern, though, and the others followed the light down paths leading to the highway. Don fumbled the saddling like many others, feeling to make sure that the blanket and cinches were properly in place. Skipper blew a warm snort in his face as if to ask what was going on. But once they moved, he seemed to have no trouble picking a path.

The first glow of dawn lit the surrounding peaks as the column gained three or four miles down the wide road descending from the pass. Voices remained hushed, and the main noises were horses' hooves crunching gravel and the wheels of the three artillery pieces in the battery. Don rode near the front with Colin McCoy and Hamway. Ardmore, Red Horse troop leader, was just ahead.

Don wondered how the special force of Red Horse troopers fared. The well-trained men should have infiltrated the city by now if all had gone well. He knew that they had also taken pigeons for reporting back to Stonegate. It was ironic that Stonegate might know more about what was happening than he did since there was no fast way for Stonegate to get messages back to him.

A scout came galloping back up the road and approached Don's banner. He reined his horse to a stop and saluted. "The scouts came upon a guard-post. We surrounded them before they could do much. They are all bound and disarmed."

Don and the others gave praise and thanks, and the lead elements broke into a trot. They came around a gentle bend and noticed a stone house by the side of the road. A half-dozen scouts waited there, and several figures were sitting, backs against the walls of the house.

Colin galloped ahead and began a conversation with the scouts when Don rode up.

The scouts gave their report. Colin and Hamway briefly questioned them, but they ordered the main column to keep moving.

"Anything unusual?" asked Don.

"They did not seem to be expecting trouble, but two were awake," answered one lad, a senior cadet. "We subdued them and then captured the others still in their beds. They had a cage of pigeons by the door, and one was able to set them free. I can't think of anything else unusual."

"Did they attach a message to the pigeons?" asked Colin. He had dismounted and looked up at Don with a frown.

"Oh, no, sir," the scout replied. "No time for that. He just stepped over to the cage and opened the door before we realized what he was doing. He shooed them out and they all fluttered away somewhere."

They left two of the younger troopers to escort the prisoners back to the camp where the artillery was emplaced. Then they ordered the scouts to continue on, and the main body followed them. "I don't like this thing about the pigeons," said Colin. "But at least they won't be carrying a message."

"The arrival of all the pigeons at once might be a message, itself," said Don. "That might be a kind of emergency signal."

"What should we do about it?" asked Hamway.

"Nothing we can do," said Don. "We just continue on."

Dawn had broken, and the sun's first appearance was near when they heard the clash of swords on shields and the cries of battle. Hamway ordered his troop to advance at a gallop and a bugler sounded "Charge." Don started ahead, lowering his spear, but he felt a hand on his arm. He looked to see Colin shaking his head.

"Time to let the young ones show what they can do," he shouted.

Don nodded, slowing Skipper to a slow trot. Gray John and the cadet troop advanced in columns of two, flowing by Don, Colin, and their five bodyguards. Don looked at one of the young men responsible for guarding him. His face was an icon of dismay. He seemed to fear missing the action more than he feared battle. *It would be nice to be young again. These lads still think they can't be hurt.*

The battle was brief as it was fierce. When Don arrived at the scene, it was already over. About fifteen Raiders still sat on their dun mounts, hands raised. An equal number of the rugged little horses wandered in circles, saddles empty. Don observed a Stonegate horse down, and a patch of blood had already stained the soil black. Don could tell that two roads joined at the battlefield, and the Black Eagle banner showed that they had met the other troop.

Hamway's horse plunged to a stop near the banner. "Black Eagle troop chased this lot down the road, and they met our lead elements here. We trapped them between us."

"What are our losses?" asked Don.

"One dead," said Hamway. "One of the cadets. Five wounded. The Black Eagle healer seems to have the bleeding stopped on the worst of these. We lost one horse dead and five seriously hurt. We will probably have to put some down."

Don asked to see the body of the cadet, and he was directed to him. He rode over to see a blonde-haired young man with his head in another cadet's lap. Don was struck at how pale the body looked as contrasted to the red faces of his friends. Tears were flowing freely.

Don dismounted and walked to the knot of grieving cadets. He knelt and wiped some blood off the quiet face. Someone had already closed his eyes. "He died well," Don said, standing up. "Remember that. There are worse ways to die."

"What shall we do with him?" asked one cadet. "We can't just leave him here."

"We will let the lightly wounded take his body back to the camp," answered Don. "Along with the prisoners."

The horse holders brought up some remounts to replace the wounded Stonegate horses. Don decided to take six of the dun Raider horses along with them, in case they would be needed to carry more captives from Prophet City. "God willing," Don said, "the Prophet will be riding one of these back this way."

†

The first look at Prophet City was striking. Don felt intimidated as he saw the large plain below, dotted by dwellings, stretching far into the distance. He could see that the road they must take had a sharp bend to the north where tall buildings gleamed in the rosy sunshine. Ruins filled more of the near distance than anything else, but the old street grid was still obvious. It formed a checkerboard pattern, and trees still stood in proud lines. He called for a halt to give their horses a rest while he inspected the scene below with his binoculars. Some other leaders had small telescopes, and they all looked intently for any signs of military units.

But all seemed quiet and peaceful. A few wagons and carts moved along, and some were even coming up the road towards them. But nothing seemed to pose a threat. He dared not delay longer and gave the order to advance at a trot. Their banners flapped in the breeze. The time for concealment was over, and they went to war under their own flags. But somehow, it seemed a bit too easy, as if a malignant force wanted them to enter, like a spider luring its prey into a carefully constructed web.

The last ten miles took an hour, and a long hour it was. They met wagons, but the civilians pulled to the side and stared at the long column, mouths agape. Some shouted oaths, but a number seemed to have the opposite reaction. One bearded farmer shouted, "You're from Stonegate, and it is about time. Go get that son of a—" Then his voice was stilled by a sharp jab in the ribs from his big-bosomed wife. But she did not wipe the smile off his face. None of the civilians offered any resistance and seemed content to be spectators in the drama unfolding before them.

As before, they passed by several outposts, which seemed to be tax collection booths, with a handful of guards at each one. They all realized that there was no sense in fighting and were quickly subdued. At the second outpost, Colin dismounted and came back with a canvas sack filled with coins. Don chided him. "We are not here to loot, Colin. Put the money back."

"I am not looting," came the answer. "I plan to give it back to the people." Don thought for a moment and then nodded approval.

The gravel gave way to flagstone paving, and the horses' hooves made a ringing drumbeat as steel shoes struck sparks from the stones. They turned onto a wide ceremonial avenue, with tall trees on both sides, which led directly to the palace. Many multi-story buildings, in good repair, lined the way, but they were all set back with green lawns before them. The city was beautiful, particularly when the temple, clad in white marble, came into view. It was Don's turn to gape. It was easily the grandest building he had ever seen. The troopers' eyes opened as wide as children at Christmas. There was not the slightest hint of resistance, and the streets remained strangely bare of pedestrians. It was as if a stage was set but with missing actors.

Then several children darted from the side streets to see the excitement, and Colin began tossing coins to them from the sack. "Take this and stay out of the way," he shouted to the youngsters. "There might be trouble." But the coin tossing drew more people out, and Don concluded that it was just going to cause problems.

A knot of old women sat by some vegetable stands, and Don pointed at them. "Throw them the whole sack, and tell them to take cover," he said. Colin complied and tossed the sack at their feet, then laughed at their astonished faces. "Go hide, mothers," he said. "This is not a time to be out and about."

†

The troopers had little need for orders as they entered the great plaza that faced the palace. Everyone had rehearsed their parts, and horse troops moved to surround the walled grounds on all sides. The gunners unhitched the guns and emplaced them about one hundred yards before the gate. Just then an enemy gun wheeled into view from a tower at the right corner of the wall, and it fired with a loud report and a great cloud of white gunsmoke. The concussion made them jump, and echoes returned from the mountains before Don's heart quit thudding in his chest. Strangely, though, the gunners had not aimed at the horsemen thronging the square, and the ball sailed harmlessly over their heads.

"Take that gun under fire," ordered Don, and the gunners jumped to comply. One gun had already taken aim and fired on the battery commander's order. The horse troopers had wisely given the guns a wide firing lane, but there was still some confusion as horses jumped, reared and tried to bolt. Again, the echoes rolled and a white cloud of rock dust obscured the tower, as another cloud of smoke from the gun billowed up before them.

The cheer from the horse troops rose before Don could observe the results, but when the smoke cleared, it was obvious that the enemy gun had taken a direct hit. The gunners began to reload as the other two guns swiveled to take aim at the large wooden gate that barred entrance to the palace grounds. It took two volleys, but the field pieces soon smashed the heavy beams to splinters. The way was now clear to enter. So far, all was proceeding according to plan.

Skipper shook his head as if his ears hurt, but at each volley he jumped less and less, as he seemed to understand that the loud noise would not hurt him. Don leaned forward to pat him on the neck and almost gave the order to advance, when armored men, armed with long pikes, streamed out of the gate. It appeared that there would be resistance after all.

Two scouts appeared from both sides of the palace walls and galloped up to him. Both had the same tale to tell, but the first to arrive shouted, "Sir, large numbers of pikemen are moving up the streets from behind the palace. I don't know how many, but it looks like thousands."

Don choked as if steel fingers gripped him around the throat, leaving him almost speechless. *Could this be a trap? Did they know we were coming? Oh, God, to be so near.*

"What are your orders?" asked Colin. "Do you want to continue the assault?"

"No," said Don. The word tasted like gall in his mouth. "We can't stand against a force like that. We will have to retreat." Hamway galloped up to him, his face set as grim as a bear trap. "Hamway," he ordered, "Pull back the horse troopers now. We will retreat the way we came in."

Hamway issued the orders and sent the two scouts to carry them to the horse troop commanders. Don turned to the battery commander. "Load with beehive rounds. We will have to cover the retreat."

Then the whole square erupted into confusion. A crossbow bolt glanced off stones next to Don, and he turned to see that the top of a building behind him had a crowd of armored men. They were in a killing box and had to get out of it. Colin shouted to the gunners, "Take up your muskets and return fire." The gunners jumped to comply, just as the guns fired a volley of the deadly beehive rounds into the foot soldiers coming out of the palace gates. They acted like a huge shotgun shell, and the deadly pellets flew through the air with a buzzing sound like swarms of angry bees. Dozens of the enemy fell, and the wall became painted in a spray of bright crimson.

Some horse troopers dropped their lances to take up their bows and return fire at the crossbowmen above them. But Hamway shouted, "Keep your lances. We will need them to get clear."

Horse troops began galloping back from both sides of the walled compound, following orders to continue back down the wide avenue leading out of the city. Hamway held the Red Horse troop to act as rear guard. Soon after the mounted troopers passed by, ranks of foot soldiers appeared on both sides of the walls, all armed with long and deadly pikes. It looked like a moving forest, but with tips of steel rather than leaves of green.

The guns fired volley after volley at the oncoming ranks, but it was obvious that they could not hold them off. There were too many, and they did not break. They kept coming, despite grievous losses. For the first ranks, it became sheer slaughter as men fell in bloody piles. But the following pikemen simply stepped over the bodies and continued to advance. Don gave the order for the gunners to hitch up and pull back.

Don had half expected more infantry to try to block their escape, so he ordered the guns to proceed at a gallop toward the head of the retreating column. He feared that they might have to fire on a blocking force if one existed. Some horses were down, hit by crossbow bolts, and some horses were carrying double, but the mail armor proved effective in preventing mortal wounds for the riders. Gradually, the square emptied as the horse troops retraced their tracks.

A few gunners, riding in wagons, continued to fire muskets at the oncoming infantry, reloading as fast as they could. Unlike the crossbow bolts, the musket balls easily penetrated enemy shields and armor, but it was like trying to kill a maddened grizzly bear with pinpricks.

Don and Colin left the rear guard and rode at a gallop to get to the head of the column. They were sure that any more threats would be in that direction, and they needed to know what was happening.

As they departed the built-up part of the city and turned south on the highway, they could see that the enemy had intended to cut off their retreat, but they had reacted too quickly for that to work. A large force of pikemen, several thousand at least, was marching south, but it was obvious that they would not arrive in time. The way ahead seemed clear, and Don began to relax. He was bitterly disappointed that their raid had ended in failure, but at least they had escaped the Prophet's trap.

They had covered perhaps five miles and had slowed the horses to a trot. A gallop is good for covering ground quickly, but a horse at that speed will tire after only a couple of miles. A well-conditioned horse can trot for many times that distance. The horse troopers had slowed to permit the three guns to be near the head of the retreating riders.

Don called a halt to allow the horses to rest. Many were soaked with sweat, and the team pulling the gun next to him had white lather around the collar. Fortunately, there was a creek nearby, and they took the time to allow the horses to take a brief drink. But they had to be careful; too much water, too quickly, would be worse than not enough.

Don thought he saw movement on the ridges ahead where the highway climbed out of the plain toward the pass. He looked through the binoculars, and a chill went through him. The movement was riders, many of them. The sun glinted off burnished armor. They were enemy cavalry, and they were blocking their retreat. He looked closer and saw a battery of guns on the point of a ridge.

Don saw that Skipper had enough water for now, so he led him away from the creek. He was preparing to mount when Hamway rode up. "Scouts report a large body of infantry moving up from the south," he reported. "I guess we know where the Prophet's thirty thousand foot soldiers are. They are all converging on us."

"They can form a blocking force, but we can move much faster than they can," said Don. "It is the enemy cavalry that has me worried."

Don handed him the binoculars. "Look at the ridges ahead. They are blocking our way, and they are on fresh horses. There are artillery batteries, too."

CHAPTER 32

†

The Great Escape

The horses' hooves then hammered- the galloping, galloping of his
stallions.
Judges 5:22 HCSB

Thomas of Longmont paced about the top of a small knoll he had chosen
for his command post. He had sent for Carla but seemed to not exactly
know what he wanted to say to her. She waited patiently while he struggled
to collect his thoughts. Then he turned and asked, "Good job escorting the
wounded and prisoners back. That showed real initiative."

"I had sent some of my archers to the ridge top to keep an eye on the
highway," said Carla, pointing to the west. "They saw two horse troopers
returning with the prisoners, so we all rode down to meet them. The troopers were keen to hurry back and catch up, but...I may have exceeded my
authority."

"What do you mean?"

"It appeared foolish to me. They would only arrive with their mounts
winded, so I told them we needed their help here. I told a white lie."

Thomas raised his eyebrows and cleared his throat as if trying to keep
a straight face. "Is that so?"

"Yes. I told them that the girls needed them as an escort. I asked them
to stay as a favor to me. They seem to hold me in a bit of awe because of
those songs. Anyway, they finally agreed, and I think it did give their spirits
a boost. They felt ashamed to have been sent to the rear..."

"I see. Well done, and we can use them. We don't have any scouts, and I need your archers to patrol to see if any enemy units are approaching. We need warning if there are."

"I left Ari and four other girls on that ridge to the west. They can see a long way down the highway, and they have a signal mirror." She pointed toward an aspen-covered hill, with a rocky, barren top."

"I am impressed," said Thomas. "Do they know the heliograph code?"

"Unfortunately, not, but they do have four codes. They can send 'all clear,' 'enemy approaching,' and 'friendly approaching.' I can also send them a signal for 'return to base.' That's all."

"Hmm. Very well. Make sure there is always someone here to receive signals from them. Have you been able to communicate?"

"Yes, they signaled that friendly forces are approaching. That was nearly an hour ago, remember?"

"Yes. I wondered at the time how we received that news so quickly," Thomas said. He gestured down toward the highway. "It appears that they are arriving now."

They walked down the hill to meet the approaching group. A dozen of Carla's archers was escorting them. A score of captured raiders, hands bound, walked in single file. But the eight wounded troopers were their first concern. Some wounds were sword cuts on the arms and legs. Painful they were, and needing sutures, but once the bleeding was stanched, they were not life-threatening. The healers had applied compression bandages, and they were able to resume their duties. But several had more serious wounds and two were unconscious and had been tied across saddles. Twenty enemy dun-colored horses were being herded by two young horse-holders. It was a large group, and Thomas issued orders to take the wounded to the healer's tent and the prisoners to a holding area. The quiet morning had changed to a scene of confused activity, all in the space of minutes.

Carla saw two gunners removing the dead lad from a Raider horse. Tears sprang to her eyes as she moved to help. She recognized the boy as a friend of Robby's, but could not remember his name. For some reason that lapse of memory was a knife twisting in her soul. *Oh God! This is so hard! Is he to be the first of many?*

Carla's archers had all been trained in first aid, and one, Ramona, had shown real talent. Fortunately, she was one of the group that escorted the wounded to the tent that was acting as a field hospital. Carla assigned her to help Wyatt, the healer. Carla personally spent a half-hour assisting as best she could. By that time, they had treated four troopers and returned them to light duty. One lad had an arrow in the throat, and the barbed tip was still in the wound.

Fortunately, he was unconscious, and Wyatt proceeded to perform surgery. He picked up a flask of alcohol. "Pour this over my hands and over this tray of instruments," he ordered.

Ramona, a slight girl with dark hair and sparkling brown eyes, hastened to comply. Carla then washed her hands in alcohol and prepared to assist.

"Now take a swab and clean his throat around the arrow."

Carla did so, washing off the black blood to make the wound as clean as possible. "Why did they leave the arrow in his wound?"

"The healer knew that he might bleed to death if he tried to pull it out. He merely broke off the shaft and put a light bandage around it to stabilize the wound."

Wyatt's hands were quick and sure as he made the necessary incision and removed the barbed point. He tied off the minor bleeds and removed foreign matter. Then he sutured the wound partly closed, but allowed a small opening for drainage.

"Why is he unconscious?" asked Carla.

"I am not sure," answered Wyatt. "He has a large knot on the back of his head. If there is damage to his spinal cord…"

"We will probably lose him?" asked Ramona.

"Probably."

†

The camp began to quiet down, and Carla proposed that she divide her archers into three groups. One would stay with the guns, one would patrol northwest up the main highway to see if there were any enemy in that direction, and the third would return the way they had come. They sent out three horse troopers with each of the two patrols. Four troopers were wounded, but they insisted that they could still fight.

Time passed slowly, but finally, the first patrol reported that the way was clear back the way they had passed before. They had seen nothing except civilian travelers but had warned them that the way ahead was dangerous, advising them to camp for a day and not go on.

Before noon, they began to hear rumbles to the west, sounding like a distant thunderstorm. Carla and Thomas broke off talking to the patrol. The commander of the culvern battery, a husky, dark-haired man from Ariel named Chad, nicknamed Beefy, frowned and shook his head.

"Is that what I think it is?" asked Carla.

"It's gunfire, if you were thinking that," said Beefy.

"Can we hear guns firing in Prophet City?" asked Thomas. "It's thirty miles away."

"Easily," said Beefy.

†

The other patrol was obviously not bringing good news. They returned at a gallop, looking over their shoulders. At first, Carla thought they were just letting their horses have a run. Then, over the ridge behind them appeared a line of armored horsemen, war spears aloft. Thomas and Beefy were a few paces away and held a huddled conversation.

Thomas shouted, "Fire all tubes. Reload with exploding shells." Beefy ran to make sure the gunners understood. As soon as the returning riders were clear, the guns began to fire on the oncoming cavalry. The ground shook and Carla held her hands over her ears. The scattered riders did not present easy targets, particularly for solid shot, but the culverns were deadly accurate. Three horses and riders were struck down like one would swat flies. A few of the friendly guns fired after a delay, caused by gunners cutting fuses to the proper length before seating the shells. These all exploded in the air over the heavy cavalry, leaving small black puffs overhead and showering a deadly rain of steel fragments. More horses and riders went down. The gunners began reloading, but before they had finished swabbing the bores, the enemy turned and fled, leaving dead and wounded behind.

The returning patrol did not slow until it arrived at the camp. Three dismounted and ran up the slope to the command post. One was a young archer and the others were two of the lightly wounded horse troopers.

The archer, out of breath, took off her helmet and brushed back her tousled chestnut hair with a free hand as she approached Carla. "We stirred up a hornet's nest," she said. "That was good shooting."

One of the horse troopers saluted and spoke at the same time. "We ran into five or six enemy horse troops and a couple of batteries of light field artillery."

"One at a time," said Thomas. "Let the young lady talk first."

She seemed surprised, but confirmed the count. "But I don't think we stopped them. They can go another way."

"There is another road heading west," said the trooper. "It runs down a valley north of this one."

"What does that mean?" asked Carla.

"It means that hundreds more may have already gone by. Heading west, I mean," said the trooper. His bandaged right arm was black with sweat and blood.

"Then they don't have to use the main highway," said Thomas. He paused for a long moment as if in thought. "They could have seen us and taken the other route."

"They certainly won't come this way now," said the trooper. "They don't have to."

Carla remembered the sketch map of the area. It had clearly shown the other road. She had not been concerned since their mission had only been to fire on anyone chasing friendly troops when they returned.

"Is everyone all right?" asked Carla. The girl nodded, and then Carla noticed that she was crying. "Jenny, what's wrong?"

"I killed a horse," she said and then her voice choked.

"What do you mean?"

"He was a beautiful sorrel, running like the wind. My arrow hit him in the throat." her voice failed there, and Carla took her in her arms. She was shaking.

"A half-dozen enemy scouts tried to cut us off," said the trooper. "They did have fast horses and came close enough to send shafts our way. I've never seen anything like it."

"What happened?" demanded Thomas.

"These girls loosed a volley of arrows at them. Four of their horses went down, and the others turned back. I don't think any of them got away unscathed. These lasses can ride with me anytime."

†

More thunder came from the west. Carla hurried back to the command post to report a mirror signal from Ari, saying they had sighted enemy troops. Thomas and Wyatt had been discussing something. In fact, it appeared to be an argument.

"What is it?" she asked.

"I was explaining that it is too dangerous just yet to allow him to go to treat the enemy wounded," answered Thomas.

"Maybe you are fine with allowing them to lie out there and suffer, but I am not," said Wyatt. He stamped off, heading to the hospital tent.

"What is it?" asked Thomas. Carla noticed that his hands were slightly shaking and beads of sweat dotted his forehead.

"Ari reports seeing enemy troops. I signaled her to return to camp."

"More troops, or the same ones our patrol saw, I wonder," said Thomas. "Why did you want her to return?"

"Because I want all the archers back here. The enemy is blocking Don's force. We have to do something."

"What? I have orders to stay here until he returns."

"But the situation has changed. We can't just sit here. We have to move the guns down the highway and try to clear a path."

Thomas stared at her, then his jaw muscles flexed, and he flushed. "Carla, you are a gifted archer, and they sing songs about you. But don't pretend to be a military leader."

"I know what I am," said Carla. "But even I know that splitting one's force in the face of the enemy is a bad idea."

"So, you know more than Don or me, is that it? You understand as much about strategy as a pig does about Christmas. I have been told to protect the culverns from capture, and that is what I intend to do."

"Protect your precious guns if they are more important than the lives of Don and his men. If you won't go to help, my girls and I will go alone."

"No, you won't. I won't allow it!"

"You can't stop us!" said Carla. She felt her cheeks burn. *My face is probably as red as my hair. I have to control my temper. What can I say?*

There was a long silence. "What about the wounded?" Thomas asked in a calmer voice. "Wyatt is worried that if we move them, they might die."

"That is up to you," said Carla. "I think that splitting our force yet again is a mistake. But we can't sit here like a bump on a log."

†

Gray John rode forward as Don was preparing to mount. "I hope it has come to your attention that a large force of infantry is following us," he said.

"I know," said Don, "And still more are approaching from the south and west. Still a good distance away."

Hamway lowered his spyglass. "That is not the worst," he said. "There are horsemen on the hills ahead."

Gray John whistled. "We are truly mouse-trapped. I thought this was entirely too easy. They knew we were coming."

"Doesn't this shake your faith, John?" asked Hamway. "God seems to have turned His back on us."

"Some kinds of faith need to be shaken," said John. He seemed to be as cool as ice. "Even if He kills me, yet will I love Him. Now let us venture something. We can't wait here."

A gust of wind whipped by, stirring up a cloud of reddish dust and flying weeds. At just that time, Don thought he heard what might be guns firing, but it was a long way away, and he was not sure.

†

More thunder rolled to the west. Carla and her archers led the column down the main highway though they sent a few horse-holders ahead as scouts. They were lightly armed, but their horses were fast, so they would have to do. But every other available man, except the gunners, had donned armor and rode ahead of the guns. The mail-clad men numbered only fifteen. With the archers, they totaled less than seventy, but they bore every Stonegate banner they found in the supply wagons. Carla hoped they made a brave show.

Wyatt was fuming about the risk to the wounded, and he rode in a supply wagon with them to give what aid he could. The three culverns came ahead of the other batteries and the ammunition wagons.

Five miles down from the pass they spotted mail-clad riders ahead. The three culverns were quickly wheeled around and emplaced and fired at a distance of one thousand yards. But the enemy did not disperse, and three light artillery batteries also emplaced and loaded their guns with beehive rounds.

The enemy cavalrymen did not lack courage. Even though they suffered losses in the first volley, they risked everything on a frontal charge. But the beehive rounds, like giant shotgun shells, shredded them. A few emerged from the cloud of powder smoke to be met with fire from the gunner's muskets and a volley of arrows from Carla's archers. At the last, the horses refused to continue, whirled and bolted to the rear. Then the entire force retreated.

Gunners reloaded with exploding shells which rained death down upon them as they pulled back. The highway was littered with forms of the fallen. It was an apocalyptic nightmare of horror and death. Carla looked around. All of her archers looked ashen, frozen in shock. When she looked back, the way ahead was clear.

✝

A ridge ahead to the west of the road showed movement. Don did not need his binoculars to see that the enemy was emplacing a light battery of three guns. He returned to consult with his battery commander. "Are they within range of the road?" he asked, pointing them out.

"I am afraid so, but we may be able to outrange them."

"When you are in range, take them under fire."

They proceeded on for a quarter-mile and then halted while the guns were unhitched and trained on the ridge. They fired several volleys, which were returned. But the enemy shells fell short, and the black blooms of air bursts appeared over the enemy guns, which immediately fell silent.

"Very well," said Don. "Good shooting. Hitch up. We have to press on."

They had not gone far when distant gunfire sounded to the east. *Now what? It sounds as if Thomas might be under attack, and we can't help him.*

✝

Carla rode just behind the culvern gunners. Their clothes and faces were as sooty as chimney sweeps, but several flashed her wide grins. Their white teeth and eyeballs made a contrast that would be humorous at any other time. *So far, our losses have been light. How long will that continue?*

It did not take long for them to hit another roadblock. As they approached a curve that bent to the right around a low ridge, they met the two horse-holders returning. "Guns just ahead," they shouted.

Beefy and Carla rode back and up the side of the opposite ridge to where they could look ahead. Through a screen of spruce, they saw the road. Four artillery batteries, twelve guns, were emplaced a mere three hundred yards past the bend. All guns were trained, waiting for their column to appear. It was a clever trap, and there was no way around them.

"God save us," said Beefy. "If we try to push guns up to fire, they will meet us with a hail of shot. We would be butchered, and the long range of the culverns will not help a bit."

"What can we do?"

"I'm blasted if I know," said Beefy. "We may eventually overwhelm them, but we might lose half of our guns doing it."

✝

The enemy infantry moved much slower than Don's horses and wagons, but the jaws of the trap continued to close. They hurried south at a fast trot, drawing near to where the road turned east and climbed up to the pass. They heard more volleys of gunfire ahead, much closer now.

"What is happening? asked Hamway. "Do you think the camp is under attack?

"It sounds quite close," said Gray John. "But sound can be deceiving."

"Our scouts are coming back," said Don. "Perhaps they can tell us something."

The news was bad. The scouts reported that the highway leading east, back over the pass, was blocked by hundreds of enemy horsemen, seemingly waiting, patiently waiting, for them to arrive. They had also emplaced guns along the ridge, ready to cut Don's force to shreds if he massed them to charge.

"Perhaps we need to abandon the guns and wagons and break out to the west. There are still gaps between the infantry columns." Gray John offered the advice tentatively as if thinking out loud.

"Our horses are tired, and theirs are fresh," said Hamway. "They are probably hoping we would do that. They would just pour out of the pass and run us down, and most likely we are outnumbered."

"And we would be going deeper into the False Prophet's territory," said Don.

"The only other choice is to try to thin out their numbers with our battery," said Gray John. "It has a longer range. Then, before the infantry gets here, we risk it all on one glorious charge. At least we will die fighting."

✝

"Beefy," said Carla. "The town guns would often fire their shells in an arch over the city walls. The gunners could not see what they were shooting at, but spotters on the wall would tell them where the shells were landing."

"Yes," said Beefy, "That is called indirect fire. But my culvern gunners are trained only for direct fire, and I am sure your gunners are trained the same way. The only indirect fire gunners are back at Stonegate." He looked at the scene below one more time. The column was halted on the near side of the ridge, and the enemy guns were still there. But a number of horsemen seemed to be forming up behind the gunners.

"I am afraid that they might be planning another frontal cavalry charge, and our guns are not ready to fire," said Carla. "They could pour over the ridge and be among our people almost without warning."

"You are right," said Beefy. "Perhaps I should ride down and order them to fall back and emplace our guns to withstand another charge."

What would be best? Either way could be right or be exactly wrong.

"Perhaps the guns and wagons should pull back, as you say," said Carla. "But if you kept some cannons in range of the enemy guns, I could direct their fire from here."

"That might work. We can try to figure out how to do it. But how would you signal us?"

"I have a signal mirror. All my girls have one. They use it for other things, too—like looking at themselves—but I can signal."

"But do you have a code for directing fire?"

"No, but I can give two flashes for shells left of target, three for right of target, and so on."

Beefy agreed, and they quickly settled on basic signals. Then he rode back down the slope through the trees to the highway. Carla waited, heart thudding, as the column began to retrace its path back up the canyon. But everything seemed to move like an ant stuck in honey. Slowly, tortuously, the column moved back. Carla realized that she should be down below directing her archers. She realized that in her absence, the girls would look to Ari to command them. *Is she up to the job? Have I made a terrible mistake? I should have had him send Ari back up here to signal for me.*

✝

Don advanced to the bottom of the highway leading back up and over the pass. He realized that the scouts were correct. There were many batteries of guns ahead, and the spaces between them were filled with hundreds of heavy cavalry. They were outnumbered at least two to one, and perhaps more waited there than he could see. He looked back toward the advancing infantry. He thought he had twenty minutes before they would converge on his force.

"Maybe we should fire a few times at the foot troops, just to slow them down," said Hamway.

"No," said Gray John. "We need to concentrate fire ahead."

Colin McCoy shouted instructions to the battery commander.

The gunners unhitched their horses and turned the guns around. The battery commander ordered, "Give them two volleys of solid shot. We have plenty of that, and I want to judge the range. Fire with maximum charge!"

Don and the mounted troopers fell back to lessen the shock to their horses' ears, just as the ammunition wagon moved forward. The guns fired, reloaded and fired again. Enemy gunners returned fire in a long volley. The entire ridge ahead was blanketed with powder smoke. But they had judged the range correctly. The enemy rounds fell short though a few came uncomfortably close. Some balls came bouncing by, but they had slowed enough so that it was possible to avoid them.

"Why don't they just charge?" asked Hamway, looking through his spyglass. "They outnumber us. What are they afraid of?

"If they charge," said Gray John, "their guns will not be able to fire, for fear of hitting their own troops. They sacrifice a great advantage, and all they really have to do is block us."

Don looked once more at the approaching infantry. Their pikes were raised, and the sun glinted off polished shafts and spearheads. It was a beautiful and terrible sight. *Time is running out. Is this where it ends? So much for the great escape.*

CHAPTER 33

†

Of Gunpowder and Poison

For their vine is from the vine of Sodom and from the fields of
Gomorrah. Their grapes are poisonous; their clusters are bitter. Their
wine is serpents' venom, the deadly poison of cobras.
Deuteronomy 32:32-33 HCSB

As Buddy Burger approached the Kolaroo River, the attitude of the people changed. Farther away from Lady Lilith, the "Dread Lady," and her domains, travelers would give him directions to her fortress readily enough. But they always included a warning to stay far away. As he drew nearer, people became more guarded and warnings ceased. He sensed their fear, hanging about them like the foul stench that lingers around a rotting carcass.

The river ran clear and swift—not easy to ford. But his way led south over an ancient bridge that still stood, its gray concrete and rusty steel beams defying the passage of time. He noticed untidy piles of rusted metal and the glint of broken glass as his horse's hooves rang against the worn surface. Someone had piled wrecks of the old self-propelled cars near the bridge abutments, put there to protect the banks from washing away in the spring floods.

He had been told to watch for a fork in the road, marked by a column topped with a black bird statue. Some said it was a raven, others an eagle, but all agreed it marked the way to her castle.

The sun was getting low in the sky, nearly kissing the range of mountains to the west, when he saw the column. The bird was a dark, misshapen thing. Its talons driven into the stone and its beak open as if screeching defiance.

Burger felt icy fingers graze his ribs as he gazed at it and was tempted to turn back, just for a moment. He shook his head, trying to clear cobwebs from his brain, and then spurred his mount to the right and uphill.

The castle or fortress was surrounded by a substantial wall, but it was not overly large. The wall enclosed perhaps two acres. The gate, topped by another eagle sculpture, stood open, and the entry was large enough to accommodate even the largest wagon. Two guards in black armor and armed with spears gazed unsmilingly at him but made no move to bar his entrance. He nodded at them and tried to put on a bold front, but did not speak.

He tossed the reins to a startled stableboy, gathered his saddlebags, and strode across the cobblestone courtyard to a door. It was ironbound and fronted the largest building. A black iron knocker met his gaze. He lifted it and let it fall against a plate, which gave a dull clang that made some doves startle and fly with excited flutters.

The man who answered the door looked rather like a scarecrow. He stood tall, with white hair, a pale face that had seen little of the sun, and large hands. His black tunic hung loosely on his thin frame. His eyes were deep-set and his cheeks were hollow. "Do you seek the ancient right of shelter?" he asked in a hoarse voice.

"No," answered Burger. "I have a proposition that your mistress will want to consider."

"I doubt that," said the man. He made no move to allow entry.

Burger tossed him a gold coin. "Why don't we let her make that decision?"

The man stared at the coin for a moment, then made it vanish. "Very well, he said. "I shall ask if she will receive you. Come into the foyer and find a seat."

He was kept waiting for a long time, perhaps an hour. But he was not surprised. The room was plain, with stone walls, and the hard chairs gave no comfort. Candles filled a few black iron candlesticks which gave a flickering light. It was not a pleasant place and was not intended to be.

†

Buddy had left his short sword on his saddle, and he was allowed to keep his belt knife. But Lady Lilith kept a young man near her, armed with a broadsword. She was obviously a cautious woman. She received him in a pleasant chamber with a glazed window that glowed with the last dim rays of evening. The floor shone with polished wood, and she reclined on a sofa. He was directed to another hard chair in the middle of the room.

"Thank you for receiving me, my lady," began Burger, with a low bow. "My name is Buddy Burger. Formerly a councilor of Steamboat, I now reside in Prophet City. I bring greetings from the Prophet."

"My, the Prophet," answered Lilith. "How interesting. A flattering beginning, to be sure. Also, difficult to verify."

"It is true enough," responded Burger. "May I sit down?"

"As you wish," she answered. She was dressed in a dark blue gown. The sleeves were long and trimmed at the cuffs in white fur. Burger sat and examined her face. Time had not been kind, though cosmetics made a valiant attempt to hide the lines. Her eyes glittered but not with the brightness of youth. She reminded him of a reptile with a strange, hypnotic gaze.

"As I told your servant, I bring a proposal that might interest you."

"Does the Prophet wish to enter a business venture?"

"Of a sort. I need your help to settle an old account. I think you will find it agreeable."

"You have a fat purse in your lap. Money is always agreeable."

"The only thing more agreeable than money is revenge, in my opinion."

"Now you spark my interest," she said, looking directly at him for the first time.

†

Ari saw Beefy ride back down the hill and immediately join with Thomas. She could not hear what they were saying, but she noticed Beefy point down the road and make a motion as if sweeping the waiting column back up toward the pass. Then Thomas shouted, "Pull back. Pull back." Beefy galloped toward the culvern battery.

Where is my mother? What is going on? Ari shouted to the archers, "Pull back. I will join you in a few minutes."

She galloped after Beefy and caught up with him as he shouted orders for the culverns to withdraw along with the rest. "What is happening?" asked Ari. "Where is Carla?"

"She is going to direct fire from up on the ridge."

"What should the archers and I do?"

"I don't care," snapped Beefy. "Just stay the hell out of the way."

Ari rode back to join the other girls. By this time the column had reversed course, moving back up the hill. The distant gunfire was much closer now, which probably meant that their friends were fighting for their lives, but they had no choice except retreat. After withdrawing a couple of hundred yards, the gunners hauled their guns around, muzzles pointing back down the road. The light artillery formed in a line extending across the valley, with the culverns behind them. Ari ordered her horse archers to extend in a wide line behind the guns.

"Why should she be our boss?" Ari noticed the voice from her left. She recognized it as coming from Golda, a merchant's daughter who was given to complaining. *Should I ignore her? What should I do?* Several of the girls glanced over their shoulders to see if she had heard the complaint. *Maybe it's not right that I was left in charge, but I was.*

She urged her horse toward Golda and saw her whispering to the girl next to her. "Golda," she said. "If you don't want to follow me, you don't have to." Her voice carried, and she meant it to.

Golda turned her horse to face her. "What do you mean? I was only…"

"Complaining?" asked Ari. "If you have a problem with me, throw your bow onto the wagon. You can help the horse holders."

Golda's mouth dropped open. "No. Please," she said. "Don't send me back."

"I can't have someone that won't follow orders."

"I'm sorry," said Golda. A tear made a clean stripe down her dirty cheek. "You are in charge. I will do what you say."

"Then keep your mouth shut."

At that moment, the culverns began to fire.

†

"Many things in life are overrated. Revenge is not one of them." The old woman named Lilith muttered, half to herself, as she arranged the golden coins into neat stacks. The leather sack that had once contained them lay flat and empty, its surface shiny from wear. The hooded eyes stared shrewdly at Burger. "Revenge has not consumed me, you know. It invigorates me. Few people have dared cross me in my life, and those few that have…" Her voice trailed off, and she stared at a distant corner of the room. Her blotchy hands quivered.

Burger waited for her to finish, far longer than his custom. Finally, he prompted her. "What happened to those few?"

"Oh," she continued. "Pray excuse me. Ha-ha. Well, you can be sure that they have paid a heavy price. But a girl deserted me once. She is clever, that one. She lives in one of the few places where I can't get to her. Pity." She returned her attention to the coins, then continued. "This is a handsome gift, to be sure, and the Prophet's enemy is another that has evaded me for far too long. I have been patient with him, but have not forgotten. No, not forgotten."

"So, you also would like to see him brought low?"

"Oh, yes. Brought low. I should have had him killed, probably, but that is too easy and it's… not elegant. Yes, that's it. Not elegant. I want him to be humiliated and die a broken man."

"I think the Prophet would rather see something more lethal."

"Don't be so quick to disagree. It so happens that I have been working on a little plan for several years now. It is elegant, and I think the Prophet would approve. It would be a small thing to finish the last details. A short letter would be all that is needed. That and a cup of special tea. I can send a messenger today to a certain lady in Stonegate."

"Tell me more." Burger was a bit surprised at how easy she had agreed to help him. *No doubt she wants the Prophet to be in her debt. That means more than the gold. Of course, no one can have too much gold.*

"How much do you know about poisons?" The old woman questioned Burger with an almost girlish laugh as though she were discussing plans for a party.

✝

Ari's horse joined the rest in jumping when the culverns began thundering. She saw the clear flashes of reflected sunlight from the top of the ridge and knew her mother was directing fire, but the flashes mean nothing to her. The muffled *crump* of exploding shells came back over the ridge, but she had no idea what effect they were having.

The ridge top ahead was still, with only a ripple in the stalks of tan grass. Then it became suddenly alive with movement as a line of horses and riders appeared with the suddenness of the swoop of an eagle. They were a magnificent sight, with bright pennons and the fish-scale gleam of burnished mail. Hundreds came at a full gallop, perhaps three hundred yards away.

Fortunately, the guns were emplaced and ready for exactly this kind of attack. The light artillery fired in a ragged volley. A few guns were loaded with ball, but most fired beehive rounds, which tore into the advancing cavalry with deadly effect. When the smoke cleared, moments later, the center of the advancing line had ceased to exist, and a bloody pile of shattered bodies lay in a crimson, twitching heap.

But the gunners, by some irrational instinct, had all fired toward the center of the line, and the wings remained untouched. They came bravely on, covering perhaps thirty feet per second. In less than a minute's time, they had reached the guns, only to be faced by the muskets and pikes of the gunners. Many of the surviving cavalrymen and perhaps fifty lightly armed Raiders were trying to ride around the right end of the line of guns to get behind them attack the gunners from the rear. The defenders' few mounted troopers moved to the left to meet a similar threat from that direction.

"To the right," shouted Ari, and she spurred her horse that way. Her fifty archers met the enemy horsemen just as they made their flanking move. The battlefield had fallen silent because the gunners had discharged their muskets and were frantically reloading. There came a ringing clash of swords as the horsemen tried to cut down the men defending the guns.

The girls needed no command to shoot. They did so as soon as they had a clear target, and a wave of arrows met the advancing enemy. The Raiders fared the worst. They only wore mail on their torso and their horses had no armor at all. Though few received fatal wounds, most were hit in arms or legs, and many of their mounts were wounded or killed.

Even the heavily armored cavalry was not immune. Their horses' heads and necks were unarmored as were their riders' faces, which was the target most of the girls chose. Their shields blocked many arrows, but they hesitated, then forgot the gunners to make an angry charge at the woman archers that goaded them so unmercifully.

"Fall back," shouted Ari. "Don't let them get too close."

The bulk of the horsemen followed after the retreating girl archers. They galloped back up the highway, turning in the saddle to fire back at their pursuers as they went. But the heavy cavalrymen apparently realized that they had no hope of catching them, since the girls wore little armor and they were a light load. Besides that, their mounts were chosen for speed. Even the remaining Raiders, who also had light armor, could not keep up.

While Ari and her archers were drawing the main threat away, the gunners were able to reload their muskets. The mail armor of the enemy gave no protection against musket balls. After several volleys, the remaining horsemen were either dead, wounded, or retreating as rapidly as they had come.

The only exception was the fifty or so horsemen chasing Ari and her girls. By this time, they were out of range of the muskets and the friendly gunners could not fire their artillery in that direction, for fear of hitting the girls. They were helpless to do anything to give aid. The few mounted troopers were still engaged with the retreating remnants of enemy horsemen.

But no help was needed. When it became obvious that they could not run the archers down, the pursuing enemy pulled their winded horses to a stop. They must have decided that there was no point in trying to face the gunners again with so few, so they turned off the highway onto a side canyon and left the battlefield. Several horses carried double and the enemy left a trail of fallen men and horses behind them.

As Ari and her excited archers returned, they took several Raiders and cavalrymen captive. All were wounded and afoot. They seemed stunned and made little resistance. As Ari's force drove the defeated men back, the scouts and a few horse holders met them and took the captives out of their hands. Ari and her horse archers neared the artillery, just as the culverns began again to engage the enemy guns behind the hill. But the guns did not drown out the cheers of the gunners as they greeted Ari and her girls.

"Poisons are an interesting idea," said Buddy Burger, sipping a cup of hot tea. "Potentially quite safe for the poisoner. But where would we find poisons?"

"My dear Burger," said Lilith, "the problem is not in finding plants that are more or less toxic. Sometimes I think the greater difficulty is in finding plants that aren't. Some of the plants used for medicine can kill in large doses. Even some of our common garden plants can make delightfully useful poisons."

"Is that so? What, for example?"

"Too numerous to mention. Rhubarb leaves can be used to make a slow-acting poison. The unfortunate victim will seem to waste away. Potato leaves, the same. There is a common shrub that unfortunately does not grow here. It is called oleander and is wonderfully toxic. The difficulty is really in finding a toxic plant that does not taste bad. Most have a foul or bitter taste. It seems that our bodies can often detect things that are bad for us."

"Perhaps the taste can be disguised. Put in something else to make it less noticeable."

"Yes, that can be done. I have made a study of this for many years, and I can say without undue pride that I am something of an expert. I have had many traitors in my dungeons, and they have made useful subjects of my experiments. Would you like another cup of tea?"

Burger suddenly swallowed, and he made an involuntary flinch. She laughed. "Have no fear, dear Burger. If I wanted you dead, there are much easier ways to accomplish that. In fact, my tea concoctions are quite well known in the East, and they are reckoned to be excellent tonics. Of course, I sell them under a different name."

Burger accepted another cup of tea even though he did so with some apprehension. "What would be a medicinal plant that could be used as a poison?"

"Strange you should mention that. A perfect example is monkshood or Aconitum. With a proper dosage, it is useful for heart disease. I have a tea that is excellent for high blood pressure. But a strong solution of the essence of the roots is fatal and quick acting. It is ideal for our purposes. Larkspur can also be used, with similar results. Although, I might use something else as well."

"Interesting. What else?"

"Buttercups cause burning of the mouth, nausea, and convulsions. Not usually fatal in small amounts, but it can cause serious distress. That might be all we need."

"You have kept me in suspense long enough, I think," said Burger. "How does all this help us get revenge on Donald of Stonegate?"

"As you might know, he is happily married to a woman named Rachel. She is a member of the Stonegate council and is the apple of his eye. I propose to make her our target."

"Why so? Why not strike directly at him?"

"Hear me out." Lilith stretched, very much like a cat. She smiled as if tasting something delicious. "She was selected as a bride for the Prophet, but Donald and some of his meddling friends snatched her away. Very humiliating. I am sure I don't have to tell you that."

"I think I have heard something of this. Another girl from Steamboat was also taken away, if I remember right."

"You remember exactly right. Now, suppose we were able to capture her again and this time make sure she is delivered to Prophet City, for the Prophet's...use. How would that sound? A perfect revenge. Imagine how our Donald would feel then? Too painful for words—worse than death, I would say."

"I see," said Burger. "As you would also say, it would be elegant. But how does the poison figure into all of this?"

"This idea has long been in my mind. Rachel has an elderly aunt that lives in the town of Estes Park. I have often gone there in the guise of a 'wise woman' of the East, with salves, cordials, and teas for sale. All harmless, and often quite useful. Rachel's aunt knows and trusts me, and my remedies do seem to help her heart and her rheumatism."

"I think I am beginning to follow."

"Yes. Well, I propose to draft a message to Rachel saying that her aunt is very ill and that she should come at once. Her aunt is elderly, and such a message will be believable. When she arrives, I will be there in her aunt's house, as an old friend and caregiver. Her aunt will be ill indeed, due to a bit of buttercup extract. A mild dose of monkshood in Rachel's tea will make her unable to give any resistance. You and five or six of my husky followers should have no problem in spiriting her away to Prophet City, and they should be able to handle any bodyguards that she might bring along. Quite simple and foolproof."

"How long would this take?"

"That is the beauty of it. I can send the message today, and we can leave for Estes Park at once. By the time she gets the message and travels to help her very sick aunt, we can be there waiting for her."

"A well-thought-out plan, indeed. I am very impressed. More importantly, I am sure the Prophet will be delighted with his long-delayed prize."

"Yes. I am sure he will. Do remind him that I have ever been a loyal ally and desire nothing more than to continue to be so."

†

The three guns in Don's battery kept up a steady rain of fire on the closest enemy gun emplacements that guarded their route of retreat. Repeatedly, black puffs of smoke appeared over the heads of enemy gunners. Cutting the fuses was a difficult art, but some seemed to be spraying shards of shrapnel where they would do the most harm to the enemy.

Don kept watching through his binoculars, but he could not be sure whether the enemy gunners were out of action or had merely taken cover. The battery commander had a spyglass and was observing as well. Suddenly, he shouted, "Sir, it appears that some of the enemy cavalry is pulling back."

Don turned his gaze towards the ranks of horsemen, and it did seem that there were fewer blocking the way. He turned to Gray John. "I think he is right,"

"We can't wait much longer," said Gray John. He gave a crooked grin. "Let's let them meet our charge. If we must die, let us die as troopers should. Not hemmed in like rats in a trap."

"I agree," said Don. "Let it be so. Bugler. Sound the charge if you please."

Don rode to the guns. "Hitch up and follow. If you must abandon the guns to save yourselves, do so. Can you blow the ammunition wagon if you have to leave it behind?"

"Yes. We can set a slow match, and it will blow sky-high after a few minutes."

"Don't leave the shells for the enemy. But you gunners are more important than the guns. Remember that!"

"Yes, sir. I'll not soon forget."

"Limber up and follow, then."

The bugles sounded, and the horses sprang forward. They loved to run, and they very well knew what the ringing notes meant. Colin McCoy rode at Don's right, and his bodyguards were to his left and rear. The Red Axe troop was in the lead in a wedge formation. Don spurred forward so that he was near the very point of the wedge, just behind a young giant on a great bay, a full seventeen hands high.

Five hundred horses at speed make the earth shake in a deep rumble like the sound of mighty waters. Only the brave can hold their position in the face of a determined charge, but the enemy apparently took comfort in their superior numbers.

The nearest guns seem to have been silenced, but as they drew nearer, distant batteries on either side began to fire. One ball hit the earth and skipped right over their heads with a whishing sound like a covey of ducks landing on a pond. He heard a *thud-crunch* behind him and knew it was a ball smashing into flesh and bone. But he did not look back. There was nothing that he could do.

As the enemy line rose up before them, they lowered their war spears and braced for impact. A thought raced through his mind: *At least, their guns can't fire now. We are too close.* But that did not apply to Don's grenadiers. Riding near the front, they used their slings to throw their missiles ahead of them, as soon as they approached the waiting horsemen. The little bombs exploded among them, deadly fragments wounding horse and rider alike. The enemy formation dissolved into confusion.

The wedge drove through the first line of the enemy like a spear through a tunic. They were outnumbered, certainly, but their force was concentrated, and the enemy spread wide. At the point of impact, it was the enemy that was outnumbered. The key was to keep pressing forward as fast as they could. If the enemy could stop them, then they would quickly be surrounded, and the greater numbers would be decisive.

Don's first opponent panicked and tried to rein his horse out of the way. All he succeeded in doing was to leave himself open. Don's spear took him full in the chest with bone-smashing impact, and he was driven from the saddle. Don absorbed the shock, then diverted the spear to the next rider before him. This time his spear glanced off the man's shield, causing his spear to miss Don entirely. Before the man could recover, Colin's axe took him on the side of his helmet, and he fell backward over his cantle.

Then they broke through the rings of defenders and the way ahead seemed open, Don reined Skipper to the right and looked behind. About one hundred of the attacking troopers had broken through, but the friction of battle and enemy pressure from the flanks had slowed the bulk of the attackers to a stop. He heard explosions to the rear. Some sounded like musket fire, and others were clearly grenades. He realized that the gunners were defending themselves and the grenadiers had held back and were still throwing their little bombs.

He realized that he could lead one hundred troopers to safety by simply continuing the charge But that would mean abandoning the rest of his command. *If I turn back, I could lose them all. Is it better to save some? Or would that be cowardice?*

†

There was a lull in the distant firing ahead of them, but an occasional enemy ball came in their general direction from over the ridge. These were unaimed but still dangerous. The friendly gunners fired a careful shot and then fired again, apparently making adjustments from Carla's signals. Then a number of friendly guns fired at once.

Following the volley there was a pause, and a hush fell. Ari's ears throbbed, and she sat her sweaty horse, wondering what was happening. Then she heard Thomas order, "Archers and horsemen to the front. We are moving out. Gunners, hitch up your guns."

Ari could not repress a wild grin. There would be something for them to do once again. "Horse archers," she shouted. "Follow me." Without looking behind her to see if her order was obeyed, she spurred forward, following their few armored troopers down the road ahead, a road now splotched by black blood and the wreckage of war.

She topped the rise to see a line of gun batteries facing her. But they looked abandoned. She galloped on, nocking an arrow to her bow. She saw the evidence of shell fire—torn earth and torn bodies. But there was movement at a gun to her right. She spurred that way to see an enemy crew trying to get their gun loaded. One man had a rammer and was thrusting into the gun's muzzle, driving a charge home.

She shouted, "Hold," and shot an arrow at him. It struck his leg. Then a shower of arrows came from the other girls following behind her. One gunner fell with several arrows through his body The rest raised their hands.

She looked to the left and saw the armored troopers falling on another crew, swords flashing red. She reined to a stop, wondering what to do with the prisoners. But three scouts rode to her side and offered to guard them. Smiling her thanks, she spurred forward, hearing ahead of her the sounds of musket fire and muffled thumps that sounded like grenades.

She topped a ridge and down below was a mass of armored men locked in battle several hundred yards away. She slowed her horse to a stop, trying to understand what she was seeing. Two scouts were at her side.

"What is going on?" one of them asked. He was a slender teen, armed similarly to the girl archers.

"It is our horse troopers fighting for their lives," answered Ari. "Go and report to Lord Thomas. "Tell him we need the guns down here and we need them right now."

†

Lady Lilith's coach was large and comfortable. The seats were well-padded and covered in red velvet. Buddy's horse was tied behind, and the four black coach horses kept a steady, ground-eating trot. The road was not as smooth as one could have wished even though the coach body rode on great springs. The potholes jarred them, but the motion was more like a ship than a rattling farm wagon. They held onto straps as they rocked from side to side.

Lilith was not given to idle chatter. When Burger tried to make polite conversation, she simply ignored him. Finally, she said, "If you don't have anything important to say, simply be quiet."

Buddy held his tongue after that. The coach was going slowly, climbing a steep highway with many switchbacks. He knew they were climbing over a high pass, and Estes Park was on the other side. The temperature dropped and he took one of the blankets and wrapped it about himself. They drew leather covers over the coach windows to keep out a cold breeze.

Despite the bumping and swaying, he nodded off. He awoke to find Lilith speaking to him. "It occurs to me that there might be one other thing that would greatly please the Prophet and cause pain to Donald of Fisher."

"Donald of Fisher?"

"Oh, yes, he goes by that name, too. It is the name he used when I first met him. But he has started a military school in Stonegate. Those young men are his pride and Stonegate's hope for the future."

"Yes, I have heard of this school."

"I have a decoction that is excellent for assassination. It does not have a strong taste and even a small amount is fatal. Best of all, the effects do not become immediately apparent."

"I can see why that might be useful."

"Yes. It does not matter much if only one or two people are the target. But for a larger number, the delay is important. Many people could get a fatal dose before anyone realizes something is wrong."

"What is it?"

"That, my dear Burger, is my secret. But I can tell you that I am proud of it. I have tested it repeatedly, and it never fails."

"Is there any antidote?"

"Not as such. Purging with an emetic might help if a skilled person suspected something amiss. But it would have to be done quickly. Feeding the victim charcoal might also help. But most likely these remedies would come too late."

"How would you use the poison? It seems you would have to have access to the kitchen."

"Yes, or the water supply. But neither is impossible. I think we should make that our next project after we spirit Rachel away."

"I rather suspect that the cadets are all in the field. I saw many young men in armor a week or so ago, and I am sure they are from the academy."

"No matter. They will return, and then we will strike."

CHAPTER 34

†

The Law of Reciprocity

Don't be deceived: God is not mocked. For whatever a man sows he
will also reap."
Galatians 6:7 HCSB

Don struggled with the idea that he should continue the charge and
so save some of his command. If he returned to carry on the fight,
he would most likely lose them all. But he could not simply ride away and
leave the trailing elements to fight their way free. *It might be logical, but it
would be wrong.*

He shouted, "Turn back and take them from the flanks." Most of Gray
John's cadet troop had broken through the lines. They had driven through
the gap that the Red Horse Troop had carved through the enemy defenses.
Both troops immediately obeyed.

Hamway and the Red Horse troopers turned to the left and returned
to attack the enemy horsemen from the rear. Don followed Gray John and
the cadets back to the right in a hook-shaped movement.

†

Skipper was not as well trained as Don needed. He felt a deep longing for his
old warhorse, Snap. But Skipper had heart even though he was not willing
to ram his shoulder into another horse like a battering ram. It was too late
to teach him that trick now.

Still, Skipper did not shy away. He leaped toward a mail-covered enemy
horse with a powerful lunge. Don's spear thrust was able to drive the cavalry-

man from his saddle. This time, however, the spear lodged in the enemy's armor, and he lost his grip on it.

Don heard a voice in his ear and looked to his right as he drew his sword. Colin shouted, "Fall back, Lord Don. Your place is to direct the battle."

Don shook his head. "My place is to lead by example. God help me!"

Then it seemed that God indeed intervened. Don entered an altered state that he had experienced in battle only once before. Time seemed to crawl, and the movements of his opponents seemed ridiculously sluggish. Another foeman, burnished mail gleaming, thrust a javelin at him. He saw the sharp point closing, the reddish whiskers and a snarl on the man's lips, all with perfect clarity. Don parried the javelin aside with his sword, then with almost a delicate touch, sliced the keen edge along the inside of the man's biceps. The wounded man's hand opened and the javelin fell to the ground, slowly, like a feather dropping. Colin, just at Don's right, slammed his axe into the man's helm. His eyes went blank, and he toppled to one side.

With surgical precision, Don and Colin carved their way into the host of the enemy, followed by Gray John and the cadet troopers. Don realized that he and the cadets were not attacking the flank as much as they were forcing back the jaws of a trap. But more of the Prophet's riders kept coming toward them to replace those that had fallen.

Don looked to the left. Despite the odds, more Stonegate horse troopers were emerging, having fought their way through the enemy lines. If they could hold the trap open for a few more minutes, the rest of his force might break free.

†

Ari ordered her girls to move out of the way as the culvern battery arrived atop the ridge and began to emplace their three guns. As they watched the teams being unhitched and the gunners manhandling the guns into position, more light artillery pieces joined them and began to do the same. Then Carla galloped from behind the ridge to join them.

"Mother!" shouted Ari. "I am glad to see you." She slumped in her saddle as tension drained from her body.

"What is going on?" asked Carla, as she calmly strung her bow. Ari answered her questions as the gunners prepared the guns to fire. Then Thomas galloped up to join them.

"Your girls did well, Carla," said Thomas. "Ari is a born leader."

"She is," said Carla. She pointed to the melee. "But we are doing little good here. I think we need to ride down and add our arrows to the battle. With your permission."

Thomas looked confused. "No. Stay out of the way. These guns will be firing."

At that moment, one culvern fired.

†

No matter how many enemies were defeated, more arose to take their place. Battle fever had kept Don going, but he was finally beginning to tire. The sword seemed to weigh as much as a bushel of corn. His helm was dented and his shield was notched. Their charge had been a gallant attempt, but it could only have succeeded if they had broken the enemies' will to fight. As it was, the greater numbers were beginning to be decisive. The battle was almost over, and Don knew it.

Then bugles began blowing. They were sounding from several directions and repeated the same notes over and over. It was not a Stonegate bugle call. The clash of blade on armor went from a din to sporadic clanging, then ceased.

Immediately, the sweaty knot of horses and men facing him began to give way and withdraw. He reined Skipper to a stop and allowed the distance between the two forces to grow wider. There was a blast like a thunderclap, preceded by the rushing sound of a cannonball passing through the air. He instinctively hunched his shoulders, waiting for the explosion. But none came. There was only a sodden *crunch* as the ball blasted through the enemy.

Then a solitary rider, carrying a large white banner, came into view. He was riding at a gallop, coming from the north. Clearly, the enemy wanted to parley. Don was willing to do exactly that. At least, he and his men could rest and tend their wounds. *Wounds? Oh, God, how many have we lost?*

Buddy had spent one night at Lady Lilith's fortress. Despite the dark and forbidding exterior, he had been shown to a rather small but comfortable room. The breakfast served was warm and filling, with cheese omelets and delicious sausages. But they had not lingered. At Lilith's insistence, they had departed early. The distance was not far, perhaps ninety miles, but it was too far to travel in one day.

They had spent the next night in a manor that belonged to one of Lady Lilith's subjects. The man was a local lord, but he was obsequious and fawning to her and provided them the best rooms he had to offer. Lilith accepted it as her due and wasted little time in conversation with him. She soon dismissed him from her presence in a peremptory manner.

But all that was behind them as the coach continued its slow descent into Estes Park. As they neared the walls of the town, the rattling coach wheels send forth echoes that returned from granite hills before they turned onto a quiet side lane. Spreading cottonwood trees lined the gravel-covered track. As soon as they stopped, Buddy Burger stepped out and gave Lady Lilith his hand to help her alight. Then he turned to look at the lodge; it was clearly not an inn.

The lodge, as Lilith called it, was a large private home that she claimed to have inherited. The housekeepers, an elderly couple, met them at the door. After they settled Lilith, they showed him to his room on the second floor. One of Lilith's armed escorts brought Buddy's saddlebags up and tossed them on his bed with an insolent sneer. Buddy considered chastening him, but his ropy muscles bulging beneath a leather jerkin caused him to think better of it.

After beating dust from his clothes and a cold-water rinse of his face and hands, he decided to return to the large parlor. His host, a stocky, dark-haired man with a full moustache, had replaced his coat with a white apron.

"What do you want, good sir?" asked the man with a shy smile and a bob of his head. "I might suggest a mug of warmed mulled wine. I have a blend of spices that I think you will enjoy."

Burger agreed and warmed his hands at a merry fire burning in the grate. He turned to feel the warmth on his back and saw an old woman walking from the back of the house toward the front door. She wore a shapeless black dress with a faded scarf tied over her hair and she leaned on a stick. A leather satchel hung from her shoulder. Her face looked somewhat familiar, but her stout, matronly body was not. She raised a trembling hand and addressed him in a quavering tone, "Do you need any tonics or potions, young man?"

"No, grandmother," said Burger. "Do I know you?"

"You should, dear Burger," the woman answered in a firm voice, standing erect. She smiled with closed lips. "Do I look like a wise woman?"

Burger gasped. "Lady Lilith!" he exclaimed. "You certainly do. I would never have recognized you. Your figure, it is so…"

"Full?" she finished for him. "Just padding. It is much easier to add fullness to a thin frame than the reverse."

"But why?"

"Estes Park is a small town. But no one has connected the kindly wise woman with the haughty Lilith. And that is my design."

"I see. Quite effective. Are you going out so late?"

"It is best. There is an hour of daylight left. Time enough to stroll through the market, sell a few of my concoctions, and send a lad with a message to a certain old lady."

"You mean Rachel's aunt?"

"Yes. I will tell her that I am in town and have more of her favorite remedies. I will say I will drop by her house in the morning."

†

The young trooper carrying the white banner had gold fittings on his armor, and his mount was hot-blooded and glossy. Don took him for a junior officer, perhaps a rich man's son.

"I have a message for your commander," he shouted when Don was still twenty yards away. "Our general would parley."

Don realized that his bloody sword was still in his hand. He wiped it on his leather gauntlet and returned it to his sheath. Colin was riding just behind him, and his four young bodyguards had also fallen in behind.

"Sir, I am Richard Roundy," the young man said by way of greeting. "Whom do I have the honor of addressing?"

"I am Donald of Fisher, commanding," said Don. "Do you desire to surrender?"

The young man flushed. "That is for my commander to say," he said. "If you would kindly order your guns to cease fire, it would make it easier to disengage and facilitate the parley."

"A good thought," said Don. He looked at the ridge above them and noticed that Thomas had wheeled more artillery into position. He called one of his bodyguards to his side and sent him up the highway to Thomas. He ordered the guns to cease firing unless the enemy resumed hostilities.

Then he turned to young Roundy. "I will meet your commander at a point halfway between our forces. I will ride to meet you when he comes out to parley."

The young man nodded, then withdrew at a smart canter. Don rode back to where his forces were assembling and had a quick meeting with as many troop commanders as he could find. He directed them to stay alert, but to give attention to the fallen. Looking around, he saw his lone battery of guns and the wagons had not been captured or destroyed, so he directed that the seriously wounded should be loaded on the wagons. There were many empty saddles.

Friendly and enemy forms lay intertwined and there was much confusion as both sides began the recovery of the dead and wounded. Don was dismayed to learn that their losses had been heavy and that the wagons could not carry them all. Then there was a shout, and he glanced up the road to see four wagons coming down, bearing white flags. Obviously, Thomas had foreseen the problem and had sent help.

"I am not sure what the enemy is doing," said Colin. "They are giving away a great advantage by asking for talks."

"True" said Don, shaking his head. "If he had pressed the attack..." They gazed into each other's eyes for a long moment. They knew they would have been defeated.

†

Rachel was pruning her roses for something to keep her hands busy when the Stonegate church bell began ringing. Her hand froze. It seemed to her that her heartbeat had stopped, and she forgot to breathe. She dropped the shears and brushed the dirt off her knees as she stood. There was a pleasant aroma in the air, but she was not aware of it.

"What does that mean, oh God?" she said to herself. She rubbed her face. "Something has happened."

She walked down a curved path leading to her house when she saw a light buggy, pulled by one horse, turning into her driveway. It was the pastor. She wrapped her arms around herself, remembering her mother's arms around her when she was little and had a bad dream. But this was no dream.

Then she ran to meet her pastor. He stepped down and wrapped the reins around the hitching rail. She grabbed his hand in hers. "Donald," she whispered. "Is he—?"

"Rachel," he said. "I wanted to come before the messenger got here. They are notifying the council."

"What! Oh, what?"

"A message just arrived by pigeon. From Thomas of Longmont. Lord Don and the horse troops have separated from the artillery units and are locked in a fierce battle. I rang the bells to call on the people of faith to pray."

"Do we know if anyone has fallen?"

"No, sister, we do not. No names were given."

She heard rapid hoofbeats on the road and knew the message was being delivered. "Let us pray, then," she said, and she dropped to her knees in the dusty yard.

†

After they finished praying, the pastor, Landon, stood by Rachel's side when the messenger approached them. He was a first-year cadet at the academy and he seemed awed by Rachel. After dismounting, he gave a low bow and handed her a folded note, sealed with a red blob of wax. She noted the "D" mark on the seal of Lore-master Duncan.

"What is this?" she asked, even though she knew the answer. As she did so, she broke the seal and began to read.

"It's...It's a summary of several messages from Lord Thomas," the lad said with a stammer. "Do you have a response?"

"Can you send a message to Lord Thomas?"

"No, but I can take a message to Lore-master Duncan."

"All right. Simply ask him to pray for our troops."

"I will, Lady," the lad replied. With another bow, he turned, remounted, and trotted his horse away.

Rachel scanned the summary. It was clear that something had gone badly wrong. For some reason, Don and his mounted troopers had separated from the guns. They were fighting without artillery support against a large force. There was nothing about the Prophet, no mention of casualties, and no word of encouragement. She handed the message to the pastor. Her cheeks were wet, so she wiped them with her hands. There was a lump in her throat.

Pastor Landon finally got her to take a seat on her porch and fetched her a glass of water and a towel to dry her eyes. He prayed for the Lord to give her strength in her hour of need. She heard a crunch of gravel and looked to see another rider approaching.

As he drew nearer at a slow trot, she noticed that the horse was sweaty. White foam had collected in a line where the reins rubbed against the horse's neck. He had been ridden for some distance.

"I have a message for Rachel of Westerly," the young rider said. When he did so, the horse danced sideways and snorted.

"I have already been notified," said Rachel. "Unless there is something new."

"You already know about your aunt?" asked the rider.

"Aunt Florence? No."

"Then, I was bidden to tell you that she is quite ill and wishes to see you."

"Oh, my. What is wrong with her?"

"I am sorry. All I know is what I have told."

†

The leaders gradually got order out of the confusion as Don's force withdrew about two hundred yards from the battlefield. They assembled about one hundred yards below Thomas and his guns. The enemy also withdrew the same distance to the north. That allowed healers from both sides to attend to the wounded. As he prepared for the parley, Don looked for Gray John but did not find him. *Where is he? Where?*

Don decided to leave Hamway in charge and rode to the meeting, again accompanied by Colin McCoy and his young bodyguards. One of the latter wore a white bandage on his forearm.

The enemy commander sat a handsome black stallion. He himself was also dark, with a heavy black beard. The man had removed his helmet, leaving it to hang from his pommel. He raised his right hand, palm forward, in greeting.

"Unless I am mistaken, you will be Lord Donald," he said. He did not smile but kept his expression neutral.

Don raised his hand, returning the gesture, which was an ancient symbol of peace. "I am," he replied. "But you have the advantage of me."

"Um…I take your meaning. I am General Davidson, and I command these forces of the Prophet. I expect that you also bear my military title, or if not, you should."

"Be that as it may," said Don, ignoring the compliment. "I assume that you are not offering to surrender. Did you wish for a parley to give aid to the wounded, merely?"

"If so, it would have been well done. Your artillery has caused us grievous losses."

"Indeed. I grieve for all those lost, regardless of the banners they fought under."

"Yet you brought the battle to us, sir. But, never mind. I just received news that may change both our futures."

What does he mean? "What… How?"

"By heliograph. No doubt you are familiar with them. The Prophet's palace is burning. There is an uprising in the city."

"That is news, indeed?"

"Humph. I wonder if it is actually a great surprise."

"I assure you, sir, that I am not a part of any uprising or a plan to burn the palace. Our incursion was intending to capturing the Prophet alive. We know he is planning to invade the East and decided to try to prevent it. Our complaint is not against the Prophet's people."

"I see. With that in mind, I plan to break off hostilities with you, if you are willing. I see no reason to sacrifice more lives to prevent you from departing."

Don thought for a long moment. *He seems sincere. But I dare not trust him.*

"Very well," Don said, finally. "I am willing. I will withdraw all our forces to a convenient spot farther up the pass. We will rest and tend our wounded."

"That is agreeable. That will give us time to clarify the situation."

"Be aware, General, if your men attempt to block our route of withdrawal, I will take that as a hostile act."

"To be sure. But honesty compels me to tell you one more thing. You launched your attack because of a large force of infantry advancing from the south. True?"

"And from the north. These forces were the main reason we mounted a frontal attack. I would have avoided attacking your forces altogether if I could."

"You may be interested to learn that the force from the south was not coming to attack you. It was coming to help you."

†

Rachel had a difficult decision. Her soul cried out to stay near Stonegate, so she could read the latest reports as they came in from the battle. But she had to accept that she could do nothing to help Don, but she might be able to help her Aunt Florence.

"Staying simply to hear the latest news would be selfish," said Rachel. She looked into the eyes of Pastor Landon. "Don't you think?"

"Perhaps, perhaps not," he answered. "It is a matter of duty. Only you can decide where your duty lies. You might be called to help make some sort of decision that affects us all. Or, you may assist your aunt. Follow your heart."

She impulsively kissed him on the cheek. "Thank you, Pastor. I will go to her."

"You can arrange to have a message sent on. Do you need to take a healer with you?"

"No, there are healers in Estes Park, I believe. She has mentioned a woman who has helped her with her aches and pains."

"Even so, don't go alone. I am sure the council would send an escort."

"I will stop by Westerly-stead when I leave. My younger brothers may have arrived. They should be returning from outpost duty any time now. But someone will go with me. Besides, I can take care of myself."

"I could go along if you need me."

"No, you have many others that need you right now. Thanks for your concern."

As Rachel packed clothes into a valise, she glanced out and saw the pastor's carriage returning in the direction of Stonegate. *Do I really need to take someone? I have my bow and arrows, and I have not forgotten how to use them.*

†

The Stonegate expedition had suffered heavy losses. Don personally helped retrieve the bodies of the fallen. All the horse troops had suffered, but the cadet troop losses seemed to be the cruelest. Eight of the cadets were among the dead, all bright lads cut down before their twentieth year. He felt drained of life like a man carved out of wood. *Oh, God, how can I face their parents? I could have saved all the young ones. Why didn't I just order the cadet troop to the rear?*

Then he noticed a murmur of a dozen voices. There was a knot of people standing near Wyatt, the healer. Don stood and walked that way. Wyatt looked up and said, "Lord Don, you may want to come here."

Wyatt was removing the helmet from a prone figure. He took up a cloth and tenderly washed the blood from the face. It was Gray John. His visage was composed but pale as if all his blood had left him. When Don knelt by his side, Wyatt had already closed his eyes. He looked as if he were in a peaceful sleep. Don covered his own face and wept like never before. Not, at least, since his young aide, Philip, had sacrificed his life for his friends.

Don was not aware of the gathering crowd as he collected himself enough to fold Gray John's hands across his bloody mail-covered chest. He bent down and whispered, "You got your wish, dear friend. You died as a horse trooper should."

CHAPTER 35
†

The Witch Is Dead

Remember my affliction and my homelessness, the wormwood
and the poison."
Lamentations 3:19 HCSB

Rachel rode in her carriage with her face to the west. With her was her younger brother, Howard, Ari's father. Howard had grown to resemble their father. A bit under six feet tall, with broad shoulders, big hands, and narrow hips, he was certainly no giant as she remembered her father from childhood, but as she looked back, she realized that they must be about the same size. Howard drove the team of small bays, which were just the right size and could keep up a steady trot for hours. He had on a thick leather tunic with a short sword at his belt. He had added a well-used crossbow in the back to go with Rachel's favorite bow. They did not expect trouble on the road, but it was best to be prepared in uncertain times.

Their younger brothers, Levi and Lucas, had been stationed at an outpost to the east, providing security for the trade route leading from that direction. It was past time for their assignment to have ended, and they had looked for them to come riding back home. But they had seen no sign of them. Rachel had planned to take Charlie with her, but Howard had insisted. He had not visited Aunt Florence for several months and was as eager to help her as was Rachel.

It would have been possible, in one long, grueling day, to have driven from Stonegate to Estes Park. But it would have been hard on the horses, so they decided to spend a night in Longmont. They ended up visiting with

Annabeth, Carla's older sister. It had been a pleasant few hours, and they had enjoyed catching up on all the latest news. But Rachel kept thinking of the struggle that was going on, far to the west. She kept looking for a messenger to arrive with more news, but none came.

✝

The causeway that bisected the blue lake just east of Estes Park was straight as a bowstring. The afternoon was balmy, and only a few puffy clouds dotted the blue, dome of the sky. Ahead of them, the mountains stood like frosty giants. As they neared the town walls, they saw that the gate was lightly guarded, with only two armored men, but it was guarded, nonetheless. Howard and Rachel waved as they entered and received nods of greeting in return. Rachel was anxious and fretted about any delay, but she had to be patient as Howard threaded a way between market stalls, other wagons, and people wandering about, oblivious to the need to keep a clear path. But they gradually left the crowds behind and traveled up a gentle hill to their aunt's home.

"Finally," said Rachel. "Aunt Florence has a stable around back. We can tie up there." She got out of the carriage as Howard continued down an alley. There was a chattering and squawking noise as he went out of sight, and Rachel remembered that her aunt had been given some guinea fowl. *Noisy birds. I wonder how she puts up with them.* She walked to the front door and knocked. She got no response, so she lifted the latch and entered. "Aunt Florence," she called. "It's Rachel."

Hearing no answer, she entered and paused to let her eyes adjust to the gloom of the front room. "Aunt Florence," she called again, wondering if her aunt had been taken somewhere else. Then she saw an unfamiliar man enter from the direction of the kitchen.

"You must be Florence's niece," the man said. "I am called Buddy."

Rachel stared at him for a moment. He was a strange-looking little man, with a face that reminded her of a rodent. He was rubbing his hands together nervously. His clothing was dark and travel-stained, and he was armed with a short sword. She might have expected one of her aunt's lady friends to be at her side, but this man made her uneasy. "Why are you here?" she asked.

"I am a neighbor. I stopped by when the wise woman, Etta, said she might need some help."

"You look like you have been traveling," said Rachel. She did not know why, but he seemed out of place.

Buddy looked down at his stained boots. "No," he said. "I have just been working in my garden. I raise some crops for market."

Rachel noticed his hands. They were clean and soft. Not at all like the hands of someone who worked in a garden.

"Where is my aunt?"

"She is in her bedroom. Etta is with her. Why don't you let me take your cloak, and I can get you some hot tea?"

Rachel walked into the kitchen and handed her cloak and shawl to Buddy. He busied himself by putting a kettle on to boil. She walked to a side table where there was a basin, a pitcher of water, and a mirror. Then she poured some water into the basin and washed her hands and face. She combed her hair with her fingers and looked at herself in the mirror.

Just then, Howard entered. "Those guineas are really making a racket," he said. "They are a better watchdog than any dog." He looked at Rachel. "How is Aunt Florence?"

"I am going in to see her right now," Rachel answered. "Howard, this is Buddy, a neighbor." The two men nodded to each other.

Rachel walked back to the bedroom, down a short hall from the kitchen. She walked in to find her aunt awake, with a strange woman dressed in dark clothes sitting by her bedside. Her aunt was pale and had a moistness about her face as if she was in distress. She knelt by the bed and took her aunt by the hand. "Aunt Florence. I heard you were ill. Whatever is the matter?

Her aunt seemed confused. "It is wonderful to see you, Rachel," she said. "I think I have some sort of stomach flu. I am feeling better."

"When did it start?" Rachel asked, patting her hand. Her eyes seemed clear, but she was obviously very weak.

"Yesterday afternoon. Fortunately, my friend Etta was here, and she has been taking good care of me. Etta, this is my niece, Rachel."

Yesterday? But that can't be right. I received the message yesterday, in Stonegate. Rachel turned to the old woman and looked closely at her. She was thickset, with a wrinkled face, and appeared to be concerned. "Thank you for your help," Rachel said.

"Not at all, dear," the old woman said. Then she quickly added. "But I fear you are a bit confused, Florence. You have been sick longer than that."

"You must have been, Aunt Florence," said Rachel. "I received your message yesterday."

"But I sent no message, dear," said Florence, rubbing her head.

Rachel moved to a chair on the other side of the bed from where the old woman was sitting. She caught Rachel's eye and made a gesture as if to say that her aunt was out of her head. But the ill woman seemed to be perfectly lucid. As Rachel was trying to make sense of it all, Howard entered the room, followed by Buddy, who carried a mug in his hand.

"Howard," said Florence. "You came, too. How nice to see you."

Buddy brought the mug and gave it to Rachel. "Here is your tea. It is just the thing to lift your spirits. I will get another for Howard." He turned and left the room.

Rachel lifted the mug to her lips and took a sip. Howard exchanged greetings with his aunt. The tea tasted of mint and something else, not entirely pleasant. She noted Etta, the wise woman, looking at her strangely, almost eagerly. Again, small feelings of disquiet nudged the corners of her mind. She put the mug on the nightstand. "Now, dear Aunt," she said, "please tell me exactly when you started feeling ill."

"It was yesterday morning," Florence said. Her voice was clear but weak. "Etta, here, had just stopped by to give bring me some salves and tonics. We were just sharing a cup of herbal tea when I noticed my mouth burning."

"I think you said that you felt the soreness in your mouth when I first arrived, dear," the old woman quickly said.

"Did I?" asked Florence. "That is not how I remember it. Anyway, I became deathly ill. But Etta is so kind. She stayed by my side, helped me to bed, and stayed with me all night."

Rachel was never sure how she grasped the truth. It was not a matter of logical deduction, but somehow, she realized that this supposed friend had deliberately given her aunt something to make her sick. And she knew her aunt was not confused. The message had been sent by someone who knew in advance that this was going to happen. *And that must mean...*

Buddy returned with another mug and gave it to Howard. Rachel stood and said, "Don't drink it, Howard. I think these two are up to no good." Just then, she heard the guineas begin to raise the alarm in the back garden.

†

The old woman smiled a smile that was more like a snarl. "You are quite right, dear Rachel. I gave your aunt poison, and only I know the antidote." She drew a gleaming little knife out of her robe and held it close to Florence's throat. Howard dropped the mug, which crashed on the floor, splattering steaming liquid in all directions. He and Buddy drew their swords and stood to face each other. Then they all froze in place.

"If you go quietly with us, Rachel, I promise that your aunt will come to no harm. We will all walk out of here. She will have the antidote, and all will be well." The old woman spoke in a tone of command. "You men, put down those ridiculous swords. My eight men will be here any moment."

Rachel gasped and pointed to a corner of the room. The old woman's eyes turned in that direction. Just then, Rachel leaped across the bed and knocked the knife away from her aunt's throat. They both began struggling on the floor. The old woman was surprisingly strong, and though Rachel had grasped her wrist, she had a difficult time holding on. She heard crashing in the room behind her and knew that Howard and Buddy were grappling with each other.

"You fool. Your aunt will die," the old crone spat the words from between her teeth, then turned and bit Rachel on the wrist. But she hung on, grimly.

Rachel began to be concerned. The old woman was possessed with a demoniacal strength and seemed to be growing even stronger while she was weakening. They both rolled to the right and Rachel found herself on her back and the old woman was above her and grabbed the knife with both hands.

"I have changed my mind," the old woman snarled. "Die, you bitch!"

"I had rather be a bitch than a witch," Rachel retorted, as she tried to bring up her other hand to halt the descending blade. Then, with a final effort, the old woman thrust the blade down, directly for Rachel's throat.

†

Rachel pushed sideways with all her strength and the blade missed her, driving all the way to the wooden floor. She grappled with her free hand, trying to get control of the blade. They rolled over and the old woman's hand slipped away. She panicked, trying to again catch hold of her wrist. But her opponent went limp, and she was able to sit up. At first, she did not know what had happened, until she saw a growing pool of blood on the floor, rapidly growing larger.

Rachel tried to shake the cobwebs from her head. *The old woman must have stabbed herself with her own blade.* She rolled her over to find the knife up to the hilt in her chest. Her eyes stared upward, accusingly. She recoiled in disgust and struggled to her feet. She looked across the room and saw no sign of Howard or Buddy, so she stood.

Just as she regained her feet, Howard rose to his knees. Blood covered his hands and arms, and his short sword dripped gore. The other man lay still. "Howard," she cried, "Are you all right?" She also noticed her aunt shaking with fear, hands over her eyes.

"I am fine," said Howard. "Only a slice on my arm."

Rachel turned to her aunt. "Shh. Aunt Florence. It's all right."

They heard footsteps in the other room and coming down the hall. It sounded like many boots. "Howard," said Rachel. "She said she had men coming. This must be them. Put something against the door."

†

Howard reached into the corner and found a stout billet of wood. "How about a bar?" he asked as he dropped it into two iron brackets. "That should hold them for a moment."

"But not for long," said Rachel as something heavy slammed against the door; it probably was a heavy shoulder. Several voices began cursing. A knock came and a man's voice spoke, "Lady Lilith. Are you in there?"

"Your mistress is unconscious," answered Rachel. "Go away."

†

Howard took hold of a heavy chest of drawers in the alcove and pulled it over to block the door, filling the space between the door and the corner. Now it would be very difficult indeed to knock the door down, even with a battering ram. While Rachel comforted her aunt, Howard parted the gauzy drapes and opened two glazed shutters to reveal stout iron bars blocking the exit. "Well, we are truly trapped," he said. "It sounds like a half-dozen men out there, at least." There was more pounding on the door.

"What is happening?" Florence asked. "Who are these people?"

"I think they are kidnappers," answered Rachel. "I am so sorry, Aunt Florence. I think they used you to try to get at me. That evil woman must have given you some kind of poison."

"Is she unconscious?" asked Florence. "Perhaps you can revive her and force her to tell you where the antidote is."

"That would be a good plan," whispered Rachel, "But she is dead. She fell on her own blade. I will search her clothes and try to find the antidote."

A heavy thud against the door shook the whole house, but the door held, even though dust blew out of every crevice. The stone walls stood as firm as a granite boulder. Howard shouted out of the open window, "Help! Robbers!"

Rachel ignored the commotion and searched the old woman's body, but found nothing. She had remembered seeing a leather satchel in the kitchen and assumed that it was her bag of remedies, but it might as well have been on the moon."

"Look, Rachel," said Howard. "This iron grill is hinged, probably for a fire escape. But it is locked."

Rachel heard a metallic rattle and stood to see Howard holding a large, rusty old padlock. She also noticed that his shirt sleeves were dripping blood. "You are wounded, Howard," said Rachel. "Let me look." She pushed up his sleeves to show several deep cuts on his left arm where he had defended himself against Buddy's sword. She tore bedclothes and hastily bandaged him to stop the bleeding. The wounds were nasty and would require a surgeon, but at least they did not look dangerous. No spurting blood meant no arteries had been severed.

Their cries for help seemed fruitless, and Rachel's aunt did not know where the key to the padlock was. They looked into every drawer and nook but found nothing. The repeated blows on the door continued. Then a voice said, "Open the door or we will set it on fire."

"What? And burn your mistress?" answered Rachel. Her response was met with silence. It was a standoff, and she could see no way out of the trap. The guinea hens began again to make a racket.

†

Rachel stepped to the window and cried again for help. This time she got an answer. "Rachel, is that you?" She looked up the alley and saw two riders. They were Levi and Lucas, her younger brothers, in full armor and mounted on warhorses. *What were a wonderful sight! Thank you, God.* Howard came to her side and shouted a welcome.

"Levi, Lucas," shouted Rachel. "We are trapped here. There are kidnappers in the house. Maybe as many as eight. Don't try to take them by yourselves. Get help."

"Yes, boys," said Howard, as the two rode closer to the house. "We are glad to see you. Do you have news of Carla, or Ari, or Don?"

Lucas rode to the window. His ice-blue eyes flashed, and his lips parted in a happy smile. Close-cropped, his beard gleamed golden in the sun. "We have news," he said. "Confusing news. There seems to be some kind of truce. We took heavy losses, but the message came from Don. We know no other names. But why don't we get you out of that room?"

Don is safe. Glory to God. "The bars are locked down," said Rachel. "No way out. But they can't get in, either."

Levi and Lucas looked at each other and smiled. "I think we can open those bars," said Lucas. He reached down and untied a coil of stout rope and passed the end to Howard. He threaded the rope through the bars and pulled the other end back. The two brothers then backed up their warhorses and wrapped the ends of the rope around the pommels of their heavy saddles. They turned so the two horses pulled on the ends of the rope like a team drawing a heavy wagon. Both horses lunged, and with a rending *screech*, the entire metal frame, bars and all, was yanked away from the window. It was then the work of a few moments to pass Aunt Florence out of the window into waiting arms. Rachel and Howard clambered out, tossing the short sword that had belonged to Buddy before them.

Rachel and Howard then ran for their buggy, to the annoyance of the guineas, which set up yet another clamor. Howard carried his aunt, whom they had wrapped in a heavy blanket. The garden was surrounded by a four-foot wall. Howard climbed over and headed for the carriage, with Rachel following. Lucas and Levi were on the other side of the wall, and they wheeled their horses around as if not sure what to do. At that moment, a gang of men came storming out of the back door. The guineas ran squawking for their coop.

The men assessed the situation and ran for the gate in the opposite wall to block the carriage's exit; then they advanced on the carriage. *It's not over yet, but maybe I can even the odds.* Rachel grabbed her bow, strung it and nocked an arrow. Howard saw what she was doing and grabbed the crossbow, putting his foot in the stirrup of the bow and pulled back the string. Before he could shoot, Rachel loosed an arrow at the nearest man. They were all armed with swords, thick leather jerkins, and steel caps. She did not know if the arrow would penetrate their jerkins, so she aimed at the man's thigh.

She never shot truer. The arrow hit where she aimed and buried deep into the thickest part of his leg. He fell to one knee and grabbed the shaft, trying to pull it out, but the barbed head did as it was designed, and he was unable to withdraw it. With curses, the other men ran towards them. Howard loosed a bolt to the center of the leading man's chest, which put him out of the fight. But the other six came on, swords raised, and gave a great shout.

Then Rachel heard a scrambling thud and saw that Lucas's mount had cleanly leaped over the wall and he was charging toward the gang of men. As she watched, Levi's mount also cleared the wall as graceful as a swallow in flight, and he followed a few steps behind.

Even though six men stood against them, the rest of the battle was never in doubt. Howard dropped the crossbow, drew his sword and engaged the nearest man. Rachel calmly loosed three arrows, always shooting at the men's legs, and disabled two more.

Howard was quite good with a sword, and his opponent was no match for him. Howard delivered a slashing cut to the man's arm, which caused him to lose his weapon, and he raised his hands. Levi and Lucas quickly cut down two others, and the rest surrendered. They knew they could not stand against two fully armed horse troopers. The brief fight was over.

They heard a clapping sound and saw that it was their aunt applauding. "Wonderful, children, wonderful," she cried. "The Lord is good. Even if the poison kills me, I can die happy."

†

But she did not die. They called in a healer, a short, bald man who had been trained in the House of Healing. He examined the residue in the cup that Florence had been given the day before. He had been puzzled at first. "I don't think this is a poisonous brew. It looks like common buttercups. You are fortunate that it did not cause convulsions."

"Will it be fatal?" asked Rachel. Her aunt was back in her bedroom, which they had cleaned as best they could. Her aunt looked anxiously at the healer who shook his head in the negative.

"No, the worst of it should be past. I expect, Florence, that you will be back on your feet tomorrow. Now, let me see this other cup of tea that they tried to make you drink, Lady Rachel."

He examined the cup, still nearly full. He smelled it and tasted a drop. "I think this is monkshood or Aconitum. Probably she meant to incapacitate you. It will lower your blood pressure and possibly cause unconsciousness. Certainly, you would have been unable to put up much resistance, had you swallowed this. No way to tell if it was designed to be a fatal dose. Not without drinking it." His eyes twinkled as if making a joke. "I don't intend to drink it to find out."

"So, you don't know if this woman, Lady Lilith, or Etta, as she sometimes called herself, mean to kill me or capture me."

"No, though I understand those ruffians claim she intended to take you to Prophet City. I suppose we shall never know for sure."

CHAPTER 36
†

A Fire in the West

Woe to those enacting crooked statutes and writing oppressive laws.
Isaiah. 10:1 HCSB

The Liberty Soldiers were waiting uncomfortably in the storm drain beneath the courtyard of the palace in the heart of the old town. They were in the central part of Prophet City. From the storm drain grate above them, it was only a matter of feet to a side entrance to the Palace. They knew that four armed guards usually manned the nearest guard-post. Twelve trained men of Gray John's special operations troops stood ready and armed behind Caleb, Elijah, Jeremiah, Josiah, and Arrow James. All were waiting for the signal to take out the guards and storm the palace.

Noah was the leader of the special operations troops and had assumed overall leadership. He was not overly tall, but his shoulders and forearms bulged. He wore blackened mail and carried a crossbow in addition to his sword. His face was lean, and blonde eyebrows shaded icy blue eyes. He spoke softly but with authority.

They were waiting to hear the gunfire which would give the distraction on which their plan depended. The tunnel was humid and smelled of mold. The grate above their head let in slivers of eerie light.

According to their map of the palace, there was an underground tunnel from the Prophet's audience chambers to the family living quarters which were in a separate wing at the northern end of the palace. The entrance to this tunnel was hidden behind a bookcase in an alcove. These family apartments had been recently built to house the many wives and children of the Prophet. One of the workmen had told them that the apartments had an exterior stone facing, but the interior was wood framed and paneled with pine, then covered with stucco. The windows were secured with wrought iron bars. A roofed corridor extended from the main palace to the new wing which was the only other entrance.

They had been waiting for several hours. The drain was a stone-walled tunnel, and the floor was a thick mass of mud and wet leaves. There was no place to sit, so they leaned against the walls and shifted position whenever the tension became too great.

"Do you think the Stonegate forces will actually come here today?" asked Caleb, looking at Noah.

"There is no way to communicate with them," said Noah. He kept his voice low and spoke close to Caleb's ear. "We might have to wait another day or perhaps two. But they should be here soon. When it gets dark, we will return to your hideout. That is, if nothing happens."

"Why can't we move back until we find a dry place to sit down?" whispered Josiah. "We could hear the gunfire just as well."

"I want to be able to move once the action starts," answered Noah. "Move quickly. Everything depends on the right moment."

Caleb and Josiah nodded and shifted position. A water bottle was passed, and everyone took a drink. Then they heard the sound of marching. A large body of men was moving through the courtyard, right over their head.

"What is happening?" asked Arrow James in a whisper.

"They are bringing in reinforcements," answered Noah.

"So, our mission is doomed?" asked Caleb.

"Not yet. Our distraction might still draw them off," murmured Noah. He made a gesture for everyone to draw back from the grill. They moved a few paces deeper into the drainage tunnel. "This might be a good sign."

The tunnel shook. Clouds of dust and sand fell from the ceiling, and they all started, gazing upward anxiously. Rapid footsteps sounded at the grate above; then the sounds died down. More explosions sounded.

"Is that cannon fire?" asked Caleb.

Noah nodded. He raised his voice. "That is our signal. Be ready." At his wave, two members of the special operations team ran forward with bars.

Two other team members hoisted them, and they began prying up the metal grille that allowed storm water to enter the drain tunnel. There was a screeching noise, and all the Liberty Soldiers flinched. The special operation team moved to the front and Noah hoisted a teammate onto his shoulders. The young man pushed up, and the grate slowly rose out of place.

"Be quick, now," ordered Noah. "Just raise up your head enough to see if anyone is looking this way." He slowly obeyed.

The young man turned his head in all directions, and then looked down at Noah. "Guards on station, but they are looking away. There are some shrubs that give us a screen."

"All right," said Noah. "Go. Go. Go! I will boost you. Tommy, give them a hand."

One by one, Noah boosted up his teammates as fast as he could. Before he climbed out, he turned to Caleb. "Wait a few minutes. Have someone check for our wave, then follow."

Caleb waited as long as he dared, then had Josiah give him a boost. He looked cautiously out and could see that the drain was next to a flower bed. He could see the side entrance to the palace. The door was open, and one of the special operations team was waving. He turned and ordered the rest to follow and climbed out. With his help, they quickly exited, then placed the cover loosely back over the storm drain. They walked briskly to the open door.

The Liberty Soldiers entered the palace and hurried to catch up. Closing the door behind him, Caleb saw blood trails where the guards' bodies must have been moved into a side room. Then they stormed down the central hallway of the palace. The startled staff, mostly women, ran screaming in all directions. The stairs to the Prophet's chambers were directly in front of them as they raced ahead.

It was surprisingly quiet upstairs. Two guards with ceremonial armor stood outside an ornate door, and with cold efficiency, Noah and Tommy cut them down. They pushed the portals open and entered the audience chamber where the Prophet, Martin Abaddon, sat with a shocked look on his face, unable to speak. He was alone, which made it easier for the men to tie his hands and wrap a scarf tightly around his mouth. They dragged him unwillingly to the false bookcase door. Caleb pulled it open to reveal a stairway down into the bowels of the palace where a tunnel led to the family quarters.

"Quick," said Caleb. "We have no time to waste. We must get the Prophet to his family quarters, find Robby, and get them out!"

"Yes," said Arrow James, as they rushed the Prophet farther along the tunnel where his fate awaited. "We will have failed if we don't rescue the son of Donald of Goldstone and return him alive and well."

The Prophet almost choked at those words, and Caleb realized that he was almost as shocked at hearing that name as his own capture. He suddenly understood that the mention of the Prophet's enemy was a cruel blow to their captive. But he held one arm firmly. Josiah held the other, and they forced him along the dark tunnel.

Dark it was, but not completely so. Small oil lamps were burning in recesses in the gray stone walls, which gave them enough light to see. There was a commotion behind them, and the special operations team stopped to listen. It sounded like voices and hammering.

"Keep going," ordered Noah. Caleb and Josiah kept dragging the Prophet along. The passageway widened, and a flight of stone stairs appeared ahead in the flickering, yellow glow. The floor below had changed to polished marble. Two larger lamps shone brighter at each side of the steps, and two large ceramic jars stood beneath them. Both jars were waist-high and nearly two feet in diameter. The air was heavy with oily smoke that had a musky scent.

Caleb felt a pain in his arm, and he lost his grip on the Prophet. A bloody knife flashed and their captive whirled free and began to sprint towards the stairs. "Watch out," Caleb shouted. "He has a knife."

Fear must have galvanized the Prophet because he ran with demonic speed toward the stairs. He had cut his bonds because he pumped his arms like a sprinter. Taken off guard, Caleb could not keep up, and Josiah lagged still farther behind. When the Prophet reached the foot of the stairs, he grabbed one of the ceramic jars and overturned it. A pool of viscous liquid spread across the floor of the passage. Ripples on the oily surface reflected orange flashes as it saturated the way ahead. With an inarticulate shout, the

Prophet stepped to the other jar and turned it over also, so that the flow became a flood.

Caleb leapt after him, but when his foot splashed into the growing pool he instantly lost his footing and fell headlong. Josiah, only a step behind, also fell so they ended up in a heap on the oily floor. It was impossible to stand up because their feet kept slipping and the way ahead was completely covered with the lamp oil.

"He's getting away," shouted Josiah in a strangled voice.

"This is worse than ice," said Caleb, almost at the same time.

"Take that, you fools," shouted the Prophet. He dumped a third jar down the steps, then grabbed a lamp from the wall and hurled it out to fall in the middle of the spreading pool of oil. Flames blazed up and a ring of fire grew wider in all directions. Caleb and Josiah struggled backwards and were able to spring clear just as the flames shot toward the ceiling. The heat drove them back, and the blaze began to draw a draft, blowing into itself with a roar. But above the noise, they could hear maniacal laughter.

Caleb and Josiah retreated still farther and rejoined the rest of their group. "How did he escape?" demanded Noah.

"We did not search him carefully enough," answered Caleb. "He had a knife. He stabbed me, and I lost my grip on him. Josiah could not hold him alone. He was possessed with unbelievable strength."

"Blast!" exclaimed Noah. "No time to worry about that now. That fire is going to suck all the air out of this passage. Pull back. On the double."

They all turned and ran from the roar and blazing heat. The air was already filled with smoke and was becoming stuffy. Choking and with watering eyes, they climbed the stairs leading to the bookcase entrance.

They threw open the portal and drank in cool breaths of refreshing air. Two guards stared at them, open-mouthed. They stood frozen for a moment and then drew their swords. Both were armed with full mail and had an outer waistcoat marked with three lightning bolts.

Noah and his special team outnumbered them, but any two could have defeated them easily. They were quickly cut down. The team looked around and saw no one else.

The only sound to be heard for the moment was heavy breathing from their small party and distant artillery fire. Caleb's mind seemed fogged, and he rubbed his burning eyes. He noticed that his sleeve was soaked with blood. Blood drops went *drip, drip, drip* onto the floor. A draft was pulling air from their room into the bookcase portal. Then he realized that the roaring sound of the fire was growing louder. Josiah pulled up his sleeve and wrapped a cloth around the gash, pulling it tight and knotting the ends. "Thanks," said Caleb. Jeremiah offered him a drink from his water bottle, and Caleb accepted it gratefully.

Arrow James ran to the window and looked out. "A nearby building is on fire," he shouted. They all ran over to see. It was true. A detached wing of the palace was clearly burning. Black smoke poured out of many windows, and flames licked skyward from the lowest floor.

"He was the fool," said Caleb. "He stopped us, but he set the entire building on fire." Then it struck him. "Oh, no! Robby is in that building."

"Is there another entrance?" asked Noah. His face was grim.

Arrow James glanced at the sketch map. "Yes, of course. See, the main entrance is here. This secret passage is noted, but does not exactly show on the map, even though we knew it existed."

Noah glanced at the map. "We have to hurry to that main entrance if we have any chance of capturing the Prophet alive and rescuing Robby. Come on. Follow me."

✝

Shakti wondered what all the commotion was. She had only just left the Prophet and was closing the door to her room when she heard women screeching. She knew the palace staff had been ordered back to their normal duties by the Prophet himself. Despite the gunfire shaking the palace, the servants had apparently obeyed, but now they were in turmoil again. She eyed her comfortable bed but reluctantly left to investigate, walking briskly toward the stairs.

Downstairs, she entered the kitchen. Pots were bubbling on the stove, but the usual cooks were not at their posts. A large pantry door was open, so she made her way there to find three terrified women huddled together in fear.

"What on earth is the matter?" she asked, confused by the image she saw in front of her. The women were visibly shaken and terrified as they clung to each other for comfort. "What has happened here?"

One of the maids managed to find her voice as she whispered, "Quiet! There are men here with swords! They ran upstairs toward the Prophet's chambers!"

"Men with swords? Surely not! You must be mistaken! Here now, I will go and check!"

"Oh, no, please don't go, Shakti! You could be killed!" said the maid in a pleading tone.

"Oh, rubbish! Don't be silly! I must go and check on the Prophet. I am sure he is fine. It must be some of his men come back from the war!"

"No!" the maid insisted. "They were not Raiders! They were all dressed in black armor and I think they killed the guards at the side entrance. One had an emblem of a red axe on his helmet. A round silver button with a small red axe."

Shakti could not stop a gasp. She had seen that emblem worn before somewhere...of course, some of the horse troopers in Stonegate. *That emblem belonged to the Red Axe troop. Can it be possible that they were here?*

"I must go and check the Prophet's chambers. Do not be afraid. I believe these men are after the Prophet and not any of us!"

Shakti ran as fast as she could up the stairway to the Prophet's chambers. There were bodies of two guards near the door. Dark red blood ran down the steps in a crimson stream. She choked and her stomach wrenched with a spasm, but she kept on and flung herself through the doors. Two more palace guards stood there, with blank looks on their faces, but there was no sign of the Prophet! The guards ignored her and she realized she could do nothing there. So, she whirled and ran towards Robby's room.

✝

The special operations team moved back down the stairs and ran down a corridor leading to the family quarters. The Liberty Soldiers followed. But as they drew closer, they knew that they were too late. They could feel heat ahead and heard the roar of an inferno. A dozen guards were passing buckets of water and throwing them on the blaze. They had stopped it from spreading to the main palace, but there was no way to enter the family quarters. A wall of fire made that impossible.

"Throw down your arms," ordered Noah. The men turned and drew their swords. They intended to make a fight of it. "Don't be fools. Your ceremonial armor is no real defense."

A tall, bearded man answered. "We are sworn to defend the Prophet to the death."

"Your prophet is dead. He started the fire himself."

"You don't know everything. There is a secret passage."

"We were in the passage when he set the fire. He didn't escape that way. Throw down your swords. We will not harm you, so you can keep fighting the fire."

One of the other guards said, "The windows are all barred for security. There is no escape that way either."

"Very well," the first man said, and threw his sword to the floor. The rest followed suit, and the Liberty Soldiers collected the weapons. Then the guards resumed their firefighting efforts. Caleb saw that other palace servants were passing buckets through a side door into the hallway that connected the two buildings.

"Oh God," said Caleb. "Robby is in there. We are too late."

They had been overheard by some of the servants. They could hear cries coming from outside. "The Prophet is dead." Caleb exited into the ceremonial gardens and walked until he had a good view. Flames were leaping out of all the windows, and curling pillars of black smoke rose to the heavens. Even the roof was fully ablaze. Some men in armor were trying to pry the steel bars off a window, but the effort was futile. Finally, they gave up.

Then Caleb heard a commotion as a mob of people entered the palace grounds. They were carrying makeshift weapons and paving stones. Some of the guards stopped fighting the fire and ordered them to leave. But the mob showered the guards with stones from all sides. Caleb realized that the mob was more dangerous than the Prophet's guards and retreated.

Inside, he reported to Noah what was going on. "That's bad," Noah said. "There is nothing more dangerous than a mob. A maddened mob is worse than a rabid dog. We need to get out of here."

The Liberty Soldiers followed Noah and his men back toward the side door that they had used to enter the palace. The few people they saw were no longer terrified of them. A woman in a black dress and white apron came running up. "Did you hear the Prophet is dead?" she asked. "Are you here to protect us from the mob?"

Arrow James spoke to her. "Yes, we saw him light the building himself. And we know a way out if you want to follow us."

Noah overheard him. "We can't get sidetracked," he said. "These people will have to look out for themselves."

"She asked for help," said Arrow James. "And if she can keep up, there is no reason she can't follow us."

Noah snorted and said nothing more. But he stepped up his rapid pace to a trot as they neared the corridor that led to the side gate. As they turned into the main corridor below the entrance stairs to the Prophet's audience chamber, they saw a familiar face.

"Shakti!" shouted Caleb. "You have to come with us."

"Caleb," answered Shakti. She smiled. Her hair had been pulled back in a bun at the back of her neck, and she wore a simple cotton dress. "Robby is in my room. I won't leave without him."

†

The battlefield had calmed, so Don left Hamway in charge of the horse troops deployed below the guns and spurred Skipper up the hill. Thomas of Longmont rode to meet him.

"General Donald," said Thomas. "I am sorry we could not give you artillery support just now. You were so locked in battle together…"

"Yes, I know," said Don. "You could not fire without hitting us."

"The casualties are still coming in. We are trying to treat them."

"Losses were heavy, old friend," said Don. "We lost many brave lads. Gray John fell. God forgive us!"

Thomas winced. He took off a leather glove and wiped his face with his hand. "A heavy loss, indeed," he said with a deep sigh. "His cadets?"

"Too many died, more wounded. How about you?"

"Losses were light. I would there were none, but that is not the way of war."

"Carla and her girls?"

"Some wounded, but none seriously, thank God. Carla and Ari are unhurt. They did well. Very well. They are all heroines to the gunners. They drew off a force of cavalry that could have hurt us."

"Thank God, indeed. I see them over there. I will ride over and speak with them; then we must talk."

"Before you go, what was the parley about? Why did they suddenly call a truce?"

"There is something going on in Prophet City. The palace is ablaze and rioting is in the streets. The enemy general is not sure which way to jump, but he no longer wants to fight us. So he says."

"Don't trust him. Still, that sounds good for us. Do you suppose the special operations team was successful?"

"I can only pray that they somehow got Robby out. But the Prophet, it seems, is dead or captured. At any rate, he is no longer in control."

†

Don rode over to Carla's group of girl archers. They had all dismounted but were holding the reins of their horses. A group of girls clustered around Carla. She had her helmet off, and her red hair blazed like hot coals in the sunlight. Ari was next to her, and her hair flashed gold. The sight of them was sweet and uplifted Don's spirit. *What would I do if we had lost one of them? These young women should not be here, yet I am glad they are. They seem to have proved themselves.*

Don reined Skipper to a stop and dismounted. He approached Carla who looked at him and smiled. "General Donald," she said, formally. "What a relief to see you."

"We were hurt badly, but the Lord spared me," said Don. "I am so happy to see you and Ari, alive and unhurt. And to learn that none of the girls were killed."

Ari ran up and gave him a hug. "Uncle Don, I was so worried. It looked like you were going to be overwhelmed."

"We nearly were," Don said, clasping her close. "If they had pressed their attack…"

Carla joined them and also embraced Don. "What happened?"

"They heard that the palace was on fire and that the Prophet was dead or deposed. The enemy general decided to make peace with us. It was a near thing, Carla, and even so, we suffered badly. Gray John is dead and many with him."

"Oh, no," exclaimed Carla and Ari, at the same time.

A tear slid down Ari's cheek. "Poor Gray John. He was like a grandfather."

They all stood still, silently grieving. Finally, Don spoke, "Thomas said your girls did well."

"Yes, they did. And Ari led them when they proved themselves," said Carla.

"Ari?" asked Don. He was confused. "Why was Ari leading them?"

"I was directing gunfire," said Carla. "Ari saved many lives and managed it with only a few wounded. She was more clever than I would have been, I think. God used her."

"I am so proud of you, Ari," said Don. "Now, stay alert. I have no idea what our next move is. I had thought that we would pull back, now that our mission failed."

"You did not capture the Prophet?" asked Carla. "But I suppose I already knew that."

"No," said Don. "They were waiting for us. But a large force is moving from the south. The enemy general says they are friendly to us, and in rebellion against the Prophet's rule."

"Really?" asked Carla. Ari echoed her question.

"I think I see the hands of our friends to the south in this; the Diné and the Sonoran Cavalry."

CHAPTER 37
†

Triumph

Violence will never again be heard of in your land; devastation and
destruction will be gone from your borders. But you will name
your walls salvation and your gates, praise
Isaiah 60:18 HCSB

The Prophet's final suicidal gesture had driven back the special team.
There was no way they could extinguish the blaze since the pools of oil
burned with blazing intensity. The fires had raged until the sun rose bright.
Daylight revealed that the family quarters were nothing but ashes and hot
coals. Stone facings still stood, but the roof had been almost totally consumed. The Prophet was dead, along with his entire family—all except for
Robby who sat alongside Shakti. They watched the last plumes of smoke rise
into the air, sometimes obscuring the view of the valley below. The special
operations team had escorted both of them through the drainage tunnel
back to the old mine in the mountains just east of the city.

"You are the only living family left now, Robby. You are the Prophet's
son, even though your heart is nothing like his. Now it is your duty to take
control of the West and its people. The riots will die down. Soon the palace
yards will be filled with the citizens of Prophet City looking for answers and
guidance, and asking questions about what will happen next. You must be
ready to address them on the balcony of the palace when the time is right.

"I heard that some of the Prophet's generals are still fighting for control,"
said Robby. "This war is not over yet."

"I know, Robby," said Shakti. She gently took his hand. "The Christians in Prophet City are sending runners with messages, and the Liberty Soldiers are trying to get an overall picture of what is happening."

"Noah and the special team have gone to find the Stonegate forces. I hope my father, Don, is well. I will always think of him as my father."

"I know, dear. If only my Charlie is with them too and unhurt."

Caleb exited the nearby cave, which was really the entrance of an ancient mine, and walked up. Shakti and Robby were sitting on the ground under a spreading tree. The city stretched out before them. Smoke did not just come from the palace, since it streamed up in thin columns from a dozen places. But it was quiet and peaceful. Sounds of fighting did not carry to their ears.

"We just got a message that a large force has entered the city," said Caleb. "It is led by the Southern people who are allied with Stonegate. There are many horsemen and thousands of foot soldiers. They are restoring order."

†

"Now the war is over," said Shakti. "The generals who are fighting will soon realize that none of them can replace the old Prophet without a long civil war. The detailed plans of the Liberty Soldiers should be enough to put you in place as the new leader of his domains."

Robby thought deeply for a moment, then shook his head in disbelief.

"Robby, this has been the plan from the beginning," insisted Shakti. "You are the son of the Prophet, so you have the best claim to take his place. None of the generals would allow another general to take power, but you would be a logical compromise."

"I have been trying to tell you that I don't want to do it," said Robby. "I just want to go back home and begin a life with Ari. I know nothing about this land. There must be factions and power struggles. I would be a fish out of water. They would eat me alive or make me a mere puppet."

"It would not be easy. You are right about that. But I know a great deal about the politics. I advised the late Prophet for twenty years. He depended on my advice. And I can help. I would be glad to. It can be done. I know it can."

"Suppose I agreed. What should I do? Right now?"

Shakti sighed. "The first thing is to allow the Liberty Soldiers to explain their plan. Many things are happening right now to pave the way for you."

"Like what?"

"Like there are nearly two hundred young men that were saved from being forced to fight. They are being sent back to spread the word that you are alive and are a Christian. Soon, crowds will gather in the streets clamoring for you to rule them."

Robby nodded but did not speak.

"The next phase will be for you to return to the palace. It would be best if the Stonegate forces could ride into town at your back."

"But, surely, that would make me seem like a mere puppet of Stonegate. How would that help?"

"The people don't think of Stonegate as their enemy. Your merciful treatment of the prisoners in the last war has not been forgotten. They would welcome a rule from a decent leader who has not been corrupted by the late Prophet's evil. I think they would see you as the best of both East and West."

"Then what?"

"Then you enter the palace and address the people from the balcony. If all goes well, the people will clamor for you to take over. Then, as you say, you will have to unite all the various factions to accept you as the leader. I will help you write your speech."

Caleb returned. "I think you both need to come with me," he said. "We have a pretty clear picture of what has happened overnight. You, Robby, are the focus of all our hopes. We want to explain why."

†

Rachel and Howard had returned to Stonegate, leaving Rachel's aunt fully recovered. As the carriage arrived at Rachel's home, Sara and Judith greeted them. Sara ran to her mother and gave her a hug. This was a day that Rachel would forever remember.

"Mum," said Sara, with an anxious look on her childish face, "a man left a thick packet for you. I think it is news about Daddy and the others. But they would not tell me anything."

"There, there, dear," said Rachel, stroking her hair. "That does not mean it is bad news." But her heart nearly stopped. *If it was good news, wouldn't they have told her?*

They all entered the house with Judith leading the way. She also was upset. Rachel noticed her hands were trembling, and her brow was furrowed.

Judith took down an oilskin-covered package from an upper shelf in the kitchen. She handed it to Rachel without a word and then stood expectantly as Rachel broke the seal and began to read. There were copies of messages from the field and a summary. It also included a note from Lore-master Duncan. Howard stood by her side, but he did not read.

"Oh, thank God," said Rachel.

"What is it, Mum?" asked Sara, her eyes brimming.

"Sweetie, your father is safe, and so is Robby," whispered Rachel. She turned to Howard. "And Ari and Carla are also well. What happy news!"

Howard's face crumpled as if he was holding back tears. It was some time before he could say a word. "Praise the Lord," he managed.

"But there is more," said Rachel. "A short note to me from Don. It says that I should plan a trip to Prophet City."

"But that is such a long way, Mother," said Sara. "Why would Father want you to do that?"

"The note is short," said Rachel. "Remember, a pigeon had to carry it. But, Howard, he said you should plan to go there too. I wonder why?"

They could say no more. Every one of them fell to their knees and thanked their gracious God.

✝

Don and Ari could hardly wait to arrive at the palace in Prophet City. Carla was riding with her troop of archers behind them. Hamway had gone ahead with two horse troops to escort Robby to the palace. Thomas of Longmont had emplaced the Stonegate artillery to cover the main approaches to the city with one horse troop providing security for the guns.

They passed a one-story brick building with a wooden signboard, marked with a red cross. Several tents were pitched nearby, and a long line of people stretched for nearly a block.

"Ari," said Don. "That must be Abel and a team from the Green River Surgery. I heard they were in the process of relocating to the outskirts of Prophet City."

"Can we stop for a moment?" asked Ari. "I would like to greet him. By the way, don't you think the city needs a new name?"

Don laughed. "You have a good point, dear," he said. "Two good points. The city needs a new name. And of course we can stop, but just for a moment."

They rode to the front door and dismounted. A harried nurse first insisted that they must wait their turn. But when they explained that they only wanted to see their friend, Abel, the healer, she hurried inside. It was not long before Abel emerged, wiping his hands on a white towel.

"Lord Don," said Abel with a smile. "Wonderful to see you! And can this be Ari?"

"It is," answered Don, as he stepped forward to clasp hands. "She is a heroine now, almost as much as her famous mother."

Abel hugged Ari with a smile. "So I heard, young lady. I am proud of you." He stepped back. "I have been hearing nothing except people saying that Robby is going to replace the Black Prophet. Is that true?"

They explained that they had heard the same thing and were anxious to see him again. After a short chat, they reluctantly said their goodbyes and went on their way.

They had also greeted Danny Yazzi on the way in, but Señor Reuben Ramos was with the forces guarding the western approaches to the city, and they had not yet seen him. It was early morning when they rode through the palace gates, now unmanned by palace guards. A group of men in mail stood by the gate and gave them a cheer as they entered. They had no idea who they were, exactly, but they were clearly friendly. The whole situation was confusing. Some smoke continued to billow up into the sky where a light breeze spread the acrid stench of death.

"It was a miracle that Robby survived this, Uncle Don," Ari said in a small voice. The thought of coming this far to learn that Robby had nearly perished in the fire was almost too much for her to bear.

"I am sure it was, Ari. Gray John, rest his soul, gave me his solemn promise that his men would rescue Robby. And they did."

The palace loomed before them in all its splendid grandeur, beckoning them to pass through its wide main entrance. The front wooden doors were slightly open, probably left ajar by palace staff. Two cadet troopers, swords belted at their waist and wearing full armor, gave them a salute and moved aside to allow them access.

Ari was puzzled. "Uncle Don," she said. "I thought the palace burned down."

"No. Apparently just one wing of the palace burned. The rest is untouched."

"Thank God."

"Come on, Ari. Let's go in. Somewhere inside we will find Robby. And it has been too long since we saw him last."

A tear rolled down Ari's cheek at the thought that any moment now she would be reunited with the one man she truly loved. "Yes, Uncle Don. Let's hurry. I cannot wait to see Robby again!"

They made their way up a staircase of polished wood. Ari wondered if this was the right way, but there seemed to be no alternative. Then she noticed that Don's limp was worse than usual. *Oh dear, this campaign has been hard on him.* A young maid appeared, looking surprised at the arrival of unknown visitors. "Can I help you?" she asked. "This palace is closed to the public for now."

"Oh, yes," Don answered. "We are looking for Robby, the lad who arrived here a few months ago, and who appears to be the son of the Prophet."

"Oh, you must mean Daniel, not Robby. Daniel came here as a prisoner, but it was soon obvious that he was the true son of the Prophet."

Don and Ari glanced at each other in momentary confusion. She wondered about the different name and hoped it was Robby after all. *Please don't let this be some horrible mistake.*

"Yes. Very well, then…can you tell us where Daniel might be?" asked Don, giving Ari's hand a squeeze. "We are his family from Stonegate."

Ari smiled at her uncle, still dressed in full armor, still flecked with dried blood. He looked like a warrior from a legend, and she was proud to be with him. The young maid looked at them with wide eyes. Ari could not tell if she was terrified or simply awestruck. She finally spoke: "I believe he is in the Prophet's chambers with a woman named Shakti. Of course, you must know that the Prophet is dead. Daniel is now his only heir. Here, follow me; I will take you there to see him."

Don and Ari let out a gasp at the mention of Shakti's name. Ari remembered that Charlie had almost given up hope of ever finding her again, but now it seemed she was here in the palace. Ari put a finger to her lips to indicate to Don to say nothing. They continued up the stairs.

Soon they arrived at a large landing and stood before an ornate door, inlaid with flecks of gold and silver. An emblem of three lightning bolts hung across the top, showing that this must indeed be the Prophet's chambers. The maid knocked loudly as a male voice called out "Come in." There was no mistaking it…it was Robby's voice.

The door opened, and Ari stood for a moment, transfixed in disbelief. Words stuck in her throat at the sight of Robby dressed in an exquisite silk tunic with finely woven wool stockings and gold chains adorning his neck. He looked like a prince and not the Robby she knew from Stonegate with a little dirt on his face after hunting.

"Is that truly you, Robby, my love?" she cried, as she raced to embrace him while her heart overflowed with joy and love.

Robby acted as if he could not believe his eyes. He stepped forward to meet her and took her in his arms. "Ari, Ari, my precious Ari. God has surely answered all my prayers."

Don walked over to hug his son and gave a low chuckle. "Thank God, you are alive, Robby. Your mother and Sara will be overjoyed to hear the good news."

"It is grand to see you, Father," said Robby as they embraced. "I was worried for you, too."

Carla must have arrived just after Don and Ari. She was escorted into the room, and she joined in the happy reunion. Ari looked around and saw that a dozen troopers from the cadet troop had taken up positions, providing security. Everyone started to talk at once. But finally, all understood that the crowds had been clamoring all day for Robby to rule in the late Prophet's place and that various generals had been reporting all morning to pledge their support.

"But, Father," said Robby, "How can I take up the burden of rule? Why should this land be ruled by one man?"

"It is not the best system, but right now, the people have nothing else," said Don, clasping Robby to his breast once again. "Devote your life to showing your people how to rule themselves. Baby steps by baby steps. They will grow in responsibility."

"Do you think I should do this?"

"With God's help, you can transform all this to a land of free people who have learned the way of self-rule."

"Father," said Robby, "I am not your blood child. I know you could not tell me that before. I understand. But my blood is tainted."

"Yes, Robby, you have tainted blood. But you are no different from anyone else. All our blood is tainted. But Christ can cleanse our blood, our heart, and our souls."

"I know, Father. He has already cleansed me."

"Oh Robby," said Ari, embracing him again. "I am so glad to hear that, my love. I am glad that we are not cousins."

"No more than I, dear Ari. I have longed to see you and tell you. I want you to be mine."

"I want that too, dear Robby," said Ari, kissing his cheek.

"I am happy for you both," said Carla. Her face flushed nearly as red as her hair as she embraced them. "You can be sure that your father and I will bless your union."

"Father," said Robby. "I have been worried about something. Can you put a monument on my mother's grave?"

"Of course, Son," said Don. His head jerked upward for a moment, and his face froze.

"Aunt Carla," continued Robby, turning to her. "What is your opinion? I will never think of her as my mother. But she gave me life and deserves our respect."

Carla patted his arm. "What a nice thought. We will make sure it is done."

Ari saw the tension leave Don's face. She smiled and turned to Robby.

Don stood back as the two young lovers embraced again. When they stepped apart, he spoke. "A wise man of the ancients said that there are two important days in a man's life. One is when he is born and the other is when he learns what he is born for."

"What was I born for, Father?

"Good question, Robby. You were born to bring glory to God. It sounds simple, but it is a profound truth. I wish I had understood it at your age. It is the beginning of wisdom because it is based on an awed respect for God. Now go out there and do your duty."

Shakti watched as the four of them spent some tender moments in the reunion with each other. Then she spoke, reminding them of the importance of the coming events. "Robby, people are beginning to arrive outside the palace. We must make our way to the balcony where you can address them and give them a show of leadership. This palace and all that is in it is now yours...and you are now the new leader of Prophet City and all the surrounding towns of this land."

"Yes, Shakti...you are right. Father, Ari, Carla, I want you to know that Shakti has been my helper since I arrived here, and we have much explaining to do about her role in all of this. But let me tell you that Shakti, although born and bred in the palace, and who was sent by the Prophet to spy for him, has been loyal to all of us in Stonegate and wants nothing more than to return to Charlie. Of course, she has agreed to help me here for a little while."

Ari looked at her, suddenly sure that she was the one that Charlie had mentioned. She knew that Charlie had never given up hope of seeing her again.

"Ah, yes," Don said. "Charlie will be pleased to find you alive and well, Shakti. And since Robby has vouched of your loyalty to us, and since you have been his helper all this time, then we accept you, of course."

The maid took a peek out of the window as the sound of cheering began to echo through the air. "Quick, it is time to see the people. They are arriving in droves, happy that the Prophet is dead, and that the war is over."

"Father, Ari, Carla, Shakti, and you too, Janetta," Robby said, beckoning the maid to join them. "You must all accompany me on the balcony as I read my speech—which Shakti wrote."

"Gladly," Don answered.

Ari could tell that he was proud of Robby. *No matter what blood Robby has, Don is his father and Robby is his son.* That thought also made her happy.

As soon as they appeared on the balcony, the crowd went into a chorus of wild cheering and clapping. There was no doubt that they knew that the Prophet was dead and that Robby was his heir.

A group to one side began singing an ancient Christian hymn. Ari recognized the words, "Glorious, glorious, glorious is Thy name, O Lord." She realized without being told that this was probably the first time that they had ever dared to gather together and sing aloud. They were a minority, of course, but she noticed that those not singing listened with rapt attention.

"Friends and citizens," Robby began as the noise subsided to a low hum. "I have come to bring you all good news. The Prophet is dead, and you are now free of his evil rule. As sole heir of the Prophet, I will be your leader, not your prophet. I will rule with kindness and compassion, encouraging each one of you to rebuild your lives in confidence. From now on there will be no more cruel, crushing taxes and forced labor. We will not be forcing men to join our armies. Political prisoners will be set free. I will use some of the Prophet's wealth to make this city bloom. And people in outlying areas will not be forgotten. We will be listening to you to learn how the government can be your ally and not your enemy. You will be free to worship in your own way. Those who wish to remain here in the West are free to do so, but those who wish to move East and live there in peace are free to go. The walls between the West and East will be torn down forever. And we can all now live together in peace and freedom!"

The crowd roared in unison. "Long live Daniel, our leader!" the crowd roared before Robby silenced them with his outstretched hand.

"That is the name the Prophet knew me by. But I wish to be called Robert, your leader. And I wish to let you know that there is to be a celebration in Prophet City in two weeks' time to which you are all invited. I wish to announce a wedding between me and my beautiful bride to be, Arielle."

The crowd applauded. A band appeared from somewhere and began playing a stirring tune, and people began to dance in the square below. A young woman ran and threw a bouquet of dried flowers. They were weighted with a wooden block and sailed up to the balcony. Ari caught them and waved them overhead. There were more cheers, and the celebration continued.

Ari blushed as Robby put his arm around her, again introducing her to the crowd. "And together, Arielle and I will give you good government, looking after all our citizens with love and compassion."

Don turned to smile at Shakti as he whispered, "And I believe we will see another wedding soon after that…you and Charlie?"

"I hope so, Don. I hope so," Shakti said, showing Don the pearl ring given to her by Charlie…a ring she had never taken off.

†

The day of the wedding dawned brightly with a sun that seemed to rise earlier than usual as if in anticipation of new things for Prophet City and the West. Don had sent a messenger pigeon from the palace to Stonegate to let Rachel and all the family know they must attend the wedding and to inform Charlie that Shakti was alive and living in the palace. It was a ten-day trip from Stonegate, which left just enough time for a large entourage from Stonegate to pack their carriages and arrive in time for the celebration in Prophet City.

The last of the Western generals had finally given up fighting each other and pledged submission to the new leader, Robert. He had not chosen a title for himself, but people used the simple title of "leader."

Charlie had left earlier by horseback as soon as he received the news. Too much time had passed without knowing where Shakti was. He rode as hard as he could without harming his good steed, longing to arrive in Prophet City as soon as possible.

It was a fine, sunny day when at last Charlie could see Prophet City looming before him. His heart skipped a beat as he galloped into the palace grounds, now mostly free of armed guards, but full of gardeners singing happily as they tended to the garden beds in preparation for a wedding.

Charlie tethered his horse as he bounded up the palace stairs. The door guards recognized him and stood aside. A smiling butler greeted him.

"Can I be of service to you, sir?" the butler asked, wondering who this unexpected visitor might be.

"Yes," Charlie answered. "I was hoping to find my lady friend, Shakti. I believe she lives here."

"And who, may I ask, are you?" the butler asked, raising an eyebrow.

"Oh, pardon me—of course. My name is Charlie, and I am from Westerly-stead in Stonegate."

"Well, then, my good man…if you will care to follow me I will take you to Shakti, who is the personal maid of Ari, our new bride to be. Are you here for the wedding in a few days?"

"Y-y-y-yes I am," stuttered Charlie. "But I have arrived earlier to see my friend, Shakti, and to see if I can be of any assistance to the groom to be, Robby."

"Oh, so you know Robert, our leader, then?"

Charlie smiled. "Oh, yes. I know him very well…ever since he was born."

The butler led Charlie upstairs to a private waiting room at the end of the hall. "If you would wait, I will let Miss Shakti know you are here."

Charlie sat down on an ornate chaise lounge with red tassels and a floral covering as he tried to compose himself and collect his thoughts. The minutes seemed like hours before he heard footsteps approaching the room.

"Charlie, oh Charlie," Shakti said as she entered, looking resplendent in a vibrant burgundy, velvet gown. He noticed tears falling down her cheeks as he stood up to embrace her.

"Oh, Shakti, I can't believe it's you. I almost gave up on the hope of finding you once war broke out, and I almost went mad with grief at the thought of losing you."

"I'm here, Charlie. I'm here. And I will never leave your side again."

†

The dark shadows under Rachel's eyes had almost disappeared by the day of the wedding. Knowing Robby was not only alive and well, but also the ruler of the West had helped Rachel relax and sleep better after the chaos of the past months.

A dozen dear friends from Stonegate had arrived for the wedding and were housed in the ample rooms of the palace where they enjoyed being waited on by palace staff. Lore-master Duncan was there and so was Marshall Jackson. Colin McCoy had not been forgotten, either. The staff under Robby's rule were treated well. It did not hurt their mood when they learned that their wages were being doubled. No guests had ever been treated with more hospitality.

The Liberty Soldiers had joined the Stonegate guests for an informal reception while the wedding party was making ready. Everyone from the East was eager to hear their story of the fall of the Prophet. At Robby's insistence, Noah and the special operations team were among the honored guests, and they were the object of everyone's admiration.

A sense of jubilation and merriment was evident, and the atmosphere was heightened by the sound of the musicians playing wedding songs. Ari had been up since dawn preparing for her nuptials, which were scheduled for midmorning. A sumptuous wedding feast waited in the palace gardens where large tables had been laid with sparkling white tablecloths, bowls of fruit and nuts and flagons of ale and wine. The palace cooks were busy preparing stewed chicken, roast venison, and platters of fresh garden vegetables baked to perfection.

A mounted ceremonial guard of Stonegate Academy cadets stood in ranks before the east gate. Their armor gleamed and their war spears were festooned with bright ribbons. Silver stood there, her white coat gleaming, and with a richly decorated saddle and bridle, in case Robby wished to ride around the plaza in grand style. Ari's gelding, Rusty, was there to keep her company, with a blanket of white lace.

Along the north wall was Danny Yazzi and his battle-hardened Diné warriors. They were also in a line, and the coats of their mounts gleamed from careful grooming. They bore their shields and weapons and all looked regal, Their black hair was glossy black, and many looked like copper statues, they sat so quietly.

Reuben Ramos and his heavy lancers had taken up positions along the south wall. They also bore their spears pointing to the sky. They looked like a steel-tipped hedge, and the bright sun reflected off their mail and breastplates.

Inside the palace, Ari's grandmother, Betty, and Carla were helping Ari into a beautifully embroidered, white wedding gown, exquisitely made with the finest silk money could buy. Sara stood by, watching with rapt attention. Ari gave her a smile.

"You look beautiful, Ari," Carla said, remembering how, only a few weeks ago, her young daughter was out on the battlefield with her bow and arrows looking disheveled and exhausted from lack of sleep.

"Thank you, Mother. I hope Robby thinks so. I have longed for this day in my heart for so long. But you know that we only had our first kiss a few days ago."

"I know, dear. But when you marry, so many things that were wrong for you will now become very right."

"Of course, Mother, I do understand perfectly."

"And today, your hopes and dreams will all come true. Today you will become Arielle Fisher, but not of Westerly-stead or Stonegate, but Prophet City where you and Robby will rule the people. So you will now be a wife, and more than a wife; you must help him govern."

"I cannot believe that God has blessed us like this, Mother. All my life I thought that Robby and I were cousins and could never marry. I never dreamed that not only would we marry, but that we would be blessed with such a wonderful life and a mission to look after the people of the West."

Carla nodded as she placed the last white flower in her daughter's hair. "We don't always know our future or our destiny. But God has plans for all of us. And Ari, this was His plan for you and Robby. Now, go out and marry that man of yours. It is time and he will be waiting for you now at the altar."

The sun was high in the sky now as Ari walked down the wedding aisle holding a bouquet of pink roses in trembling hands. All she could see through the mist of her happy tears was Robby…waiting patiently for her to become his wife.

BE STRONG AND COURAGEOUS; DON'T BE TERRIFIED OR AFRAID OF THEM. FOR IT IS THE LORD YOUR GOD WHO GOES WITH YOU; HE WILL NOT LEAVE YOU OR FORSAKE YOU.

Deuteronomy 31:6 HCSB

†

THE BALLAD OF CARLA

When Carla was a lass, she rode the mountain pass.
She hunted far for game.
With Rachel by her side, she wild and free would ride,
Until the Raiders came.

The Raiders came and burned, to steal what others earned.
They stole six beauties fair.
But brave men rescued them, and they returned again.
And escaped that evil lair.

The beauties made a vow, they would never cow.
The next time they would fight.
The Raiders well might try, but they would rather die,
Than live under evil's might.

The day was clear and bright, when Carla had to fight.
Rachel rode there as well.
The evil men gave chase; it was a desperate race.
They fled the fiends from hell.

Though their mounts were fast, they cornered them at last.
They put arrows to their strings.
The Raiders gave a sneer; they saw no cause for fear.
They laughed at arrow stings.

Against the evil band, they had to make a stand.
They let their arrows fly.
They pierced them through and through. Their shafts flew straight and true.
The foe made an awful cry.

The Raiders ran away, their dead they left to lay.
They knew they could not win.
They climbed the mountain crags, with their tails between their legs,
Back to the West again.

So Carla came to be the Pride of Westerly.
Her fame spread from town to town.
With help sent from on High, she was not afraid to die.
We shall ever sing of her renown.

AFTERWORD

The tale of Stonegate takes place a bit more than a century in the future after the collapse of civilization in North America. After decades of recovery, the society is in some ways similar to the medieval period in Europe. There is a common language, related to English. Many of the crafts and trades found here would be familiar to our ancestors. But with the progress beyond subsistence existence, the old scourge of mankind, war, also makes a reappearance.

The affairs of humans have drastically changed, but the landscape, climate, flora, and fauna remain largely the same. Walled towns have taken the place of some of the old cities. Stonegate is the transformed town of Fort Collins. Hightower once was called "Denver." Junction was formerly known as "Grand Junction." The resort town of Steamboat Springs has had its name shortened to "Steamboat." Bethuel and Ariel have no earlier counterpart. Lady Lilith's keep is near the town once known as "Kremmling."

Terrain features have also changed names. The Front Range of Colorado is now known as the "Western Wall." The Colorado River has been corrupted to "Kolaroo." Likewise, the Cache la Poudre River changed to "Cash River." Vail Pass is called by people in Ariel "First Pass." But the descriptions of these places is intended to faithfully represent what would be found on the ground.

The Prophet and his new religion are not intended to be typical of anything that existed before. They represent a corruption and perversion of some 21st Century beliefs, but that is all they are intended to represent.

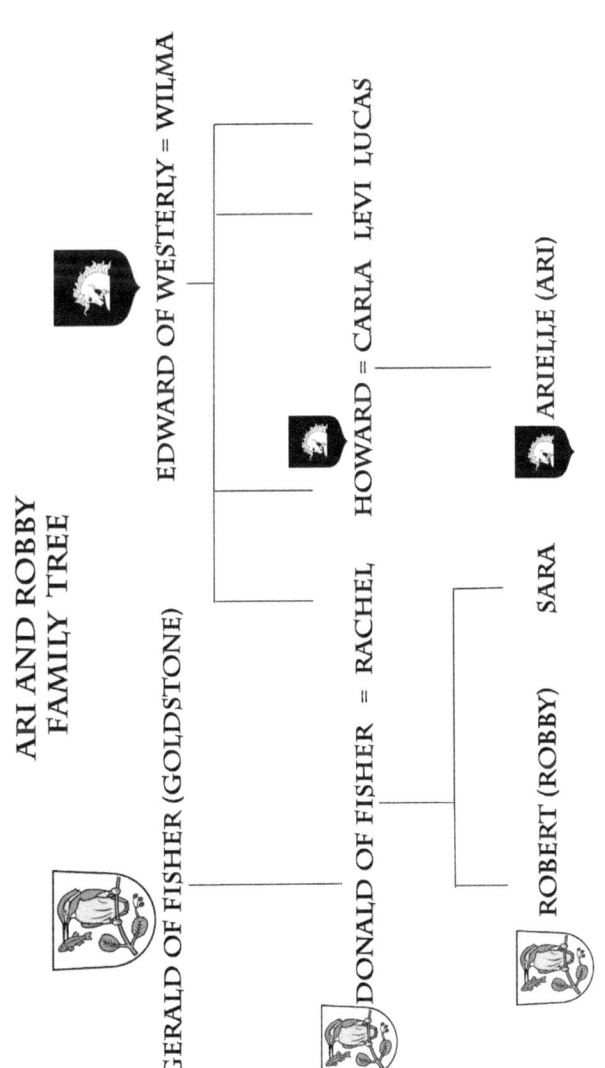

ARI AND ROBBY
FAMILY TREE

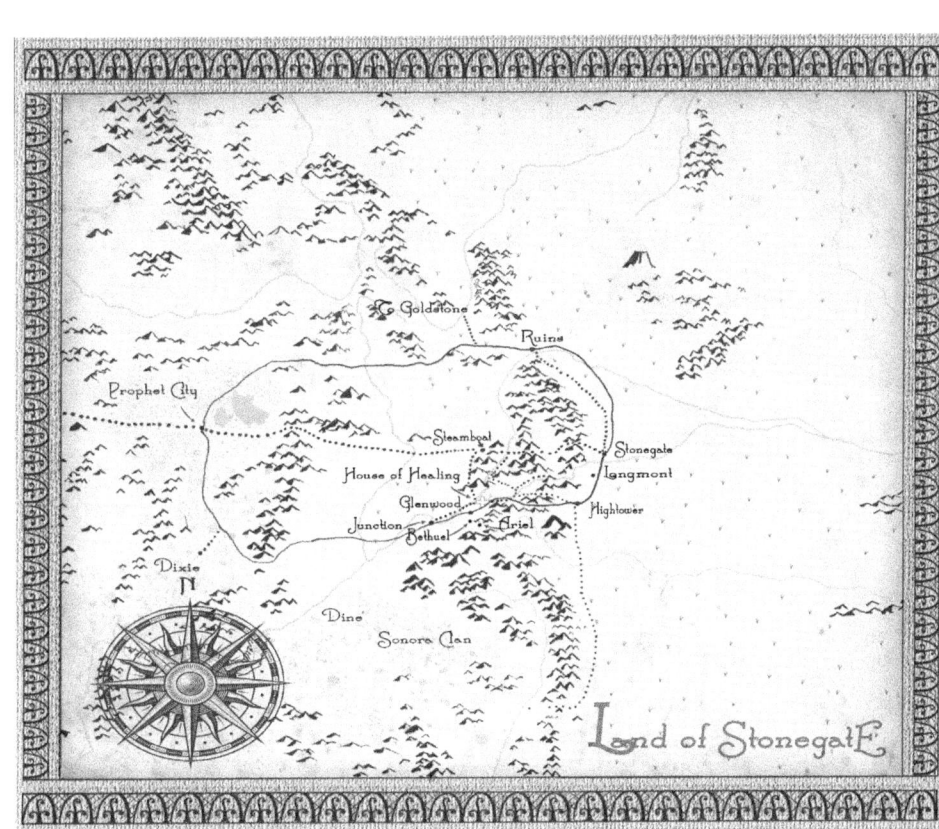

To Goldstone

Ruins

Prophet City

Steamboat

Stonegate

House of Healing

Langmont

Glenwood

Highlower

Junction

Ariel

Bethuel

Dixie

N

Dine

Sonora Clan

Land of StonegatE

www.ingramcontent.com/pod-product-compliance
Lightning Source LLC
Chambersburg PA
CBHW071157100726
47908CB00002B/415